NOTTINGHAM

THE TRUE STORY
OF ROBYN HOOD

ANNA BURKE

Bywater
BOOKS

Ann Arbor

Bywater Books

Print ISBN: 978-1-61294-165-3

Bywater Books First Edition: January 2020

Printed in the United States of America on acid-free paper.

Cover designer: Ann McMan, TreeHouse Studio

Bywater Books
PO Box 3671
Ann Arbor MI 48106-3671
www.bywaterbooks.com

For El, who fought for a better world
and
for Tiff, who stayed by me through these woods

In the year 1194, Duke Leopold V of Austria imprisoned King Richard the Lionheart as he was returning to England from the Third Crusade. The tax levied to pay his ransom nearly beggared the kingdom.

Chapter One

The roar of the crowd drew Robyn away from the narrow side streets, made narrower with market stalls crammed with the last of the autumn harvest and a scattering of hopeful chickens. She'd been on her way to the fletcher's shop, but the noise emanating from the town square drew her toward it like a lodestone. Dread tightened her stomach. She picked up her pace, taking care to conceal the limp rabbit hanging from her belt beneath her cloak. Killing a rabbit hardly constituted a crime, but she wasn't about to give the sheriff another excuse to breathe down their necks. She saw Old Widow Gable hobbling down the street ahead of her, elbowing her way through the outer fringe of the assembly, and above her gray head rose the gallows, ominously empty in the chill fall air.

"What is it?" she asked the older woman as she caught up to her. Widow Gable glanced sideways at Robyn from beneath the tattered corner of her headscarf, and the corners of her eyes crinkled with dark amusement.

"Don't let the sheriff catch you looking so guilty, Robyn Fletcher," she said. "Now put those young elbows to good use so we can find out."

Robyn obliged her and forced her way past her fellow townsmen and women, Widow Gable on her heels. Their progress was halted halfway to the center by an impenetrable press of bodies.

"Morning, Tom," she said to the broad young man beside her. His bare forearms were streaked with soot from the forge, and his younger sister, Lisbet, perched on his shoulders, chewing on a hunk of brown bread with single-minded intensity.

"They got Bill Gibbons," he said, frowning at the gallows.

"Poor bastard." Robyn shook her head to hide the relief that flooded through her at his words. Bill wasn't her brother Michael, and for the moment that was all that mattered. "What did he do?"

"Stole a pig from Marcia. He should have known better. They're saying someone had to pull her off him before she killed him herself."

"Might have been better for him if they had just let her finish him off," said Robyn.

Tom grunted in agreement. "How's business?"

"You know how it is." Robyn touched the lump beneath her cloak for comfort. The feud between her brother and the sheriff of Nottingham was common knowledge. They'd courted the same woman, and Michael, a fletcher, had won in spite of the sheriff's wealth and status. Gwyneth was just the lovely daughter of a serf. Unfortunately for Michael, the sheriff's foresters made up the bulk of Michael's customers, and the sheriff had not forgiven him the slight. The arrows Michael and Robyn crafted piled up in their barrels while Gwyneth grew round with child and the threat of snow hovered over the distant hills.

"Look," Lisbet said from her vantage point atop her brother.

"Look at what?" Widow Gable stretched her bony neck in an attempt to see over the crowd. Her efforts were rewarded as a scrawny figure stumbled onto the scaffold, led by a brutish man in a forester's uniform. Robyn recognized the forester: Clovis, the sheriff's favorite thug. He smirked as he led Bill to the noose and remanded him into the care of the waiting hangman.

"I'd like to see that bastard hang instead," said Tom.

"Fat chance of that," Robyn said as Clovis ripped the hood off Bill's head and revealed the man's pinched and hungry face. The crowd jeered. Robyn saw the hangman motion for Clovis to step

4

back, and Clovis held up his hands in a mocking gesture of placation that set her teeth on edge. Clovis never missed an opportunity to overstep the executioner's position.

Still, she had little pity for Bill. Poaching was one thing; stealing from your neighbors was another, especially with winter coming on. The only dissenting voice came from his wife, who screamed and pleaded from somewhere near the front of the crowd. A rotten onion flew from elsewhere, hitting Bill in the chest and splattering across his face. Another caught Clovis squarely in the jaw.

"He'll be smelling that all week," said Widow Gable with a cackle.

Robyn itched to be out of the crowd. Now that she was sure her brother was not at the receiving end of the sheriff's justice, all she wanted to do was get the rabbit back to the shop and house she shared with her brother and his wife. Leaving, however, wasn't an option. The crowd surged against her as the hangman settled the noose over Bill's head, bloodlust whipping them into a frenzy. A pig was worth more than a man's life with winter coming on.

"Bill Gibbons." Robyn's fist clenched as the familiar voice silenced the crowd, and she followed the sound to its source. There, appearing from behind the gallows and dressed in a fine surcoat of flawlessly dyed green and red wool with a sober expression on his handsome face, stood the sheriff of Nottingham. Thick hot hatred boiled up inside her at the sight of him. No one dared throw another onion; hated he might be, but here he was the living embodiment of the king's law. She tried to tune out his voice, but the words penetrated her skull like grave worms.

"You have been found guilty of the theft of a sow by the court. As is my duty to Nottingham and to the Lord our God, I hereby sentence you to death by hanging. May God have mercy on your soul."

Bill's wife shrieked and flung herself at the gallows. The crowd pulled her back, aided by more of the sheriff's brutes, and the buzz of the crowd cut off her screams as the sheriff's hand dropped. The lever sprung; the trapdoor opened; the noose tightened with a jerk, and Bill dropped, twitching, his legs beating the air as they searched for solid ground. Robyn looked away. Death by hanging was quicker than some of the punishments meted out in this square, but that didn't make it any easier to watch. Some citizens dealt with it by working themselves into a frenzy. Others, like Tom and Robyn, watched because it was required, doing their best to hide their disgust behind stony faces.

The crowd grew bored after the initial jerks faded into subtler spasms, and the crush separated into pockets of individual conversations as business resumed. Robyn overheard a group of men haggling over the price of a team of oxen, while another cluster debated the rising price of wheat.

"Well," Robyn said to Tom, "the pigs around here will be safer now."

"Can't say I'll miss him."

"But I'm sad to see him go," they said in unison. It was what the two of them always said after an execution, and the rote words released some of the tension from Robyn's body. Her fists relaxed by her sides.

"Come by the forge some time," said Tom as she turned to leave. "I'm tired of only seeing you at hangings."

"I will. Might need more arrowheads one of these days. Keep an eye on your brother for me, Lisbet."

Lisbet nodded around a mouthful of bread, then shot Robyn a doughy grin. The grotesque image surprised her into a laugh, but the sound of Bill's wife's wails stayed with her as she pushed her way out of the commons and back into the warren of streets. Merchants hawked their wares, hoping to catch the wandering attention of the dispersing crowd, and Robyn skirted around a flock of geese and their errant goose girl, a towheaded child who seemed more interested in her bare feet than her charges.

"Look lively, Maeve," Robyn said to her, giving the child a light rap on the head.

"Ma says I'm to ask you if you want the feathers," Maeve said, catching hold of Robyn's sleeve.

"Tell her I'll stop by tomorrow."

"When's Gwyneth having her baby?"

"Another month or so."

"She's so big, though," said Maeve. "Like a goat." She mimed a pregnant goat's gait, holding her arms out to suggest a pendulous belly.

"Better a goat than a goose girl," said Robyn, reaching out to give the girl another gentle cuff around her ears. Maeve ducked and darted away, scattering her flock.

Gwyneth did look a bit like a goat around the middle, Robyn thought as she ducked into the shop a few streets later. Not that she would ever say as much. Her sister-in-law sat with her legs spread to accommodate her pregnancy, which threw off the symmetry of her slender frame and caused the backaches and the headaches and the sore feet that Michael and Robyn took turns rubbing.

"There you are," Gwyneth said. She rose awkwardly and held her belly as she embraced Robyn with her other arm. "I was about to send Michael out to find you."

Robyn relayed the news of Bill's execution as she gutted and skinned the rabbit for the evening meal. Gwyneth had already set the stew pot over the hearth, and it bubbled with carrots, parsnips, and cabbage from their small plot of common land, filling the room with fragrant steam. Robyn breathed it in.

"Where is Michael, anyway?" she asked, washing her hands in a bucket.

"He went to talk to Aaron at the fletcher's guild, but he said he'd be back soon," Gwyneth said as she helped Robyn toss chunks of rabbit into the stew. "Not that your brother understands the meaning of the word." Her smile pushed the shadows out of Robyn's mind, and she felt the chill left by the hanging melt away.

"It's not like Aaron can do anything," said Robyn, but it was hard to feel bitter about their situation in Gwyneth's presence. So what if the sheriff hated them? They had each other, and soon they'd have the baby, and that was all that mattered.

"He told Michael he might be willing to buy some of the back stock."

"At a loss," said Robyn.

"A loss is better than nothing, which is what we have now. Cut that chunk up a bit more or you'll choke on it later."

Robyn sliced the offending piece of rabbit into smaller slivers. "Baby's not even born yet, and you have to mother something?"

"You hardly need mothering. Keeping you and Michael alive is more like herding wild boar."

"I'll tell him you said that."

"It will hardly surprise him." She snatched the rabbit from Robyn and dropped it into the pot with a flourish. "There. It will be ready by the time he gets back, and now no one will choke."

"We're forever in your debt."

"And don't you forget it," Gwyneth said, picking up the pelt Robyn had set aside. "This will make a nice blanket for the baby."

"It's just that Aaron wouldn't know the pointy end of an arrow if it stuck him in the arse."

"And he's the only other fletcher in the city." Gwyneth caught Robyn's eye and smiled. "The sheriff has to let it go eventually. People will forget, we'll be fine, and everyone will remember what wonderful fletchers you and Michael have always been."

Robyn didn't think Gwyneth believed her own words, but she couldn't bring herself to disagree. "When did Michael say he'd be back?"

"Soon," Gwyneth said again, shaking her head.

With the rabbit cooking and Gwyneth's soft voice humming as she scraped the fat from the rabbit skin, Robyn allowed herself to relax, and rested her elbows on the table as she watched Gwyneth work. The cat at Gwyneth's feet meowed plaintively.

"What?" Gwyneth said, smiling as she glanced up from tossing the innards to the tabby.

"I was just thinking that I hope the baby looks like you."

"I hope it looks like you and Michael." She brushed Robyn's cheek with the back of her hand, careful not to smear rabbit blood across Robyn's face. "Your eyes and Michael's nose. Unless it's a girl. Then she can have your nose too."

Robyn wrinkled the nose in question. Both she and her

brother had the same thick dark hair and hazel eyes, and Robyn also shared her brother's height. Gwyneth barely came up to her chin, which sometimes made her feel like a lumbering ox in comparison, and other times made her grateful that she could shield Gwyneth from the threatening world with her body. "Midge says hello," she said to change the subject. "I stopped by the mill on my way home."

Midge, Robyn's cousin and closest friend, had actually asked her to tell Gwyneth to push out her baby before the rest of them had to roll her around in a barrow, but Robyn opted not to relay that part of the message.

"I don't suppose she gave you any honey cakes?"

"Robyn!" A child's voice shouted from the shop before Robyn could answer, and then Maeve pushed through the curtain that divided the rooms and came to a panting halt before them. "It's Michael," Maeve said between breaths.

The blood drained from Gwyneth's face, and Robyn's heart stalled in her chest.

"Where?" Gwyneth dropped the rabbit skin and clutched Robyn's hand. Blood and fat cemented their grip.

"The square."

They ran, Robyn half pulling, half carrying Gwyneth with her as Maeve darted in front of them, throwing up clods of dirt each time her bare heels struck the street. He was at the guild, Robyn repeated to herself with each breath she drew. *The guild.* Not the forest. Even if he had gone hunting, they'd have to put him on trial first, and everyone loved her brother. No one on the jury would convict him. The sheriff couldn't just hang Michael—not, she thought with rising terror, that anyone would try to stop him if he did. Beside her, Gwyneth whimpered, a high animal noise escaping her as she clung to Robyn while trying to support her belly. She shouldn't be running, Robyn thought, but she didn't dare slow down.

Their street opened onto the larger central road running through the city to the castle, and as before, the stalls stood mostly empty of people save for a few watchful hawkers keeping

9

their eyes open for thieves. She could hear the roar of the crowd rising, and she looped her arm more securely around Gwyneth's waist and picked up their pace.

People parted like soft curd as they rounded the corner onto the common. She didn't have to elbow this time. The crowd melted before Maeve, some innate instinct for spectacle greasing their way until they came up hard against the rough arms of the sheriff's foresters. Michael knelt on the ground a few feet away, his face bruised and his dark hair damp with sweat.

"Michael!"

He looked up at Robyn as his name was ripped from her throat, and she saw the mute panic in his eyes. Clovis stood behind him holding the rope that bound his wrists. Robyn tried to muscle her way past the forester in front of her. She was vaguely aware that she knew his name, but it wouldn't come to her. All she knew was that she had to get to her brother before this nightmare went any further. "Michael," she screamed again, slamming her forehead into the forester's nose. She felt it crunch as he released her, howling, and she threw herself past him and onto her brother.

"Robyn," he said as she wrapped her arms around his neck. The ground was cold and damp against her knees. She choked on all the words she might have said, her throat paralyzed with the crushing certainty of the gallows.

"Get up, girl," said Clovis, grabbing her by the hair. She ignored the sharp pain and clung to Michael until Clovis's boot caught her in the ribs and sent her sprawling. A second kick, this time from the man whose nose she'd broken, collided with her shoulder. The crowd fell silent as she stumbled to her feet, and the only sound was the wheezing coming from her throat and Gwyneth's sobbing breaths.

"He didn't do anything," she managed to say as she regained control of her diaphragm.

"Robyn," said Michael, shaking his head in warning. "It's too late."

"He was at the guild." She was shouting, she knew, her voice rising hysterically as Clovis leered and the weak autumn sun cast unfamiliar shadows over faces she'd known her entire life.

"Robyn. Enough." The defeat in Michael's voice silenced her. "Listen to me. Promise me you'll take care of them. Take care of my child."

"Do it yourself." She clutched her ribs. "You're not dying. I won't let you."

"Tell Gwyneth I love her more than anything."

Robyn heard Gwyneth arguing with the sheriff's men to let her through, but she didn't have Robyn's height or strength, and all Robyn could see of her sister-in-law was the bright shine of her hair.

"I'm going to get you out of this."

Clovis laughed. She ignored him, fixated on her brother's face.

"I love you too, little bird," he said.

"Stop it. Goddamn it, *stop*."

A disturbance stirred the crowd somewhere to her left. She turned to look, desperate for help from any quarter, and saw instead the sheriff of Nottingham astride his black horse, followed by the hooded executioner.

"Michael Fletcher," he said as he dismounted. "You stand accused of poaching in the king's wood, and you've been found guilty."

Murmurs rose from the crowd. Some of them had bought meat from Michael, and others had looked the other way, but none now spoke in his defense. Robyn hated them for their cowardice. Michael would have spoken up. Michael would have pointed out the breach in justice had it been one of them, but they just stood there.

She took a deep breath despite her aching ribs. "You can't. Not without a trial." Robyn stared up at the sheriff's face. Handsome, yes, but his cheeks and nose bore the red stain of ruined veins, and while his shoulders and arms were hard with muscle, his stomach protruded over his belt, a testimony to his position of favor in Prince John's court. He slapped the end of his reins against a meaty palm as he considered her.

"You must be the sister," he said. "And you will address me as 'my lord.'"

She placed herself between him and her brother and glared up at him. "You can't hang him without a trial. My lord."

"Do you always hide behind your women, Michael?" A few people laughed at the sheriff's words. "Although your sister's tall enough to be a man herself," the sheriff added with a curl of his lip.

"Enough, Robyn," said Michael. "Ed turned me in."

"Ed?" Affable, smiling Ed, who always had a kind word for Robyn when she passed him in the street? She refused to believe it.

"They caught him with a leg of deer."

And he'd named Michael to save his own skin. Michael's eyes, so like her own, contained a weariness so profound that she whirled around to find Ed's face in the crowd, intending to break it beneath her fists, anything to hide from Michael's weary acceptance, and instead saw Gwyneth.

"Please." Gwyneth's voice carried over the laughter, and the sheriff's sneer stiffened. Robyn turned to look at her sister-in-law. Gwyneth stood behind the barrier of men with her chin tilted up and her eyes blazing with unshed tears. "Please let him go," she said, and the arms holding her back dropped away from her as if she'd burned them.

Hope surged in Robyn. Gwyneth stepped forward, still holding her belly as if it pained her, and placed her hand on the sheriff's wrist. His eyes softened as he looked down at her, but then his gaze traveled to her stomach and the child within, which was not his, and Robyn knew her brother's fate was sealed. It didn't matter if the sheriff broke his own laws. Who would punish him? The prince? Their distant king?

"You know why he had to poach," said Gwyneth. "You gave him no choice."

"Gwyn," said Michael, but Gwyneth paid him no heed. She, too, seemed to know his fate was sealed, and the hatred in her voice should have flayed the sheriff's skin from his body.

"You only hang him because I spurned you."

"Silence, woman," said the sheriff.

"You sicken me. You sicken us all. It's no wonder no good woman will have you, and—" Clovis handed Michael's rope over to the executioner and slapped Gwyneth hard enough to send her to her knees. Robyn fell at her side and put her arms around her shoulders to forestall any more punishment.

"Hang him," said the sheriff of Nottingham, and the crowd opened its mouth and howled, in protest or in triumph. It didn't matter. She sought her brother's eyes. They were glued to his wife, but he glanced up as if he, too, had heard the sound of Robyn's soul splitting down the middle.

Robyn carried that look with her all that winter. It hovered over the bed as Gwyneth screamed in childbirth, blood soaking the sheets and the midwife shaking her head as the hours passed and Gwyneth strained, and still the child didn't come. It waited behind her eyes each time she blinked the weariness away, stroking Gwyneth's sweat-soaked brow, and it was there on the midwife's face when at last the boy ripped free of his mother's womb in a surge of blood, so much blood, the boy too large for Gwyneth's frame and his little face red with the rage and grief Robyn felt each time she woke up in the bed she now shared with Gwyneth, because Michael was gone forever.

Chapter Two

Marian listened to the wind howling outside the Edwinstowe Priory walls and settled deeper into her chair. The sky had been clear when they left Harcourt Manor, but the weather around midwinter was always unpredictable, and now icy rain lashed the roof and battered the shutters. She contented herself with the satisfying knowledge that they would likely have to spend the night, and possibly the next night too if the weather didn't relent, which put even more distance between her and her father.

She turned her attention away from the window and back to the parlor. The Lady Emmeline of Harcourt sat by the hearth with her sister, the prioress of Edwinstowe, but where Emmeline was willowy and fair, the Reverend Mother was broad and ruddy, dwarfing even the two mastiffs that accompanied her everywhere. The sisters bore a striking resemblance to each other all the same. The curve of the prioress's cheeks held up her wimple with the same mischievous grin Marian had seen on Emmeline's face all throughout their girlhood. It seemed impious on a nun, and yet the nuns of Edwinstowe Priory had elected her prioress unanimously. Marian didn't blame them. She dispensed sound advice to all who asked, delivered sympathy to those who needed it, and knew when a penitent required compassion or a firm word. Women from nearby villages, towns, and manors sought her counsel regularly.

This was partially why Emmeline had braved the winter roads

today with Marian, Willa, and Alanna in tow. Midwinter's long night crept closer, and with it all the despair attendant to the season. A fire had destroyed some of Harcourt's grain reserves, and the mood on the manor was grim. Mead, prayer, and the prioress's blessing would settle Emmeline's mind.

Marian studied Emmeline over the lip of her goblet. They'd grown up together after Marian's mother had died. Emmeline had been the daughter of a wealthy lord in Lowdham before she married the Earl of Harcourt, and Marian's father had sent her to Lowdham to serve as Emmeline's handmaiden when he was appointed sheriff of Nottingham. "I will not have you running wild in Basford while I am in the city," he'd told her. Marian smiled at the memory, pleased with the irony. She might have learned her station better on her father's estate, instead of riding over the countryside with Emmeline and her brothers.

Now, however, Emmeline looked every inch the lady. Marian curled her feet more tightly up beneath her and smoothed the blue wool of her dress over her knees. In the chair beside her, Willa of Maunnesfeld twirled her goblet of mead and arched a red brow, either noticing the nervous habit or the impolite way Marian had been staring at Emmeline. Marian dropped her eyes to her own goblet and took a sip. The heady, summer-sweet liquid burned away the last of the cold still lingering from their ride. It did not burn away Willa's eyes. *You don't need to be here, Willa,* she thought uncharitably, but Emmeline always brightened when Willa came to stay with her at Harcourt, and so Marian reminded herself she should be grateful that her friend was happy.

Willa, like Marian, was seventeen and ripe for marriage. Unlike Marian, Willa was the daughter of a duke, a man who outranked Marian's own father by several degrees of peerage. The Maunnesfeld estate bordered Harcourt, and Willa visited Emmeline as she pleased. Willa would marry the duke or marquis of her choice, while Marian would have to be content with her betrothal to Lord Linley, the Viscount of Nottingham, as if any woman, alive or dead, as were his two previous wives, would be content with marriage to that—*no.* She stopped the thought before it ran away with her like a pair of poorly trained carriage horses. The wedding wouldn't take place until the autumn. Richard would be back by then, and she could appeal to him to make her father see sense.

Richard wasn't a friend exactly; he was her king. He spent little time in his own country, but he liked to see Marian when he was home. They often shared a drink at banquets, and he'd walked with her through the Nottingham castle gardens on summer evenings, talking of music and politics and horses. Some of the court women had made insinuations about their relationship, but the rumors never managed to spread far. Too many real scandals occurred at court to make much of something that wasn't there in the first place. She just had to hope his affection ran deep enough to foil her father's plans. Maybe he could even convince him to let her join the Edwinstowe Priory. She could help the Reverend Mother brew mead from the priory hives and illuminate manuscripts with delicate brushstrokes in the scriptorium, and she wouldn't have to worry about dying in childbirth like her mother.

"Daydreaming?" Willa said.

She glanced up. With her red hair, green eyes, and lean face, Willa looked like a fox, and right now her lips shared a fox's predatory cruelty. Marian felt her face flush beneath her scrutiny. Willa was bored, and when she got bored, her teeth came out.

"I was just thinking it would be nice to join the priory."

"You? A nun?"

"Why not?" She knew what Willa was thinking, but she wasn't going to give her the satisfaction of saying it.

Willa saved her the trouble. "Because Jesus can't put a viscount's baby in your belly."

"Willa," Emmeline said, whipping her head around to glare at her friend. "Can you blaspheme outside the church?"

"It's cold and wet out there."

"But hot and dry in hell," Marian said under her breath, but not so quietly that Emmeline couldn't hear. She thought she saw her lips twitch in a smile.

"Forgive me, Reverend Mother," said Willa in a tone that noticeably lacked contrition. "And excuse me. I'm going to go see where Alanna wandered off to."

"Yes, go find your minstrel. No doubt she's in the stable, singing to the horses." The prioress waved Willa's apology away and leaned back in her chair, clasping her hands behind her head in a sprawling gesture that strained the fabric of her habit. Marian couldn't shake her memories of the young woman the prioress had been when Marian had first come to stay with the family. Then, she had not been a holy sister. She'd been Tuck, the girl who could outeat any of the men at her father's table, and who outdrank them too, when given the opportunity. Gossips claimed the lord of Lowdham had sent his eldest daughter to the priory because no suitor dared bed her out of fear of her voracious appetites. Marian knew better. Tuck was her father's favorite, and when she'd asked to join the church, he'd acquiesced.

If only I was half so lucky.

Marian watched Willa leave with a surge of bitterness. Willa, Tuck, even Emmeline. They had choices—or at least more choices than Marian. She would marry Linley because Linley's position in Prince John's court was secure, and because a man of his rank was more than her father had dared dream for his only remaining heir. She listened to Tuck and Emmeline talk of festival days and honey harvests with half an ear and hoped Willa would bring Alanna back soon. She could use a song.

Alanna wasn't Willa's minstrel, despite Tuck's phrasing. She served Emmeline and Harcourt and had since Emmeline's wedding. Marian, however, couldn't deny the affinity Willa and the minstrel had for each other. Sometimes, Marian wondered if Willa came to Harcourt to visit Emmeline, or Alanna. Only one was proper. *Not that it's any of your business.* She couldn't even blame Willa. Everyone liked Alanna. Marian just didn't understand what Alanna saw in Willa—or what Emmeline saw in the redhead, for that matter.

"Marian," Emmeline said.

Marian snapped her head up. She wasn't sure how much time

had passed while she'd been brooding, but the fire had burned lower than she remembered. "Yes?"

"Can you go find out what has happened to Willa and Alanna? It's getting late."

"Of course." She stood and braced herself to leave the warmth of the room for the drafty corridors of the priory.

Outside in the hall torches guttered as the wind blasted through chinks in the mortar. She wished she'd thought to grab her cloak. At this hour, most of the sisters would be in bed, or else holding private vigils in the Lady chapel. She hoped, for the nuns' sake, that none of them were on their knees on the cold stone tonight. Her breath spun a frosty veil in front of her as she walked.

She passed the door to the kitchen and resisted the urge to nip inside and warm herself by the banked coals of the ovens before braving the outer courtyard on her way to the stable. Then she retraced her steps. Cutting through the kitchen would save her the longer walk through the refectory. Bolstered by the promise of temporary warmth, she put her hand on the latch.

Willa's voice drifted through the oak. Something about it gave Marian pause. She'd never heard Willa sound like that. It sent a shiver down her spine, and she opened the door cautiously, uneasy and unsure of the cause of her unease, knowing only that she didn't think she wanted to know what lay over the threshold. But she was unable to stop herself from looking.

Alanna and Willa stood on the far side of the shadowed room. A single torch flickered in its sconce, and Marian blinked as she puzzled to make sense of the scene before her. Willa leaned against the wall with her head thrown back, and Alanna stood so close she seemed pressed against her. She *was* pressed against her, and her lips were on the fair skin of Willa's neck. Marian glanced down. Willa's skirt was hiked up past her thighs, and she said Alanna's name again in that low, throaty voice as the minstrel's hand moved.

Marian swallowed against the sudden dryness in her throat. She no longer felt cold. Heat had flooded her body, and she stared, transfixed, as Alanna moved her lips up to Willa's cheek and then to her ear, where she whispered something that made Willa gasp. One of Willa's hands buried itself in Alanna's dark hair. The other braced herself against the wall as she cried out in such obvious pleasure that Marian felt her own body respond.

The unfamiliar feeling brought her back to her senses. She knew she should leave. This wasn't for her to see, and she still wasn't even sure of what, exactly, it was she was seeing—just that she had to get away from the sight of color peaking in Willa's cheeks as her breathing came faster and faster. She took a small step backward, and as she did so, Willa opened her eyes.

The green flash fixed Marian to the spot. She waited for Willa to scream at her, or cover herself, or at least push Alanna away. Instead, Willa held her gaze as Alanna's hand moved beneath her dress, the rhythm rising to a crescendo that parted Willa's lips in a cry of rapture. Her eyes fluttered shut as her body arched against the woman who was, beyond any shadow of a doubt, despite the impossibility of it, her lover, and the severed eye contact at last broke Marian free of her paralysis. She whirled and fled. Her cheeks flamed as she bolted down the hallway, and she ran until she came to the door that opened into the cloisters and stepped out into the winter storm.

The covered cloisters blocked the worst of the freezing rain but did nothing to break the wind. It cooled her face with icy blasts, and she half fancied she felt steam rising off her skin. Her heart pounded faster than the run had called for, and there was an uncomfortable heat between her legs that made her want to douse herself in the frozen pool in the center of the cloister garden.

Willa. Alanna. She couldn't make sense of it, and yet it had seemed to make perfect sense to them. She squeezed her thighs tightly together as the pressure between them built. She'd heard of women who engaged in unseemly acts. Somehow, though, she couldn't reconcile what she'd just witnessed with the horror in those whispered voices as the tellers related sordid tales of women with male parts preying on fair maidens. Neither Willa nor Alanna had any unusual bits of anatomy, as far as she'd seen, nor had they looked as if they'd needed any. She closed her eyes to try to block out the images that still seared her retinas, but that only made it worse. With her eyes closed, she could hear Willa.

"Our Father who art in heaven," she began, but the prayer felt inappropriate on her lips and she stopped at once. She took several deep breaths to calm herself. As the seconds passed and the cold leached away her body heat, some of the uncomfortable need inside her dissipated too, and her head cleared enough to think.

Emmeline's husband was away in the Holy Land with Richard on Crusade. In his absence, Marian slept with Emmeline and her young son, as was fitting for a handmaid in Marian's position. It was warmer that way in the winter, and Emmeline liked to talk at night after little Henri fell asleep. Sometimes, Marian woke up with Emmeline's head resting on her arm or her legs intertwined with her lady's, but that was different from the embrace she'd just witnessed. There was no desire between her and Emmeline.

She raked her memory for some precedent. She knew that women sometimes developed friendships that raised eyebrows at court, though they mostly went ignored by husbands too busy scheming to care overly much about their wives. What she'd seen, however, would have given Willa's future husband plenty to worry about. Was this what went on behind those closed doors? Given her intimate role in Emmeline's household, Marian had seen men and women together often enough to know the sights and sounds of pleasure, and Willa certainly had looked like someone in the throes of passion.

The image disgusted her. Or, at least, she thought it did. Her mind struggled to provide her with a label for the conflicting emotions welling up inside her. Part of her wanted to burst into hysterical laughter. Sinning so boldly in a priory was exactly the sort of thing Willa would do, and a part of Marian admired her for it. Another, stronger part worried for the stain this placed on both of their souls, as well as the position they'd put Marian in. Should she tell someone? Who? And what would she even say? All she wanted was to be back in the parlor with Emmeline and

Tuck and her own sour mood, worrying about her marriage and finishing her mead. Perhaps she could slip back in and say she hadn't found them. It wasn't like Willa would dare contradict her.

The realization that she would have to face Willa again brought a rush of terror. Willa had seen her watching. Worse, Marian hadn't left or spoken when Willa met her eyes, and instead had been . . . what? A part of it? She shivered again. All I did was watch because I was confused, she told herself. Anyone would have done the same.

She repeated that to herself until she almost believed it. By then, her teeth chattered from the cold, and her shivering was entirely a result of the winter air.

"There you are."

Marian jumped. Willa stood by the door, looking composed and calm and entirely unabashed. Marian, on the other hand, felt her cheeks flame again.

"You'll freeze out here," Willa continued in a conversational tone.

"I'm fine."

"Don't be stupid. Come on."

Marian shook her head. She couldn't go near Willa. Not when her body had suddenly reminded her of everything she had just tried to suppress.

"Emmeline will start worrying."

"Just leave me alone. Please."

Willa let the door swing shut and walked toward her. Marian backed away until her foot hit a stone pillar and rain pelted the back of her head and shoulders. Willa moved closer, stopping only when a handsbreadth separated them.

"I thought you might be like me, but I wasn't sure."

"I'm not like you." She wished her voice would stop shaking. It's the cold, she told herself. Still, she wondered what Willa had seen in her face.

Willa's lips curved in a mocking smile. "No? Then why did you watch?"

Marian opened her mouth to tell Willa that she was wrong,

and that she had only watched because what she had seen hadn't made sense; she had been confused, not curious, and no part of her had wondered what it might be like to touch or be touched by another woman. She couldn't bring the words out into the winter air. Willa's smile deepened in satisfaction, but she moved away, and Marian let out the breath she'd been holding. It hitched when Willa grabbed her hand.

"Seriously, Marian, it's freezing out here. Come on."

"Let go of me." She snatched her hand out of Willa's and stalked toward the door.

Willa reached it right on her heels. Aware that slamming it in her face would reveal just how much Willa's words had upset her, she held it open, and so it was that together they saw the nun escorting a messenger in the prince's livery toward the prioress's chamber. They exchanged a worried look. There were only a few reasons a messenger would travel through this sort of weather, and none of them were good. Marian and Willa broke into a run and burst into the room just as he delivered his message.

"King Richard has been captured by Duke Leopold of Austria."

Marian saw Emmeline's face freeze.

"It is against public law to detain a Crusader," Tuck said. "Has anyone notified the pope?"

"I assume so, Reverend Mother," said the messenger.

"And his men? What of them?"

He passed a hand over his damp forehead. His clothes were soaked from the icy rain, and Marian would have pitied him if she hadn't felt like he'd dumped a bucket of ice over her head with his words. Richard couldn't be captured. It wasn't possible. It *couldn't* be possible. He was the king!

"Captive also, or on their way back to England. No one seems to know."

Emmeline turned her face to the fire. Willa went to her side, leaving Tuck to see to the messenger's needs while Marian stood with her boots frozen to the flagstones.

"Perhaps captive is better than fighting?" Willa said to Emmeline.

Emmeline stared into the flames with a blank face. "It is not Connor I'm worried about," she said, naming her husband. She sounded older than her twenty years. "He can take care of himself. But if Richard is delayed for too long, it could mean war."

The sound of the crackling flames filled the pause that followed her words. War, and worse than that, worse than anything Marian had allowed herself to consider even in the darkness of deep night: the possibility that Richard might not return in time to intervene on her behalf. Prince John favored Linley, and Linley had been all but promised an earldom should John succeed his brother on the throne. Such a rise in station should have pleased her. Instead, Viscount Linley's face filled her vision: cold gray eyes, patchy dry skin, and lips as thin and bloodless as a rat's tail.

"There's no one left to fight," said Willa. The Saladin Tax the previous year had taken most of England's able-bodied fighting men, as fighting was preferable to beggaring one's estate, and all that was left were youngest sons. Marian guessed Willa was thinking of her twin brother, but she couldn't bring herself to care. Alanna would comfort her. Marian had her own problems.

"They'll turn the country into a convent," said Emmeline. "There will be only women and children left."

"Would that really be such a crime?" Tuck placed her hands on Emmeline's shoulders. "We could start over, raising boys who won't grow up into their father's sins."

Emmeline shook her head and sagged back into Tuck's embrace, leaning her cheek against the other woman's chest and closing her eyes. "I would not wish for my son to grow up without his father, but you're not wrong, Tuck."

"All will be well. We shall pray tonight, but not, I think, for too long. Prince John will expect you at court soon and that will take some doing with the roads as they are. You need rest."

Court. Marian twisted the silver ring on her middle finger

23

hard enough to leave a bruise against her knuckle. If she was lucky, her horse would slip and send her tumbling into some bottomless ravine in Sherwood Forest, where she'd grow moss instead of hair and fade into the trees. If she wasn't lucky, neither God nor all the saints would be able to stop her father's machinations, and she'd be married to Viscount Linley before harvest time.

Chapter Three

Wind snatched the warmth from the eaves of the thatched roof and whistled through cracks in the walls. The drafts sent sparks up from the hearth as Robyn paced the small room. Gwyneth lay in the bed by the fire with Symon asleep in her arms, swaddled in his rabbit-skin blanket. The quiet unsettled Robyn almost as much as the child's tears. Both the baby and Gwyneth shared the same pinched, exhausted look, and her feeling of impotency grew with each shallow breath that passed Gwyneth's lips.

"There must be something you can do," Robyn said to the midwife, resisting the urge to shake the woman.

"She's lost too much blood. Her body is weak, and her milk isn't flowing like it should."

"So make her stronger."

The midwife gave Robyn a pitying look. "Find the child a wet nurse. Or a goat."

"And Gwyneth?"

"You need to prepare yourself, Robyn. If she survives the fortnight, then the odds will turn in her favor."

"If she survives?" Robyn repeated the woman's words in a rising voice. "What are you saying?"

The woman didn't answer right away. Instead, she packed up her herbs and salves and stared at Gwyneth's sleeping face. "The child was too big for her body. Things tore that should not have torn, and she needs rest and food. Broth and bread, meat when she can take it. And prayer."

"You don't understand. I can't lose them. My brother . . ." She couldn't finish the sentence.

"Good meat. Soak the bread in broth and see that she eats it and give the child goat's milk when her milk runs out. I've left you willow bark for her fever. The bleeding has stopped, at least, which is something."

"I can't lose them." All it seemed she could do was repeat words that had already been said. Michael was gone. Gwyneth and the baby were all she had left of him, and if they left too . . . Panic seized her throat.

"Pray, then," the midwife said as she took her leave.

Pray. When had prayer ever helped her? She continued pacing. They'd been struggling already before Michael's death. There was never enough to eat, which was why he had taken the risks he had in the woods, hunting game larger than the rabbits and squirrels Robyn brought down with her slingshot. That meat had turned into food and cloth and medicine, for there was always a market for game.

Now they had nothing. In the dead of winter, the energy she would spend hunting rabbits wouldn't be worth the meager reward, and leaving Gwyneth alone in the house terrified Robyn even more than starvation. She couldn't bear the thought of returning to another death.

Symon stirred, and his face reddened as hunger woke him. Robyn scooped him into her arms and cradled him against her breast, rocking him back and forth as she pressed her lips to the fine hair on his head. The song she hummed came from some-place far away. *Sleep,* she begged him silently. *Sleep so she can rest. Sleep so I can think.*

Symon whimpered and nuzzled against her, searching for her breast. "I wish I could," she told him. Her body ached as her nephew's whimpers turned into frustrated sobs, then subsided. He slept in her arms, but his face remained screwed up in dis-content, and she almost woke him up just to hear him scream

26

with her. He slept because he didn't have the strength to keep on fighting. He slept, and so did Gwyneth, and Robyn wished more than anything that she, too, could close her eyes and wake to a kinder world.

"A goat," she said, turning the words into a quiet song. "I'll find you a goat."

Even if she found someone willing to sell milk to her, she'd have to find a way to pay. She could go to her uncle, the miller, but he had more mouths to feed than there were days in the week. That left the church. The Nottingham priests, however, were in the sheriff's pocket, and while she could set aside her pride to ask for their aid, she doubted even they had a spare nanny goat still in milk this late in the year.

"Michael," she said into the down of Symon's head. "I need you."

Gwyneth turned against the pillow, her golden hair limp and dark with sweat. Her eyes flickered beneath their lids as the fever rode her dreams.

"There's more to fletching than feather and wood," Michael's voice said from the depths of Robyn's memory. It had been her twelfth name day, and he'd taken her to a grove of young oaks just past the border of the forest. "You need to know how the arrow will fly."

"But how . . ." She hadn't finished her question as he placed a slim bow in her hands. The wood was light, suited for a boy, not a man, and as soft as velvet where he'd oiled it. Robyn thought it was the most beautiful thing she'd ever seen. She had nocked the arrow he handed her with reverence.

"Sight down the shaft. Yes, just like that. You see that tree, twenty paces east, with the burl? The one that looks like Aunt Mildred's face on market day? See if you can hit it."

She remembered how clumsy her fingers had felt on the bow-string, the familiar arrows clunky and foreign as she let the first one fly. She'd missed, of course. Everyone missed their first shot, according to Michael, but something had stirred in her blood that morning while her brother smiled encouragingly and the pads of her fingers itched from the snap of the bowstring. She had missed her first shot, true, but she had not missed her second.

"It's a shame you're a girl," Michael had told her as they slunk out of the forest, careful not to attract the attention of the foresters. "I've never seen anyone shoot like that their first time. You're plenty strong. You've been holding out on me, little bird."

She felt the tears on her cheeks as the memory faded. Not the crippling sobs that had racked her body as she'd thrown herself against the crowd, struggling to reach her brother as the executioner led him to the scaffold. These were small tears, just salt seeping from a wound too deep to measure. She clutched her brother's son more tightly to her chest and watched the fire burning. That same bow waited for Symon, one day, and his small hands would grip the wood where hers had, sweat and spit binding them as surely as the blood that ran in both their veins.

All the boy had to do was live.

"Robyn," Gwyneth said. Her voice was hoarse and thin, and it cut Robyn further open. She came closer, careful to keep rocking the child in her arms. "When is Michael coming home?"

Gwyneth's eyes were glassy, and her cheeks unnaturally flushed. More willow bark, Robyn told herself.

"Soon," she answered. Gwyneth would remember the truth when the fever broke.

"Is it raining?"

"Outside, yes."

"I hear screaming," said Gwyneth.

Robyn sat at the edge of the bed so that her body touched Gwyneth's, hoping the solidity of her presence would soothe her sister-in-law. "I hear it too."

She'd hear it forever. The sound had flayed her throat as Michael swung, and Gwyneth's voice had risen in a horrible harmony with her own.

No, she swore. Gwyneth would not die, nor would the child. Whatever it took.

She set out for the Papplewick mill later that afternoon, running past houses dark with rain and streets slick with ice. The wind picked up as she ran and propelled her forward almost as if it grieved with her, shrieking through the winter trees as its hands shoved her roughly toward her uncle's house.

"Midge," she said, gasping for breath when she arrived. Her cousin caught her by the shoulders and dragged her inside. Robyn's bevy of cousins stared at her with open mouths for the space of a heartbeat, and then concern poured out of them all at once.

"Is it Gwyneth?"

"The baby?"

The questions came hard and fast until she held up her hand for silence. "I need someone to stay with Gwyneth."

"I'll do it," said Midge, just as the rest of her sisters burst out with questions about where Robyn was going.

"For God's sake, will you lot be quiet?" Her uncle's bellow silenced the room. "Robyn. What do you need?"

Her lungs burned from her journey and her face was numb with cold, but she managed to force out her next words. "I'm going to talk to the sheriff."

Her uncle didn't need to shout for silence, this time. No one spoke until Midge said, "I'll get my cloak."

"The sheriff?" Uncle Benedict looked down at Robyn with concern. Robyn didn't try to guess what he was thinking. The sheriff had levied an especially harsh tax on her uncle after Gwyneth had married Michael, carrying his grudge down Michael's bloodline.

"Michael is dead," she said flatly. "If the sheriff truly loved Gwyneth, perhaps he will help us."

Benedict sat down heavily at the table and rested his hands palms up on his knees as if the answers lay within. "Are you sure that is wise?" he asked her at last.

"If he would just let us sell our arrows, Gwyneth would stand a chance."

"Is she any better?"

Robyn stared at him, unable to answer, and settled for a short shake of her head.

"But he killed Michael," said Midge.

She'd had the same thought as she ran, each footstep pounding that bitter truth deeper into her bones. "I know. But I can't let him kill her too, or Symon."

Her uncle lent them his elderly cart horse and gave Robyn enough coin to stable him in town. It was more than he could afford, she knew, but she was grateful for the speed and the warmth as she and Midge rode double on the gelding's bony back. It was only early evening, but sunlight failed to pierce the clouds, and they rode through freezing mud in the half-light of dusk, tree branches whipping against their clothing. Midge wrapped her arms around Robyn's waist and hung on as the cart horse stumbled and righted himself time and again. They both let out a sigh of relief when the lights of Nottingham came into view, and the gate guard waved them through hurriedly before ducking back into the shelter of the gatehouse.

"I'll stable the horse," Midge offered as they dismounted outside the shop. The wooden sign with its painted arrow creaked above them in the wind.

Robyn nodded, her throat too tight to speak. Her hand hesitated on the latch as Midge led the horse away. "I was only gone two hours," she said to herself, and pushed the door open. The shop lay in darkness. Arrows and bow staves cast long, thin shadows on the walls as she walked past barrels of curing wood and piles of sawdust blown about by the storm. Warmth greeted her when she entered the living quarters. The fire had not died, at least, and the dark outline of Gwyneth's body lay against the glow.

"I'm back," she said as she fell to her knees beside the bed. Gwyneth's eyes were open, and Symon nursed fitfully at her breast. Robyn tucked a strand of hair behind Gwyneth's ear.

"Where did you go?"

"To get Midge."

"Did you find Michael?"

"No," said Robyn, swallowing.

"Oh." Gwyneth's face slackened. She no longer looked like something out of a minstrel's song. When Michael had first

30

courted her, Robyn had thought she resembled a wood nymph or a goddess. Now she looked tired and old and heartbreakingly mortal.

"I'm going to get help," she said. "I promise."

Midge arrived a few minutes later and hung her soaking cloak by the fire to dry. "How's my littlest cousin?" she cooed as she peered around Robyn to see Symon. Gwyneth managed a weak smile.

"Can you brew some willow bark tea?" Robyn asked.

"Of course." Midge busied herself with the kettle.

Robyn said, "I'll be back soon. I promise."

She tore her eyes away from the sight of her family and made for the door, shivering in her damp clothes. The wind had redoubled its earlier efforts when she strode into the street. It flung her cloak around her and swiped the hood from her head, catching her hair and snarling it with icy fingers.

What am I doing? she asked herself as she forced her way up the hill and left the narrow streets for the wider thoroughfares of the wealthy. The castle loomed above her with its pennants snapping. She didn't want to know what Michael would think of her, begging for mercy from the man who had sentenced him to death. She didn't even know what she thought. That's not entirely true, said the part of her that knew better. Her nails dug into her palms. If killing the sheriff would bring Michael back and feed Gwyneth, she would do it. If seeing him drawn and quartered and ripped into pieces in the cardinal directions would resurrect her brother, she would watch. She would have watched anyway, the sweet taste of justice in her mouth, but none of it would mean anything if Gwyneth died.

Rain blew into her face. So much would be different if Michael had fallen in love with someone else. She allowed herself to savor the bitterness of the thought for a moment before discarding it. Michael could not have fallen for another woman, just as Gwyneth could not have loved the sheriff. She'd seen the way her brother and his wife looked at each other. There was enough leftover warmth to include Robyn, and her heart stirred

31

helplessly as she remembered the easy grace of their shared lives. Her brother, singing off-key as he fletched an arrow. Gwyneth, trimming feathers plucked from one of Maeve's geese with a smile on her lips as she caught Robyn's eye, brimming with love for them both. Few families were so lucky. All of that was gone now.

The door to the sheriff's townhouse stood before her long before she was ready to face it. The oak gleamed in the last of the stormy light, and behind it somewhere was the man who had taken her brother away. I can't, she thought, biting her cheek hard enough to draw blood. *I can't, Michael.* She would die before she asked this man for help. *I can't.* She would die, taking the sheriff with her, and then . . . Gwyneth would still lie there, fevered and weak, and Symon would pass out of the world without a fight. *I must.* What she did now she would do out of sight of pride and vengeance.

She raised her fist and knocked.

A servant answered the door after an eon and scowled at Robyn. "What do you want?"

"I'm here to see the sheriff."

"His lordship doesn't have time for the likes of you."

"It's about Gwyneth."

The woman's scowl deepened. "Wait here," she said, not bothering to invite Robyn inside. The door slammed in her face. She stared at it, her mind curiously empty save for the repeating litany, *I have no choice I have no choice I have no choice.* When it opened again to reveal the sheriff, she bowed her head, hiding the murder in her eyes behind lowered lashes.

"Robyn Fletcher."

"My lord."

"To what do I owe the honor?"

The quiet mockery in his voice made her stomach threaten to throw up what little was in it. This was the man she had gone to for aid. This was the man . . . *no.* She steeled herself. "Gwyneth is near death, m'lord."

He waited, perhaps enjoying watching the rain run down her face as it plastered the hair to the back of her neck.

"I've come to ask that you bury with him the grudge you bore my brother."

"Do you, now." It wasn't a question.

"Gwyneth needs to eat, and I cannot feed her if I cannot sell our arrows."

"I hardly see how that is my problem."

He wants you to kneel, she told herself, but her knees refused to budge. "Everyone knows you hated my brother. But your foresters need arrows, and ours fly true. I could sell them to you."

"My men have no need of a poacher's arrows."

Robyn focused on the muscles of her thighs and willed them to let her bend her knees. They remained rigid. Gwyneth, she reminded herself. *Think of Gwyneth.* Instead, she saw her brother's face, turning red then purple as the rope dug into his neck and the blood vessels burst in his eyes.

"Would you let her die, then?" she said, her voice dropping. She met the sheriff's eyes and noted the cold calculation in their depths along with the pleasure he did not bother to hide at her humiliation.

"Of course not. I heard she was near her time. She need only marry me, and she will want for nothing. I'll even raise your brother's child as my own."

Ice poured down Robyn's back, only to be replaced with white-hot flames that licked at her insides and sent smoke across her eyes. Gwyneth, marry this man? The world tilted as she staggered and caught herself on the door frame. It was unthinkable. Symon would not grow up in the house of his father's killer, nor would Gwyneth submit to him while Robyn still drew breath.

"Never," she said, venom filling her mouth. "She would die before she married you."

"Then so be it." He dropped all pretense of congeniality. "But when she does, know this, girl. No one in this town will ever buy from you again, and your brother's brat will beg for scraps in the street like a dog while you slum with the whores for your daily bread."

Robyn lunged for him, but he caught her by the front of her

tunic and shoved her back into the street. She landed in a half-frozen puddle to the sound of his laughter. Slops and night soil soaked into her clothes and squelched through her fingers, but none of that mattered. The sheriff had shut the door on her and her hopes, and she sat in the downpour until the numbness in her limbs eased the ache of failure.

That's it, then, she thought, ignoring the curse of a man on horseback as he reined up sharply to avoid running her down. None of them would survive the winter. She'd only made things worse by coming here. She stared at the closed door and willed it to burst into flames. If only she had brought a bow, she could have shot the sheriff, which would have at least avenged Michael's death before condemning the rest of them.

Night fell in earnest as she stood on shaking legs and walked slowly through the darkened streets. When she arrived home, the shop sign swung overhead, and the arrow flew of its own accord as if to taunt her. Inside waited all those useless arrows. She could use them for kindling, maybe, when they ran out of firewood.

Or you could use them to hunt. The thought stopped her short, and she hesitated with her hand on the door. Yes, Michael had been hanged for that same crime, but she wasn't Michael; she was stealthier. She would be more careful. The sheriff wouldn't expect her to repeat her brother's mistake, and while he gloated over his victory, she would keep her family alive. She straightened her shoulders and stepped into the warmth of the shop as a grim determination curled around her heart.

Chapter Four

The stiff fabric of her court dress hung around her arms, and the irritatingly long sleeves threatened to catch on everything she passed. She eyed a freestanding candelabra with suspicion and veered around it to avoid entanglement, grateful that her dress, at least, was not as ornate as Emmeline's or Willa's. Willa wore enough brocade to weave a tapestry. Her red hair was wrapped in green ribbons, complementing the pale yellow ones in Emmeline's honey brown locks. Her father's wealth spilled from the jeweled mantle on her shoulders. Marian avoided meeting her eyes. She would have avoided Willa entirely if she could have gotten away with it, but Willa went where Emmeline did whenever possible, and Marian, as Emmeline's companion, had no choice but to follow.

Marian wore blue. She always wore blue. Her father had confiscated a great bolt of good cloth from a merchant last summer, and as a result all her court dresses were the same shade—a fact that the seamstress had done her best to hide with clever paneling, trim, and inserts. She didn't mind. Blue suited her, and her goal in court was to draw as little attention to herself as possible. Bland wardrobes, combined with a proximity to Willa's sharp tongue, nearly ensured this.

Emmeline walked beside her as they made their entrance to the receiving hall, her arm resting on Marian's and her other hand firmly closed around her son's. He shot Marian a dubious

35

look, fidgeting with his collar as he struggled to keep up with his mother's limping gait. When she was sixteen, Emmeline had suffered a riding accident that left her with a bad leg, a fact that only seemed to encourage her preference for riding over walking. Marian wished they could ride away now.

Willa left them to stand a few yards away with her father and twin brother, who slouched beside his sister with a bored expression that did not seem to please their father. The hall smelled of sparingly washed bodies and perfume, and the latter failed to conceal the former. Tapestries and heraldic banners muffled the sound of the courtiers' voices, and the susurrus of soft-soled shoes moving over the rushes whispered underneath the conversations. Marian scanned the faces of Nottingham's nobility. Most she recognized by name, and the rest she had seen in passing. She didn't see her father or Lord Linley.

"Emmeline," a thin woman with graying hair said as she kissed Emmeline on both her cheeks and stooped to bestow the same honor on Henri. Marian tried to fade into Emmeline's dress, an illusion Lady Margery seemed only too happy to oblige as she attempted to engage Emmeline in the latest gossip. Around them, the assembled peerage cast curious looks at the empty dais while incense and smoke from the torches shaped twisting patterns in the high vaulted ceiling.

"There you are," said a voice in her ear.

She turned, fearing to discover one of her father's cronies, and smiled in relief as Alanna slid into her customary position to Marian's left. The relief faded as the suffocating memory of the scene in the priory settled over her again. She did her best to stifle the urge to pull away from the minstrel. It had not been Alanna who had held her eyes during . . . whatever that had been. Alanna was her friend. She had only ever showed Marian kindness, and there was always the chance that Willa hadn't told her that Marian had witnessed their tryst. Sin, she corrected herself. Alanna hadn't changed the way she acted toward Marian, nor had she made any insinuations that Marian was anything like Willa, whatever that meant.

It was also impossible to hold any sort of hard feelings against Alanna for long. It wasn't just that her unornamented brown hair and plain features offered Marian a refuge amid the brightly painted faces of the nobility, or that she'd known her for years. When Alanna spoke, ripples of silence fell around her as passersby stopped, entranced by the low musicality of her tongue and the rich warmth that infused her words. When she sang, even the dead listened.

"Any sign of the prince?" Marian asked.

"He's here somewhere, along with Isabella. You know how he likes his entrances." Alanna hooked her arm companionably through the arm not occupied by Emmeline's, which earned Marian a mocking glance from Willa.

"Have you seen his herald?" Marian asked Alanna.

"Fat old fraud. I think he's losing his sight. Half the time he can't even tell who he's announcing."

"But he is loud."

"Which is really all that matters." Alanna pursed her lips in professional disapproval. "And how is Lady Margery?"

"Pretending I don't exist," said Marian, turning her face to hide her words from the lady in question.

"Well, she wouldn't want to give you ideas above your station, baroness. You might try and snatch up her son."

Lady Margery's son fidgeted as he waited for his mother to return to his side. At fifteen, he had the complexion of a parsnip and almost as much personality.

"I wouldn't dream of reaching such lofty heights," said Marian as she suppressed a strong urge to laugh.

"Margery might not have heard you two," said Emmeline when Lady Margery departed, "but I certainly did. Alanna, the word incorrigible comes to mind."

"My lady. I'm honored."

"You shouldn't be."

"And yet she never seems to let that stop her," said Marian.

"Indeed. No, Henri, you cannot play with the other children." Henri left off tugging on his mother's arm and pouted. Emmeline was spared the need to further chastise her entourage by the slightly off-key trumpeting of the herald.

"I think he's losing his hearing, too," said Alanna.

The prince's herald was an elderly man with a stooped back and wispy mustache that fluttered as he spoke. "His Royal Highness, Prince John, Count of Mortain, and the Lady Isabel of Gloucester."

The assembled nobility fell silent as the doors swung open and the prince and his wife strode down the aisle to the dais. John cut an imposing figure in his fur mantle and ceremonial garb. He lacked his brother's towering height, but there was something about his eyes that set Marian's teeth on edge. Richard might have been nicknamed the Lionheart, but John walked with a predator's easy gait as his eyes roamed the audience. Marian kept hers averted. John favored her father, but she did not plan to give him any cause to give her so much as a second glance. She had seen what happened to the women who played that game.

John took his seat on the throne and held out his hand to his wife, who smiled demurely.

"I wonder why Isabel looks so pleased," Alanna said. Marian wondered the same thing but did not get a chance to dwell on it further, for the prince began to speak.

"It is with great sorrow that I must announce the capture of my brother Richard. As many of you know, Duke Leopold has . . . delayed . . . Richard's return, which grieves us all." But John looked neither grieved nor greatly concerned by his brother's mishap. "We do not yet know where, exactly, my brother is being held, but I have been assured that our good regents are looking into the matter."

Heated whispers broke out amid the court, which John allowed to grow into a cacophony of speculation.

"He looks as if his prayers have been answered," Willa said, breaking away from her family once more. Marian wished she would stay where she belonged.

"Perhaps they have," said Emmeline.

According to court gossip, Richard had been on his way back to England after signing a truce with Saladin when bad weather drove his ship to port in Corfu, and then more bad weather on the next leg of his journey wrecked his ship near Aquileia, forcing him to make his way over land. Marian could picture him standing on shore in the middle of the wreckage, mustering his forces for a trek through unfriendly territory. How his pride must have stung when he was discovered. No demands had arrived from the Duke, but the prospect of civil war stirred the air, fanned by the speculations of the peerage. She toyed with the brocade on her sleeve.

"We won't hear much in this weather anyway." Emmeline accepted a goblet of wine from a passing servant and took a long swallow. Marian knew the damp irritated her bad hip, and suspected Emmeline was in considerably more discomfort than she let on.

"Your father's here," Alanna said, touching Marian's arm lightly and pointing toward the dais.

She followed the gesture. Her father, the sheriff of Nottingham, had his head bowed beside the prince's, and he appeared to be listening intently to whatever John was saying. His face was flushed from drink, just as it had been ever since her mother had died, and Marian felt a familiar surge of pity. He needed a wife. Not only would it be good for him, but it might make him more amenable to other prospects for Marian. Prospects, for instance, who didn't have a habit of picking their teeth at table and beating their wives.

A minstrel struck up a tune on the other side of the crowd. Alanna's head jerked, and her eyes lit up, distracting Marian from her thoughts.

"Perhaps this isn't a total waste of our time after all. Dance with me?" Alanna caught Marian's hands and pulled her into a jig, twirling her until Marian laughed despite herself as the song wound down. Breathless, she broke free, and Alanna gave her an exaggerated bow before turning to Willa. "And you, my lady? Would you do me the honor of a dance?"

Willa curtsied, playing along, but Marian didn't miss the smoldering look the redhead shot the minstrel. Nor, Marian realized, did Emmeline. Marian saw the crease in her mistress's brow and wondered what she knew of her best friend's dalliance with her singer. Did she think it harmless? Or did she, like Marian, see the danger in the way Alanna's hand brushed Willa's hip?

Marian bent and swept Henri up in the music to distract herself, eliciting a giggle from the boy. Perhaps it was wrong to dance so soon after the news of their captured monarch, but the rest of the court seemed more than eager to shake off the tension, and as the evening unfolded into a tumult of music and wine, Marian allowed herself to hope that all might yet be well. The pope would intervene, and Richard would return, and when he did she'd remind him of his affection for her and beg him to persuade her father to arrange another match. Until then, she'd do her best to stay out of her father's way. Her eyes met Willa's again as she whirled a giggling Henri around. Besides, she thought, jerking her gaze away, she had plenty of other things to worry about.

Chapter Five

The roe deer couldn't have weighed more than three stone, but after a quarter of an hour in the warm spring air, three stone felt like fifty. Robyn crouched in the shadow of a large elm with the deer's small head lolling against her chest and its delicate forelegs resting almost companionably across her knees. The sweet close smell of the meat made her mouth water and heightened her awareness of her empty stomach. Game had grown scarce as winter waned, and with the child nearing four months old and still as ravenous as ever, this deer was an unexpected boon.

Foolish, she told herself. She was too close to the edge of the forest to have risked a deer. She should have taken a few cuts and abandoned the rest of the carcass to the wolves, or, better yet, shot a rabbit instead. Sweat dripped off her upper lip. There was still time to hide the carcass. She could take the haunches and the loins, leaving the rest for the crows and wolves, and consider herself lucky.

"Luck favors the rich, little bird, and no one else," she knew her brother would have said if he were there.

She'd be damned if she fed the crows today. Using the stave of her unstrung bow to haul herself to her feet, she continued back along the game trail toward Nottingham.

Foolish, trilled the birds high up in the budding branches, but it was hard to feel fear beneath the trees with bluebells carpeting the forest floor as far as the eye could see and sunlight piercing the new green of the canopy in lazy shafts, trickling like mead where it glazed trunks wet with sap. She passed a cluster of mushrooms, dewy white and begging to be sliced into venison stew. The burning in her shoulders and thighs kept her moving. There would be time for gathering mushrooms later, when blood from the young buck was washed from her hands and the deer was hidden in the musty dark of her uncle's mill.

Foolish, her uncle would undoubtedly agree. She could almost hear his gruff voice lecturing her as he swung a bag of rye meal over one shoulder. "Your father would never have stood for this. First Michael, now you. Have you no respect for his memory?"

He'd take the deer regardless, she knew, as he always did. Besides, it wasn't her father's memory that drove her out of the shop and into Sherwood, time and time again.

Robyn wiped another drop of sweat from her brow and glanced around the woods. Nothing moved besides the occasional bird and skittering squirrel, but the hair on the back of her neck prickled uncomfortably.

A branch broke further up the trail. She spotted a large, twisted oak a few yards off the path that promised some protection from prying eyes and made her way toward it as quickly as she dared, her thighs burning with the effort of crouching low to the ground beneath the deer. Around her, a chorus of birds rose in alarm. Michael had taught her the meaning of the more important of the forest's bird calls, and right now, this was the only one that mattered. Fear soured her mouth and her heartbeat pounded in her throat as she laid the deer down in the bluebells and pressed herself against the trunk of the tree. Slowly, her hands shaking with barely suppressed panic, she slipped the bowstring out of the pouch at her belt and strung the bow. The wood felt smooth and warm, and the leather grip, dark with oil from her brother's hands, calmed the worst of the shaking. Her fingers brushed the feathers with a fletcher's care as she loosed an arrow from her quiver and willed her heart to slow.

The unmistakable sound of footsteps drifted toward her on the breeze. She recognized the tread; this was someone who was comfortable in the woods, and who knew how to avoid the reaching roots and low-hanging snags that tangled the inexperienced. She was lucky that branch had snapped at all, given the ease with which this person trod the forest. Luck is for the rich, she reminded herself, and willed the stranger to keep walking. The bowstring hummed very faintly against her forearm as she nocked the arrow. *Don't look this way. Don't stop.*

The penalty for poaching the king's deer was death. Pheasant, hare, or smaller game demanded lesser punishments, but Prince John loved his deer, as reportedly did his brother, King Richard, assuming he ever made it back from the continent.

There is no difference between a man and a deer, she told herself. *They are both just skin stretched over organ and bone.* Accidents happened all the time in the forest. Outlaws roamed these woods, like the bastard Siward and his band, who made a habit of stealing sheep from those who most depended on them and raping any woman they caught alone. No one would think to trace a dead forester back to her.

The footsteps drew parallel with her hiding spot, then paused. She heard the rustle and creak of leather boots and jerkin as the stranger knelt and ran a hand over the leaves near the ground, and in that soft rustle of bluebells she realized her mistake.

Blood.

The man exhaled in a short burst, and Robyn thought she could hear the pieces falling into place in his head as he took another step and knelt again, this time closer, perhaps to examine the soft imprint of a booted sole in the deep loam of the forest floor.

I have no choice, she realized, and with the certainty of that thought held firmly in her mind, she moved out from behind the tree and leveled the arrow at the man's heart. He looked up from his crouch, and she watched surprise registering across his broad, weathered face. She might have faltered, then, if he had been anyone else.

Clovis.

Her vision narrowed to a howling tunnel as his expression

twisted from surprise to malicious satisfaction. She remembered the way he'd jerked the rope that bound Michael's wrists as he led him to the gallows, forcing him to stumble up the steps, denying him what little dignity remained in those last few minutes of his life. She remembered, too, the roar of the crowd around the platform: a hundred people watching, a hundred people who could have stormed the gallows and cut Michael down, and instead did nothing.

Her bowstring twanged. The arrow sprouted from Clovis's leather jerkin almost of its own accord, and silence filled her ears as the shaft buried itself almost to the fletching. Clovis's eyes widened as he tilted forward, and he collapsed into the blue sea of flowers, driving the arrow the rest of the way through. The metal arrowhead glistened redly in the morning light from the exit wound along his spine.

"Collect your arrow, little bird," Michael's voice whispered in her head. "Don't leave any signs behind."

She took a step toward Clovis, then another. Her head spun as she watched his body twitch once, twice, and then lie still as the life leaked out of him into the earth, just as Michael's had leaked down his leg. You left piss behind, she wanted to tell Michael as she stared down at the warm corpse at her feet. *Piss, and me.*

The minutes trickled away from her as the birdsong returned, but she couldn't make herself touch the body. Leaving the arrow in him wasn't an option. Her arrows were recognizable to anyone who knew what they were looking for, and too few people bought them to rely on numbers. Take it, she urged herself, but she couldn't shake the memory of Clovis laughing as he gave Michael one last shove, even though the man lay dead at her feet.

He will never laugh again. The thought did not bring her the relief she'd hoped for. Clovis still laughed in her mind's eye. He would always be there, laughing, and Michael would always trip, and he would always die, no matter how many times she killed this man. The unfairness of it wrapped around her chest like a vise.

"Don't move," said a voice from behind her.

Robyn froze. She could hear the man edging around her, his breath coming quickly as he fought what she could only assume was a strong urge to shoot her then and there. She caught a flash of red hair, followed by pimples that glared angrily even from her peripheral vision. Not a man. A boy.

"Robyn?" His voice rose an octave and he flushed a maroon that rivaled the color of his hair.

"Cedric," she said, searching for words that did not come. Of course it would be Cedric. He was the only forester who still purchased his arrows openly from her, and he had made his intentions toward her clear with each tortured glance from his cornflower blue eyes.

"You shot him."

She shrugged, unable to speak. She and Gwyneth had laughed at his bumbling attempts at courtship and the way his boyish voice cracked whenever he spoke to her. Laughing at him was easier than resenting him, for they relied more heavily on his patronage than Robyn cared to admit. Now one of her arrows, sister to the ones in his quiver, had killed one of his fellows, and all the laws of Nottingham dictated that he bring her in for justice.

"Why?" he asked.

She shrugged again, helplessly, then pointed at the tree. He would be able to see the deer from here, and even Cedric could put two and two together.

"Stand up," he said, clearly forcing himself to speak more firmly than he wanted to.

"We were hungry, Cedric." She did not try to hide the pleading note in her voice. His weakness for her might yet save her life, her pride be damned, but she would shoot him, too, before she let him take her back to Nottingham. "You don't know what it's been like since my brother died."

"You should have come to me. You know I would have helped you."

"What could you have done?"

Sweat broke out on Cedric's brow as he looked back and forth between her and Clovis. "You could have married me."

She flinched at his honesty. True, she could have married Cedric, leaving the bed she shared with Gwyneth and the baby for his and letting him rub the stubble of his sparse beard against her face as he grew to slowly hate her for her silence and for her indifference, but then again starvation was a surer way to die.

Lie to him, little bird.

"I still could," she said, but the words sounded forced even to her own ears and she saw the doubt in his eyes.

"Why'd you do it, Robyn?" he asked again.

"You know no one will buy from us."

"Then take a rabbit, or a bird, or Christ, some mushrooms. But a deer?" He lowered his bow. "Do you want to hang? And Clovis . . . Clovis."

"Clovis was a brute."

"Clovis was a *forester*. And a good man."

She laughed bitterly. The sound echoed in the forest, silencing the birds. "My brother was a good man."

"Michael was a poacher."

"And you've never hunted a deer in your life?"

Cedric's face turned the same shade of red as his pimples. They both knew he had. He'd brought Robyn and Gwyneth gifts of game this past winter once or twice when Robyn had been close to giving up, and none of those gifts had been sanctioned by the king.

A distant shout interrupted Cedric's reply. His shoulders stiffened, and Robyn's fingers spasmed on the bow. I could shoot him too, she thought, but she discarded the notion as soon as it crossed her mind. Clovis she would murder again, but Cedric had been kind to her. *Please, Michael, if you're up there, put in a good word for me,* she prayed, meeting Cedric's eyes. He closed them in frustration, and when he opened them, she knew her prayer, or at least the threat of blackmail, had found its mark.

"Go," he said. "I won't tell them it was you. I swear it on my life."

There was no time to thank him—nor to wrench her arrow from Clovis's torso. She could see the flicker of movement through the trees heralding the arrival of more men, and the only thing that would keep her out of the noose at this point, even with Cedric's head start, was speed. She raced off back the way she had come, feet flying over the familiar trail and toward the dark, tangled depths of Sherwood Forest.

Robyn surveyed the open stretch of moonlit ground between the trees and the mill. Going home to Gwyneth, who was no doubt beside herself with worry, was out of the question until she was sure Cedric would keep his word. That left her aunt and uncle. Robyn didn't want to bring trouble down on them any more than she did Gwyneth, but no forester alive stood a chance against Aunt Mildred when she was in a temper.

The burble of water drowned out the murmur of the forest and made it impossible to listen for sounds of pursuit. Her body ached from running and from several hours spent perched in a tree overlooking the trail back toward home, and the thought of doing any more running tonight made the muscles of her legs quiver in protest. Most of the family would be asleep at this hour, but Robyn knew that Midge slept lightly. She mimicked the cry of the small white-faced owls that lived in the mill's rafters.

Nothing. She whistled again, this time louder. Long minutes passed, and she was just about to make a dash for the darker shadows along the riverbed when the cottage door creaked open and a slight figure slipped out, wrapping a shawl around her shoulders. One last whistle drew her cousin to the edge of the woods, and then Robyn risked a whisper.

"It's me."

"Robyn?"

"Keep your voice down."

Midge reached out blindly, and Robyn caught her hand, pulling her into the trees.

"What are you doing here?"

47

The memory of the arrow protruding from Clovis's back caught up with her at last and she sank to her knees to vomit the remains of her breakfast into the dirt.

"Come inside," Midge urged when Robyn finished retching. "It's not safe."

"Any safer than us standing out here? Don't be a fool, cos."

Robyn allowed Midge to lead her across the rutted yard to the mill, where the familiar smells of baking bread, herbs, cabbage, and mutton pies overwhelmed her. Midge poured her a mug of ale and tore off a sizable hunk of bread from a cooling loaf.

"There's cheese, too," she offered. In the dim light of the low fire, darkness carved new hollows out from Midge's round cheeks and tamed the wild abundance of hair that escaped the confines of her braid to curl perpetually around her ears. Robyn took the block of hard cheese in silence and downed the ale, thirst taking precedence over hunger.

"Should I get my father?" Midge asked.

Robyn shook her head. Uncle Ben would wake soon enough, followed by her aunt and the rest of their brood. Now that she was here, she found she wasn't quite ready to face him, not with the severity of her crimes hanging over her head.

"Did something happen to Gwyn? I thought she was better."

Robyn shook her head.

"The baby? Robyn, you're scaring me."

"Cedric caught me."

"Cedric caught you what?"

Robyn forced the words out one by one, her earlier bravado evaporating like mist over the morning river as she stumbled over the grisly details. When she finished, Midge didn't speak. Instead, she took away Robyn's cup, grabbed herself one, and filled them both with her mother's supply of strong ale.

"I don't know what to do," Robyn said when Midge sat back down at the table.

"Cedric promised you he wouldn't say anything."

"What if he changes his mind, or the others realize he is lying?"

48

"He cares for you. He's helped you before."

"That was before I shot a forester. And even if he never says a word, what then? He'll always have that over me."

"Cedric's too sweet to use it against you." Midge wrapped the end of her braid around her finger and tugged at it periodically in agitation.

"He's still a boy. Who's to say he stays sweet?"

"What were you even going to do with a whole deer, Robyn? I thought you promised to stick to small game."

"I didn't plan on it, but it practically walked into my arrow and Gwyn—"

Midge laid her hand on Robyn's, cutting her off. "Don't worry about Gwyneth."

"How can I not?"

"Because right now you have to worry about yourself. My father will take care of Gwyn and Symon."

"But—"

"She's family, Robyn."

Robyn hesitated. If Cedric betrayed her, as she had to assume he might, the sheriff's wrath would fall on all he perceived had thwarted him—her uncle included.

"Why don't you sleep here tonight?" Midge said, oblivious to Robyn's growing panic. "We can figure out what to do tomorrow. If Cedric hasn't said anything by this point, he isn't likely to before morning. It's not like there is any other way they can trace you."

Cold fear spilled over Robyn. *The arrow.*

"What?" Midge's eyes widened in alarm.

"I left the arrow."

"Well it's not like they'll know it's yours."

"They will if they take it to the guild." Her arrows bore her mark, unless by some slim chance the shot had damaged it.

"Say you sold it to somebody. The only people who know you're a fair shot are me and Gwyneth."

Robyn let the words soothe her. Maybe Midge was right. Maybe Cedric could be trusted to keep her secret, at least for now, and she could return home. *And if Cedric gives you away? What will happen to them then?*

She knew the answer. Her nephew would grow up haunted by the crimes of his family, and Gwyneth would end up marrying the loathsome sheriff to save her son or even worse, because the sheriff held Robyn's life over Gwyneth's head as a bargaining chip. Better Robyn had died in the forest than leave them to that fate.

"I could marry Cedric." The words left poisonous fumes in her mouth. "He would see to it that Gwyneth was taken care of."

Midge held her eyes. "You could," she said, but her tone contained all the doubts that clouded Robyn's mind.

As much as she wanted things to be different, Robyn knew she could not marry a forester. Foresters had killed her brother, and even if it bought Gwyneth time, it still might not be enough to protect her from the sheriff. She would have thrown her life away for nothing. Robyn wished she could go back to that winter day before the sheriff's door. Instead of begging him for mercy, she would thrust her knife through the place where he should have had a soul. She'd let herself believe that she could save them and that she had choices. She knew better now. There were no choices for people like her when men like the sheriff made the rules.

"No," Midge said, narrowing her eyes at Robyn. "I know that look, and whatever you're thinking, stop right now."

There was no other way, though, was there? She'd known that since she looked up and saw Cedric standing over her in the forest. She'd known it all her life really, ever since Michael had laid that bow in her hands and she'd felt the arrow sing to her as it left her fingers.

"Midge," she said, "I need you to do something for me."

"No."

"You don't know what I'm going to say."

"I know I'm not going to like it."

"I need you to visit Gwyneth tomorrow. Don't tell her you've seen me, but you have to find a way to steal my good tunic. The yellow one," she added in case Midge didn't remember.

"I can give you one of—"

"I need you to take my tunic and dump it in the river. Get it good and muddy."

"No." Horror laced her cousin's words as understanding dawned across her round face.

"You will then go back to Gwyneth and tell her that you saw my clothes in the river on your way home to the mill. She will know it is mine when you show her, and she will assume that I've drowned."

Midge clapped a hand over her mouth. "You can't do that to her," she said into her fist. "Robyn, that's—"

"People need to see Gwyn upset. *Cedric* has to see Gwyn upset. He'll think I've drowned myself, and everyone else will just think I got unlucky, even your parents."

Midge shook her head, wordless.

"It's the only way I can keep them safe."

"She'll hate you for this, assuming it doesn't kill her."

"Maybe. But if I'm dead, they can't use me against her. I can hunt for all of us, like Michael used to, but I won't get caught again." She would be more careful, this time. She'd hunt deep in the woods and only bring game home under the cover of darkness. She would . . . Midge's voice interrupted her planning.

"This is stupid, Robyn. There has to be another way."

"Do you have any better ideas?"

"I will if you would give me time to think."

"There isn't time."

"What if there is, and you throw everything away? You don't get to come back from the dead once you're dead. I would have thought you knew that after Michael."

The glare that passed between them was the sort that started tavern brawls.

"I'll stay the night then," Robyn said, dropping her gaze as guilt won out. "But in the mill, not here. I can hide in the eaves the way you used to. But I'm leaving in the morning."

"Where will you go?"

Robyn pulled an arrow out of the quiver still on her back

and laid it on the table, running her finger along the smooth wood of the shaft where it met the feathers and over the maker's mark that her father had passed down to his ill-fated children. "Sherwood."

Midge opened her mouth to argue, no doubt thinking of her sister Mary, who had been assaulted by Sherwood bandits. Her eyebrows furrowed as she turned this new idea over. "That bastard Siward's out there," she said, her eyes transfixed by the arrow between them. "You know what he did to Mary. And there are foresters, and wolves, and all sorts of other things."

"It's a place to start, at least. It's almost May. There will be plenty to eat between now and harvest time, and by then I'll have figured something else out."

"What about the outlaws?"

"Isn't that what I am?"

"Not technically. Nobody has ordered your arrest. You're drowning in the river, remember?"

"It's the sheriff that worries me right now. Not Siward." She made herself sound braver than she felt. "And the foresters don't usually go into the deeper parts of the forest, according to Cedric." Cedric had also explained that this was, in part, because the outlaws in Sherwood's heart were better armed and better woodsmen than the sheriff's men, but she didn't think that was something Midge needed to know at the moment.

"What about me?"

Robyn glanced up, startled. "What do you mean?"

"How will I find you?"

"You won't. It would be too dangerous." She regretted the words as soon as they were out of her mouth. Midge's eyes flashed, and she stood, drawing herself up to her diminutive height.

"If it is too dangerous, Robyn Fletcher, then you shouldn't be out there."

"That's not what I—"

"Here's what is going to happen. If, and only if, I do this for you, you will tell me exactly how to find you, and if you are not where you say you will be, so help me God, Robyn, I will hang you myself."

So be it. She did not have time to argue. Robyn took her cousin's hands in hers and gave them a firm squeeze. "I promise, Midge, that you, and only you, will have the privilege of hanging me."

The cry of an owl woke her the next morning. Midge, she thought, opening her eyes. Two large yellow orbs stared back at her as the disgruntled former occupant of the eaves hopped closer. Outside, songbirds stirred sleepily, the threat of swooping owls past. Robyn, however, gave the cruel, curved beak a nervous glance. Starlight and the first gray glow of dawn filtered through chinks in the thatch. Her uncle needed to get it redone this year, and Robyn had already promised him she would find time to help. *Too late for that, too.*

The owl, apparently deciding that she wasn't a threat, side-stepped further down the broad beam and settled in for the day. She watched it for a while and tried to force herself not to think about Gwyneth and the baby and the shafts waiting to be fletched on her table, or the wooden staves curing in the corner, the shape of the bows-to-be clear in her mind's eye. Michael had some skill as a bowyer, too, and she'd been learning the craft from him before the sheriff had hanged him without a trial and forced her to live by the bow, instead of by making them. The baby would be fussing by now, and Gwyneth would have already risen to kindle the breakfast fire, perhaps hoping to find Robyn curled up on the workbench beneath Michael's old cloak.

I'm sorry, Gwyn. She willed the words to find their way down the rutted path from Papplewick to Nottingham, along the River Leen and through the gate to the town below the castle on the hill where her sister-in-law no doubt paced the floor, fear souring the morning.

Another owl cry floated through the warm air of the mill. The owl to her left tilted his head, intrigued by the promise of mate or foe. Robyn whistled back. This earned her a startled hoot from her feathered companion, and then the owl took off for a less occupied rafter as Midge clambered up onto the beam.

"I'll do it," she said, not meeting Robyn's eye. "But you will owe me for this for the rest of your life."

Robyn didn't bother mentioning that the rest of her life might not be such a long time. "I know."

Midge hauled a sack up beside her. "I brought you a few things."

Robyn couldn't make out much of her face in the dark, but the tone of her voice spoke volumes. "Did you sleep at all?" she asked her cousin.

"Just promise me you'll be careful. You should go, now, before my father wakes up."

You should go, little bird. Michael's voice echoed Midge's, gruff and sweet and familiar. She heard it more clearly than she'd heard it since his death, and with it came a curious weightlessness as the future she'd labored over with every waking breath slipped out of her reach forever. "Meet me in two days," she said, still floating. "Follow the river until you come to the first stream, then follow that until you see a hill covered in chestnut trees, about two more miles. I'll be waiting."

"We will take care of Gwyneth. Just promise me you'll take care of yourself."

"I promise. And, Midge, be careful."

"Can I bring you anything?"

Robyn thought about this before answering. What did she have that couldn't be left behind? The little wooden robin Michael had carved for her could go to Symon, and she still wore her brother's hunting clothes. They would serve for now. "Arrows, and a second bowstring if you can manage it," she said, resisting the urge to ask for something to remind her of Gwyneth and the baby.

"I will manage."

Midge clambered down. Robyn followed, and they stood in the predawn light avoiding each other's eyes until the sound of a screaming infant penetrated the stone walls of the mill.

"Two days, Robyn."

"I'll be there."

Shouldering the satchel, she eased open the door of the mill and followed the riverbank into the forest. Her body ached worse than it had yesterday, bruised from an uncomfortable night spent crammed below the thatch, and she itched on top of it—probably the parting gift of the biting insects that made the roof their home. Gwyneth would tell her not to irritate the bites. Her heart ached at the thought, but the weightlessness continued to buoy her as the mill faded from sight and the dark shadows of the forest enveloped her.

I killed a man. I lost my family, my business, and my future. She repeated these things to herself with every step, but a different thought kept trying to surface as she brushed cobwebs from her face.

I'm free.

Noise ahead of her broke her out of these thoughts. The cheerful voice of a pig herder urged his charges down to the water to drink, and the pigs scattered ducks and wading birds before them as they snuffled and grunted at the water's edge. Robyn disappeared as best she could into the trees and gave the pigs and their keeper a wide berth. This part of the forest was open, grazed by swine and sheep and goats, and harvested by the people she'd grown up with. That glen there was where the best chanterelles grew, and broad clearings fed the herds of red and roe deer that roamed the forest under the protection of the king. Here by the river flourished the best blackberries and raspberries. Her arms bore the faint scars of years of picking berries with Midge and the other village children, and she touched the nearest bramble, letting the thorns catch at her fingers.

She walked until the sun began its descent toward the western horizon, keeping the river always to her left. The trees grew closer together here, and moss-covered boulders sprouted among their roots like sentinels, watching her. This was deeper into the woods than she'd ever been. The forest road lay somewhere to the east, bisecting Sherwood and cutting through the small village of

Edwinstowe that lay in the forest's heart, but between the road and the borders of the woodland spread vast tracts of wilderness. Lose her bearings, and she would be hard pressed to meet up with Midge, let alone find her way out of the woods ever again.

The massive corpse of a toppled great oak caught her eye. The roots reached halfway up the trunks of the nearby trees, moss clinging to them, and the trunk promised shelter from the heavy clouds rolling in. Robyn poked at the hollow with the stave of her bow, not wanting to disturb anything with teeth, and settled herself in the soft loam to examine the contents of her sack.

Bread, more cheese, and some hard sausages wrapped in cloth were tucked beside the shriveled remains of the last of the winter apples. A flagon of ale sloshed at the bottom. She tried not to dwell on how long it would last her. She had her knife and her bow, and the wool of her brother's tunic was thick enough to withstand the damp, chilly night ahead. The past two days had soaked it with her sweat, but she could still catch a lingering whiff of her brother if she buried her face in the sleeve. His clothes fit her well. Both she and Michael had inherited their father's height, and testing out the new bows she had made over the past year had filled out her shoulders. Sturdy boots, made from rich dark leather, were laced up her calves. She checked the laces for signs of fraying. The cobbler's work held. As long as she kept the hood over her face and wore her dark hair loose like a boy, she might pass for a man from a distance. Walking in the deep woods as a woman carried risks she didn't like considering.

The reality of her situation hit her the next day. Birdsong filled the woods and roused her from troubled sleep, and she watched dawn break over the forest from her nest of leaves. Noon came and went. She got up to urinate, then returned to the shelter of the trunk and observed the passage of wood lice over its rough surface with dispassionate interest.

Images of Gwyneth's grief filled her mind. Symon, at least, was too young to understand what was happening, but she knew Gwyneth would never forgive her, nor could she forgive herself. All she could do now was wait for Midge to make sure her family was safe, and then she would vanish.

Chapter Six

Spring came early that year. Marian woke to golden light and the soft sound of Emmeline's snores as she extricated herself from her embrace, easing Henri's arms from around her neck in the process. The large featherbed held the three of them easily, plus the sleeping body of Emmeline's favorite sight hound, and while normally Marian burrowed deeper beneath the covers if she woke before Emmeline, something about the morning light caught her breath. She slipped into a robe and rekindled the fire before opening the shutters to a cacophony of birdsong.

Harcourt Manor lay inside the borders of Sherwood Forest. The road to the manor always felt like an adventure, with its twisting oak trees and brambly hedges. Once home, though, it was easy to believe that this was the only place in the world. She could see the trees in the distance, past fields green with spring wheat and glistening with dew. A low line of mist still hovered at the edge of the forest, but the sun had already burned it off from the fields. Serfs tended to their crops, and she could hear the bustle from the manor kitchen garden.

"Good morning," she whispered, smiling into the light as the scent of soil and sap flooded her lungs.

She fetched water and tea for Emmeline, returning before her mistress woke. The light teased the golden strands from Emmeline's hair and lit red fires in Henri's brown curls.

"Rise and shine, little lord," she said to the boy as she stroked his head. He blinked at her sleepily and extended his arms, begging to be lifted. Marian scooped him onto her hip and winced at the weight. "You're getting too big for this," she told him. He sucked on his thumb in response. "Shall we wake your mother?"

He nodded, his eyes roving toward the bread and jam on the breakfast tray.

"Emmeline," Marian said, resting a hand on Emmeline's shoulder. She hated waking her. When she slept, Emmeline still looked like the young girl who had led Marian in secret games of chase around her father's manor, pilfering fruit from the kitchen and riding her father's old warhorse whenever the grooms were distracted. These days, worry had etched new lines in her face, and Marian ached to see it. Emmeline opened her eyes and promptly shut them, squinting in the sunlight.

"Wake up, mummy," Henri said from his perch on Marian's hip.

"Tea?"

"God bless you, yes." Emmeline sat up and let her unbound hair fall heavily over her shoulder and into her lap. Marian smoothed a lock behind Emmeline's ear and cupped her friend's cheek where the imprint from the pillow had left a memory of its weave on her skin. This was the life she wanted. Friends, the sweet warmth of Henri in her arms, and a glorious spring day ahead of them.

This was what she was going to lose.

She fetched the tea, a task that was complicated by Henri's refusal to leave her arms, and handed the mug to Emmeline. Emmeline sighed with satisfaction as she took a sip.

"I want tea," said Henri.

"You don't like tea," Marian pointed out.

"Then I want jam."

"Would you like bread with that jam?"

Henri considered this solemnly, then nodded. Marian prepared them all thick slices of bread smeared with some of the previous season's blackberry preserves, enjoying the warm breeze that wafted through the open window. She licked her fingers clean and extricated herself from Henri, seizing his mother's hairbrush from his sticky fingers.

"Mmm," Emmeline murmured as Marian settled behind her and gathered her hair for detangling. Emmeline had thick, soft tresses that shimmered beneath the brush strokes as Marian worked out the knots. The simplicity of the motion soothed them both. She gathered the hair into two parts and rose on her knees to begin braiding. Her fingers wove the strands from memory, and Henri flopped into his mother's lap to stare up at her, making animal noises for reasons known only to him. Marian's hands brushed the skin of Emmeline's shoulders as she worked, and she retrieved a rogue strand from Emmeline's bosom with an expert flick of her fingers.

Willa's unwelcome words crashed into her as her eyes traced the visible swell of Emmeline's breasts beneath her shift. She blushed, grateful that Emmeline could not see her, and bit her lip as she finished braiding. She was not like Willa. She was not like Willa at all, and she wished the redhead had never spoken those damned words. She would not have taken note of Emmeline's figure otherwise.

Emmeline sighed as Marian finished, and leaned back into her arms. Emmeline's body, still heavy with sleep, melded into hers, and she tilted her head back against Marian's shoulder. Marian stiffened. Henri, never one to miss an opportunity for cuddling, curled up in his mother's lap like a puppy. Emmeline plucked at his ringlets with an idle hand.

The feel of Emmeline's body flush against hers was familiar, and yet today felt different. The smell of Emmeline's hair, perfumed with rose oil and redolent of sunshine and honey from yesterday's visit to the manor hives, made her head swim, and the warmth radiating from Emmeline's body seemed to pool between Marian's thighs. Emmeline sighed in contentment and began speaking of the needs of the day. Marian tried to listen, but there was a buzzing in her head that had nothing to do with memories of bees and everything to do with the way Emmeline's hips felt between her legs: soft and solid and strong.

60

Fear closed her throat. This was wrong. This was Emmeline, her closest friend, the woman who had brought her into her family and made Marian as much a part of it as Connor or Henri, and she should not be having lustful thoughts about her.

I'm not, she told herself. I've never wanted her. Not once. Not in all the nights we've spent together have I thought of touching her the way Alanna touched Willa. Now, though, she wondered what it might be like to bury her face in Emmeline's hair, not as her handmaid, but as . . . as what?

"Excuse me," she said, interrupting Emmeline's discussion of the recent litter of sight hounds. She detached herself from the tangle of limbs, not looking at Emmeline as she made an excuse about the latrine.

Outside in the hall, she pressed her face against the cool stone wall and felt the prick of shameful tears. *What is wrong with me?* She felt polluted, as if what she'd witnessed between Willa and Alanna had planted a seed inside her, and now it put out roots and shoots and curled around everything that mattered. A passing servant threw her a concerned glance, and she waved him away.

I will rise above this. This was simply a test, and with enough penance perhaps she could weed it out. *And if I can't?*

I will. I am not Willa. I cannot be like Willa.

Chapter Seven

Robyn fidgeted with a stick as the afternoon light waned. If Midge didn't get here soon, her cousin would be walking home in the dark, and Midge didn't know the woods well enough to make that journey safely. The hill afforded her as clear a view of the surrounding countryside as one ever had in the forest. She could see the silver ribbon of the river below and the vast expanse of treetops spreading out in either direction, tendrils of mist rising over distant glens. It looked like a tapestry from here, plush and uniform, gentle even. She could wrap herself up in a view like this.

Or suffocate.

At the top of the hill stood a circle of ancient standing stones, green with moss and lichen, no taller than her hip. Walking through them raised the hairs on her arms. There was something about these particular stones that felt oddly sentient.

A flicker of movement from below caught her gaze. She crouched behind one of the chestnut trees and squinted at the small figure approaching. When it did not get much larger as it grew closer, she knew it was Midge.

"I got lost," Midge said, sinking to the ground when she reached the top of the hill. "I told my mother I went to visit Gwyneth, though, so if I don't make it back tonight she won't worry."

Robyn found she couldn't bring herself to ask after her sister-in-law.

"I brought more arrows, like you asked. And ale and some pie the baker sent over when he heard that you, well, you know."

"I can't eat my own funeral pie."

"Suit yourself. I'll eat it. Everybody else is too upset to eat. But I did carry it all this way."

"I just meant—"

"I know what you meant." An unpleasant silence fell between them. "She will hate you for this, Robyn."

Robyn dropped her head to her knees and willed the world to stop spinning around her. "I didn't have a choice."

"I saw Cedric. He wouldn't meet my eye, and he looked like he'd been crying, so you don't have to worry about him anymore, I reckon. My mum's a wreck. You better hope she never finds out you're still alive, because she'll give you a slower death than a hangman's noose. She practically whipped me for bringing her the news in the first place and told me I was mistaken, which was almost funny, seeing as you are still alive after all. All of them were crying. It was awful. I have half a mind to stay out here with you."

"You can't."

"That's the other thing. You don't get to tell me what I can and can't do, ever again." She pulled out a hand pie and bit into it. "You've lost all moral authority."

"Midge . . ."

"Don't 'Midge' me. I feel like shit, and it's your fault. Figured out what you're going to do yet?"

"Not yet."

"So what have you been doing?"

Robyn contemplated telling Midge that she'd spent the better part of the last two days asleep under a log, then thought better of it. "Laying low."

"Got any meat?"

Robyn produced three pheasants and two plump rabbits, which Midge shoved into the sack she'd just emptied.

"Have you chosen a place to camp?"

"I found a log."

Midge closed her eyes. "A log?"

"I didn't want to get lost either," Robyn said in her own defense. "I wanted to find my way back here to meet you."

"Well, you've met me now."

The ugly silence fell again.

"How . . . how did she take it?"

"How do you think she took it, Robyn?" Midge fussed with the kerchief covering her curling hair and avoided Robyn's eyes.

"I shouldn't have shot the deer."

"No," Midge agreed. "You shouldn't have, but you did. You can't take an arrow back once you've loosed it. Isn't that what your dad always said?"

"Something like that." She took the offered pie and forced herself to eat. "Midge, I don't know what to do." Saying it out loud brought an odd sort of relief.

"I know you don't."

Slanting sunlight cast long shadows behind the stones. Midge would have to stay here tonight, and Robyn didn't bother trying to hide her gratitude as she watched the twilight settle over the forest around them.

"Are there wolves nearby?" Midge asked as she followed Robyn's gaze.

"Probably." Wolves hadn't been at the fore of Robyn's mind as she lay despondent in the leaf litter, but now that Midge was here, she eyed the darkening forest with apprehension. Wolves usually preferred sheep and deer to men. Usually, however, didn't offer the same level of comfort beneath the trees as it did beside a warm hearth. "Fire would scare them off, but we're too close to the river."

As if on cue, a distant howl shivered in the air.

"What about a small fire?" Midge inched closer to Robyn. "We don't know for sure if there are people out there, but now we definitely know there are wolves."

Robyn hesitated. Alone, she would have climbed a tree and done her best to sleep tied to a thick limb. She couldn't risk Midge falling out of a tree, however, and so she relented despite her trepidations about Siward.

"A small fire. But not up here. It's too visible."

They climbed down the far side of the hill, putting the bulk of rock and earth between them and the river. Robyn chose a spot in the middle of a cluster of trees and began to claw at the dirt with her hands.

"What are you doing?"

"If we lay a fire in a hole it won't be as visible."

Midge scrabbled a stone free from the roots of a nearby tree and knelt to help. The end result wasn't very deep, but it was better than nothing, and they parted ways briefly to gather fallen wood. That, at least, was within the law. Robyn scanned the forest for signs of movement, animal or otherwise, but the only things she saw were a stoat about its business and a nervous rabbit returning late to its burrow.

Their fire, meager though it was, kept the darkness and its attendant thoughts at bay. Neither of them spoke much. Robyn's thoughts careened between guilt, despair, and relief, and back again. Midge kept her own counsel.

"I'll take the first watch," Robyn offered, laying her strung bow beside her.

"Okay." Midge made no move to lie down to sleep. "Will you promise me something?" Across the fire, her eyes loomed huge and dark in her young face.

"What?"

"Promise me you won't disappear."

Robyn shifted where she sat and tried not to let Midge see the flash of guilt that had crossed her face. Disappearing would be easier for everyone. She couldn't tell Gwyneth she was alive. She saw that now. It was too risky and too cruel. Better Robyn left her family to grieve and move on instead of worrying about her. Gwyneth would only blame herself if she knew Robyn had risked so much, and the thought was more than she could bear.

"I'll tell Gwyneth if you do."

Midge's threat hit its target. "You can't," Robyn said, meeting her cousin's eyes with horror.

"Then don't do anything stupid. Promise me."

A chunk of wood shifted in the fire pit, sending a shower of sparks up into the night air.

"What do you want me to do, stay here forever?"

"I don't know. I just don't want to lose you." Midge's voice broke.

"Fine. I promise."

The weight that settled over her as she said the words pressed her down into the earth at last, a bitter seed unwillingly planted.

Robyn scanned the stream bank several days after she escorted Midge home, fingering the quarterstaff she'd cut for herself. Her bow hung unstrung on her back. She'd found that otherwise it tangled with the undergrowth as she moved through the forest, impeding her progress and making more noise than was wise. She only strung it for hunting purposes now, or whenever she thought she heard the sounds of something larger than rabbit or deer moving toward her.

This stream marked the outer boundary of the territory she'd explored so far. She kept her progress gradual, bordered always by a landmark she knew so that she did not become hopelessly lost. The exercise gave her purpose, and she'd even dared set up a series of snares, though this was risky. All a forester had to do was wait by her snares long enough to catch her checking them and she'd be dead again.

The stream was just wide enough that she'd have to wade through it in order to cross, and too deep in places to cross comfortably. Centuries of spring floods had worn a small ravine between the hills here, but a stout log lay over the water only a few paces from where she stood.

Something about the log bothered her. It was too conveniently placed, and the trees on the far bank stood closely together. Anybody could watch the bridge from behind the scruffy branches of the squat pine, not that anyone in their right mind would be walking this deep in the woods.

I don't need to cross here, she told herself, but the thought seemed silly. There was no reason for anyone to lie in wait here when there were forest roads and paths that received more foot traffic than the occasional deer. She stepped out from behind her tree and set one foot on the log. It held, and she stared down past the mossy bark to the rocky streambed below. The fall would hurt if she slipped, but wouldn't break anything. She tucked her staff under her arm and made it a few more feet across before a gruff voice stopped her mid-step.

"No farther."

A burly man wearing a patched tunic beneath a stiff leather jerkin placed himself between her and the opposite bank. He too held a quarterstaff, and Robyn noticed with unease that his bore the scars of frequent use. She did not dare speak for fear of giving herself away, and so she waited for him to elaborate on his position, with sweat prickling her skin.

"These woods are ruled by Siward Ironarm," he said, and Robyn noted through the jolt of fear those words sent through her that the man's head was shaved like a Dane: short on the sides and long on the top.

"I thought these woods belonged to the king." She pitched her voice low in an attempt to hide her sex, but it had been nearly a fortnight since she'd last spoken to another human. The words cracked like a boy's.

"These woods haven't seen a king in half a century."

"And Siward, does he think himself a king?"

The man laughed. It was not a wholly unpleasant sound, and something about it gave her the impression that he did not much care for Siward.

"We're rich in kings these days and poor in everything else. What's your name, boy?"

"My name is my own business."

"Fair enough. You're not a forester."

"Neither are you," she said.

"Siward might have a place for a likely lad if you're down on your luck and don't mind kneeling in the dirt."

"I don't need another king."

The man shrugged. "Suit yourself, but I'll be taking you to him nonetheless. Can't have you running off telling stories."

Robyn didn't bother arguing. She turned to run, and it was only when she emerged, sputtering, from the cold water of the creek that she realized he'd flung his staff between her legs. Her own staff was nowhere in reach, and she wiped the hair out of her eyes as she struggled to free her bowstring from its pouch.

"None of that, lad." The big man landed in the shallows and sent a splash of water into her face as she staggered to her feet. Two staves twirled idly in his hands; one of them was hers.

"You could just let me go," Robyn said, backing away from him until the roots protruding from the bank dug into her spine.

"I could," he said, "but . . ." He trailed off, and Robyn followed his eyes down to her chest. Her wet tunic and half-laced jerkin clung to her breasts, leaving little to the imagination.

"God's toes," he said. "You're a bloody woman." The big man dropped the staves. The motion was so deliberate that Robyn's hand hesitated over the knife in her belt, though her heart still pounded. When she didn't move or answer, he spared a glance over his shoulder, then lowered his voice. "You need to get out of here."

Robyn nodded and edged along the creek bed. The man spared another glance into the forest, cursed, then picked up both staves and followed her.

"I'm not going to hurt you," he said. "What the hell are you doing out here? No, never mind. I don't want to know. I'll get you out of Siward's territory, and then I'll leave you be. Hurry up now."

Robyn's boots slipped on the roots as she clambered up the bank, and she contemplated making a run for it. The man moved quickly, however, and so she accepted the proffered staff in silence. He set off back the way she had come. His boots were nearly soundless on the forest floor despite the water that dripped from his clothes. Robyn left a trail of puddles in her wake and her feet protested the sudden abuse of sodden leather with the promise of blisters.

"Stay on this side of the River Maun," he said, pausing twenty minutes later. "More foresters here, but trust me when I say you'd rather meet one of them than Siward's boys." He gave her a critical look. "And bind your chest for Christ's sake."

"Thank you," she said, resisting the urge to cross her arms over her breasts.

"Don't mention it." He gave her a quick smile. "And I mean that. It'll be my hide if you do."

"Why do you follow Siward then?" she asked as she wrung water out of her tunic. "You don't seem overly fond of him." And he's a raping bastard, she added to herself. Antagonizing him didn't seem like a wise idea, however, so she kept her simmering anger under wraps.

"There's safety in numbers out here, even if the company is filth."

Robyn thought about the days she'd spend in the forest, jumping at every breaking branch, and, though she hated the thought, understood why a decent person might settle for safety over morality if they grew hungry and scared enough.

"You should go home, girl."

Robyn gave a short, humorless laugh. "Do you think I'd be here if I had anywhere else to go?"

"Bind your chest and do something about your hair then if you want to live out the month."

"How long have you been out here?"

"Too long." He turned to leave, shaking his head, and Robyn placed two fingers on his wrist to stop him. The gesture seemed to surprise him. He froze, muscles cording beneath her touch, and Robyn pushed aside a sudden, vivid memory of Michael. Something about this man's kindness reminded her of her brother.

"You said there was safety in numbers," she said, speaking quickly. "Are there others like Siward out here?"

"A few."

"Where?"

"It's hard to say. There's a small group a few miles south you'll want to steer clear of, but they'll leave you alone more likely than not. Siward's the one to watch out for."

"I know," she said, releasing her grip on the muscled forearm. "He's robbed my uncle's village four times in the past two years. Raped my cousin, too." She turned to leave, not wanting to think about Mary, but the stranger spoke again.

"Wait." He rubbed the back of his neck as he appeared to weigh a decision in his mind. "Damnit," he said. "My name's John."

"Robyn."

"You're going to die out here or worse, Robyn, unless I come with you. I can't have that on my conscience."

"What about Siward?"

"He won't miss me."

"Why should I trust you?" Robyn crossed her arms and met the stranger's brown eyes. "How do I know you aren't just as bad as Siward?"

John rolled his shoulders, then sighed. "Look closely," he said.

Robyn studied him in confusion. He had a square jaw and a crooked nose that looked as if it had been broken several times, and the muscles cording his neck and arms reminded her of Tom the blacksmith. Nothing about him revealed anything that made her feel much better.

"I don't see anything."

John looked over his shoulder before lifting his damp shirt.

At first, she didn't understand what she was seeing. A bandage was wrapped around his muscled torso, and his hairless stomach was just as chiseled as the rest of him.

Bind your chest and do something about your hair, he'd said. She examined his face again. Dirt smeared his cheeks, making it impossible to tell if there was stubble on his chin, but a clean-shaven outlaw seemed improbable, somehow, even with his shaved head. Much easier to just grow a beard. He was handsome, in a rugged sort of way, but it suddenly occurred to Robyn that what was pleasing about his face was the contrast between his broken nose and his youthful skin, skin that did not quite belong on a man of his size.

"God's nails," she said, taking a step back. "You're a woman, too."

"No," John said. "I'm not. Call me John. That's who I am. Forget it, as others have before you, and I'll leave you to fend for yourself."

"But you . . ." she trailed off.

"Look like an ox?"

Robyn hadn't been thinking of those words exactly, but the description fit. "As strong as one anyway," she ventured.

"That's what my late husband called me. Joan the Ox."

"I . . . I'm sorry?"

"Don't be. I got the last word."

Robyn wondered exactly what had happened to Joan's husband. John, she corrected herself. He'd said that was who he was, and it was no business of hers to decide otherwise.

"Can you use that bow?" he asked.

"Yes."

"Good. Out here you'll need it."

Chapter Eight

Marian knelt in Harcourt's small chapel. The church was empty of people, and the only sounds were the bleating of a nearby flock of sheep and the fluttering of the swallows in the eaves. She breathed in the emptiness and tried to pray.

Lord, please cleanse me of impure thoughts. No, that just made her think more of them. Emmeline's lips. The way Willa's body had arched against Alanna's touch. She stared up at the cross and tried again. *Merciful God, please let my father choose a different husband for me or let me join the church and serve you.* A life of quiet contemplation, of prayers and gardening and sisterhood— that was what she wanted. It wouldn't matter, then, if she thought of Willa's blazing green eyes or the creamy swell of Emmeline's breasts. Every day would be a penance. She'd be safe.

The chapel door opened and shut behind her. *Dammit,* she swore, profaning her mind still further.

"Marian?"

She squeezed her eyes shut and willed Alanna to leave her alone. Unsurprisingly, it didn't work. The minstrel knelt on the stone beside her and placed a warm hand on her shoulder. "Are you all right?"

"Of course. I just felt the need—"

"To bruise your knees? I've never seen you here on your own before."

"I pray," said Marian, doing her best to sound indignant instead of guilty.

"And I come for the acoustics." Alanna sang a few bars of Marian's favorite ballad. The music swelled in the still air, and even the swallows stopped their swooping to listen. "See?"

"Keep singing."

Alanna opened her mouth. Honey poured from her throat and filled the church with golden light. It soothed the ache inside Marian. Nothing that pure could be a sin. Then again Alanna sang, not like an angel, but like a pagan goddess of old. Her voice carried timbres and melodies that invoked heartbreak and ancient forests, craggy heights and gentle rivers, love and loss and everything in between, all of it holy, all of it true in a way Marian felt to her marrow. A tear ran down her cheek as the minstrel finished her song.

"Now, why are you really here?"

Marian thought of Linley and the betrothal she yearned to be free of, but some of the song still lingered in her chest. It urged her to speak truth.

"I saw you."

Alanna raised her brows. "I see you right now."

"I saw you and Willa. At the priory. In . . . in the kitchen."

"Ah." Alanna drew out the word in a long breath and rearranged herself to sit cross-legged in her minstrel's breeches. "Marian—"

"It's wrong. What you did."

"Perhaps."

"I would never. I don't want that."

"Am I saying that you do?"

"Willa said—"

"Willa says a lot of things, usually without thinking, first. Whatever she said to you, put it from your mind. You know your own truth."

Marian chewed her lower lip until it split. Blood trickled from the cut and down her throat, metallic and calming. *You know your own truth.* It sounded so simple, and yet . . . "What if I don't?"

Alanna's brown eyes caught hers, and she couldn't bear the compassion in their depths. She stood before Alanna had a chance to answer. "I should go."

"Marian—"

"Thank you for the song." She fled down the aisle and past the stone pews until she burst out into the green stretch of grass in the churchyard. A startled lamb leapt out of her path. Alanna didn't follow.

She kept running. The dirt road that led toward the fallow fields reserved for the autumn planting tumbled out before her feet like unspooling yarn. Peasants stopped to watch her, and it occurred to her that her flight would arouse questions she would later have to answer, but she didn't stop until she came to the brook by the common fields with the stand of willows. Two women harvested willow withies further upstream, but they did not approach Marian as she sank beneath the shelter of the trailing boughs.

Truth. What good was truth? And how could Alanna be so calm about her own truth? Didn't she worry what others might think, or what could happen to her and Willa if their truth was discovered? Men were punished for such transgressions. Marian had never heard of a woman being hanged, but there were other consequences. Spiritual consequences.

Then again, she thought as she pulled apart a willow leaf, a priest would urge her to focus on the duty she owed her father, which of course meant Linley. The thought of the older man touching her sent a shudder of revulsion through her body. Linley repulsed her far more than Willa and Alanna. Why couldn't he have been old, but kind? That she could have dealt with. Instead, he watched her like a cat with a mouse, and she knew he would expect her to share his bed. Gone would be slow, sunlit mornings with Emmeline and Henri.

The leaf disintegrated beneath her assault. When Willa married, she could continue seeing Alanna and her husband would be none the wiser. She would get to have love and passion and station so long as she wasn't caught. And even if she were caught, the worst that would happen would be a few years of penance, the shame of her peers, and separation from Alanna.

The last thought stopped her cold. Yes, Willa could have everything, but that also meant she had everything to lose. Marian had seen the way the women looked at each other: like the other was bread and salt and air. The emotion that strangled her breath this time was not desire.

Want, yes, and hunger, and envy.

Chapter Nine

Robyn sighted down the arrow, aware of John's eyes on her. When she loosed it, taking the pheasant before it had a chance to pump its wings, he let out a low whistle of approval.

"You weren't kidding. Where did you learn to shoot like that?"

"My brother."

"And where's your brother now?"

"Dead."

John didn't say anything to that. He nodded, as if confirming something, and scanned the forest for signs of human activity before retrieving the pheasant. Robyn watched him and marveled at the way he moved silently over the ground. She accepted the bird and checked her arrow for signs of damage before wiping the blood from the head and shaft and replacing it in her quiver.

"What did you do, then, before you came here?" he asked Robyn.

"I was a fletcher."

He nodded again. "You'll be wanting those feathers."

Robyn tucked the pheasant into her game bag. The thought of roasted fowl made her mouth water, and she absentmindedly eyed the surrounding forest for mushrooms and young green onion shoots.

This was farther into Sherwood than she'd ever been. John seemed to know where they were going, but Robyn didn't like being entirely at his mercy, and the reappearance of the Rain-worth river ahead was more reassuring than she cared to admit.

Dark and swollen with the recent rain, the water raced past the banks, carrying leaves and branches. John knelt on the rocky bank and scooped a handful of water into his mouth. Robyn set her pack and bow down and cast a furtive glance around her as she did the same.

"You look too much like a woman. It's not a problem, necessarily, but the trouble is you don't look like the kind of woman who enjoys snapping a few necks before breakfast if you take my meaning."

"It would be hard to miss your meaning, good sir." Robyn tried to banish that image from her mind. "So, what should I do?"

"That's up to you. You might pass as a youth, with a little work, at least from a distance. It's easier that way. Less chance of an unpleasant encounter."

Robyn didn't need to ask for clarification. "Do I have to shave my head like yours?"

"No, but you can't have hair past your waist, either."

"It isn't that long." Robyn pulled her braid out from her tunic. It lay in her hands, dark and heavy with sweat.

"Cut it and keep your hood up. Nothing I can do about your face." John gave her a critical look. "I suppose I could break your nose, but I don't think that will do much either. You're too pretty."

"Thanks?"

"It's not a compliment. Pretty faces get remembered."

Robyn tried to remember the last time anyone had called her pretty. Gwyneth, maybe. Barring that, she tried to recall the last time she'd felt anything besides tired. She pulled her knife out of her belt and sawed at her hair, watching the fat locks fall into the water. John didn't comment at the hack job, nor did he offer to help.

"Is this better?" Her hair felt odd, floating several inches above her shoulders, and she shook her head experimentally.

"Better. Do you mind?" He knelt beside Robyn and pulled the top portion of her hair back and secured it with a strip of leather pulled from his own hair. The end result kept the hair out of

Robyn's eyes and was so unlike anything that any self-respecting woman would wear that Robyn figured she would pass on that assumption alone.

"Try not to wash your face too much, if you can. You don't have my build, but you're broad enough in the shoulders. And keep your hood up."

"I will."

"What's your name?"

"It's Robyn. Like I told you."

"No. It's Robyn Hood. That hood needs to become as much a part of you as your bow. Do you understand? There are a hundred youths in Sherwood, but if a forester gets wind of a woman with an arrow that doesn't miss, you're worse than dead. There's a clearing downstream that I found when I first came here. It will do as a camp, for now."

Robyn shouldered her pack again and stood, staring downstream. Midge's home lay that way, and beyond Midge, beyond Papplewick, lay Nottingham and the narrow house she had shared with Gwyneth and the baby.

John clapped a large hand on her shoulder as he looked down at her. "Whoever you're missing, let them go."

"I would love to get you behind a long bow," Robyn said later that day as she watched John bring his ax down on the body of a fallen oak, hacking off some of the smaller limbs with long, even strokes that sent wood chips flying. His muscles bulged beneath his threadbare tunic. Robyn had a bow stave curing in the shop that would make a perfect weapon for his frame, and her mind turned over the gentle curve of the notch and the smoothness of the grip. John could punch through plate mail with a bow like that.

"I've never been much of a shot."

"You wouldn't need to be," she said, still dreaming of wood polished smooth and oiled.

"You going to gather wood or just stand there?"

"I need to tell you something."

John wiped the blade of his ax on his leggings to remove the worst of the sap and tucked it into his belt. "I'm listening."

"There are people I have to take care of."

Haltingly, she told John about the events that had led her into Sherwood, and the responsibility she still had to Gwyneth and Symon.

"The sheriff of Nottingham wants to marry your sister-in-law?" John asked when Robyn finished.

"I'll kill him first."

"I brought a case against my husband, once. The sheriff laughed me out of court. Didn't believe a . . . woman," he said, biting off the word with venom in his voice, "my size was capable of fearing a man like Peter."

"Peter was your husband? What happened to him?" She thought she already knew the answer.

"He came at me when I had a hammer in my hand. That's the thing about oxen," he added with a glint in his eyes. "They don't know their own strength."

Robyn didn't need to ask whether Peter had survived the encounter. John's presence in the woods, combined with the satisfaction on his face, told her everything she needed to know. A blow from John's hammer would split a man's skull like a pumpkin. She just wished she could do the same to the sheriff.

"I need to keep hunting. Gwyneth and the baby need meat, and without me . . ." She didn't finish her sentence.

John thought for a moment, his eyes narrowing. "Coin is easier to smuggle into town than meat."

"I don't have coin."

"True. But there are all kinds of things to hunt in Sherwood."

"Are you out of your mind?"

Robyn flinched as Midge's voice cut shrilly through the forest. Their meeting was not going as well as she had hoped.

"You'll like him."

"I thought I told you to stay away from outlaws. What about Mary?"

"Midge, I am an outlaw."

"Take me to this *friend* of yours."

"Absolutely not."

"Robyn, I won't be able to sleep at night thinking about you running around the woods with some vagabond blacksmith. It's bad enough that I have to deal with Gwyneth—" Midge cut herself off and glanced up at Robyn guiltily.

"What about Gwyneth?"

"She's . . . She misses you, Robyn. I don't know what you expected. I keep telling her you're in a better place now, but it seems I'm lying."

Robyn stared at her cousin, torn between exasperation and disappointment. She'd made her meeting with Midge by the skin of her teeth, leaving John back at their camp, and the last thing she wanted was to get Midge more involved in her crimes. "Midge," she began, but Midge shot her a look full of disgust.

"What are you doing, Robyn? How is this helping? How much longer do I have to keep lying to everyone? And what happened to your hair?"

Robyn opened her mouth, shut it, and gave up. "You want to meet him? Fine." She turned, leaving Midge to follow or not as she chose, and stormed off through the woods.

What did Midge expect her to do, find a new life for herself without leaving the forest? She couldn't just saunter into a new village, expecting to find work, without questions being asked that she didn't have answers to. Besides, she couldn't leave Gwyneth until she knew Gwyneth was going to be okay without her. That was the one thing she'd promised Michael.

"Robyn, wait," Midge called out from somewhere behind her, but Robyn didn't slow. Midge would keep up or she wouldn't.

John's arm across her chest stopped her before she burst into the clearing. She paused, panting, glaring up at the big man as the sounds of Midge's clumsy pursuit drifted through the leaves.

"I take it that is your cousin, making more noise than a boar in rut?"

Robyn looked over her shoulder, still leaning on John's arm, and nodded. No words could possibly prepare John for Midge.

"Robyn," Midge shouted, stumbling to a halt in front of them. Her eyes widened as she took in John.

"Is this him?" she asked, puffing herself up like an angry hedgehog.

"Midge, this is John. John, this is my cousin, Midge."

Midge stalked around them and looked John up and down. Twigs clustered in her hair, making her look half wild, and despite her ire Robyn felt a surge of affection for her cousin.

"Pleasure to meet you, miss," John said.

Midge scowled. "I didn't bring enough ale for three."

"John can have my share."

"Are you a poacher too?" Midge asked, ignoring Robyn. "Or a murderer? Heretic? What?"

"Murderer. Poacher too, I guess, these days, and I can't say I have much faith left."

Silence fell around them, and Robyn waited for her cousin to blow her top. Midge, however, seemed to take this news in stride. "Who'd you kill?"

"A wife beater."

Midge cocked her head, looking for all the world like a disgruntled owl. "Did he deserve it?"

"There is no doubt in my mind."

They ended up letting Midge drink all the ale. She blinked at them out of bleary eyes, light from their small fire flickering over her face and shimmering off the grease stains from the ducks they'd roasted over the coals. The meat and ale had gone straight to her head, and she lay with her head in Robyn's lap, blinking at the flames.

"You're too tall," Midge said to John. "I'm going to call you Little John."

"Will that make you feel better?" John asked her.

"Yes."

"Then call me whatever you like."

"Robyn wrote a song about me," Midge said, hiccupping. "Sing it, Robyn."

Robyn stroked her cousin's hair, feeling a smile creep onto her lips. Drunk Midge was her favorite Midge. She cleared her throat and sang the first verse.

"Midge, Midge, last and least
Barely a smidge of flour and yeast."

Midge hummed along, then broke in, adding a second verse in a warbling voice.

"Midge, Midge, last of her brood,
Tiny and fearsome and always quite rude!"

John let out a low laugh. "Is your cousin always this charming?"

"I'm afraid not."

"I like you." Midge waved her hand at John. "Little John. Keep my cousin safe. She's horrid to look at, but we're all quite fond of her."

Robyn and Little John, for Midge did not forget the nickname she'd bestowed upon him, accompanied Midge closer to Papplewick than Robyn had dared venture since her flight. Midge picked at John like a woodpecker after a bug deep in the bark of a gnarled oak, teasing out tidbits of information as her short legs struggled to keep pace.

"Do you miss working in the forge?"

"Sometimes."

"How many burn scars do you have?"

"I lost count at forty-two."

"Can I see them?"

"Here." John rolled up his sleeve, revealing a forearm corded with muscle and riddled with smooth ridges of puckered skin. Midge tucked an errant strand of hair behind one ear and leaned in closer to look. Her chin barely came past John's waist, forcing her to keep her head perpetually tilted up, and Robyn saw the smile that hovered around John's lips as he looked down at her.

"That one looks like a wolf's head."

"So it does."

"And this one, maybe a cat?" Midge leaned closer, frowning as her small hands traced a scar at the base of John's wrist.

"If you say it is a cat, then a cat it must be."

"We're almost at the road," Robyn said, interrupting Midge's exploration.

Midge shot her a glare. "I can see that."

"Be careful." Robyn touched Midge lightly on the shoulder. "Can I see you next week?"

"Only if you bring enough ale for the rest of us," said John.

"And don't take any chances," Robyn told her cousin. The woods here were carefully coppiced and crisscrossed with trails. New shoots sprang from the bases of trees harvested last fall, and their straight and slender limbs obscured her view. Anybody could be out here harvesting fallen branches, plants, mushrooms, and herbs, not to mention the ever-present foresters. The chances of Robyn running into someone she knew were far too high for comfort. She missed the darker, wilder woods, where the foresters rarely ventured and the trees grew wide enough to hide her and her bow. She hugged Midge, torn as always between anxiety and loneliness at the prospect of watching her cousin walk away.

"Wait," said Midge, pausing before taking her leave. "What about the spring fair?"

"What about it?"

"You should come."

"That sounds like a terrible idea, Midge."

"No one will recognize you, and there will be so many people there anyway that you'll be safe."

"Midge, I—"

"And then there's the archery contest."

"And also the sheriff."

"You could see Gwyneth."

That took Robyn's breath away. She glanced at John for backup, but he seemed intrigued by the idea.

"There will be a lot of traffic on the road to the fair," John said. "And more leaving, once they've had enough to drink."

Which will make them easier to rob, Robyn realized as she followed John's train of thought. It was risky. Far riskier than poaching, but what was the worst that could happen? They'd be caught and hanged, which wasn't exactly a change of circumstance.

"I'll think about it," said Robyn.

This seemed to satisfy Midge, for her face split in a wide smile and she gave Robyn a quick hug. "Be safe," she said. "I'll see you soon."

"You're lucky to have family like that," said John as they watched Midge leave.

"Trust me," Robyn replied. "I know."

Chapter Ten

Harcourt joined Maunnesfeld for the first hunt of the season, along with most of Nottingham's nearby nobility. Prince John himself kept a hunting lodge north of the River Maun, and while the prince was notably absent, his master of the hunt had promised plump hares and yearling deer fat with new grass. Rumor held that John had taken a trip across the channel for reasons that, while unknown, were suspected to have everything to do with his brother's continued absence.

Marian didn't think he'd gone to save him.

Damn you, Richard, she thought.

Spring rains had left deep ruts in the road. They caught unwary ankles and caused her horse to snort in irritation as the mare picked her way along the lane, following the rest of the hunting party. It wasn't a real hunt, more of an excuse for the hounds to stretch their legs than anything, but Marian shared their enthusiasm. A warm breeze riffled her hair, bringing with it the smells of early flowers, fresh grass, and new leaves. She nudged her mare beside Emmeline's and didn't bother to chastise the animal for champing at the bit. The bay mare's head tossed prettily, and the motion cast her long black mane into the wind.

"Thank God," said Willa from Emmeline's other side as she checked the hood on her hawk. "If I had to spend one more day listening to my brother moaning about the cut of his clothes, I was going to fling myself from the tower."

85

Both Emmeline and Willa had taken their goshawks from the mews, and Marian eyed the birds with both admiration and distrust. Emmeline's hawk's sharp beak had drawn its fair share of human blood, and while Willa's hawk appeared to be more even-tempered than her mistress, Marian took no chances. Her own wrist was empty. Her hawk had died over the winter, and she hadn't had the heart to replace it yet. Instead, she concentrated on the fresh air and the heavy scent of honeysuckle on the soft spring wind.

"Does your brother still fit into your clothes?" asked Alanna. She rode a plain palfrey, but the horse responded to her hands attentively and kept its composure, unlike Willa's temperamental courser.

"I haven't seen him trying, but who knows?" Willa said. "Ever since he grew a beard, he's been insufferable."

"You mean ever since he grew a beard you've been unable to trade places," Emmeline corrected.

"What is the point of having a twin if you can't make good use of it?"

A few of the hunting party's unwed sons paused their horses by the three of them to exchange pleasantries and flirt. Emmeline deflected their attentions, safe in her marriage vows, but Marian and Willa were not so lucky.

"Come ride with us," a comely youth urged Willa, letting his horse arch its neck and prance in place. Marian thought she recognized him. Perhaps he'd competed in last year's tournament, for he rode with the self-assurance of a warrior and his young face was scarred. But you didn't join the Crusade, she thought, which makes you richer than the rest of us. Emmeline's husband wasn't the exception; many of the nobles had chosen to go on Crusade instead of paying the Saladin Tax exacted by Richard.

"I'd hate to embarrass you," Willa said to him. Her red hair spilled over one shoulder and was bound with green ribbons calculated to bring out the eyes Marian still couldn't bring herself to meet. "Your horse hardly looks capable of matching mine."

"I like a filly with spirit."

Marian stifled a laugh at his lack of ingenuity, and Alanna raised an eyebrow.

"But do the mares like you?" Willa asked him.

The youth rode off after a few more unfortunate overtures, oblivious to the glare Willa shot at his back.

"I like a filly with spirit," Marian mimicked.

Emmeline laughed and patted Willa on the arm with her free hand. "I do not envy the man that tames you," she said.

Marian looked away from Willa. Alanna's expression never slipped in these moments, but Willa lacked a courtier's tact despite her birth. The awkward silence that fell was interrupted by another young man, who flashed a smile at Marian.

"Care to join me?" he asked.

"I fear my mistress needs me," said Marian.

"Lady Emmeline, could you spare your companion?" he asked, bowing in the saddle. He had a perfectly oiled mustache that reminded Marian of a weasel.

"I fear she is essential," said Emmeline. "I simply can't get by without her."

"Surely your minstrel can see to your needs," he said.

"She said no, Joss." Willa jogged her horse between theirs, giving the man a playful shove. "I realize that might be a first for you, but I'm sure you'll find some other girl to pester before too long."

"Like you, Lady Maunnesfeld?"

"I think not. Now go before my mare bites you."

Joss galloped away, showing off his horse's speed, and left the four of them alone again.

"Nothing ruins a hunt like feeling like the quarry," said Willa. "Don't they have other things to chase?"

Alanna laughed, and Marian saw the flush of happiness the sound brought to Willa's cheeks. Something in her chest twisted painfully. *I am not jealous.* "Let's run for a bit," she suggested, eager to clear her head.

"Are you sure you can keep up?" Willa had not boasted without cause. Her father bred some of the fastest horses in all of

Nottinghamshire, sought after by the king's messengers and not entirely suited for the hunt, but that didn't stop Willa from taking out her favorite mare whenever she pleased. White as spilled milk, the mare floated over the fields, ears cocked back for the sound of her rider's voice. Emmeline's horse, a fine-boned black mare with a white snip on her nose and a tendency to kick everyone but Emmeline and the stable boy, rolled her eyes.

Marian preferred her placid mare. She lacked the fine breeding of the other two, but she nuzzled Marian whenever she entered the stables, and her soft brown eyes and gentle demeanor never wavered. Even on her friskiest days, like today, the mare rarely did more than toss her head.

"Worry about your own horse," said Alanna, and spurred her mount into a canter. Willa followed in a spray of mud, and Emmeline joined them with an unladylike whoop. Marian's horse did her best to keep up, but soon fell behind, just as Willa had prophesied.

Marian slowed her horse to a walk as Sherwood loomed before them and let her hand run over the bark of passing trees as she allowed her mare to pick a trail from the hundreds that crisscrossed the forest floor. She thought she saw a small herd of deer take flight in the distance, alarmed by the hounds, perhaps, or merely aware of the presence of more humans in the forest than was usual.

"Let's head for the clearing by the river," Emmeline said when Marian caught up with them. "Let the birds stretch their wings."

The warmth of the day sent sweat trickling down Marian's neck. She didn't mind. Sweat was better than rain, and there were few enough flawless days during the English spring. Birdsong rose and fell around them. The hawks shifted their heads beneath their hoods, sensing prey, and Alanna broke into a sweet song about a dove that lilted through the air. Marian hummed along, content, until her horse sidestepped without warning.

She didn't have time to shout. The source of her mare's discomfort roared to life, and she had just enough time to register the hornets' nest dangling from a recently split tree trunk before the cloud of angry insects engulfed her. She dropped the reins and clutched at her saddle with one hand and threw her other arm over her face to shield it as her mare took off at a gallop.

Branches tore at her as her horse surged through the woods, maddened into previously inconceivable speed by the stinging insects. Marian felt welts rising on her arms, neck, and face, and did her best to stay on despite the pain. She managed for what felt like miles until the sharp crack of a low hanging branch collided with her skull and knocked her from the saddle and from consciousness.

Chapter Eleven

Robyn edged down the game trail, hunger warring with caution as she teased back a tangle of ferns to reveal a cluster of mushrooms growing along the length of a decomposing oak. She scooped them into her game bag with a vivid fantasy of another roasted duck, sprinkled with some of the wild onions she'd found earlier that day.

Crouching, she parted another bank of ferns and froze. A woman lay in a heap of crushed undergrowth, her arm thrown out to one side and her riding skirts tangled around her. Every inch of her was covered in angry welts, and Robyn recognized the work of Sherwood's busiest residents in the stings swelling the fair skin. Robyn whistled their warning call as she knelt beside the crumpled shape. John appeared a few moments later, quarterstaff gripped firmly in his hands, and frowned at the body.

"Who is that?" he asked.

"I don't know." The swelling made it impossible to determine so much as the shape of her nose. Her hair had come undone from its bound ribbons and snarled about her face, and her arms were scratched and bruised.

"Look at her clothes," John said.

Robyn could tell that beneath the dirt the clothes were finely made. This woman, whoever she was, wasn't a commoner.

"We can't just leave her here," she said, reaching out to touch the woman's shoulder. It was still warm, and her breast rose and fell with even breaths.

John knelt to examine the woman's injuries. "She's alive," he said. "Just insensible. But how do you think she's going to react when she wakes up and sees us?"

"Better us than a wolf."

"People will be out looking for her. We can't risk it." John stood and motioned for Robyn to do the same. "We can carry her to a path if it makes you feel better. She'll be easier to find at least."

Robyn might have agreed had the woman's eyes not fluttered open at that moment. "She's awake," Robyn said.

"Then we need to go. Now." John stepped back, but Robyn didn't follow.

"Can you hear me?" she asked the stranger.

"Yes." The words slurred out of her mouth past swollen lips.

"Do you know where you are?"

The woman—girl, really—shook her head, then winced and touched her face gingerly.

"We need to get her to the river. Mud will help the stings. Can you walk?"

The girl nodded, winced again, and tried to stand. Her riding skirt tangled around her legs and she tripped, landing hard on her knees.

"Here." Robyn lifted the girl and wrapped one of her arms around her waist. John moved to her other side, and despite his frown, Robyn noted that the hand he placed on the girl's elbow was gentle.

Each step seemed to jar the girl in and out of consciousness. Robyn was tempted to ask John to just pick her up and carry her, but there was a grim determination to the way their new companion set one foot in front of the other that stopped her. Upper class or not, the girl had grit. She also weighed nearly as much as Robyn, and they both let out a sigh of relief when the river came into view.

"Here," Robyn said when they arrived, pulling up a handful of

mud. "This will help." She daubed it on the girl's face, careful not
to put too much pressure on the swollen flesh.

"The river will help, more," John suggested. "The cold water
will bring down some of the swelling."

"He's right," Robyn said. "Did they sting you anywhere else?"

The look the girl gave her might have been sardonic. It was
hard to tell, with one eye swollen half shut and her cheeks puffy
and slathered with gray mud.

"I'll help you with your boots," she offered, and when the girl
didn't protest she unlaced the leather boots and pulled them off.
The leather had protected her calves and feet. Robyn had time to
observe the rounded muscle of one leg before the girl pulled her
legs to her chest.

"She doesn't want to undress in front of us," Robyn said as she
recognized the sudden fear in the other woman's posture.

"I wouldn't either," said John. "But, little dove, you're not much
to look at, at the moment, and neither of us are inclined to take
advantage of a woman. If we were, we wouldn't have bothered
carrying you this far, would we?"

The girl's eyes narrowed as much as the swelling allowed. "I'm
not your dove," she managed to say.

"Just wear your shift. Here." Robyn knelt behind her and
undid the belt at her waist and coiled it in her hand. The cord
was soft. Not silk, but not the rough wool or flax Robyn was used
to. The stranger let Robyn pull the tunic over her head. More
welts covered the girl's back. The dress, a soft blue thing made of
lightly spun wool, clung to a few bloodied scratches, but all in all
the worst of the damage had been done by the hornets.

"Thank you." The girl rose awkwardly to her feet and limped
toward the river with strides that quickened the closer she got,
until she was nearly running. The minute the cool water washed
over her she let out a long groan.

"What are we going to do with her?" John asked below the
burble of the river.

"Make sure she doesn't pass out again, get some of the swelling down, and take her to the border of the forest. Someone will find her."

"They might be looking now," said John. They both glanced over their shoulders, straining for the sounds of human traffic.

"We helped her, and she doesn't know who we are." Robyn spoke the words with more confidence than she felt. John's anxiety wormed its way under her skin, and she couldn't help jumping every time a branch cracked.

The girl stayed in the water for a long time. Robyn was just beginning to wonder if she'd passed out again when she emerged, shift clinging to her body, to sink once more onto the bank. Robyn found her eyes wandering over the girl's curves and forced herself to look down. "How do you feel?" she asked.

"Better."

"Put mud on the other stings."

The girl scooped up a handful of slippery mud and rubbed it over her arms, chest, and neck. The dark mud glistened against the light gray of her shift. Something about her seemed familiar. Robyn studied her, trying to see past the swelling and the mud to whoever lay beneath.

The girl wasn't a peasant, that much was clear, but she wasn't acting like a silly highborn lady afraid of dirt on the hem of her dress, either. Still, only the gentry or merchants with money or social standing rode through Sherwood. People like Robyn walked. Better not to know her name, she decided, picking up a smooth stone and tossing it into the river. If she was someone Robyn knew from before, Robyn's reaction might give her away.

She jumped when she realized the other woman was studying her with the same intensity.

"I know you, I think," the girl said, confirming Robyn's worst fears. "But I can't place it. Are you from Nottingham?"

She doesn't know you're a woman, Robyn reminded herself. Her eyes drifted again to the soft swell of breast the shift revealed. "Not recently," she answered. "And you?"

"Not recently?" she asked, ignoring Robyn's question. "But you are from there?"

"Do you always ask so many questions?"

"Only when I ride into a hornet's nest." The girl pressed her hands to her face, prodding at the swelling. "Ouch. I feel . . . I don't feel right."

"I wouldn't touch that if I were you."

The girl explored her lips, which were swollen to three times their normal size, and Robyn's mouth tingled in sympathetic pain.

"I must look like a fright."

"You certainly gave us one." Robyn found herself grinning. The whole situation, though fraught with the possibility of discovery, was ludicrous. Robyn Fletcher didn't sit by the banks of the river exchanging pleasantries with the gentry. Robyn Hood, on the other hand, apparently did.

"My horse?"

"I didn't see one."

"I should thank you. I will, but my head . . ." she touched it again. Robyn could barely make out the slits of her eyes, but something in the sudden slowness of the girl's speech warned her. She had just enough time to catch her as she slumped back into unconsciousness.

"Seven hells," John swore, looming over Robyn as she cradled the girl in her arms. "Now what do we do with her?"

Chapter Twelve

Marian woke to the sound of crackling firewood, the smell of roasting meat, and an ache that covered her from head to toe. She lay on what had to be the ground, judging by the lumps jutting into her back and hip, and a coarse wool cloak covered her while another bundle of cloth pillowed her head. Something with multiple legs crawled across her arm.

This was not Harcourt Manor.

Hornets. She remembered that much. Hornets, and the pounding of her horse's hooves over the forest floor as the mare fled in terror. That pounding continued now in her skull, a dull, insistent ache that suggested she'd hit her head at some point.

"Are you hungry?"

Marian looked up into a pair of striking hazel eyes framed by a short fall of tousled dark hair. Firelight flickered across the boy's skin, and she blinked as she tried to place him. Something about the bow of his lips looked familiar. Then she glanced away from his face and around the firelit clearing, her pulse quickening. None of the other members of the hunting party were in sight. "Where am I?"

"Sherwood Forest, m'lady."

"M'lady?" Marian frowned as she repeated her title, trepidation adding to the ache in her skull, then regretted it as the motion sent ripples of pain through her swollen skin. She reached up to feel her face gingerly. The skin felt tight and hot to the touch, crusted beneath a layer of—*mud?*

"Well, you're not a swineherd."

Marian pushed herself into a sitting position, and the cloak fell off her bare shoulder. That wasn't right either. She had a detailed memory of selecting the blue tunic to match Emmeline today. Now she was in her shift, alone with a strange youth in the middle of the forest, without horse or friend. "Where are my clothes?"

"Right there." The boy pointed at the cloth she'd been using as a pillow. She recognized her tunic and riding skirt, then wrapped the cloak more tightly around her. "You don't remember?" he said.

"Remember what?"

"We found you near the river. The mud is for the stings, m'lady." The boy grinned each time he said "m'lady," she noticed.

Mud. Right. That would explain why her skin crackled every time she moved, and while it didn't feel like anything was broken, which was good, Emmeline would be worried sick about her. She pictured her friend pacing the rush-covered floor with her bad leg, perhaps barking orders at her huntsman to send out another search party.

"I'm in service to Lady Emmeline of Harcourt. She'll be looking for me," said Marian, another sentence hovering at the back of her throat. She bit down on the words before they could escape. A lady's protection might go further than her father's, out here where he hunted outlaws like vermin.

"I don't doubt that," said another voice.

Marian jerked her head around—another painful mistake—and scrambled away from the bull of a man crouching by the fire.

"He's mostly harmless," said the youth, correctly interpreting her alarm. "And we've already had this conversation, although it's clear you don't remember. If we wanted to hurt you, we wouldn't have gone to the effort of bathing and feeding you. Speaking of food, there's roasted goose and some mushrooms."

Marian took a steadying breath. She was alive, relatively unharmed, give or take a pint of hornet venom and a massive headache, and whoever these men were, the boy was right—they hadn't done anything to her. Yet. She could fare worse in Prince John's court, she reminded herself, and the goose did smell delicious.

"Thank you." She sat up a little straighter and decided to ignore the chill of the night air on her bare shoulders, not that she could feel much of it beneath the layer of mud and the hot press of the throbbing stings.

"Excellent. John? Ready to eat?"

"I was born ready to eat."

The youth snatched the goose from the coals and blew on it to cool it down before slicing off a drumstick for Marian and placing it on a broad leaf along with a handful of mushrooms. Marian popped one of the mushrooms into her mouth, ignoring the way it scalded her tongue, and accepted the waterskin the youth handed to her.

"It's good," she said, meeting the hazel eyes again.

"You haven't even tried the goose."

Marian bit into the leg and let the grease run down her chin. What was a little grease when her face was already covered in mud and monstrously swollen? The meat sang on her tongue notwithstanding her headache, and she licked her lips, smiling her approval despite the odd way her cheek muscles moved underneath the swelling. "It's good, too."

"You hear that, John? Our cooking is good enough for the gentry."

Marian looked closer at the boy, trying to figure out where she had seen him before. The memory shimmered in the flames just out of reach. A flash of hazel. Defiance. Eyes locking across a crowded Nottingham street.

"Speaking of the gentry," said John, gesticulating with a wing, "we'd be much obliged if you didn't mention that we found you."

"You don't want a reward?"

The two exchanged pointed glances at her words.

"Reward us with your silence, lady," said the youth. "As well as the pleasure of your company."

There. That look, wary beneath the sparkle of mischief. She cradled the drumstick in her hand, the meat momentarily forgotten. She'd seen that look before, and it hadn't belonged to a youth. Those smooth cheeks had never felt the prick of a beard, and there were women at court who would kill for eyes that shape and color. Her heart pounded a little faster. Perhaps she wouldn't have seen through the façade if she hadn't spent so much time around Willa and her brother. The twins had switched wardrobes until their father beat them out of it, and the youth in front of Marian now looked like Willa had then, wearing clothes slightly too large for her as she questioned the place the world demanded she fill.

This youth was a girl.

"I won't say anything," Marian said, questions bubbling up as her rescuer smiled. She wanted to ask the stranger her name, and she wanted to ask what had driven her into the woods and what she was hiding from, for she was certainly hiding. The stolen meat and the dirt across her cheeks were proof of that. Instead, Marian took another bite of the goose and tried to wrap her throbbing head around her situation.

She was the daughter of the sheriff of Nottingham. Her father made his living hunting down men and women like her rescuers, and Marian knew exactly how far his gratitude would extend for their intervention on her behalf. He'd thank them as he hanged them. I won't tell them who I really am, she decided. That would eliminate any foolish notions of asking for a reward or a pardon.

"We'll bring you to the edge of the forest tomorrow," the woman said, licking her fingers clean as she finished her share of the bird. Marian caught herself staring at her mouth again. It seemed impossible now that she'd mistaken the woman for a youth, and her curiosity mounted. Thunder rumbled to the south. She pictured the clouds gathering above the rolling hills of the forest, towering above Nottingham castle and flickering with summer lightning. She edged closer to the fire.

"Any news worth sharing?" the big man asked her. He, too, had finished his share of the goose, and his hands turned over a piece of wood. Shavings fell in delicate curls from his knife, and she wondered what he was carving. A spoon, or perhaps a bird.

"Have you heard about the king?"

"The bastard got himself captured," said the big man. "That's what comes of leaving good English soil."

"Any idea what they plan to do with him?" asked the woman.

"All I know is that Prince John wishes they'd keep him indefinitely," Marian said.

"I bet he does. Do you spend a lot of time in the castle?"

Marian ate the last of her mushrooms and touched her face again. The swelling seemed to be going down, and though she knew she must look frightful with her face covered in mud and her hair in tangles, the food and the fire and the sounds of the forest and the distant storm were oddly comforting. "Lady Emmeline doesn't like attending court, but yes."

"Such a tragedy," said the woman. "The food and the music must be truly awful."

"Do you know the difference between sex with a king and holding court with a king?" Marian repeated one of Emmeline's favorite jokes. She would not have dared say it in polite company, but here it seemed fitting, and she wanted to match her rescuer's teasing tone.

"I am pleased to say I do not," said the woman.

"Sex is over quickly and at the very least you can close your eyes."

The big man's laughter surprised Marian, and she felt inordinately pleased with herself when his companion gave her a crooked smile. By all rights she should be terrified, but something about the outlaw reminded her of Alanna and Emmeline, and Marian trusted them implicitly. Or maybe the fall had just knocked all the sense out of her head. The latter was by far the likeliest explanation.

"So, you're what, a lady's handmaid?"

"Yes." She didn't bother correcting the assumption to include her title, or explaining that she was more companion than handmaid at this point. The luxury of anonymity, of no one looking at her sideways because she was the sheriff's daughter, was refreshing.

"And what exactly do you do?"

"I see to her needs," said Marian.

"I've always wondered what needs a lady has that the rest of us don't," said the woman. The man watched the exchange with a frown that twitched upward periodically as if he was trying to contain a smile.

"I mostly keep her company," Marian admitted. "And I care for her leg. She had a bad riding accident when she was younger, and I oil it at night to relieve the ache." She had a sudden vision of herself rubbing the smooth muscles of Emmeline's thigh, and something about the way the woman studied her face brought the blood to her cheeks. The mud, at least, concealed her blush. "She loves hunting, though, so I ride out with her and her hawks, and I fetch her whatever she needs and help her dress."

"What would you do if you had someone to help you dress?" the woman asked the man.

"Tell him to kiss my ass while he's at it."

"It's a good position," said Marian, annoyed at their ribbing.

"I'm not saying it's not." The outlaw sat with her hands clasped loosely around her knees, and she turned her eyes back to Marian. Marian shivered slightly as they passed over her. "It just seems like a waste of a good pair of hands."

"I spin and sew," said Marian. "I am not idle."

"Let's see your hand, then."

The outlaw reached out and gently pried her fist from its grip on the cloak. Marian let her open her fingers, her chest suddenly tight as the woman's sun-browned skin brushed hers. The contrast between her smooth palm and the woman's callused one proved the woman's point. Still, she felt a strange reluctance to pull her hand back into the safety of the cloak. The gentle rasp of the outlaw's touch lulled her further into the warm circle of the fire, and she found she couldn't take her eyes off the other woman's face.

"You must be tired," the man said, interrupting her trance. "And you're still sick from the sting-poison. Get some rest. We'll keep a watch, and no one will harm you."

Marian lay down by the fire. The warmth of the flames eased the ache of the stings, and she closed her eyes. The outlaws didn't speak for a long time. She had almost drifted off to sleep when the woman spoke, softly, as if she didn't wish Marian to hear.

"I couldn't just leave her, John."

"I know."

"You didn't leave me behind."

"You weren't a lady's maid."

"You wouldn't have helped me if I had been?"

"I might have tossed you over my shoulder and sold you back to your father."

Marian opened her eyes a sliver in time to see the woman shake her head.

"She'll be off our hands tomorrow." The fire cast her face in shadow.

"Good."

"What's that supposed to mean?"

"You've made yourself far too memorable already for someone who's supposed to be dead. What if she recognizes you?"

"How would she recognize me?"

"The fair," said the man.

"Well, I'll keep my hood up. It isn't like I'll be anywhere near the nobility."

"Do that. And stop flirting with her."

Marian turned the words over as she drifted off, wondering how she was going to explain any of this to Emmeline, let alone her father. A night in the woods wasn't the sort of thing her father would want to hear about. Anything could happen in the woods. Anything at all. *Stop flirting with her,* the man had said. A pair of hazel eyes drifted through her dreams, and the faint rumble of thunder vibrated through the earth beneath her as she slept.

Chapter Thirteen

Robyn watched the girl sleep the next morning while John removed what was left of the goose from the little pot they kept tucked in the coals and divided it into three portions.

The swelling on her face was almost gone. Her dark hair lay over her mouth, and her breath disturbed the heavy brown curls. Robyn found herself comparing the curve of the girl's cheek to Gwyneth's. Where Gwyneth was fair and slender, this girl was dark and lithe, the swell of her hip and her rounded shoulder hinting at strength as well as beauty. A girl like that wouldn't break beneath the weight of a market lamb, nor would her breath come too quickly after a run through the fields. It isn't Gwyneth's fault, Robyn reminded herself, her heart aching as it always did when she thought of her sister-in-law's frailty. She wished Gwyneth were here now. She would know how to make this girl feel comfortable.

"Wake her up," said John as he tossed Robyn a hunk of breast meat. "The sooner we get her back to her people, the safer we'll be. We've waited too long already." The first light of the morning filtered over his face as he spoke, and Robyn saw the fear there beneath his stoic expression.

"All right," she said, wolfing down the meat and kneeling next to the girl to shake her shoulder. The girl blinked, her long lashes weighted down with mud, and looked around with large brown eyes. "Time to wake up, m'lady." Robyn offered the girl her hand. "You look better today. Your mistress might even recognize you."

The girl let the cloak slide off as her gaze swept around the clearing, pausing on John, and then swinging back to Robyn.

"You do remember what happened, don't you?" Robyn asked, worried for a moment that the girl had had another lapse in memory. She must have hit her head hard when she fell off her horse. "The river's not far. Eat something, and then we'll get the worst of the mud off and see you home safely."

The girl accepted the goose and ate quickly. The grease shone like beeswax on her full lips as she took Robyn's hand and rose to her feet. Standing unsupported, she was only a little shorter than Robyn. Tall for a woman, and once again Robyn's eyes lingered on her too long. She'll be gone soon, she told herself as she released her hand. The sooner the better. The feelings stirring in her chest were dangerous.

They made their way to the river in relative silence. Neither John nor Robyn wanted to make any more noise than was necessary, and the girl followed their lead. "Here," Robyn said, pausing at a part of the river obscured by reeds.

The girl tied her shift in a knot about her knees and bent to wash, running the water through her hair and letting it sluice down her arms. John placed a hand on Robyn's shoulder, forcing her to tear her eyes away from the sight. She raised an eyebrow at him.

"Let the lady wash in peace."

"I'm not—" Robyn began, and then she paused. John held her eyes for longer than was strictly necessary. *I wonder who he thinks about when he's lonely. Men? Women?* "I'm keeping guard."

John said nothing, but Robyn kept her eyes averted for the rest of the girl's ablutions.

"My clothes?" the girl asked when she finished.

Robyn handed her the bundle and tried not to stare. Without the mud and the grotesque swelling of the stings, the girl looked older. Not a girl, Robyn thought, grateful for her disguise. A youth might blush before a young woman like this, but a fletcher's daughter had no such excuse—or at least none that a priest would condone.

"Let's go. We've a ways to walk before we get to the road," said John, his knuckles white on the quarterstaff. Robyn adjusted her grip on her bow and fell into step beside the girl.

"I'm in your debt," the woman said after a half hour of silence punctuated only by the sound of their breathing.

"Don't worry about it," said Robyn.

"You could have just left me there. Or worse."

Robyn made the mistake of looking at her again. Welts from the stings still marred her cheeks, but she had the sort of face that gave a person pause. Her dark hair and darker eyes shifted beneath the dappled light of the trees, and Robyn thought that a great many people probably let their gazes wander on before snatching them back a few moments later, searching for her in vain. Her allure was delayed, but once noticed, impossible to ignore.

"What, do you think there's no honor among thieves?" she asked.

The woman gave her a small smile, dimpling one cheek. "So you are a thief."

"A thief of geese maybe, but you can hardly blame me for that. They're not very fast."

"And they are so very tasty."

Robyn warmed to the wry tone in her voice as she held a branch out of the girl's way. "Next time you fall off your horse, make sure you bring some preserves."

"Gooseberry or black currant?"

"Best to bring both, just in case."

"I'll have a hard time explaining why I only ride with jam in my saddlebags from now on."

"Think of something." Robyn paused, watching the girl out of the corner of her eye. "What are you going to tell them anyway?"

"About the jam?"

"No," Robyn began, but the girl waved her words away.

"I'll tell them the truth. I fell off my horse near the river and hit my head. When I woke up, it was morning, and I followed the river as best I could until I found the road, and then I followed that. I was terrified the entire time, of course," she added, batting her lashes in an uncanny impression of a delicate noblewoman. "Everyone knows there are outlaws in the forest."

"That must have been quite a trial for you."

She clutched at her breast and mimed a swoon. "You've no idea. Wine. I must have wine."

"Is your mistress like that?"

"Emmeline? No. She's tougher than horsebread. And kind. She'll be worried."

"And we'll have you back to her in no time, unless the two of you can't be quiet long enough for me to hear myself think," said John with a scowl.

Robyn made a face at him behind his back, and the woman laughed, then pressed her hand to her mouth. The urge to make her laugh again almost overrode Robyn's better judgment, but John was right. Silence was survival.

They came upon the forest road sooner than Robyn would have liked. She stared at the deep ruts while John surveyed the nearby woods, acutely aware of the woman standing close behind her. "Well," she said, keeping her voice low, "it won't be long now."

A hand brushed her forearm. She felt the touch through her entire body.

"I'm Marian."

"Marian?"

"Just Marian," she said, tilting her head slightly to one side. "And you?"

Robyn leaned against a tree and crossed her arms as she weighed her options. She couldn't give the girl her name, but she also didn't want to lie to her. "If I see you again, perhaps I'll tell you," she said at last.

Marian gave her a smile that sent a slow burn down her chest and into her stomach. "Perhaps you will," she said, and Robyn resisted the urge to tell her right then and there, just to hear Marian say her name.

"Do you often get lost in these woods?"

"I confess this is the first time."

"Then I shall count myself lucky," said Robyn.

"And why is that?"

A horn sounded further down the road.

"That's Emmeline's huntsman," Marian said, and Robyn hated the huntsman and his horn for ripping Marian's attention away.

"You should go," she told Marian as she caught sight of John's expression. "You're safe now."

"Am I?" Marian's smile faded, and the look that came over her face held none of its earlier coy sweetness. "Thank you." She reached out and took Robyn's hand for a fleeting moment, just long enough for the tips of her fingers to burn against Robyn's wrist, and then she was gone. Robyn watched her walk down the road and fought a disquieting desire to run after her.

Chapter Fourteen

Gregor saw her first. His white mustache lifted in a smile as he reined his horse up sharply. "Here," he called over his shoulder before dismounting to stand before her. Marian knew she still looked nightmarish, mud staining her clothes and her face puffy and bruised, but she didn't care. She collapsed into Gregor's arms, startling him, and burst into tears. She'd learned long ago tears were the best way to avoid unwanted questions, and the relief in her throat wasn't entirely feigned.

Emmeline arrived moments later. "Marian," she said, pulling Marian to her. "We thought we'd lost you. We found your horse, but there was no sign of you, and the hounds lost your scent in the rain. Look at you." And with that, she folded Marian into a fierce hug. Marian let herself relax into the embrace as the familiar smell of Emmeline's perfume washed over her.

Since they had not brought Marian's mare, she rode pillion with Emmeline back to the castle. The sky once more promised fair weather, and soft brushes of clouds swept the arc of blue. Marian glanced back over her shoulder as they rode. She could not make out the outlaw's silhouette amid the trees, nor had she expected to, but her eyes scanned the trunks anyway.

If I see you again, perhaps I'll tell you.

She hid her smile in Emmeline's back.

Emmeline ordered a bath drawn and attended Marian herself

when they returned to Nottingham as the maid looked on askance at this breach in protocol.

"You poor, tragic thing," she said, sponging the dirt off Marian's wounds and working oil into her hair. "I feared the worst."

"The worst may yet come if my face does not return to normal."

"Hush. You were too lovely by half as it was, although . . ." and here she paused, eyeing Marian's swollen eyelids. "You do make a lovely cyclops."

"You wound me."

"Alanna says she will play whatever you like. I've been a monster since you left. The kennel master has half a mind to drown my hounds just to be rid of me, and even Willa was beside herself. She stayed another day to make sure you were recovered."

The promise of food and music, combined with the luxuriant feeling of Emmeline's hands on her hair and the draught of wine she'd drunk to banish the lingering chill nearly lulled her to sleep. She let her eyes close as Emmeline sluiced hot water over her hair to rinse it. The outlaw's face rose before her. Marian remembered the straight arrow of her nose, the proud chin, and the slight slant of her hazel eyes. *I will find a way to repay you*, she decided, even if she had to wander the forest on foot. *Whoever you are.*

"Come, put on something dry and I will fetch Alanna."

Marian rose from the copper tub and allowed the maid—who looked relieved, at last, to be doing something—to pat her dry, and then she slipped into a soft wool tunic. The fabric did not chafe against the scrapes, and she gave a little shudder of pleasure at the feeling of clean cloth against her skin.

Food arrived, along with Willa. "You look terrible," she said as soon as she saw Marian. "Did you run into a tree?"

"I think, perhaps, a tree hit me. I don't remember doing much running."

"Your horse did that for you. I did not believe her capable of such speed."

"I wish she hadn't been. I might have made my way back sooner." Marian touched the sore spot on the side of her head.

"Be nice to her," Emmeline ordered Willa. "I will not have you goading her today."

"I do not goad," said Willa, looking affronted.

"I am not blind, nor am I deaf. Now pass me that cheese and for goodness' sake, pour the wine before we die of thirst."

Marian sank into the couch and listened to the familiar sounds of Emmeline and Willa's good-natured bickering.

"M'lady," said a servant, opening the door enough to peek her head around. "Alanna is here."

Alanna pushed her lyre into the startled servant's hands and wrapped her arms around Marian. "We were worried sick about you," she said into Marian's ear. Marian held on to the strength of Alanna's slender frame, grateful for her friends and even willing to forgive Willa, albeit temporarily. "Tonight I'm all yours. Whatever you want to hear I'll sing, no matter what Willa says."

"Excuse me?"

"Ignore her," said Alanna as she retrieved her lyre.

Marian settled back onto the couch and ran her hands through her damp hair. They all wore their long hair loose, a luxury allowed only in the company of women and small children. Henri played in the corner and made small chirruping noises as he galloped his wooden horse over the rushes.

"Fine. Marian, what do you want to hear? After all, you had a harrowing night alone in Sherwood Forest," said Willa.

"Alone?" Alanna strummed the lyre's strings gently. "They say the forest is thick with thieves."

"Perhaps my swollen face scared them all off," said Marian.

"I know a lay about a maiden, taken by outlaws, who falls in love with the leader of their band."

"Let me guess, he turns out to be a knight, wrongly denied his due by his vassal lord?" said Willa.

Marian laughed, hoping to cover the blush that spread over her cheeks. Her memory of the conversation she'd overheard by the fire was hazy, distorted by the blow to her head, but she remembered the man telling the woman to stop flirting with her. She remembered, too, how the words had made her feel: light, almost drunk, as if she'd downed a flagon of French wine. My head, she tried to tell herself, but the way the outlaw had held her gaze reminded her uncomfortably of the way Willa looked at her—more curious than courtesy allowed. Unlike Willa's gaze, however, the outlaw's hadn't made her want to run for cover. Quite the contrary. She'd wanted to stay there in that hazel glow despite the mud and pain and the worry her absence had surely caused.

Emmeline gave her a shrewd glance. "My dear, you're blushing."

"The wine, m'lady. It always brings up my color."

"I think we'll hear that song," said Emmeline as she refilled their glasses. It was good wine, stronger than the watered stuff they drank at meals, and Marian savored the spices. "Perhaps we shall rewrite your story. A night alone in the woods is perilous, but a night with an outlaw . . ." She trailed off suggestively.

Marian shook her head at her mistress as Alanna began to play, but thoughts of Sherwood, the outlaw woman, and all else fled her mind when Alanna opened her mouth. Her voice filled the room, rich and low, then sweet and high, as versatile as the lyre in her hands and twice as lovely. Marian closed her eyes and let the music wash over her while her heart soared with the notes.

The music ended abruptly with a sharp knock on the door.

"My lady," said Gregor from the other side of the oak.

"Come in." It might be improper for Gregor to enter Emmeline's solar, but the tone of his voice suggested this was an occasion that merited exception. He bowed upon entry, taking note of those assembled and then dropping his eyes respectfully.

"There's been news."

The peaceful look brought on by the music left Emmeline's face, and the lines returned. "Tell me," she said.

"King Richard is now with the Roman emperor." Gregor paused as if considering whether to continue.

"And?" Emmeline prompted.

"He's demanded a ransom of 150,000 marks."

"150,000 marks? That's more than the crown draws in a year. What does Eleanor say?"

"The queen regent means to pay it."

Marian saw the words hit Emmeline like a blow. The Saladin Tax had taken her husband, and now the crown was after more. This time no husband or son would suffice; the crown needed money, and estates like Harcourt would provide it. Her own plight seemed small in comparison. That didn't stop her stomach from plummeting. It would take months to raise that much money, if it could be done at all. Months Emmeline didn't have.

Emmeline clenched her jaw and nodded to herself as she smoothed the fabric of her dress over her lap. "Thank you, Gregor."

He hesitated, then bowed his way out of the room and shut the door behind him. Emmeline let her head fall into her hands the moment the latch fell into place. Stunned silence settled over the four of them. Henri looked up from his toy in confusion, the wooden horse in his hand forgotten.

"Well," Emmeline said eventually through her fingers, "we had better hope for a good harvest."

"Even with a good harvest that will beggar the kingdom," said Willa. "How can she hope to raise that much?"

"I don't know."

Marian didn't say anything. The messenger had just killed the small hope she'd harbored for Richard's swift return, and she cradled its corpse, too beaten to even cry. Her dowry would be a boon to any suitor now, and her father would want to make good use of the opportunity. She knew he thought that marrying her far above her station would serve her well. Sometimes she didn't even blame him for not seeing beyond the viscount before Linley's name, and the earl he thought would come. To be a countess—that should have been all she wanted. Her children would inherit lands and titles, and she would have influence. What did it matter if Linley repulsed her? He would give her sons and daughters, and if she survived childbirth, he would eventually leave her alone and take his pleasure elsewhere. She was a woman. This was her lot.

Why, then, did her soul scream for something more?

Chapter Fifteen

"Raise it higher," John instructed. Robyn adjusted her grip on her quarterstaff as sweat dripped down her back. The sun beat down on them in the clearing near the stream. Every farmer knew the basics of handling a quarterstaff. Staffs kept stray dogs away from livestock when the wielder did not have a bow, and in a pinch they kept away thieves of the human variety, too. Robyn understood the basics. Block, strike, block again, sweep.

John took this to another level.

"I thought you would use a hammer or an axe," she said, panting as she narrowly blocked another strike. "Seeing as you're a blacksmith."

"I like to keep my enemies at arm's length," said John. "And a staff can be used like an axe too." He swung it up and over his head in a two-handed grip, then brought it down in a chopping motion. Robyn threw herself out of the way as it hit the dirt.

"I suppose I should be grateful that all you did was toss me in that stream."

John leaned on the staff and grinned.

Two weeks had passed since they'd returned Marian to the city, and so far it seemed she had kept her promise. No one came to hunt them down to hang them—or to thank them, and John no longer frowned whenever Robyn mentioned Marian's name. Instead, he made her go through quarterstaff drills. Robyn wiped a sheen of sweat from her brow and made the most of the breather.

"Hold up," John said, tilting his head to one side as he listened to something in the distance.

Robyn heard it. Footsteps: one person, coming toward them at a fast pace. Her first instinct was to climb the nearest tree and string her bow, but John shook his head and faded behind a tree trunk. Robyn did the same.

The footsteps neared, followed by the sounds of someone breathing heavily. Something about the quick panting breath sounded familiar.

"Midge?" Robyn said, stepping out from behind the tree as her cousin barreled into the clearing. "Midge, what are you doing here? What's wrong?" Branches tangled in her cousin's hair and her face was red from exertion.

"I had to tell you," she said, gasping for air.

"What?"

Midge shook her head, too out of breath to continue for the moment.

"Let her breathe," said John, placing a hand on Midge's shoulder. "Get her some water."

"The king," Midge said after she had taken a long swallow from Robyn's waterskin. "The German king set his ransom for 150,000 marks. They're demanding a quarter of all property value for nobility, freemen, and the church. No exceptions."

Robyn felt the air leave her lungs as her throat closed in panic. "Gwyneth," she said, gripping her cousin by the forearms. Never before had she wished to be a serf, but now, with that impossible sum hanging over their heads, she wasn't sure the small plot of land they owned was worth it.

"That's why I came."

John looked between them in confusion.

"There's no way she'll be able to 'pay.' Not that Midge's family will either, but the sheriff will use this to press his suit, and Gwyneth will have no choice but to accept." Her hands tightened around Midge, who shook her off with a glare and rubbed the skin that Robyn had bruised.

"Gwyneth will accept for Symon's sake," Midge agreed. "Though if I were the sheriff, I would sleep with one eye open."

The only person Robyn knew who hated the sheriff as much as she did was her sister-in-law, but Midge was right. Gwyneth would do it for Symon. She would do anything for Symon. Robyn turned and slammed her fist into the nearest trunk. The bark bit into her knuckles in a glorious burst of pain, splitting them, and she rested her head against the trunk as she struggled to control her breathing. All this time, she'd thought she'd spared Gwyneth the worst of it by running. Instead, trouble had rushed in to fill the space she'd vacated. Gwyneth thought Robyn was dead. With no other hope she'd have little choice but to marry, and if she chose anyone besides the sheriff, he would bring his wrath down on her new husband just as he had the old.

"I will kill him," she said, the tree doing little to muffle the venom in her voice. "I will hunt him down and send him back to Prince John in pieces. This I swear."

"Hear, hear," said John.

All the anger that she'd held tight to her chest since her brother's death rose to blur her vision. The sheriff had taken her brother and driven her out of the only home she'd ever known, and before that he'd done everything in his power to make her family suffer.

Now it was her turn to make him pay.

"Midge," she said, taking her by the shoulders and looking straight into her eyes. "Nobody is going to starve this time. Do you understand me?"

Midge frowned.

"You keep asking me what I'm going to do." She searched her cousin's eyes. "We're going to take back what belongs to us. We're not going to run like rabbits. We're going to fight, and we're going to steal, and we're going to take from the sheriff what matters most."

"Which is?" asked Midge.

114

John answered for Robyn. "His pride."

Midge looked back and forth between the two of them, then drew herself up to the limits of her height and gave Robyn a short nod. "I'm in."

Robyn opened her mouth to tell Midge that it was too dangerous, but held her tongue. Midge understood the stakes. *And besides,* the part of Robyn that still blazed with anger said, *it is her fight, too.* "We need to start being more careful, then," she said at last. "We can't leave any signs for the foresters to follow, and we need to plan."

"Midge can help with that," said John. "Keep your ear to the ground. Listen to everything, even if it doesn't seem important."

"My sisters already do that," Midge said. "They're the worst gossips in town, and there are a hundred of them."

"A hundred?"

"Eleven," Robyn corrected. "But they might as well be a hundred."

"They eat that much," Midge muttered. "And Gwyneth?"

The urge to punch another tree nearly overpowered her. "The only thing that will help her now is money."

"Why can't she just join you?"

"Here? In Sherwood?"

Midge shrugged, and Robyn let the fantasy play itself out for a moment. "She wouldn't last the winter. I'm not even sure *I'm* going to last the winter. And besides, Symon will cry, and nothing brings people running faster in the woods than a crying baby."

"We could shove a stocking in his mouth," said Midge.

John laughed. "Spoken like someone with too many nieces and nephews."

"You have no idea." Midge gave a shudder. "Anyway, I ran all the way here, and I'm starving. Do you have anything to eat?"

Robyn wrapped her arm around her cousin's shoulders and led her back toward their camp, where a brace of rabbits hung from the branches of a tree, out of reach of scavengers and just waiting to be roasted. She pictured the sheriff hanging like the rabbits, then discarded the image. Hanging was too good for him.

"You know," said Midge, glancing up at Robyn. "There's always the fair."

"What?"

"The purse at the fair. For the archery contest. It's practically a dowry, and if you gave it to Gwyneth, she might even forgive you for pretending to be dead."

Robyn tripped over a root, and the only thing that prevented her from falling headlong to the ground was her cousin.

"Now that would certainly wound the sheriff's pride," said John, twirling his quarterstaff thoughtfully. "You're smarter than you look, Midgeon."

"What did you call me?"

"Midgeon. Offspring of a pigeon and a midge."

"Better a midgeon than a great ox."

Robyn let the sounds of their teasing soothe her as she contemplated Midge's words. Stealing the prize right from under the sheriff's nose would not only wound his pride, but also be fitting. He'd hanged her brother for a mislaid arrow, but he'd failed to realize his mistake: he hadn't hanged her too.

Chapter Sixteen

Marian breathed in the afternoon air and paused to wipe her face with her apron. Emmeline's manor overlooked the forest, and from the top of this field Marian could see the river snaking through the distant trees. She could also see the road. Three figures on horseback trotted down it. Marian thought she recognized the rider on the milk-white horse. Hair that shade of red was uncommon.

"Emmeline," she said, stepping over a freshly raked windrow of hay to where Emmeline toiled beside the other women of the manor. The manor was small enough that every hand was needed during harvest time, even noble ones, and though Marian had protested for the sake of Emmeline's leg, Emmeline had not been swayed. She pointed toward the road. "Riders."

"Seven shillings it isn't good news." Emmeline flipped the rake, leaning on the handle for a walking stick, and began the walk over the fields back toward the keep. The dirt track wound around the strip fields of the manor, packed by boots and hooves. The fields that belonged to the manor burgeoned with produce, for the weather had been fair, and the tenants' fields looked equally prosperous.

"I hope it is not another summons to court," Emmeline said as they walked.

"I shudder at the thought." Marian took another breath of air. No perfume. No sewage. Definitely an improvement on Notting-ham Castle.

Emmeline's steward met them in the yard. "Guests, m'lady. The lady Willa and her men-at-arms."

"Willa?" Emmeline frowned down at her clothing as she handed the rake to a passing stable hand. "I'll see her now. Take care of her men and horses."

"Would you like to freshen up first?"

"Willa, unlike you, does not stand by propriety. She won't faint at the sight of me, I promise, Samuel. A basin for my face and hands will suffice. And send for Alanna."

Emmeline's receiving room showcased what little wealth her husband's family had retained. The coat of arms hung over the hearth, and the chairs were all finely crafted, if old. Willa paced before them. Her long strides ate the floor and disturbed the rushes. "Emmeline," she said the moment the door shut behind Emmeline and Marian.

"Willa, are you quite all right?"

Willa shook her head, lips pressed tightly together, and raised her hands in a hopeless gesture. "I am to be married. To Lord Barrick."

Marian's fists clenched in horror.

"Oh, my love," said Emmeline. She took a few limping steps toward Willa and attempted to draw her into a chair, but Willa shook her head.

"I'll die of it," she said. "Or I'll kill him."

Marian remembered Lord Barrick. He had tried to corner her on several occasions, his breath reeking of garlic and ale. Sloppy, old, and prone to lashing out with his blackthorn stick at servants, children, and women alike, Barrick made Linley look like a lamb. The idea of Willa married to him was almost laughable it was so grotesque. Youth and beauty and spirit wed to a poisonous toad.

"Have you spoken to your father?" Emmeline asked.

"He won't see reason. He's too caught up in counting coins, and Barrick is the richest suitor in this part of England. He's offered to help my father with the tax as part of the contract."

Opportunistic bastard. No woman would have Barrick willingly, and no father would happily give his daughter into Barrick's

118

keeping. The ransom tax afforded men like Barrick an opportunity that made Marian's stomach roil.

"What about a convent?"

"Barrick's name is better than ours, and my father doesn't dare renege on his word. Or so he says."

"When are you to be married?"

"Just after Midsummer."

"But that's only a month from now," said Emmeline, the color draining from her face. "Why the rush?"

"Perhaps so that I do not have time to kill myself before he plows me." The bitterness in her voice could have soured wine. Marian watched Emmeline draw Willa's hands into hers, her fair hair damp with sweat and her face luminous with anguish for her friend.

"My love," she said, and Marian recognized the tone. It was the same one she used with Henri, sweet and full of boundless compassion. Willa's lower lip trembled.

"I don't know what to do," she said.

Marian dug her nails into the palm of her hand. There was nothing Willa *could* do. She would wed Lord Barrick just as Marian would wed Lord Linley, and their fathers would profit from their daughters' sacrifice. For the first time in her life, Marian found herself wishing her hands gripped a sword instead of the linen folds of her dress.

Alanna entered the room a moment later. The easy smile slipped from her face as she saw Willa's expression. They stared at each other wordlessly, and despite the horror of the situation Marian felt that now familiar pang of envy. No one had ever been able to read her own thoughts as clearly as Willa and Alanna understood each other.

"Who?" Alanna asked.

"Lord Barrick," Emmeline answered curtly for Willa, who didn't seem capable of saying his name.

The color drained from Alanna's face, and she crossed the room with slow, uncertain steps. Willa turned away from her. "I should have been my brother. I'd make a better man than he ever will."

The idea hit Marian with the force of a mule's kick. She wondered at how quickly it had come to her, and how much of her own longing for escape played a role. Willa *would* make a better man than her brother, William. She, at least, enjoyed the company of women, which was more than could be said of him. She had her twin's height, too, and stubborn jaw. Marian had a sudden image of Willa dressed like the hazel-eyed outlaw, with her long red hair cropped and her brother's sword in her hands. Willa could even wield a blade, thanks to her twin's abhorrence for violence. The two had switched places during lessons for most of their childhood, at first to spare William, and later because Willa enjoyed it.

As much as Willa vexed her of late, and as much as she wished she could rid her mind of Willa's taunting words and haunting eyes, she could not bear to think of her friend broken. Lord Barrick was a death sentence. He'd put three wives in the ground already, and it was rumored they had not died from natural causes. Anything was better than that.

Even outlawry.

Could she find the woman again? The forest was vast, and the outlaws knew it well. Marian stood no chance of tracking them. But, she remembered with a jolt, they had said something about the fair. It was a chance. Slim, but a chance nonetheless, and that was more than Willa had right now.

"Will you stay the night?" Emmeline asked Willa.

"Yes. And then I must return or else my father will think I've run off, and had I any place to go you can be sure I would."

Marian turned over the idea during dinner. So much could go wrong. She hated that her plan required taking advantage of Emmeline's generosity in a manner that could end with Marian herself drowning for treason, though as she was the sheriff's daughter she found this unlikely. Or she could ask Emmeline for help outright. Emmeline would aid in any way she could. That much she knew without question, but Emmeline and the people under her protection had far more to lose than Marian did.

I can't involve her in this, she decided. Not yet.

She knocked softly on the door to Willa's chamber later that night. The rush light in her hands cast greasy shadows over the walls.

"It's Marian," she whispered when she heard no response.

The door creaked open. Willa's eyes were red-rimmed and puffy. Alanna stood behind her with her hand on Willa's waist. The gesture of intimacy would have made Marian flinch a few days ago, but tonight it served only to deepen her resolve. She could sort out her conflicting feelings later.

"What do you want, Marian?"

"I want to help you. May I come in?"

"How can you help me?" Willa said, but she stepped back and let Marian into the small guest room.

Marian wet her lips with her tongue as she searched for the right words. Willa's glare challenged her, and for a fleeting second, she considered leaving her to her fate. It passed. They had been friends, once, before she'd walked into that kitchen. What she'd seen there wasn't enough to condemn Willa. She squared her shoulders. "I lied about what happened to me in the forest. I wasn't alone. Someone found me."

"I don't see what that has to do with me."

"Hush, love," said Alanna, her eyes fixed on Marian's face with the terrible brightness of hope. A part of Marian broke as she looked at Alanna. However wrong, however sinful, the love in the minstrel's face made her want to weep.

"I think I might know someone who can help you."

Chapter Seventeen

Robyn tested the pull of the bow and sighted down an imaginary arrow toward the road. "What if we see somebody we know?"

"Don't make eye contact," said Midge, strolling along between Robyn and John. "Everyone will be drunk, anyway. Win the archery contest, give Gwyneth the purse, and we can be on our way by nightfall."

"There's no guarantee I'm going to win, Midge." Her fingers itched as she spoke, and the thrum of the bowstring vibrated along her bones. She *could* win. A few weeks of shooting every day had honed her skills from excellent to superb, and the lure of winning the purse from under the sheriff's nose and then presenting it to Gwyneth beat in her temples like drums. Ten pounds would save her family.

"You do realize Gwyneth might kill you. If I were you, I'd take my chances with the sheriff."

"Then perhaps I'll make *you* tell her I'm alive."

"Lighten up, cos. There will be dancing, music, hot pies, and ale, and once you've told Gwyneth, the worst will be over and all you'll have to worry about is staying alive."

"You're such a comfort, Midge."

"That's me." She broke into song, her voice carrying through the coppiced woods. "Midge, Midge, balm for the soul—"

"Until they found her half dead in a hole," Robyn finished for her.

"That was not where I was going with that."

"And yet it is where you will end up if you don't shove a loin-cloth in that mouth of yours."

Her threats fell on deaf ears. Midge hummed to herself as they walked out of the woods and up the road toward the fields outside the city where the festival awaited. Robyn didn't begrudge Midge her high spirits. Well, not entirely. It wasn't lost on Robyn that the stress of keeping her secret wore on Midge almost as much as it did on her. At least Robyn didn't have to live with the human consequences.

Nobody hailed them as they joined the throngs outside the city gate on the flat plain where trestle tables and tents stood, and merchants had set up their wares. Livestock bleated in pens, tended by children with long sticks, and Robyn glimpsed a troupe of minstrels and acrobats on the outskirts, practicing their routines to gleeful shouts and applause. The press of bodies overwhelmed her. She sidled closer to John, taking comfort from his bulk, and pulled her hood further over her head.

Midge vanished into the crowd and reappeared with foaming tankards of ale, her eyes alight with excitement. "There's a bear," she said, pointing behind her into the crowd. "And someone said there might be jousting later since the prince is here."

Good, thought Robyn. That will hold everyone's attention.

Twice she thought she saw Gwyneth ahead of her in the crowd. Each time she realized with relief that she had been mistaken, but as they milled about, listening to the minstrels and stopping to watch a few plays, her anxiety mounted. Gwyneth was here somewhere. She had to be.

"Robyn," Midge said, pulling her toward the archery contest. "Look."

Robyn looked. At first she didn't understand what Midge wanted her to see. The judges' pavilion bordered one side of the field, and men and women milled about beneath it. Robyn started. One of them looked familiar. True, the last time she'd seen that face it had been swollen and battered, but there was no mistaking Marian's figure, even from this distance.

123

"Do you see it?"

"Huh?" Robyn tore her eyes away from Marian and followed Midge's finger to the prize, which was being touted above the heads of the crowd by a brawny giant. The fat purse gleamed in the sunlight, the leather oiled and visibly bulging with coin. *Her* coin. The certainty of victory pulsed through her veins.

"Wish me luck," she said to Midge, and approached the man in charge of the lists.

"Your name?" he asked.

"Robyn," she said without thinking. *By God's blood, you're an idiot.* "Robyn Hood."

"Take your mark, then. You've come just in time."

Robyn noticed the other archers queuing and hesitated, looking back over her shoulder at her companions. Midge mouthed encouragement. John gave her a small nod, his eyes wary. She understood the unspoken words. John had her back, and if the worst came to pass, he would get Midge out of there.

The contest was arranged in a large field. Later, the ground would be sundered by the hooves of warhorses during the joust, but for now the grass remained green. Sheep dung spotted the verdant stretch between the rope strung across the near side of the field and the straw targets opposite.

"Take your mark," the man repeated. Robyn strode out onto the field with the others, taking her place in the middle of the line of archers opposite a target. The broad shoulders of her competition blocked the pavilion from her sight, and besides—she couldn't afford to think about Marian right now. Not with the straw target looming in the distance.

"Nock."

Archers slid arrows onto strings. Some men fumbled, while others nocked with practiced ease, and Robyn noticed another woman down the line wearing a look of concentration almost as intense as the one Robyn felt on her own face. May the best woman win, she thought to herself, pleased that she was not alone.

"Draw."

She pulled the bowstring back to just below her ear. The

fletching tickled her jaw. Around her, the world stilled as it always did before she made a shot, and the target occupied her entire field of vision.

"Loose."

Her first arrow hit the bull's eye just a little off center, but still within the mark. She waited for the spotters to jog across the green to call out who had made it into the next round. It felt strange to shoot at a stationary target after weeks of hunting game, and she adjusted her grip, calm settling over her while the archers who had not shot as well as she trickled off the field. The other woman, she was disappointed to see, was one of them.

"Nock."

She selected her second arrow. The head glinted in the sunlight.

"Draw."

Again, she took her aim.

"Loose."

Another hit. She wiped her forehead with her sleeve as she chose a third arrow, not bothering to see who had left the field. It was almost too easy. The breezes that wafted by were gentle; she could not have asked for better shooting conditions. No leaves obscured her target, and it did not bound away when the wind shifted and delivered her scent.

The announcer called for a third round.

Her arrow thunked beside the other two. Grumbles arose from some of the men around her as they trudged to retrieve their arrows and depart, their loss no doubt quickly assuaged by drink. Let them go, she thought. She'd sold arrows to men like them: weak-willed, unwilling to put in the focus required for brilliant shooting, or men who didn't need to shoot, didn't need the deadly accuracy required for poaching or deterring wolves from a flock. Arrow after arrow left her quiver as the field shrank around her, until the rough voice of the announcer jerked her out of her trance.

"Gather closer together," he ordered, shooing her nearer the pavilion. She jogged down the field to collect her arrows before

125

joining the others. They would be judged on their last shots in the final rounds. This first bout had merely been elimination.

Several spotters moved the targets farther back, increasing the difficulty of the shot. Robyn grinned. She couldn't help herself. Certainty sang along her bowstring. These men were good, but they were not her. They did not understand their arrows with the intimacy of a fletcher. She knew each one personally, had tested its flight and christened it with the sweat from her hands. Her lungs filled with air and she exhaled. An errant breeze whispered past her ear and into her hood. No one stopped her. No one told her she should not shoot because she'd been born a woman. Was this how men felt? Free? She thought of Michael, and some of the fierce joy bled out of her. Freedom had limits.

A large crowd had gathered by this point to watch. Their eyes bored into the back of her head, prickling against her shoulder blades as they chattered about the competitors' chances. She ignored them. They were nothing more than leaves, and the target was all that mattered.

A flash of blue moved in the corner of her vision. It drew her eye, involuntary though the motion was, and she closed her hand around her arrow as she met Marian's gaze.

Fire licked her insides.

Color flushed Marian's cheeks as her lips parted in recognition, and the sight went to Robyn's head faster than a mug of ale. She winked, and Marian's lips curved in a smile Robyn knew she'd see later that night as she tried to fall asleep back in the safety of the forest. She enjoyed the feel of those dark eyes on her as she took her mark.

"Nock," said the announcer. Robyn nocked her arrow alongside the four other remaining competitors.

"Draw." She could still see Marian out of the corner of her eye. She forced herself to concentrate on the target.

"Loose."

Her shaft landed dead center, but so did three of her competitors'. The fourth swore violently and stepped back, waiting to fetch his errant arrow until the contest finished.

Robyn nocked another arrow. Some of the certainty of victory had faded with her lapse in concentration. Things felt less sure, and she steadied her breathing. She needed this. Gwyneth needed this. The world narrowed once more to the target, and when she let her arrow fly she sent part of her heart with it. Please, she prayed. Let me win.

It landed beside its sister arrow, the shafts so close she could hardly tell them apart. One of the judges took the field to inspect. Robyn eyed the other targets with frustration. Once again, the three of them had shot in tandem, too close to call.

Robyn set her jaw. It was time for what Michael called "cocky shooting," wasteful, the sort of thing done by wealthy yeoman with money to spare. She squinted, not at the target, but on the first arrow. Blue tinted her gaze. She let it, and Marian's dress melded with the sky as she released her last arrow.

She knew she'd won before the judge announced it. She'd split her first perfect shot down the middle, ruining the fletching and blunting the head, but none of that mattered. The crowd roared. With a jolt, she realized they were chanting her name.

"Robyn Hood, Robyn Hood, Robyn Hood."

She turned. Midge's face grinned back, supported by John's quieter smile. *I won.* The chant accelerated, along with her heartbeat. If she lingered much past this, she'd have men offering to buy her ale, and she couldn't risk that, no matter how wonderfully strange it felt to hear her chosen name on the lips of the men and women she'd grown up with.

"Archer," one shouted. "Where do you hail from?"

She waved him off and looked to the announcer for guidance. He gestured for her to retrieve her arrows, and when she had them in hand, split though one was, she knelt before the pavilion.

"Wonderful shooting," said a woman's voice.

Robyn looked up to see Marian standing before her. She wore a simple blue dress, but Robyn had a sudden recollection of the smooth skin beneath it, and the curves revealed by the rushing water of the stream that day in the forest. She met Marian's brown eyes slowly and savored the current of energy that passed between them.

127

"May I see your arrows?"

"Of course, m'lady." Robyn handed them over, not bothering to hide her satisfaction.

"These are of fine quality," said the announcer from beside Marian. The crowd strained to listen to his voice. "Who made them?"

I did, Robyn thought, but the impossibility of her answer slowed the passage of time as she struggled to grasp the precariousness of her position. Admitting that she'd made the arrows was as good as admitting her identity. Anyone who examined her arrows closely, however, might recognize the craftsmanship, which left her only one option. She swallowed, wishing she had a moment to pray, and tossed the dice.

"I bought these arrows the day before last, from a widow in your city, but the price she charged was far too low." She paused, her eye falling on the purse. "I think, perhaps, that I shall give her the prize in exchange for another quiverful."

The crowd loved this. Marian, however, pursed her lips, giving Robyn a measuring look as the announcer nodded, clapped Robyn on the shoulder, and departed.

"The purse is yours to give to whomever you choose," she said, handing two of the arrows back to Robyn. "But I would like to keep this."

Robyn's gaze fell to the ruined arrow in Marian's hands. "It won't fly far for you, m'lady."

"Does it need to?"

"That depends on where m'lady aims."

"Perhaps it has already found its mark."

"Marian," called a voice from the collected nobility. A flicker of annoyance passed over Marian's face, but she hid it quickly, motioning for Robyn to rise.

"I would speak with you before you leave," she said, and her hand brushed Robyn's as she turned, a small gesture, lost in the folds of her gown but hot as a brand against Robyn's skin.

Robyn didn't have time to dwell on this. The giant tossed the purse in the air, causing the coins inside to jingle dramatically, and Robyn caught it.

"Thank you," she told him. "Have you seen the fletcher's widow?"

"She's over there," he said, pointing to a face white with shock a few yards away. Robyn's heart stopped as Gwyneth covered her mouth with her hand. Symon gripped his mother's golden hair in tight fists, and Midge was doing her best to prop them both upright.

"Never mind." She pushed past him and approached the woman she would have gone to the ends of the earth to protect from the hurt that shone out of her pale blue eyes.

"Keep it together," said John into her left ear. "Smile. Remember, you don't know her well."

Several onlookers had lingered to observe the exchange, the generosity of Robyn's gift piquing their curiosity. Robyn wished them all death by a thousand cuts or perhaps, in the interest of time, something more immediate. "You undersold your arrows," she said to Gwyneth in a lame attempt to continue with her falsehood.

Gwyneth did not speak.

"My cousin is in shock, sir," said Midge, taking Gwyneth's arm. "It is such a generous gift."

Robyn resisted the urge to scoop her nephew into the air as she used to and surprise a long string of giggles from his little belly. Her heart ached. No, her entire body ached at the nearness of them, but she knew she could come no closer. "Might we buy you a drink?" she said instead, gesturing at herself and John.

At last, Gwyneth managed a brittle smile and nodded, clutching the child to her, and they made their way toward the edge of the crowd on the far side of the green. John bought a flagon of ale from a leering alewife, who looked as if she would be willing to give him far more than a jug for the pleasure of his company, but he fended her off with uncharacteristic brusqueness.

"You are supposed to be *dead*," said Gwyneth, holding Symon so tightly that his face began to darken with infant rage.

"Gwyn—" Robyn began, but Gwyneth cut her off.

"You are supposed to be dead. I thought you were dead for weeks. Why didn't you tell me?"

"It wasn't safe," Robyn said, wishing she had just let Cedric shoot her. "I had to protect you."

"By lying to me?" Her voice rose, and Midge placed a warning hand on her arm.

"She didn't have a choice, Gwyneth," said Midge.

Gwyneth turned on her. "And you. You knew?"

"I—"

"Robyn." Tears filled Gwyneth's blue eyes and spilled down over porcelain cheeks. Robyn wanted to hold her, anything to ease the anguish, but she knew that would only make things worse.

"I killed a man, Gwyneth, and Cedric saw."

"You think that is an excuse for leaving me alone to mourn you? Men die all the time, Robyn. We know that better than most."

"You were in danger. I didn't know what Cedric would do, and I thought you would rather I run than hang." She hadn't meant the last words to sound so harsh and instantly regretted them.

"Of course I would rather you lived. I just wish you had seen fit to tell me, instead of playing me the fool."

"Gwyneth, I'm sorry."

"And I don't suppose you're coming home, are you?"

"I can't. Not now."

The baby began squalling, forcing Gwyneth to spend a moment cooing into his beet-red face. None of the sweetness lingered in her eyes when she lifted her gaze again to Robyn. "Thank you for the purse, Robyn Hood. Now, if you'll excuse me, I think I'll take my son home."

"Gwyn, please."

"I loved you as my own sister. Every day I prayed that you'd come back, and now I find out that you've been on this earth the whole time. Do you care so little for us?"

"I couldn't tell you and keep you safe."

"And so you chose to let me live in hell."

"I had no choice," she said, her voice breaking.

"There is always a choice, Robyn. You've made yours clear." She snatched the money from Robyn's hands, glaring at Midge and John as she did so, and turned on her heel.

"Gwyn," Robyn called out after her, but her sister-in-law did not look back.

"We have to go with her," said Robyn. "She isn't safe with that purse." As she spoke, however, she saw another familiar figure approaching Gwyneth: Tom. Lisbet dogged his heels, and Robyn almost shouted out to them. She remembered herself in time. Tom would see Gwyneth home. Perhaps he'd even marry her. She waited to see how that idea would settle with her brother's ghost, but all she felt was worry. Tom was a friend. If he cared for Gwyneth, he was at risk. *And there is nothing else I can do right now to protect them.*

"Well, that went well," said Midge, scowling at Gwyneth's retreating back.

"She will never forgive me."

"She might yet," said John. "Here, drink this."

"I'm not thirsty."

"I don't care. Drinking will keep the mug in front of your face and give your hands something to do in case anybody's watching. Besides, that went better than I was expecting."

Both Midge and Robyn gave him looks of horror. He raised his hands in a placating gesture. "Anger is better than tears. If she has the strength to hate you, she has the strength to survive. I think she will come around. You didn't see the way she looked at you when she first realized who you were. But you can't go back to the way things used to be. She's got to find her own strength, unless you want to drag her and the baby back into the woods. And you've given her business and money today, along with the knowledge that you're alive."

"When did you get so wise?" Midge asked John.

"I've left my fair share of people behind, little one."

"Archer." A group of men with expectant faces approached. "Let us buy you a round."

"Thank you," said Robyn, "but I've just topped off."

"Drink it then! There's plenty more."

"Perhaps another time," said Robyn.

The men exchanged disappointed looks, which quickly soured

into resentment. She didn't want to wait around to see what they'd say next. She had to get out of Nottingham. It wasn't home. Not anymore. Not without Gwyneth. She repressed a painful memory of their house with its cheery hearth and worn wood table, Gwyneth singing as she spun by the fire while Robyn fletched in the dim light and Symon gurgled from his cradle.

"Wait," said Midge, placing a hand on Robyn's arm.

Robyn shook it off. "We should never have come."

The crowd let out a roar as the next contest began, and Robyn heard the clack of wood on wood: quarterstaffs. If they left now, no one would notice. No one except Marian.

I would speak with you again.

Gwyneth. Marian. The ties that bound her to this city. Their faces blurred before her, one dark, one fair, and the same reckless feeling that came over her when the wind turned the leaves silver before a storm ripped through her. Marian wanted her. It didn't matter that she thought Robyn a youth. Right now, she needed to be wanted by someone, and if she couldn't have the love of her family, then she'd settle for a pair of brown eyes and a slow smile.

"Fine. We'll stay a bit longer, if you want to see the bear that badly. I have something I need to do." She caught a glimpse of Midge's hurt expression as she walked away and saw John place a hand on her cousin's shoulder. Let him comfort her, she thought, aware that her anger was misplaced, but too lost in it to care.

The fair swallowed her. She saw the maypole rising off to her left. Its brightly colored ribbons shimmered as girls danced around it. Robyn had always hovered on the outskirts of the May Day festivities, avoiding the boys who might have tried to lay her down on the spring grass or sought a kiss and a promise. As a craftswoman, she had not had the same pressure to marry as most women, though it would have made her life easier. The thought had filled her with dread. She knew what she was and who she wanted, and she knew emphatically what she didn't want: a man in her bed and a child in her womb. She loved

Symon, but dying in the birthing bed like her own mother, and like so many of the women she knew, held no allure. She had watched the dancers and her eyes had followed them the way the men's eyes had, and she'd swallowed that along with everything else she knew she couldn't have. Perhaps she might have married Tom. He was a good man. She could have lived with that, though he might not have been happy.

The life she could have had walked beside her like a shadow. She bade it farewell. None of those worries belonged to her anymore.

Traders shouted over each other, and spring foals bucked and kicked beside tolerant mares as she passed through the crowd. Merchants from other towns hawked spices and cloth while tinsmiths sold pots, and beer and ale flowed from Nottingham's alewives, casks resting on the backs of wagons or held up by the women themselves while stray dogs ducked around legs and squabbled over scraps. A flute played a lively tune to her left, and Robyn nearly collided with a group of dancing girls. They giggled as they spun away, a few trying to catch her eye. None were Marian.

She'll be with the nobility, Robyn reminded herself, and made her way back toward the tents where the nobles rested in the shade. A group of drunken men loitered between her and the tent. Robyn paused, pretending to examine a barrel of early parsnips.

". . . and then I asked him, 'what does a goat and your sister have in common?' He didn't know, so I told him, 'I'd suckle on both.' You should have seen his face."

One of the men jostled against Robyn. She backed away, aggravated but unwilling to draw attention to herself.

"What about the sheriff's daughter?"

This gave Robyn pause. She didn't know the sheriff's girl, but any mention of the man made her itch to nock an arrow.

"You don't want him to hear you talking about her. I heard he's aiming to marry her off above her station. An earl or something. Viscount at least."

"Not if I plow her first."

"Seems like she wants to get shafted by someone else if you take my meaning. You know what they say: the longer the bow . . ."

Robyn shook her head, glad of her hood, and dodged the men. She pulled her hood lower as she skirted the brightly colored banners and silks fluttering in the breeze, seeking a blue dress in the riot of perfumed bodies ahead.

"Robyn." Marian detached herself from a group of women with a smile. Robyn turned away so that her companions could not see her face and took refuge behind a teetering pile of sheepskins. The smell of lanolin grounded her, obliterating the lingering whiff of perfume.

"I wasn't sure if you'd come back for me," Marian said, smoothing the skirt of her gown and looking over her shoulder.

"I wasn't sure I would either."

"I'm hurt. You'd give a purse to a perfect stranger, but you'd scorn me the pleasure of your company?"

"Pleasurable is not exactly how my company is usually described, m'lady."

"Then what do they say?"

"I wouldn't dare use that kind of language in front of you."

The smile slipped on Marian's face. "To hell with courtesy. If I hear one more courtly phrase, so help me God, I will take both halves of your arrow and gouge out my eyes." Marian leaned against the sheepskins. The white wool brought out the red highlights in her dark hair.

"Gouging out your eyes won't stop you from hearing them."

"It might change the subject."

"Oh, fair lady," Robyn said, raising her voice to mimic the affected speech of the nobility, "then however will I see myself reflected in your fair visage?"

Marian gave a snort of laughter that seemed out of place with her carefully ribboned hair and rouged lips. "You sound like you've spent some time at court."

Robyn crossed herself.

"So," said Marian, looking up at Robyn through her lashes.

"You wouldn't tell me your name, and yet you were quick enough to tell all of Nottingham today, Robyn Hood."

"Perhaps I was trying to be mysterious."

"Perhaps you're just rude."

"No, you're thinking of my cousin. I'm the soul of courtesy."

"Modest, too," said Marian. "Is Robyn Hood your real name?"

"It is now."

"What did your mother call you?"

"A mistake, more often than not."

"You're incredibly vexing."

"You're incredibly lovely." Robyn bit her lip, but there was no taking the words back. Words, like arrows, could not be recalled.

"Do you really think so?" Marian tilted her head and shifted her weight toward Robyn ever so slightly. Robyn had seen the same gesture from women countless times before, usually where her brother was concerned, and had scoffed at how easily men were moved by it. Now that she was on the receiving end of it, however, she found herself struggling to catch her breath.

"Well, especially compared to the way you looked at first," she said, hoping to regain some of her leverage. "Your nose is much smaller than I recall."

"Yes, well, it's amazing what river mud can do, isn't it?"

A vivid memory of Marian in the river further spurred her heart rate. "Perhaps it will be all the rage at court."

"Or perhaps they'll be talking about the youth who won the archery contest, only to give his prize away to a beautiful widow."

"Is she beautiful? I hadn't noticed."

"Hmm."

"M'lady, are you jealous?" Robyn found herself desperately wishing this was so.

"Just curious. Are you always this generous to strangers? Or is the widow special?"

"I am sure she is special to someone." Talking about Gwyneth with Marian made her jittery. They belonged in different worlds, and she wanted to keep it that way.

"Of course."

"You must have someone. Special, that is," said Robyn when Marian didn't say anything more.

"Oh, I think I might," she said, her smile cutting and her expression impenetrable from beneath her lashes.

"Is this why you wanted to see me again? To ask about the fletcher's widow?"

"No."

"You could have fooled me."

"Which is funny since you haven't fooled me at all." Marian moved closer as she spoke, silencing Robyn's protest with the heady force of her proximity. I'm a woman, Robyn reminded herself. She doesn't want me, she wants the person she thinks I am. That didn't stop her from wishing fervently that Marian would close the remaining gap between them. "I wanted to thank you again for saving my life."

"It's nothing."

"It's something to me. And, as I am already indebted, I wanted to ask you for another favor."

"A favor?" Robyn couldn't take her eyes off Marian's lips. "I think I should remind you that I'm an outlaw," Robyn forced herself to say. "I am in your debt for your silence, if nothing else."

"I gave you my word I would say nothing."

"Words are . . ." Robyn made a vague gesture that she hoped conveyed her ambivalence toward oaths. Marian caught her hand and laced her fingers through Robyn's.

"My word means something."

"Yes, m'lady. I won't forget that."

"Will you help me then?"

I should say no, Robyn reasoned, her mind coming up with a long list of all the things that could possibly go wrong by agreeing to involve herself with Marian any further. Then again, when was the last time things had gone right, despite her careful planning?

"I'm yours," she said, hoping Marian didn't understand just how much she meant it.

"My friend, Will, is at the convent in Edwinstowe."

"Will?" A deep suspicion filled her, fueled by Marian's amused smile.

"I think you'll find Will interesting, and perhaps the two of you will have more in common than you think."

"And what am I to do with him?"

"Whatever you please, although I had hoped you might see fit to take him with you."

"With me?"

"Into Sherwood."

"You do realize that Sherwood is a dangerous place, don't you?"

"Not half so dangerous as life at court." She slid her hand out of Robyn's and took a step back. "If you ever wish to see me again, you can find me when the Lady Emmeline is in residence at Harcourt. Do you know it?"

The Harcourt estate, small as it was, bordered the region of Sherwood that Robyn and John had taken to haunting. She nodded, her mind already concocting reasons to venture near the manor. "Does that mean, m'lady, that you wish to see me again?"

Marian touched the tip of the broken arrow tucked into her belt and smiled as she backed away. "I would have thought that much was obvious, Robyn Hood."

John favored Robyn with a puzzled glance when she slid into step beside him.

"Where did you go?"

"I'll tell you later. Where's Midge?"

John pointed toward a group gathered around a pair of jugglers. Midge watched with a rapt expression a few feet away. "She knows you and I are leaving, and I've told her when and where to meet us next. Don't say good-bye. You're being watched."

Robyn forced herself not to look over her shoulder. "Who?"

"A forester."

"Where?"

"Ten paces away to your left."

Keeping her hood over her face, Robyn turned just enough to glimpse a whey-faced man with a constellation of pimples across his cheeks. "God's nails," she swore. "Cedric."

"Pray tell, who is Cedric?"

"He's the one who saw me kill that forester." She stole another glimpse. A frown wrinkled his brow as he studied her, but she did not see any flash of recognition. Suspicion, yes, and something bordering on understanding, but he had not yet put two and two together. If she lingered here much longer, however, he would.

"Then it's time for us to get the hell out of here."

"Yes."

"We need to lose him," said John. "Follow me."

He made a show of laughing at the jugglers, then waded through a flock of sheep. Robyn dodged around the animals and followed. John's quarterstaff cut a swathe just wide enough for her to slide into his wake as he used the sturdy oak to prod drunken men and women out of his way. A few looked as if they might protest, but after glancing at his face turned back to their companions. They wove through the crowd like a tapestry needle: back and forth, pausing to admire a black colt, savoring the smell of a pie-seller's wares, and always moving. When Robyn at last dared to glance behind her, Cedric was gone.

They joined a group of villagers departing Nottingham for the forest road. John made small talk with a man leading a donkey laden with hides, while Robyn let a girl of six or seven touch the arrows in her quiver.

"Are you the archer?" the girl asked. "I saw you."

"I am."

"I'm going to be an archer someday." The girl's tangled brown hair escaped her kerchief and reminded Robyn strongly of Midge. Her younger brother bounced alongside her.

"I'm going to be an archer too. And kill infidels."

"No you're not," said his sister. "Da says you're going to be a farmer."

Robyn smiled as they argued back and forth. Had she and

Michael ever been that young? It hurt to think about, but the hurt felt good. When it came time for her and John to part ways with the villagers, she knelt before the siblings.

"Take care of each other," she said. "And take these." She pulled two wing feathers she had meant to use for fletching from her belt pouch. The children accepted the goose feathers with reverence. She wished she could give them something more, but they smoothed the striped feathers with their plump, strawberry-stained fingers and gazed up at her with adoration.

"Make some friends?" John asked as they turned down a narrow track.

"They were curious."

"Hmm." He measured her with his brown eyes. "This is a good spot."

"For what?"

John pointed at the road along the River Leen, partially visible through the trees. Robyn nodded her understanding as the muscles in her stomach clenched.

"What about Cedric?"

"Trust me. We won't be the only highway robbers on the hunt today."

The sunlight felt suddenly oppressive. Speaking about stealing and actually doing it were, Robyn reflected, very different animals. Poaching did not have immediate human consequences. She did not have to look anyone in the eye as she slit a deer's throat or broke a rabbit's neck.

On the other hand, Midge's family needed money, and so did she and John. The world was inherently unfair; Michael had understood that when he first went into the woods, and nothing that had happened since had changed Robyn's mind. She needed to make her own justice. Today, that meant taking coin from those who had it, to give it to those who did not.

She remembered how it had felt to kill Clovis. He'd been so still when she left him. Empty. And yet, the part of him that she hated, the part of him that had taunted Michael at the last, lived on inside her.

That knowledge did not undo the momentary exultation that had come with the snick of her bowstring as the arrow took him in the heart.

"I'm ready," she said to John.

"I know."

They waited by the road in the shade of a chestnut tree. Robyn mulled over her conversation with Marian as villagers strolled homeward. I'm yours, she had told her, and there had been a truth there that sent a ripple of fear through her mind, followed by a recklessness that should have terrified her, but did not.

"This one."

Robyn jerked herself out of her thoughts. A man led a pack-horse with empty panniers. He hummed to himself as he walked, and a woman in a yellow dress ambled alongside him with her arm looped through his. Both seemed to have difficulty walking a straight line, but Robyn noticed the short sword at the man's hip and the long knife the woman carried. Drunk, perhaps, but by no means easy prey.

"Are you sure?"

"Look at his purse."

The dark leather at the man's belt bulged. Robyn thought she could make out the press of coin against the sides, and hunger stirred within her.

"Follow my lead. I'll do the talking for this one. You just keep an arrow on the woman."

"The woman?"

"Trust me."

"But—"

"Chances are she's more dangerous than him by half, but he'll want to protect her."

John strode into the road at an easy pace, twirling his quarter-staff. "By God's balls," Robyn swore under her breath as she fumbled an arrow to her bow and followed.

The man stopped humming when he saw them. Robyn had expected the woman to shrink with fear, for the cut of her cloth-ing suggested she belonged to the merchant class, but all she did was tighten her grip on her companion as she stared at the tip of the arrow.

"Good afternoon," said John. "It seems you did well for yourselves."

"Good afternoon," said the man. "And God bless." His face whitened around his lips.

"I'm not sure God would bless me, and I don't think today that he has looked too kindly on you," said John.

"What do you want from us?" said the woman.

"Your purse looks heavy. We'll be taking half of it."

Half? thought Robyn. The man seemed to share her confusion. He dropped a hand to his waist to pat the contents.

"Half is the price you might have paid for a guard. As it is, you'll find you attract less attention without it, which amounts almost to the same thing. Give it here or we'll shoot your wife."

Robyn forced herself to meet the woman's eyes. They were a light shade of hazel, more green than brown, and they stared at her with muted fury. *Could I shoot her if they call our bluff?* She didn't know. Nor did she know if John was truly bluffing. Did he expect her to take this woman's life over a few coins?

"You don't have to do this," the woman said to Robyn.

"Your purse, man." John's voice cracked like a lash. The man groped at the strings, not daring to take his eyes off Robyn's bow, and let it fall to the ground.

"Kick it over here."

The man obeyed John's order. Robyn saw sweat darken the sides of his tunic. She kept her arrow level on his wife and reminded herself of Midge's family, and tried not to think about how much these people might have needed the profit from their wares.

John tipped half of the contents of the purse into his belt pouch. When he finished, he tossed it back. The man trembled as he stared at it, and Robyn saw fear, gratitude, and frustration twist his features. They might have taken everything. Most thieves would have, from his coin to his horse and possibly even the boots from his feet. His wife, too, could have suffered a different fate,

141

though Robyn didn't think any man who tried to force her would get far. The set of her jaw suggested a generous capacity for violence.

"Safe travels," John said. "And Godspeed."

Robyn backed off the road, still keeping her arrow on the woman. Only when the trees were shielding them did she remove it and shove it back into her quiver.

"What now?" she asked John.

"Now we run."

Behind them, the couple sent up the hue and cry, and answering shouts echoed through the forest. Robyn wasn't concerned. Her feet carried her down the game trails and into the wild heart of the woods, and each step felt like flying.

Chapter Eighteen

Twilight settled over Harcourt like a shroud of velvet, the stars pricked out in careful needlework against the violet sky. Marian and Alanna edged along the manor wall, hands tracing the wood as they tried to avoid notice.

"Who is at the gate?" Marian asked again, quietly.

"Rourk."

"And will he let us pass?"

"He will if he knows what is good for him."

Marian chewed her lip. She'd trusted this part of the plan to Alanna, something that now seemed misguided at best and suicidal at worst.

"And why will he let us out?"

"Because I've seen what he gets up to with the priest."

"What?"

"Shh," Alanna said, turning and pressing her fingers to Marian's lips. "Trust me, you don't want the details."

Marian tried not to think about Father Derrick and his quivering jowls as she followed Alanna toward the gate.

"Gate's closed," said the bored-looking youth in the gatehouse. Then Alanna lifted the edge of her hood and he straightened, swallowing nervously.

"Tell anyone you've seen us, and I'll have to go to confession," Alanna said, her melodious voice poisonously sweet.

"Right. Hang on." The boy didn't even glance at Marian in his haste to open the smaller door in the gate to let them pass. Marian stifled a smile at his expense, even though her heart threatened to leap out of her throat. Sneaking past the manor gates at nightfall wasn't something she did. Ever. Alanna grasped her hand and pulled her over the threshold and out onto a road already lit by the rising moon.

"We've miles to go," Alanna reminded her.

Marian settled more deeply into her cloak and wished for a moment she had stayed behind. Alanna could have easily taken the journey to the priory alone. The chance that Robyn might be there, however, had been too much for Marian to resist. Fear and longing needled her at the thought. Robyn was a woman. A woman passing as a youth, not particularly well, but still a woman.

And I am not doing anything wrong. She was allowed to make new friends, and Robyn had saved her life. The warmth that filled her chest when she thought of Robyn could simply be the thrill of the danger she posed. Outlaw. Sheriff's daughter. Their worlds should never have collided, and yet they had met twice now as if it had been preordained. *Or Robyn could be a test of faith.*

There was a temptation there that she didn't have a name for. The outlaw's quick smile and wary eyes met hers each time she blinked, as if she'd stared into the sun and couldn't shake the afterglow. That in itself was no sin. Even flirting, though thrilling, had just been a game. Neither expected anything from the other. No harm had been done.

It's Willa's fault. She put these doubts in my head. And now here she was on her way to make sure Willa had arrived safely at the priory, where she would meet Robyn, and Marian might never see either of them again. *I should be going with them.* She tried to stifle the thought as a tide of panic followed it. Leaving meant giving up everything, and there was still a chance she could convince her father to change his mind and betroth her to someone else, or let her join the priory. You're a coward, she told herself. Perhaps she was a coward. Perhaps this was an opportunity she was foolish to pass up, but she was not Willa, and her father was not a duke. He was the sheriff of Nottingham and Marian was his only living heir.

144

He would never stop hunting for her. His pride would not allow it. And even if she could somehow find a way to evade him, what would she do in the forest? She could not wield a blade, and while she'd shot a lady's bow on the hunt, she had no illusions about her usefulness to a gang of outlaws or about how long she would last. Besides. They wouldn't want the sheriff's daughter in their ranks. That would get them hanged for certain.

They eased into a steady pace, keeping their eyes on the black shadows of the forest around them. Every cracking branch sounded louder than normal, and every shadow seemed to reach for her. She kept Alanna's hand clamped firmly in her own.

This is madness, she told herself as they walked. Madness, and it is all my fault. How would Emmeline react when she found that both Alanna and Willa had vanished in the night? Would she believe that Marian didn't know anything about their whereabouts? For that matter, could Marian stand to watch Emmeline grieve for a friend who was very much alive and well? Although perhaps "well" was a stretch. She considered the reality of what she'd set in motion. Willa and Alanna would be on their own beneath these trees with no walls to protect them and no roof over their heads. Robyn, too, was out here in this unforgiving darkness, listening to the rustling of leaves and the quick footfalls of the forest creatures going about their business, each noise a possible threat. Outlawry had seemed simpler back at Harcourt as she lay awake at night beside Emmeline remembering the curve of Robyn's lips.

Tuck's priory was only an hour's walk, but in the darkness the trip seemed to take years. An owl swooped low over their heads and hooted. They both squeaked in alarm. Alanna shot her an embarrassed smile in the moonlight.

"I guess I'll have to get used to that," she said.

Marian swallowed past her dry throat. "Is that something you can get used to?"

"I'll let you know."

Talking calmed her heart. "Are you sure about this, Alanna?"

"Of course not. But I can't let Willa do this alone, and she can't stay at Maunnesfeld."

"There are other places you could go, though."

"Like where?"

"Maybe a place with houses and walls and fewer owls."

"But here we'll be close to you. We can always leave later on."

"You could also be killed out here, or worse," Marian pointed out.

"I could be killed anywhere. Here, though, I can be with Willa."

The way she said it made it sound so simple, as if being with another woman were natural, easy even, once obstacles like propriety and impending marriages were out of the way. Marian was grateful the moonlight hid her flush. I am not like them, she told herself, but she remembered the feel of Robyn's wrist beneath her fingers.

"What's it like?" she asked.

"What is what like?"

"Being . . . being with a woman."

Alanna slowed her pace but didn't turn to stare at Marian, for which she was grateful.

"Have you ever been with a man?" Alanna said.

"Of course not. Have you?"

"Yes. It's different. Not better or worse really. That depends on the lover, not their sex."

Marian felt her face might light the forest. Alanna rarely spoke of the personal life she'd led before coming to Harcourt, but she'd been apprenticed to a minstrel of a grander estate, and her stories were full of bright clothing and brighter personalities sparking against one another like flint and steel. "Oh," she managed to say.

"With Will, though," Alanna said, shortening Willa's name affectionately, "it's something else entirely."

"And?" Marian prodded when Alanna trailed off.

"I could sing you a thousand songs about love, Marian, but until you've been in love you won't believe me. Willa isn't perfect. I know that even better than you, but she's mine and I am hers, and the rest of the Earth could burn so long as we have that."

"You don't worry about what other people will say, though?"

"I'm a minstrel. I make my living off spinning rumors into song. They can say what they want."

146

Brave words, now that she was leaving all those people behind, Marian didn't point out. "But you knew Willa was going to get married eventually."

"And had it been to a nicer lord, I would have begged Emmeline to let me leave her service and gone with Willa."

"You make it sound so easy."

"Love isn't easy. You just eventually figure out that some things can't be fought. Once I accepted that, I just did what had to be done. If that means leaving my place at court, abandoning my career, and running away to live like an animal in the forest, then that's what I'll do."

The lights of the priory flickered through the trees ahead of them on the path, sparing Marian the need to come up with a response.

Instead of the usual novice, Tuck met them at the gate and pulled Marian into her ample bosom. "The roads aren't safe," she said, shaking Marian gently. "Especially for you, you silly girl. Sheriff's daughter," she added under her breath as she shook her head.

"Is Willa here?" asked Alanna.

"Yes, which is how I knew to expect you. Does my sister know you're here?"

Marian stared at her feet as she shook her head.

"I thought as much. Now get inside before somebody sees you. As my church has apparently turned into an inn without anyone telling me, I may as well see that you're comfortable."

"We don't want to obtrude on the hospitality of the convent," Marian began, but Tuck waved her into silence.

"Willa has already invoked the right of sanctuary. For the next forty days, I am bound to protect her."

"How can she invoke sanctuary if she hasn't committed a crime?" Marian asked.

"Has she committed a crime?" Alanna asked a second later.

"There are those who might hold that disobeying one's father is crime enough. Treason, it is called. The rest you'll have to ask her yourself."

147

They crossed the moonlit courtyard with its kitchen garden, the smell of herbs strong in the night air, and followed Tuck into the priory public dormitory. It was a small stone room with several pallets arranged around the walls. A woman and child occupied the pallet farthest from them, and a tall youth jumped to his feet when Tuck opened the door.

Marian's jaw dropped. Willa stood before them, but she looked so much like her brother that Marian had to blink several times to convince herself it wasn't William. Willa had given herself a rather brutal haircut, which she'd covered with a cap to hide the worst of, and she wore a pair of breeches that looked like they'd been pilfered from the stable, judging by the stains around the knees. A sword belt hung around her waist and the pommel gleamed in the low light of the fire. That, Marian was sure, had not been stolen from a stable boy. William's squire, however, might have some explaining to do when one of his lord's blades turned up missing.

"Willa?" Marian said.

"Could you really not tell?" Willa asked with a grin.

Alanna reached up to touch Willa's shorn hair and shook her head in disbelief. "Who knew hair made such a difference? Although really, Will, what did you use to cut it—your sword?"

"I was in a hurry."

"I'll fix it for you later."

"Now," Tuck said, interrupting their reunion, "would one of you be so kind as to explain to me what is going on?"

Marian glanced at the woman in the corner, unwilling to speak in front of strangers.

"Gwyneth will be joining our order soon enough. She pledged herself this morning, but with the baby I thought it best to house her here for now. I was not expecting additional visitors."

The woman raised her head at the sound of her name, and Marian started. She recognized her: she was the widow Robyn had offered the purse to after the archery contest. Her blond hair was covered by a scarf and her eyes were shadowed, but beauty like that would have shone even on a corpse. Gwyneth met

Marian's eyes impassively, then turned her gaze back to the face of her sleeping son.

"That's wonderful," said Marian, unsure of the truth of her words.

"I can't go home, Tuck," Willa said. "I asked my father to let me pledge to the priory, but he refused."

"Shall I quote what the Bible has to say about obeying fathers?"

"Only if you believe it."

"Fair enough. But at the end of your time here you will have to go somewhere."

"Marian knows someone. He's supposed to meet us."

"And this man—is he trustworthy?"

"Yes," said Marian before Willa could speak. "He saved my life once."

Tuck raised her eyebrows. "You still have not yet explained why Willa arrived on my doorstep with a sword in her hands."

"It was in my scabbard."

"Technicalities do not interest me right now, Willa of Maunnesfeld."

"Even Marian had trouble recognizing me. My father will be looking for a woman, not a boy, and I've made sure he'll never find me."

"I see." Tuck adjusted her wimple as she considered Willa. "And I suppose Alanna is going with you, judging by the sack she's carrying?"

"Yes," said Alanna. "But I assure you, I will take more care with my hair, should I choose to cut it."

"And I also suppose that you have informed my sister of all of this, have you not?"

Silence met her words, which seemed to confirm her suspicions.

"They will question Emmeline," Marian said at length. "I thought it was better if she didn't know right away, for her sake."

Gwyneth made a scoffing noise in the back of her throat. They all turned toward her, and she met their eyes defiantly. "Trust me when I tell you that your Emmeline will not agree."

149

"And why should we take your word for it?" said Marian. I have no reason to dislike this woman, she told herself, but God help me, I do.

"Marian," Tuck said in warning. "If you will not speak with courtesy to my guest, how do you expect me to extend the same courtesy to you?"

"I am sorry," she said.

"Very well," said Tuck. "I will not lie for you. Neither will I go out of my way to tell the truth. That will have to suffice."

"Thank you." Willa offered Tuck a bow. Marian covered her mouth with her hand to hide her amusement at the sight.

"Well, make yourselves comfortable," Tuck said, gesturing at the other pallets. "The fewer people who see you, the better."

"Good night, Reverend Mother," said Alanna. Her voice seemed to soothe Tuck, for the nun's face softened as she motioned for Marian to follow her out the door.

"I had thought to stay," said Marian.

"And worry my sister? I think not. I will take you home myself."

"But—"

"This is not negotiable."

Marian hugged Alanna tightly. "Be careful," she said, letting go. "Promise me."

"I promise."

Willa chewed on her lip as she stared at Marian. "Take care of Emmeline," she said at length.

"I will."

"And Mare—"

"What?"

"Thank you."

When Marian joined her, Tuck already had her walking stick in hand, which was suspiciously near the same height and thickness as a quarterstaff.

"This is not well done," the nun said as she led Marian out of the priory and into the night. "Emmeline will worry, and what of Willa's family?"

"Do you know Lord Barrick, Tuck?"

"By reputation. I would not wish him on Willa, but what about her mother?"

"What about Willa?"

"Outlawry could be worse than a bad marriage."

"It could also be better. You don't understand. You're free here."

Tuck turned at the heat in Marian's voice. "I serve the Lord."

"Yes, but you don't have to worry about dying in childbirth or your husband beating you. You do as you please. I know you do, Tuck. Willa and I—"

"Do you wish to join my order? I would have you."

"My father won't hear of it." She kicked at a rock and sent it flying into the undergrowth. The outburst and ensuing throb in her toe felt good.

"I shall pray that he changes his mind."

Marian listened to the sounds of the forest. She wished she could believe her father might be persuaded to let her live out her days behind the priory walls, but she knew better. Another owl hooted.

Disappointment cloyed her throat. She had not seen Robyn. That should not have felt like a spear thrust to the gut, and yet she hated Tuck in this moment for dragging her back home. Knowing Tuck was right didn't make it any easier to swallow.

"Who is this man to you?"

"What?"

"This man you've entrusted Willa's life to."

Midnight wrapped her in velvet darkness. "He's . . . not a man."

"Is he a goat?" Tuck's voice dripped with tartness.

"No. He's a woman. Dressed as a man. For safety, I think. I don't rightly know."

"If she's in the woods, that would be safest, yes."

"She won the archery contest at the fair and rescued me when I fell off my horse, and she gave Gwyneth her winnings." The words tumbled out of her mouth.

"Ah." Tuck sucked her teeth. "Yes, I wondered where she had gotten the money for admission."

"She gave you the ten pounds?"

"Normally we expect more, and we rarely accept commoners, but I took pity on her and the child."

Marian wondered if Robyn knew where the money had gone, or if that had been her plan all along. Now she wouldn't get to ask.

She wanted to scream.

"Here you are," said Tuck when they finally arrived. "I expect I'll be seeing you and my sister quite soon."

"Good night, Reverend Mother."

Tuck touched her shoulder and Marian lifted her eyes to the nun's.

"You're a brave woman, Marian. Go with God."

Chapter Nineteen

"I have no idea what this is about, as I have told you countless times already," Robyn said as they walked down the track toward Edwinstowe. She felt naked without her bow, which she had stowed in a hollow tree nearby, but with their staffs and increasingly ragged clothing they looked less like outlaws and more like beggars, which served their purpose.

"I do not see why you have to do this woman's bidding."

"I am not doing her bidding. I am . . ." Robyn trailed off. She didn't have a good reason for helping Marian—or at least not one that John would accept.

"And this boy. Will. What are we supposed to do with him? Is he wanted for stealing?"

"I don't know, John."

"She has a fair face," John said, stopping to face Robyn in the road, "but I do not like the hold she seems to have over you. We do not know who she is, Robyn."

"She has no hold over me, and we do know who she is. She's a lady's handmaid. Her fair face has nothing to do with it, and I would be much obliged if you dropped the goddamned subject."

"Why would a lady's handmaid collect your arrows after the shooting match? Have you thought of that?"

"She recognized me. That is all."

"Handmaids stay with their ladies. They don't play at judge."

"She was not playing at anything."

153

"She approached you in front of all of Nottingham. Have you thought about the questions that will raise? The consequences it could have for Midge or Gwyneth?"

"All I do is think about consequences." Robyn's shout startled a few birds out of a nearby tree.

John held up a hand to sue for peace. "I have said my part."

"You have said more than your part." Then, guilt squeezing her stomach, she tapped him with her staff. "And I value your advice, John. You do not have to come with me if it troubles you."

"Yes, it is a mark of value to be ignored," he said, but he grinned at her as the trees parted and they entered the clearing that held the small fields, handful of cottages, and the nunnery at Edwinstowe.

A few sheep bleated at them as they walked along the lane, and Robyn's mouth watered at the prospect of cheese. Meat was all well and good and had been hard enough to come by in her old life, but now she missed cheese and bread and ale. She eyed a gaggle of geese longingly. She needed feathers for fletching, too. Pheasants didn't have the long, thick feathers she was used to working with.

The villagers they passed shot wary looks in their direction as they came into view. "Not much used to strangers, here, are they?" said Robyn.

"Not strangers like ourselves at least. The Royal hunt passes through here, but they bring coin. We just look like we bring fleas."

Robyn scratched her head as surreptitiously as possible as they approached the convent. The low wall around it crawled with ivy, and the arches looked as if the stonemasons had done their best with what they had to work with, which was, put bluntly, not enough stone. Sheep clustered outside the gate, and the convent's fields hummed with bees and the voices of the novices working in them, sleeves rolled up over their arms and their habits bleached from the sun.

"Doesn't seem like such a bad lot," Robyn said as she studied the women in the fields. "At least they don't have to worry about childbirth."

"Christ is a gentle bridegroom. They say you can hardly feel

154

it." John held up his fingers to indicate the size of their savior's heavenly parts.

"There is a special place reserved in hell for you," said Robyn. "Do we just knock?" They both eyed the priory door, aware they were under the scrutiny of a few watchful peasants and a particularly curious goat.

"Looks like."

Robyn raised the knocker, which looked as if it too had suffered from the neglect of an errant mason, and let it fall. A few long minutes later, during which time the goat nibbled on the tattered hem of John's tunic and Robyn had to fend off a lamb from making a similar attempt on her pants, the door jerked open to reveal the strangest woman Robyn had ever seen. Round red cheeks beamed at them from a wide face enclosed in a wimple, and the nun's belly, equally broad, protruded a few inches ahead of her feet beneath a massive bosom. The arm that held the door was nearly as muscular as John's, and the woman exuded a terminal kind of health and good cheer that made Robyn want to take several steps back, lest it be catching.

"Good afternoon," said the nun. Robyn felt the vibrations from the woman's deep voice through the soles of her boots. "What brings you here?"

"We're looking for a boy."

"Then you've come to the wrong place," said the nun, winking at Robyn.

"His name is Will?" She couldn't help the question that crept into her voice. God help the man who tried to force his way into this nunnery, she thought, wondering if the woman had ever wielded a staff, and if so, how much faster Robyn could run than the powerful thighs concealed by that woolen habit.

"Oh, you mean Will." Her face brightened further, which didn't seem possible, and she cracked a jovial smile that revealed a row of gleaming white teeth. "Come on in. You'll find Will in the sanctuary, but first, let me offer you something to drink. Mead, perhaps? Our bees are most productive. Or some of last year's cider, although that is getting down to the dregs."

155

John and Robyn followed her into the convent. The door shut behind them, walling them in, and Robyn glimpsed a meticulously tended kitchen garden through one arch and a small orchard through another before the woman brought them into a courtyard crisscrossed by flower-lined stone paths. The flowers, too, looked unusually robust, and Robyn guessed the nun accompanying them tended to these beds herself.

"Wait here," said the nun, vanishing through a wooden door.

"Wow," said Robyn when she was sure they were alone. "That is quite a woman."

John opened his mouth, shut it, tried again, and then settled for shaking his head in mute disbelief. They stood together in silence.

Robyn had never had cause to set foot in a priory. Convents were for the devout or, more realistically, for the unmarriageable daughters of the nobility, widows, and the occasional oddity who craved an education—and isolation—over a husband's wealth. The priory at Edwinstowe had been constructed in her grandfather's lifetime and finished when her father was a young man. The years since, few as they were, had seen the forest send out ivy shoots to scale the walls and moss grow at the base of the stone in the shadows where the sun rarely touched. The sound of feet on flagstones jerked her attention back to the door in time to see the nun return, balancing a tray on one hand and restraining a massive dog with the other.

"Hope you don't mind," she said, releasing the beast.

Robyn stifled the instinct that urged her to leap onto John's shoulders and stood as if rooted like the ivy to the ground as the brindled mastiff lunged for them. The dog skidded to a halt bare inches from bowling them over, lips wrinkled in a snarl, and let out one loud, slavering bark. Robyn received a distinct whiff of fish and blinked through the spray of slobber across her face.

"This is Sister Mercy," the nun explained with a wicked grin. "Brother Patience is in the orchard, or else he'd be here to greet you too."

Robyn uttered a silent prayer for this small grace and stifled a scream as Mercy rose on her hind legs to place her paws on Robyn's shoulders and deposit a wet lick across her mouth. Thus satisfied, she dropped once more to haunches rippling with muscle, thrust her muzzle into John's hand for inspection, and circled back to sit at the nun's feet.

"We get all sorts here in Sherwood," she explained. "Mercy and Patience help deter the more unsavory ones. I am the Reverend Mother here."

"I'm Robyn, and this is Little John."

The prioress looked John up and down. "Is he now?"

John's cheeks reddened and he cleared his throat, clearly uncomfortable.

"He's not little where it counts," Robyn assured the nun, taking the opportunity to get back at John for his earlier comment about Marian. She ignored the murderous glare he sent her way.

"God does love his little jokes." The prioress extended the finger bowl, and first Robyn, then John, dipped their hands and washed the worst of the dust from their faces and fingers before Tuck distributed the dirtied water between the nearest flowers.

"Now." She produced three small mugs from the folds of her habit and poured a golden stream of mead into each. "Tell me why I should entrust Will into your keeping."

"Why . . .?" Robyn trailed off, too confused to continue.

"Will has requested sanctuary, and I am therefore bound to honor that request and prevent the long arm of the law," here she paused to pinch John's arm, "from knocking down the priory doors."

"We're not employed by the king," said John, apparently more offended by this suggestion than by any of Tuck's previous insinuations.

"Are you related to Will, then?"

"We've never even met him," said Robyn. "We're only here because Marian—"

"Yes, Marian. You made quite the impression on her, didn't you?"

Robyn didn't know what to make of the searching look the nun gave her.

157

"See?" said John under his breath.

"She asked me to help her friend."

"And why would you want to do that?"

"Because I keep my word." Her temper flared.

"Very well." The nun whistled over her shoulder. The door swung open again, this time admitting a slender youth with hair redder than a fox's coat and eyes as green as a cat's, followed by a young woman with a plain face and dark hair. Robyn recognized the hauteur of nobility in the youth immediately. It was in every line of his body and stitched into the very fabric of his clothes. You're a damn fool, Robyn, she told herself. There were only a few reasons Marian might have asked Robyn to look out for the spoiled progeny of the ruling class. The most likely, and the one that sent a dull ache throughout her chest, was that this boy was her lover, and she'd taken Robyn for the fool that she was in the hopes of sparing her beloved from whatever crime he'd committed. *What did you expect?*

"Hello," said Will.

Robyn listened to the sounds of the forest birds twittering in the distance and remembered what Tuck had said a few moments before. God does indeed love his little jokes, she thought, and this one was on her because if his voice was any gauge, the boy leaning against the door frame wasn't any more a boy than she was.

"God's blood," John swore.

"Please," said Tuck, pointing a finger at the sky. "Do not defame the Lord where he can hear you."

"I thought he could hear me everywhere," John said.

"Then don't do it where I can hear you."

Robyn drank some of the mead in her mug. The honey exploded on her tongue, but it didn't wash away the acrid taste of uncertainty.

"You must be Robyn," the noblewoman said.

"I am." Although, she reflected, it might have been better if she wasn't.

"What in bloody hell are we supposed to do with her?" John

158

asked Robyn. Sister Mercy growled low in her throat. "Beg your pardon. Our Lord in Heaven, please send me guidance, because I am in sore need of it."

"Was that really so hard?" said the Reverend Mother.

"I'm not sure I understand." Will had a cold, clear voice. Robyn guessed she used it frequently to order servants around.

"What are we supposed to do with her, Robyn?" John repeated.

Robyn wished she knew. More than that, she wished she knew why Marian had thought to send Will to her in the first place because the most logical explanation was that she had seen through Robyn's disguise just as easily as Robyn now saw through Will's. And if Marian had seen through her, then that meant others might have too.

"What, exactly, did Marian tell you about me?" Robyn asked Will.

"Well, I guessed that you'd be taller."

"What is that supposed to mean?"

"The way she talked about your shooting, you would have thought you were a god."

"Will the blasphemy never end?" said the nun in despair.

"I heard you calling on the blessed virgin's teats this morning, Tuck."

"A most holy relic indeed."

"And you told Sister Meredith to mind her tongue or you'd beat her with, I repeat, the goddamn holy cross."

"It left an impression, didn't it?" The nun chuckled at her own joke.

"Marian didn't tell me you were a woman," said Robyn.

"Surprise."

"Sherwood is no place for a noblewoman."

"Why not? I've been hunting these woods my whole life. Legally."

"With a soft bed and a full table waiting for you when you returned, and someone to lay your fire and fetch your water," said Robyn, bristling at the barb.

"I'm not weak, if that's what you're saying."

159

"You don't even know what weakness means." Words boiled out of Robyn's mouth. "You've never gone hungry. You've never had to watch a child starve to death because you couldn't feed it, or seen your brother hanged for the crime of trying to feed his family." John laid a heavy hand on her shoulder.

"Noblewomen die the same as any other. With me around, though, at least *you* won't hang."

"Is that a threat?"

"Peace, Robyn," said John. "She has a point."

"I don't see it."

"My father won't hang me, and he won't hang you as long as you're with me. I can give you the protection of my name, so long as you protect me from him for as long as you can."

Robyn wanted to hurl more accusations at Will, but John's hand now gripped her shoulder with a fierceness that promised to leave bruises if she didn't cooperate.

"We can't protect deadweight in Sherwood. You'll have to do your part."

"I can fight, and I have a hawk."

Robyn examined Will's belt and noted the rub on the leather where a scabbard normally hung. A sword might be useful as long as the girl could do more than wave it around. Or, it could get them all killed. "How long have you been at the priory?"

"Three days."

"Then you have four more weeks before you run out of sanctuary. If I were you, I would stay here. Forget whatever Marian told you. She had no right to make claims on my behalf."

Panic flashed across Will's face and supplanted her earlier arrogance. Her eyes darted from Robyn to John, then back to Robyn. "I have nowhere else to go."

"An argument could be made that you have everywhere else to go," said John, looking down at Will without a shred of pity. "I assume you realize that you can't go home again? Or do you fancy that this is a jaunt in the park, a game to amuse yourself until your father comes around? What did he do anyway, beat you?"

"He sold me to a man who's laid three wives in the ground already. I am dead either way."

Robyn pushed away any sympathy, refusing to think of Gwyneth and the sheriff. This girl was a liability. "So you've run away to the woods, is that it?" she asked.

"An argument could be made," said the nun, echoing John's words, "that both of you have done exactly the same thing." The Reverend Mother's voice retained its infectious good humor, but Robyn noted the way Sister Mercy's brown eyes studied Robyn and John, and thought that the dog revealed more about her mistress's mood than the woman herself.

"It's hardly the same, Reverend Mother," said John.

"Does it matter how the sentence is delivered if the end result is death?" said the woman who had followed Will, speaking for the first time. Robyn looked at her more closely. Her face might be plain, but her voice held a richness that promised something deeper than any surface beauty, and Robyn had to shake the spell of her voice off before she could fully comprehend her words.

"And who are you?"

"My name is Alanna of Dale."

"Well, Alanna, it does matter." Robyn shrugged off John's hand and stepped closer to Will and Alanna to look the other women in the eyes. Her temper drained out of her as she noted the dread and exhaustion in their faces. Gwyneth had looked that way when Robyn last saw her. *Seven hells.* "It does matter," she repeated more gently. "Especially if one death is swift and clean and the other slow and torturous. I can offer you the first, if it comes to that, and I will do what I can to spare you the second." She stuck out her hand and waited for Will to accept the gesture, half convinced that this was madness, and entirely certain that she couldn't walk away from these women now any more than she could have walked away from Gwyneth, or Marian, or anyone else with the same hunted look in their eye that Will tried and failed to conceal. "Collect your things and meet us where the forest joins the road at nightfall. The fewer people who see you leave here, the better. I assume you're coming too?"

"Yes, if you will have me," said Alanna.

"Before you go," said Tuck, stroking the mastiff's head, "one of our mules went lame this morning. We could use a blacksmith. You know the trade by the looks of you."

John let out a long sigh and rubbed the shaved side of his head, muttering something under his breath that sounded like "women" and "eternal damnation."

A knock on the door made the fugitives jump.

"Come in," said the nun.

A young nun burst through the door and stumbled to a halt before her. "Reverend Mother, he's here."

"Who?"

"The sheriff."

John's hand was back on Robyn's shoulder so quickly it might never have left, and it was the only thing that stopped her from shoving the nuns aside and running toward the man herself, for all that she was armed only with a staff.

"No," John said, tugging Robyn back. "Not like this."

"Christ on a biscuit," the prioress blasphemed. "Will, Alanna, get them to the cellar, then find Sister Gwyneth and the child and bring them with you. Now."

John dragged Robyn with her as Will turned on her heel, and the four of them bolted into the dark halls of the convent. Will stopped at the top of a low flight of stairs and pointed toward the door at its base. "Through there. Past the casks is a second door. Alanna knows how to open it."

Alanna motioned them down while Will took off again. When she shut the door, they were plunged instantly into darkness.

"Seven hells," said John.

"Try not to trip over anything. Keep your feet under you." Alanna's voice came from farther back in the cellar, and Robyn and John did their best to follow it, keeping their hands outstretched before them until Robyn ran into something soft, warm, and human.

"Sorry," she said.

"It's fine. Watch your head. It's tight back here."

162

Robyn ducked beneath a low lintel and into a room that smelled oddly of cedar and damp straw.

"We'll be hidden here," said Alanna. "At least until the sheriff leaves. This door is almost impossible to see unless you know it's there."

"Why is the sheriff here, anyway?" asked John. "What did you do?"

"We haven't done anything."

"We wouldn't judge you if you had," John said.

Footsteps sounded beyond the door, which opened with a scrape. Robyn couldn't see who entered, but she heard the sound of several people breathing and moved back to make more room.

"You're safe," Will said, but Robyn got the impression she wasn't speaking to them.

A child whimpered, and a woman hushed it. The voice made the hair on her arms rise, and she remembered what the prioress had said: *find Sister Gwyneth.*

"Gwyn?" she said hesitantly. The darkness thickened as she waited for a reply.

"Robyn?"

"What are you doing here?" She was already groping her way across the space as she spoke, searching for Gwyneth and Symon with her hands. Gwyneth met her with a small sob. "Hey there," Robyn said, finding Symon's tiny cheek with her thumb. "Gwyn, what happened?"

"After the fair I took the purse home. I sat up all night with it thinking, because I knew why you'd given it to us, and even though I don't think I can ever forgive you for lying to me, I understand why you did it. I also knew I didn't have much time. Pierrot would have found a way to take the money from us if I didn't marry him."

Robyn shuddered at the sound of the sheriff's given name leaving Gwyneth's lips.

"All I want is to be left alone to raise my son, and since I can't come with you, finally I realized there was only one place that would take me. I took my vows two days ago."

163

"You're a nun?"

"A novice, for now. Yes. There are worse things to be."

"That's not what I meant. I just . . . I didn't realize it was that much money." Most convents took only noblewomen because the large dowries they provided kept the convents running.

"It wasn't. Not quite. But Tuck is a good woman, and Symon will be pledged to a monastery when he comes of age."

Robyn wished the nun were here now so that she could thank her a thousandfold. "Gwyn," she began, her throat tight with unshed tears, "I'm so sorry I got you into this."

"I'm not." Some of the anger slipped back into her voice. "Pierrot would have found a way to force my hand eventually, and there was nothing you could have done to stop him while you were within the law. That still doesn't make what you did to me right, but you've saved our lives, Robyn. I know that." Her hand cupped Robyn's chin, and Robyn leaned into the touch, overwhelmed.

"That's why he's here then, isn't it?" said John. "He's figured out where you've gone."

"I believe so. Either that or he's looking for her ladyship," Gwyneth said. "Or should I say, m'lord?"

"You can just call me Will." Will's tone suggested this was an argument they'd had before. "Alanna, can you sing for the baby?"

"Shouldn't we be quiet?" asked Robyn.

"They shouldn't hear us unless they come into the cellar, but they might hear a screaming child." Alanna began a slow, low lullaby, and the notes hovered in the close air, breathing a little tranquility into the tense atmosphere. Alanna had a phenomenal voice, but Robyn wished she could listen to the conversation taking place between the prioress and the sheriff. More than that, she didn't like being penned down here like a rat in a hole. If the nun decided—or was forced—to turn them in, there was nowhere to run.

"Shouldn't one of us be trying to listen to what they are saying?" Robyn said, interrupting Alanna.

"Tuck will tell us," said Will.

"And if she doesn't tell us everything? I'm not saying that I don't trust a woman I just met, but there are things she might overlook that are important. Things we need to know."

"Things worth risking your life for?" asked Gwyneth.

"If it will help you, yes."

"Robyn—"

"I need to know what's happening."

The others shifted uncomfortably around them, until Alanna cleared her throat. "All of us are too easily recognized."

"She's right. It's not worth the risk," said John.

"But," Alanna continued, "would the sheriff recognize you in a habit, Robyn?"

"Absolutely not," said Gwyneth, making the connection before Robyn did.

"That could work," said John.

"No," said Gwyneth. "You'll have to rip it off me."

"Please," Robyn began, but Will hushed them all with an urgency that rendered silence immediately. Footsteps echoed in the chamber beyond.

"Search the place."

"Yes, by all means, turn my priory into a tavern if it suits your needs."

"You can't hide her forever, Mother," rumbled the bass voice of the sheriff.

"Well if I do, I assure you it won't be behind a cask of mead. Sister Angela, raise the torch a little higher so our good friend can complete his search. The sooner he leaves us, the sooner I can write to the bishop to demand an explanation for why my priory has been overrun."

"Gwyneth," he bellowed, ignoring Tuck.

Symon gave an uncomfortable whimper, which Gwyneth stifled with a rustling of cloth and her breast.

"Are you quite done, my lord?"

"Mark my words, Mother, I will make you pay for this."

"Me? Whatever for? She came to me scared and able to pay, and now she has taken holy vows. Had you but come a few days

165

earlier, we might have spoken reasonably, but now my hands are tied. She belongs to God. Not you."

"She never belonged to you," Robyn said under her breath. "You will let me see her."

"I will not, sir. You have already violated the sanctity of these walls. If our lord Jesus were on Earth, he'd send you to the pearly gates himself. As it is, I feel quite confident that I could give you a kick in the right direction."

"I will remember this when I come to collect the ransom tithe, woman. If you truly wish to protect the women in your charge, you'd do well to treat me with more respect."

"Small men make big threats. You will leave this place now, before I have a mind to release my dogs on your men. Unless there is another cobweb you would like to look beneath?"

"My lord, perhaps we should look beneath her skirts. She's large enough to hide three women, don't you think?"

"Shut up, Alfred," said the sheriff with a viciousness that surprised even Robyn. Heavy footsteps retreated, plunging them again into stillness, which was shortly punctuated by Symon's muffled sobs.

"Hush, little dove," Gwyneth cooed to her son, but her voice was unsteady.

None of them spoke until Tuck opened the door some time later, the torch in her hand momentarily blinding them.

"He's gone," she said. "And I've opened a new cask of mead."

Gwyneth let Robyn put her arm around her shoulders as they exited the hidden room. Symon quit his fussing as he looked up at Robyn, and his face broke into a smile as he recognized her.

"I wish you could stay," Gwyneth said softly enough that none of the others should have been able to hear.

Robyn kissed the top of her sister-in-law's head, her heart twisting. "Me too, Gwyn."

Tuck lit several more of the sconces, lighting up the cellar. Stone arches supported the ceiling, and lining the walls were casks and barrels filled with mead, cider, and ale. Several more doors to what Robyn assumed were other storerooms remained shut, and when she turned to look behind her, she saw the nearly seamless wall of stone where the door to their hiding place had been.

A long trestle table occupied the center of the room. Tuck pulled several mugs down from a shelf and filled them one by one, passing them around as she went. They drank without speaking for a few minutes before Robyn broke the silence.

"Thank you."

"Think nothing of it. Badgering that man gives me more joy than it should, Lord knows."

"He doesn't make idle threats," said Gwyneth. "He'll tax you higher than he should for this, and it is my fault."

"He'll tax us either way, my dear, and what is it that they say? 'You can't get blood from a stone.'"

"He could," said Robyn. "The son of a whore."

"No matter, he's gone for now, though it might be best if you stayed down here for today, in case he left someone standing guard. I can get you on your way before first light. Assuming you are still leaving?"

Robyn glanced at John, trying to read his expression. John merely folded his arms and waited for Robyn to deal with the mess she'd gotten them into.

"So," Robyn said, turning to Will and Alanna. "You can still change your minds. In fact, you should change your minds. We'll probably all be dead before harvest time, and while I can't promise to keep you safe, I can promise you cold, discomfort, hunger, and sore muscles."

"I've been on the road before," said Alanna.

"Exactly. You've been on a road," said John. "We tend to avoid those, seeing as they have people."

"We can manage," Will said.

"Any chance you can use that sword?" Robyn asked her.

"I'm a fair blade."

"You'll need to be more than fair. What about you?"

Alanna whipped a knife out of her belt and sent it thudding into the cellar door. Robyn blinked.

"I won't slow you down," said Alanna with a hint of a self-satisfied smile. "I bring my lyre too, which I've found is even better at discouraging violence. I can also pass as a boy. I used to when we traveled, and I'm more convincing than Willa. Or you, for that matter."

Robyn considered responding, then decided Alanna had meant it honestly.

"One more thing," said John, lowering his brows forbiddingly. "We need to know who might come looking for you."

"No one," said Will, squaring her shoulders. "I made sure of that."

"How sure?"

"Sure enough that I could invite you to my funeral, if you had a mind to go."

Robyn saw Gwyneth stiffen out of the corner of her eye and cursed Willa for her poor timing.

"And you, Alanna?"

"I'm just a minstrel. You don't need to fear the hounds on my account."

No, thought Robyn. Perhaps not. But the hounds may find us anyway.

Chapter Twenty

Heavy afternoon light filtered through the manor window and illuminated the lady Emmeline as she paced across her chamber, heedless of her limp. "I don't believe it," she said to Marian. "No matter what they found, I don't believe it."

Marian set aside her needlework and smoothed her face as best she could. The missive Emmeline had discarded lay between them on the floor, but Marian was shaky with her letters, and Emmeline had not calmed down enough to tell her what the lines contained. Marian had a feeling, however, that she knew. No news had come from Maunnesfeld yet, and while Alanna's absence could be excused a little longer, Emmeline's credibility had limits. A sick relative either lived or died, and either way Alanna would have sent word.

"My lady?" Marian ventured.

"They found her horse," she said, her hands white and clenched at her sides.

"Whose horse?"

"And a forester came across a soiled gown in a ditch, along with a handful of red hair."

"Willa?" Marian didn't have to muster feigned horror. She hadn't asked Willa what, if anything, she'd done to cover her tracks. If she had, she would have broken the news to Emmeline herself before she let her believe Willa dead.

"Her father has written to me to ask me to aid him in bringing his daughter's killers to justice, as my lands border the forest, and as he so kindly points out, it was most likely to me she was running."

"My lady . . ."

"I don't believe it." Emmeline muttered the words to herself as she continued her pacing.

"How do they know she's dead? Did they find a body?"

"Not yet, but her father seems to think it's a foregone conclusion. Had he sent for my help days ago when she first went missing, perhaps we might have found her alive."

"You know Willa, Emmeline. Is it possible that this is just some sort of, I don't know, pretense? Alanna's been gone for some time, too. Perhaps they ran away."

Emmeline shot her a piercing look. "Do you really think so?"

"I don't know what to think." *Except that I refuse to let you believe she's dead.* "It just seems like something Willa would do."

"She would have told me."

"Not if she thought it would put you at risk."

"Did she say anything to you?"

"I don't think so," said Marian, hating the lie, but if Willa's father was already casting stones, she needed to maintain it for a little longer. "Neither did Alanna."

"I just can't believe it." Emmeline sank into her chair and buried her head in her hands.

"Can I bring you anything?"

"I think I need to be alone, Marian. If you would."

Normally, this kind of dismissal would have stung, but Marian backed out of Emmeline's chambers buoyed by a wave of relief. She needed time of her own to think, and so she made a beeline for the small herb garden past the manor kitchens. Bees droned in the lavender, but no one tended the tidy beds. Marian sank to the base of the smoothly fragrant bay laurels on the northwest wall and wrapped her arms around her knees.

She hoped Robyn had kept her word and met Will and Alanna at the priory. If not, Emmeline would find out soon enough the next time she visited her sister, and then Marian would have to answer for her own lies too.

This was my idea, she reminded herself, but that didn't make it any easier to swallow. Emmeline's pain was her doing just as surely as it was Willa's. Besides—of the two of them, Marian was beginning to think Willa had gotten the better end of the deal. She was out there with her lover, while Marian was here, forced to pretend to grieve. What was it Gwyneth had said? Emmeline would not thank them for lying, or something like that?

Gwyneth. Her jaw clenched as she recalled how unnecessarily attractive the other woman was, with her blue eyes and thick blond hair. Robyn clearly thought so too, for why else would she have given her enough money to buy her way into a convent? And why did that bother her so much?

You know why it bothers you, her heart informed her. But lie to yourself if it makes you feel better.

"I am not in love with an outlaw," she said to the empty garden. "I hardly know her."

Her mind provided her with a list of things she did know: hazel eyes lined with dark lashes and a mouth that was quick to smile; strong, callused hands; shoulders broadened from pulling a bowstring; and a voice free from the affected French accents of court. Marian closed her eyes and tried not to think about what Robyn might have noticed about her, or how she compared to Gwyneth.

She didn't compare to Gwyneth. Not well, at least. Maybe that was why the widow had joined the priory. There, she'd be closer to the woods, where it was easier for Robyn to see her. Stop, she told herself. It didn't help. Her mind raced on without her, and Emmeline's grief and her own jealousy vied for her attention with each new sordid image that paraded before her, until she shoved the palms of her hands against her eyes and wept.

Sleep evaded her for a long time that night. When it came at last, long past midnight, she dreamt of Robyn.

Marian walked in a clearing in the woods. Bluebells carpeted the forest floor, and she thought, in the half logic of dreams, *the bluebells will be gone soon for it is nearly June.* She did not hear the footsteps approach; she knew them anyway. Robyn's arms encircled her waist, and she felt her breath on her cheek, warm and fragrant with blackberry wine. It was so easy to turn in those arms, as if she'd done it a hundred thousand times before, and so easy to touch that face.

Robyn tasted of blackberry. The tart sweetness sent heat spilling down her throat as Robyn pulled her closer and then down to the sea of blue blooming above the small meadow. She smelled crushed stems and bruised grass, so real her sleeping self ran fingers over her sheets to feel the brush of petals against her palm. Robyn's lips moved over hers, slowly at first, and then with a hunger that answered the burning need in Marian's bloodstream. It coursed through her in a fever that rose to spiraling heights until a release so sweet she cried out broke it, leaving her spent and sated and surrounded by flowers.

She woke up smiling in the gray light of dawn. Her body felt heavy and languid where it lay tangled in the linen sheets. Emmeline snored gently beside her with her son in her arms, and her exhales stirred his ringlets.

Memory fell upon her from the shadows above the bed. Her own breath died in her throat as alternating waves of desire and shame boiled her in her shift. Damp hair stuck to the back of her neck in the same places she'd dreamed of Robyn's mouth, and she extricated herself from the bed with barely suppressed panic. Her dressing gown hung beside Emmeline's on the wall. She snatched it and pulled it on as she eased the door open, careful not to strain the hinges lest Emmeline wake and ask her what was wrong. She climbed down a stairway to an empty storage room that had once housed bolts of cloth and salted skins. A few empty crates remained. She sank onto one and let out the shaking breath she'd been containing.

It was a sin to crave the touch of a woman as one should crave a man's. The church rarely spoke of such things, but Marian knew them all the same. Sex was for marriage. Marriage took place between a man and a woman. Without a husband, a woman depended on the charity of her family, unless she was a widow.

Widows, at least, might inherit businesses and estates and rule in their own right, but few other options besides the church presented themselves.

I could marry Linley and then poison him. First, however, she'd have to consummate the marriage, and that carried the risk of pregnancy and death.

Who am I becoming?

This was why such things were sins. She'd jumped from lust to murder, all in the space of a night, and before that she'd committed treason by helping Willa escape her father's will. If only she had never come across them at the priory.

If only she had never fallen from her horse and looked up into a pair of eyes that held the forest at their heart.

If only her very blood had not been contaminated by this devastating *want*.

She felt in the pocket of her dressing gown for her knife. The delicate lady's blade, used for slicing fruits and trimming threads, slid through the tender skin of her thigh as she tried to bleed out the devils inside her as the doctors recommended. The pain scored a brilliant line across her sight. The opening between her legs was still slick with the memory of dreams, and she drew the tip of the blade upward toward it. Beads of blood blossomed and dripped. Her hand shook as she reached the innermost part of her thigh. With her shift hiked up, she could see the curls that sheltered her, and she let one finger touch herself. The shock of pleasure sent a flash of blue across her vision. Her blade fell to the ground. She stared at the blood she'd let and willed it to cleanse her, even as her body trembled beneath her hand as she sought a different kind of purity.

When she surfaced, she noticed that the shutters over the window in this room had come unlatched at some point during the spring. Rainwater pooled beneath it, flanked by a bank of moss. Pale gray light reflected off its surface and danced on the opposite wall. Marian watched dawn shiver over the stones. I should be on my knees praying, she thought, but the panic had receded. In its wake was stillness.

What had Alanna said? Only Marian knew her truth?

She stared at the blood staining her shift. This, then, was true: she wanted a woman she had met only twice, wanted her with a fierceness that made her wish to shed her skin and run through the forest like a wolf, ripping with her teeth and laughing a wolf's laugh at the hunters who pursued her, all the while howling.

I could sing you a thousand songs about love, Marian, but until you've been in love you won't believe me.

A bird landed on the sill and trilled a greeting to the rising sun. Marian looked at its red chest and blue wings and laughed. The sound startled the bird, and she named it to herself as it flew away on wings of inevitability.

"Robyn."

Chapter Twenty-One

Robyn woke before dawn with a start to find a large shape towering over her, only barely discernible from the darkness around her.

"Rise and shine," said the prioress.

Right, Robyn reminded herself. After the sheriff's departure and a healthy serving of bread and cheese smeared with honey and preserves, along with too much mead, Tuck had asked John to see to a mule, then some poorly repaired plows, and finally a difficult piece of forging that John had done his best to patch with the limited priory foundry and tools. By the time evening fell, it had been easy enough to convince them to spend the night, and Robyn had been loath to leave Gwyneth and Symon even with the added danger her presence posed to them.

John groaned and sat up beside her.

"I've packed some bread and sausage and strawberries for you, along with some cheese and a flagon of mead to break your fast," Tuck continued.

"Thank you," said Robyn. The fare the night before had been simple but plentiful, and her stomach still felt pleasantly full. She let herself remember a soft goat cheese mixed with blackberry preserves with a shudder of pleasure.

"I've got to be on my way as well this morning, so I'll walk you to the forest with Sister Mercy and Brother Patience." The dogs, never far from Tuck's heels, panted their approval.

"Hello, Patience," John said as the male mastiff presented its rear for him to scratch.

"Where are you headed?" Robyn couldn't help the suspicion that filled her voice. The nun had hid them yesterday, but she'd had the night to change her mind.

"Not to Nottingham, if that's your worry. I keep a few hives in the woods, and early morning is the best time to pay them a visit."

Robyn glanced around the room. Alanna stirred, but she saw no sign of her sister-in-law or, for that matter, Will. "Where's Gwyneth?" she asked, panic filling her chest.

"She helped me pack the food, and right now she's waiting in the courtyard should you decide to get out of bed before sunrise."

Robyn bolted past Tuck and down the hall, brushing past startled nuns clutching beaded rosaries on their way to morning prayer, and into the faint light of early morning. Stars still studded the sky, and mist lay upon the ground of the courtyard in a thin blanket. Each step she took kicked up tendrils of fog.

"Gwyn?" she called out.

"Here."

Robyn's gaze darted around the cloisters until she saw Gwyneth leaning against an arch, several satchels at her feet and Symon bundled in her arms. The nun's brown woolen habit and starched white wimple looked strange on her, covering her hair and neck so that only her face glowed in the predawn light. Panting slightly from her run, Robyn approached, waiting for a hint of Gwyneth's mood. Gwyneth, however, kept her face composed and closed, a sure sign that all was not yet forgiven.

"Will you be happy here?" Robyn asked her.

"Does anyone really know how to be happy?" Gwyneth looked away. "I can raise my son in peace, and he'll be safe from Pierrot and the king's wars in a monastery when he's grown. That is enough."

"Michael would have wanted more for you than that."

"Michael is dead, Robyn, and you're gone. At least here I will have time to grieve."

"I . . ." she trailed off. Not even in the days following Michael's death had Robyn seen Gwyneth so bitter. "I never meant for it to happen."

"You and Michael, always trying to protect me, never realizing the only things I ever needed from you were love and trust. You're my sister, Robyn, not my caretaker. You should have trusted me with the risks you took. Both of you. Or did you think I wasn't strong enough to bear it?" Her chin rose defiantly, daring Robyn to confuse her frailty of body for frailty of spirit.

"I don't think you're weak."

"Don't you? Because your actions tell me differently."

"Gwyn, please listen to me. I was scared. I didn't want to hang, and I didn't want you to see me hang. I almost lost you too, you know, when Symon was born. How could I bring that kind of trouble down on you?"

"Because we're family."

Robyn felt the words like the slap they were intended to be. "Okay," she said, her voice rough. "Okay. You're right."

"I need you to promise me something: never lie to me again. I can't bear it. Not after this. I need someone to trust, Robyn."

"I promise."

"And Symon needs an aunt."

"I'll be there for him."

"You better." Gwyneth wiped her eyes with the hand not holding her child. "And you better visit us."

"Nothing could keep me away."

"Fine. Come here then."

Will's arrival ended their embrace as her shadow separated itself from the priory wall with a rustle of feathers. The large goshawk riding on her shoulder shuffled her feet, turning a hooded head toward Robyn, Gwyneth, and Symon. Alanna, John, and Tuck followed behind, along with the dogs.

"Shall we?" Tuck opened the small gate and looked at the rest of them expectantly.

"We shall," said John, watching Robyn.

"Right. Um. Let's go, then," Robyn said, conscious of John's gaze as she tore her eyes from Gwyneth.

177

Tuck closed the gate carefully behind them again with a practiced flick of her walking stick. "Sister Gwyneth will lock up behind us. We don't want any rogues getting the wrong idea, now do we?" She led the way down the road at a startling clip, her legs eating up the ground and her dogs trotting at her side, tails wagging back and forth. Robyn and John followed, with Will and Alanna trailing behind. Robyn glanced back over her shoulder at the priory. Gwyneth would be safe there, which was more than she had dared hope for. Her spirits rose as she remembered the fury in the sheriff's voice.

"What are you smiling about?" John asked her.

"I was thinking about our good friend," said Robyn. "Do you think he slept as well as we did last night?"

John snorted. "Not if he dreamt about Tuck. I wish I could have seen his face when she told him she could kick him halfway to heaven."

"Hardly an empty boast," said Robyn, pointing at the nun's calves, visible above sturdy boots through the cloth of her habit as it swirled around her on the path ahead of them. "Think you could beat her in an arm wrestling contest?"

"Not without losing an arm." John kept his voice low. "I'll wager quite a few men were relieved to see her married off to Christ. Those thighs could snap a man in half."

"Still, I bet he'd die happy."

Tuck came to a halt a half a mile down the forest trail. "This is where I leave you," she said, her face somber in the gray light. "But if you ever need anything, don't hesitate to find me. We could always use a blacksmith. And Willa, remember what I told you. I will not lie to my sister on your behalf."

"I remember," said Will. "Thank you for everything." Robyn detected a trace of hesitation in the girl's voice and wondered what she thought about the future looming like the branches above her.

"No need to thank me. Just keep yourself safe."

They watched her leave in silence. Will shifted her feet and rubbed the hilt of her sword, her eyes boring into the side of

Robyn's skull. Robyn felt Will's anxiety mounting but didn't assuage it.

"Where do we go now?" Will asked when neither Robyn nor John spoke. Alanna seemed content to let Will ask the questions, for now at least, and looked around her with interest.

"Before we go anywhere, we need to get a few things straight," said Robyn. "You make one wrong move and we'll bring you back to the priory before you can say 'Nun Tuck.'"

"I'm not—"

"You're a liability. You don't know what you'll do out there," said John. "None of us do until we're living it. But before we go one step further, I want to make sure you know how to use that blade. Give your bird over to Robyn. Minstrel, step back and don't interfere with any of those flashy knives of yours."

Robyn accepted the hawk with caution and held the slender chain tightly in her fist. Birds had loyalties, just like people, and even fewer qualms about ripping into human flesh.

John hefted his staff and circled around Will. Robyn watched as Will's feet shifted lightly over the ground, feeling for even footing in the early morning light, and tried not to think about the sharp point of the blade reaching John. The bird shifted on her wrist, then settled.

Will lunged. John parried, bringing the staff down to swipe at Will's feet, but Will leapt over the sweeping end and brought her sword up to block John's next blow. Oak and steel met with a dull thunk, then separated. John feinted for Will's head, but Will merely crouched, sword at the ready, as John's real blow struck at her stomach.

The flash of steel and the blur of oak danced around the small clearing. John tried to force Will into a copse of trees where her sword would be of little use, but Will ducked out of the way, quicker than John on her feet, which surprised Robyn. Will, however, did not have John's stamina. John bore down on her, relentless, until at last the sword fell from her hands as John backed her into a snaking tree root, intentionally tangling her feet.

"Well done," he said, tapping the sword with the butt of his staff. "But you've never faced a real opponent."

Will's face flushed a brilliant scarlet as she scrambled to her feet, panting. "I've had training," she said, her tone adamant.

"Short bouts here and there. But you're not strong enough, and you tire easily."

"I—"

"I'm not done yet." John poked her in the middle, making the girl gasp. "Still, you're not half bad." The staff tapped the girl's shoulder, and this time she let out a low growl.

"How dare you."

"I'm not going to hurt you. The same can't be said for anyone else you'll meet out here, present company excluded. Just remember that you'll always have an advantage with a blade if you can get a decent opening, so long as you are not afraid to strike the throat or belly."

"It might be useful to have a swordsman," Robyn said. "If only as a visual deterrent."

Will's lips thinned with further outrage.

"If you stay, then you drill every day, and you do what we tell you to do. Think you can do that?" said John.

Will nodded, though the effort of keeping her mouth shut seemed to cost her.

"You're noble born, so I'll ask you again. Can you take orders from two commoners without question?"

"I said I could."

"On your knees."

"But—" Will protested, and then she dropped, realizing her mistake.

"What if that was all the warning he'd given you about an arrow?" Robyn moved to tower over Will. "You'd be dead."

"Robyn—" Alanna began, but Will spoke over her.

"Please," said Will, her cheeks still scarlet. "Please don't turn us away."

Robyn considered her scarlet face. The minstrel didn't concern her the way Will did. Alanna seemed steady, whereas Will carried herself with an incendiary attitude that Robyn recognized only too well. It was how she felt much of the time: like tinder, ready to burn. Robyn looked at Alanna again, and hoped she knew how to control her friend for all their sakes. "Stand up and take back your bird before she slits my wrist. We've got ground to cover before sunrise."

Will stood and held out her hand for the bird. Robyn handed it over gratefully, then clasped Will on her birdless shoulder. "Welcome to Sherwood," she said.

"And one more thing," said John, a wicked grin splitting his face. "You blush a pretty shade of pink. From now on I'll be calling you Will Scarlet."

"So, this is where you live?"

Robyn looked around the clearing that served as their camp and wished she'd had the foresight to avoid the Nottingham fair, Gwyneth, Marian, Will, and Alanna altogether. Will stood by the base of the oak that dominated the stand of nearby trees with her fist clenched tightly around the jesses of her hawk and her other hand wrapped around the hilt of her sword. Alanna unslung her lyre from her back and examined the instrument, running practiced fingers over the strings.

"Yes," said Robyn, dropping her satchel next to a chestnut tree several years past its prime. She tried to see the clearing as Will and Alanna must: a shallow fire pit dug into the center, shielded from wind and view by low wickets masked with ferns. A small lean-to, covered with moss and barely waterproof, huddled against another oak. They'd have to extend it, now that Will and Alanna also needed a place to sleep, and as her eyes grazed the crumpled undergrowth, she realized the other complication. Additional bodies would add more foot traffic, and foot traffic meant pathways, and in a matter of weeks they'd have to move. The clearing already looked too lived-in for Robyn's liking.

"When you have to shit, make sure you do it as far from camp

181

as you can, and bury it," said John. "You'd be surprised how quickly smells build up. And smells attract foresters."

Will wrinkled her nose. "We've been to Nottingham. We know all about smells."

"We've got food for today, but we should hunt anyway. It's always better to hunt on a full stomach than an empty one. Do you know how to set up a snare?" Robyn asked.

Will shook her head. Alanna nodded.

"Good," she said to Alanna. "Will, I'll teach you. We'll gather wood while we're out, along with anything else we find, like mushrooms, eggs, or greens. We'll have berries soon, but we need to start thinking about winter. That means baskets for storing nuts, which also means harvesting reeds and willow branches, and we'll all need furs to wear and sleep in. Once winter sets in, we'll be safer in a camp, and we can settle in. The foresters don't like to break trail through the snow."

"We can start setting watches, now that there are four of us," John added. "It will make raiding easier, too."

"Raiding?" Will's eyes widened.

"We're going to need coin, and that doesn't grow on trees."

"But first we need food." Robyn waved a hand at Will. "Leave your hawk. I'll show you a few things while John ..."

"... John will be busy cutting new quarterstaffs," John finished for her. Robyn nodded and set off into the woods, intentionally forcing Will and Alanna to keep up. She paused after a few seconds.

"You're making too much noise, Will."

"I'm trying to keep up."

"Move quietly. Watch me and Alanna. If that means walking more slowly, walk more slowly." She set off again, listening. Will improved slightly, but Robyn still heard the sound of snapping twigs and grinding dirt. "Okay," she said, taking a deep breath to temper her impatience. "Every time you break a stick, all the animals in earshot know we're here. That means we can't kill them, and if we can't kill them, we don't get to eat." Will's cheeks colored in what Robyn assumed was either embarrassment or anger, but the other woman held her tongue. "You need to watch where your feet are as well as what's around you. Step on moss or rocks or roots when you can, and try to avoid soft ground. We don't want to leave too many prints if we can help it."

Will improved marginally as the morning passed, although Alanna's whispered pointers and encouragement probably had more to do with it than Robyn's snapped commands. Robyn stopped them now and then to point out a landmark or to adjust Will's footing until they came to a brushy open area inhabited by an unusually large rabbit warren. "We'll set some snares up here. See this trail?" She knelt by a low tunnel of brambles. The sun broke through the trees in this part of the forest, and it warmed her shoulders as she plucked a tuft of rabbit hair from a thorn and held it up for Will to inspect. "Watch."

"How often do you check your snares?" Will asked as she studied the way Robyn tied the thin cord around two sticks, setting up a trip wire over the trail.

"Once a day, twice if I can help it. And we never set snares near camp in case a forester finds them."

"May I try?"

"Yes, but not here. We'll practice away from the hotter trails so that you don't have to worry about leaving too much of a scent. There. This line here triggers the snare, which will send this branch," she tested the spring of the sapling she'd commandeered, "into the air, hopefully either breaking the rabbit's neck or keeping it out of reach of a fox."

She backed away from her handiwork and pulled another length of string from her pocket. They'd need to make more cord soon, too. "I'll show you how to set one up here, but first show me how you set yours, Alanna."

Alanna's hands were not quite as deft as Robyn's, but she worked with confidence, and the end result made Robyn nod with satisfaction.

"I was in charge of finding dinner when we traveled," Alanna explained. "Before I joined Emmeline's court. You try, Will."

Robyn studied Will as she worked. The woman had quick

fingers, but she couldn't quite master keeping the tension on the little sapling she'd chosen. She also chewed on her lower lip in a way that reminded Robyn of Midge. Her cousin would visit soon. *And what will she think of these two?*

"So, what, your father wanted to marry you off?"

"To Lord Barrick."

"I haven't heard of him."

"Lucky you. His estate is to the south, and he's rich enough that my father overlooked the three dead wives before me."

"How rich?" Robyn asked, wondering if Will knew enough about Barrick to relieve him of some of those riches.

"Richer than my father."

"Couldn't you have joined a convent or something? You and Tuck seemed to get along just fine."

"I wish. Convents still want your dowry, and they don't boost the family name. Barrick was willing to take me for half of what a convent would expect, and with the ransom tax . . ." Will trailed off.

"At least you'd have enough to eat with Lord Barrick," she said, unable to stop the judgment from creeping into her voice.

"I'd rather starve."

"Spoken like someone who's never had to starve before."

Will's fist closed around the string, and she glared at Robyn. "I can't help my station any more than you can help yours. Hate me for my name if you like, but I'm here the same as you."

"Not quite. Your brother is still alive."

"My brother is a sad fop who'd rather be diddling his squire than his wife, but no one cares so long as there is a baby in her belly and he has the good sense to bribe his servants. Yes, he's alive, and I'm sorry your brother isn't, but whatever happened to him isn't my fault."

"Will," Alanna said in warning. Robyn didn't miss the way Alanna watched the two of them. She didn't like how much those dark eyes picked up on.

"He was hanged for poaching by the sheriff."

184

Will had the good sense to glance uncomfortably at the snare in her hand. "I'm sorry to hear that," she said. "I wish your brother was alive, and I wish my father loved me more than he loves his coffers. But since we can't have either, perhaps you should teach me how to catch these goddamn rabbits. I'm no forester, but I'm guessing we've scared off everything for a mile around by now."

"That's the beauty of a snare. It'll be here when everything comes back," said Robyn, biting back the urge to goad Will further. "So, how do you know Marian?"

"Marian?" Will made another clumsy attempt to set the snare as she spoke. "She's a baron's daughter and Emmeline's handmaid and companion, now that her husband's on Crusade. Emmeline is a good friend of mine. Our estates border."

"And I served as Emmeline's minstrel," said Alanna. "Marian is a friend."

When neither of them spoke further, Robyn contemplated strangling Will with the snare. She searched her mind for something else to ask that wouldn't reveal the depth of her interest or discomfort.

"It's just—" She snatched the snare from Will, set it, and stood. "It's just that you're a woman."

"So are you."

"Does Marian know that?"

Will remained crouched on the ground, looking up at Robyn through disconcertingly green eyes. "Yes," she said at length. "Which is what gave her the idea that you might help us."

Robyn recalled the way she'd flirted with Marian: shamelessly, as if it were the most natural thing in the world. Marian had responded in kind. Had she known the whole time? And if not, when had she guessed? Why had she said nothing? Had anyone else seen through Robyn's disguise?

"She won't give you away if that's what you're worried about," Alanna said. "She's kept our secrets."

"I'm not worried." Robyn did not bother asking about the

secrets Marian had kept for Alanna and Will. "Come on. We'll set more snares on the other side of the thicket. Can either of you use a bow?"

"I'm passable," said Will.

"I can't, but I can use a slingshot," said Alanna.

"Then we'll need to find two bow staves, too. You can't hunt with a sword. Slingshots are good for rabbits, though, and I can teach you how to shoot, Alanna. Or Will can."

They circled the thicket, Will moving more quietly than she had thus far. Robyn's thoughts were still on Marian as she watched Will set up the next snare without assistance. It was clumsy, but passable, and Robyn gave a nod of approval.

"What is John's story?" Alanna asked when she finished.

With a start, Robyn remembered that John had not trusted them with his past. Without that knowledge, however, the reality of living near a powerfully built, unknown man would understandably unnerve the newcomers. She brushed off the momentary burst of pity. They'd get used to it. John's past was not her story to tell.

"He was a blacksmith. Now he's not."

"She means, why is he here," said Will.

"I know what she meant."

"But you trust him?" Will fidgeted with a hawthorn leaf she'd plucked from a low branch and avoided Robyn's eyes.

"I wouldn't be here with him otherwise."

"All right." Will held up her hands defensively, the leaf crushed against her palm.

"Look, Will," she said. "When I first met John, he disarmed me and knocked me into a stream. He could have brought me back to the outlaw gang he was running with, or he could have killed me, or worse. But he didn't. He's the reason I'm still alive out here. There are plenty of bad men in the world. John isn't one of them."

Will still didn't look convinced. Robyn didn't blame her; trusting too easily got a person killed anywhere, not just Sherwood. Will and Alanna would have to make their own decisions about John, just as Robyn would have to live with her decision to trust Marian. Even if that meant helping Will. "What's your real name, anyway?" she asked.

"Willa. Willa of Maunnesfeld."

Robyn swallowed hard. "Maunnesfeld? But you said your father wasn't rich."

"He owes a lot of money to the crown," she said, dismissing Robyn's incredulity. "And my brother will inherit the estate, along with the debt, and my younger brothers after him. I have three older sisters who married well, and I am not . . . I am not 'biddable.'" She spat out the last word.

"Good," said Robyn, feeling more sympathetic toward Will than she had thus far. "I don't like biddable women."

"Really?" Will shot Robyn a grin. "I thought you said I had to follow your orders."

"That's just to keep you alive. You can be as difficult as you want with anyone else you meet."

Alanna gave Will a light smack on the arm. "Don't let that go to your head," she said, smiling at Will in a way that made Robyn suddenly uncomfortable, though she couldn't quite put her finger on why.

Chapter Twenty-Two

Marian knelt by the bank of the river. The water felt delightfully cold on her hands as she beat the stains out of her clothes with a smooth stone. Early morning sunlight stained the fields gold behind her, and she could hear the farmers calling to one another across the rippling wheat. She did not need to wash her own clothes. The washerwomen had made that plain with their horrified expressions, but she felt the need to cleanse something even if she could not cleanse herself. Watching the current carry the soiled particles away soothed her.

"That's the last of it," Marian said as she pulled the shift out and wrung it dry. She had not quite been able to remove the bloodstain.

"I should hope so," said a servant named Maude. "And you don't need to be helping with this again, m'lady. Get back to her ladyship or she'll have my hide for turning your pretty hands to lumps like these." She held up her chapped hands for Marian to see.

"I'm quite all right."

The basket of damp clothes weighed as much as Henri when she hefted it onto her hip. She settled into the weight and began climbing the slope back toward the manor house. She hadn't gotten more than a horse length before a stone whistled past her ear. Frowning, she turned back to the river. Another stone landed at her feet.

Marian searched the reeds on the far bank. Motion caught her eye. A person stood in the shadow of a willow, and as she squinted to make them out, a flash of white teeth from beneath a hood sent her heart racing. *Robyn.*

"I'll be on my way shortly," she called over her shoulder to the serving women. "Don't wait." Used to the arbitrary commands of the nobility, they obeyed. She made a show of examining the rushes by the water's edge as if she were merely contemplating a future harvest. When she was sure the women had passed out of earshot, she set her basket down and stared at Robyn.

The outlaw didn't speak. Marian became extremely conscious of the way her hair escaped its braid and the muddied hem of her dress. *She's an outlaw. She doesn't care about mud on my clothes.* "I didn't think you'd come," she said.

"I thought you might like to know that your friends were safe."

"You might have left word with Tuck."

"You told me I could find you here. I keep my word." Robyn remained concealed in the shadow of the tree, but Marian thought she heard the grin in the other woman's voice. You should go back to the manor, the sensible part of her mind cautioned. The cut on her thigh itched. Sensibility hadn't gotten her anywhere so far. She pulled off her boots and her stockings, hiked her skirt over her knees, and waded through the shallowest part of the river.

Robyn grasped her hand and pulled her up the bank when she emerged.

"You're going to think I spend all my time in rivers," Marian said as she entered the sanctuary of the willow boughs.

"There are worse ways to spend your time."

"Like what?"

"I don't know, outlawry?"

The hood shadowed Robyn's eyes. All Marian could see of her face was the mocking twist of her lips—lips that she vividly recalled kissing in her dream. Her body warmed despite the lingering chill of the river.

"Lower your hood."

"Is that a command, m'lady?"

Marian thrilled at the low timbre of Robyn's voice. "Yes."

Robyn lifted the thin supple leather from her head and let it drop. Dappled sunlight fell across her eyes. Marian's breath caught as she beheld the outlaw's face for the third time in her waking life, though she saw it often enough when she closed her eyes.

"Tell me something," said Robyn. "When did you know?"

"Know?" Marian thought of her dream and licked her suddenly dry lips. "Know what?"

"That I was a woman."

Relief coursed through her, and she laughed. Robyn could not know what was in her head. "You're prettier than any boy I've ever seen."

Robyn's eyes widened, and Marian was gratified to see that she, too, was capable of blushing. It made her feel slightly more in control.

"I knew I should have let John break my nose," said Robyn.

"Please don't." Marian laid a finger alongside the perfect line of it, feeling the warmth of Robyn's skin beneath her fingertip. She couldn't bear the thought of anything happening to this face. "It's lovely."

Robyn didn't pull away from her touch. Marian let her finger trace its way down Robyn's cheek and jaw.

"Lovely things get remembered."

"Would you rather I forgot you?" Marian asked.

"I—" Robyn rubbed the back of her neck as the corners of her mouth curved upward. "No."

"I don't think most people would notice. People see what they expect to see."

"And you expected to be rescued by one such as me?"

"Hardly. But, if you recall, I had just received a blow to the head. My expectations were . . . distorted."

"That does explain a great deal. Normally, baron's daughters don't stoop to speak to my sort."

"Have you met many baron's daughters then?" she asked.

"Just your friend Will."

"Willa is the daughter of a duke."

"Which is obviously very different. Dukes and their daughters are notoriously gracious to outlaws." Robyn shifted her weight to lean against the tree, and Marian fought an impulse to push her up against the trunk and press her lips to hers. The strength of the desire left her out of breath. She hid it behind a feigned interest in a passing butterfly.

"That reminds me. I still haven't repaid you for your help."

"And as I told you, I do not require payment," said Robyn.

"Is there nothing I can give you?" Marian raised her eyes to meet Robyn's as she spoke. The intensity she found there stole the ground from under her, and she floated, tethered to the earth only by the amber green of Robyn's irises.

"Perhaps there's something."

She could not tell if Robyn's voice was getting softer, or if the sound of her heart hammering was simply drowning it out. "Name it, and it's yours."

Robyn's lips parted as if she were about to speak, and then she gave her head a slight shake and looked down. The broken eye contact left Marian reeling.

"Name it," she repeated.

Robyn stared into the forest. Marian caught her hand in frustration, desperate to know what Robyn had decided not to say, and the outlaw's eyes once more met hers. This time, the green had turned the dark of pines in shadow.

"I would like to know you better, Marian."

Her fingers tightened around Robyn's. Those words could mean so much, and also so little.

"Marian?" A voice called her name from across the river.

"God's teeth," she swore, and Robyn laughed. Marian hadn't heard her laugh before, and a molten glow spread out from her chest to fill her body.

"You should get back," said Robyn.

"I know. But I—" She broke off. She wanted to say too many

191

things, and there was too little time. Instead, she leaned in and pressed her lips to Robyn's cheek. Her kiss brushed the corner of Robyn's mouth, and Marian pulled away before her body betrayed her.

"I'd like to know you, too, Robyn Hood," she said as she slid through the willow curtain and darted back into the river.

Her father's summons came as a relief from Emmeline's moods. The guardsman Gregor escorted her on her ride back to Notting-ham, and while Marian suspected that he, too, was glad to be out of the shadow that had fallen over Harcourt in Willa and Alanna's absence, neither of them mentioned it. Neither did they mention the looming prospect of war or the tax that Harcourt could not afford to pay. They spoke instead of the heights of wheat and rye and the first of the ripening plums, speculating about the harvest to come and the prospect of midsummer.

"Did you ever go to the bonfires?" she asked him, observing his white mustache out of the corner of her eye. It twitched in a smile.

"I did a great many things in my youth," he answered. "I'll answer for some of them in heaven, but not to you."

Marian laughed, delighted at the image of a younger Gregor courting anyone, let alone someone who was now as old as he was, perhaps stooped and hook nosed and still dreaming of summers past. It was a far more pleasing prospect than what lay before them or behind.

"You should stay away from the fires," he said, fixing her with a serious look.

"I doubt I'll be given a choice." Dancing around the mid-summer bonfires wasn't something the sheriff's daughter or Emmeline's handmaid would be allowed, even if she'd wanted to go. Still, the idea of total heathen abandonment had its appeals, especially when she thought about Robyn. She replayed the conversation they'd had the day before as she rode, remembering the feeling of Robyn's cheek beneath her lips.

Her smile faded as the forest road brought them out into the fields and pastures surrounding Nottingham. She didn't know why her father had summoned her back to the city, but she had a feeling it was not for the pleasure of her company.

"Ease up on those reins," Gregor said.

She looked down at her hands. They gripped the reins with white knuckles, and her horse tossed her head uncomfortably at the pressure on her mouth. She relaxed her hands and patted the horse's neck. "I'm sorry, girl."

A few people hailed them as they approached the city gates. Marian didn't recognize any of them. She hadn't spent much time in Nottingham since her childhood, and most people didn't equate her with the seven-year-old child clutching her father's hand at her mother's funeral.

Her father lived just beneath the castle. Here, the winding refuse-clogged streets gave way to wider avenues lined with the houses of the wealthy. Even the chickens looked plump and content as they scratched through piles of manure for seeds.

"I'll be at the Stag's Head," Gregor said as she dismounted and handed her mare to the freckle-faced boy who had appeared the moment they halted. The last time she'd been here the stable hand was Tomas, a sullen youth with a stutter who had a way with animals that made up for his recalcitrance. Freed from her mare, she stared at the oak door of her father's house, gathering her courage. At last, she raised the bronze knocker and let it fall.

"Marian," said Eliza, the straight-backed housekeeper with an iron jaw. "We've missed you."

She allowed herself to be led inside the hall and into the sitting room, where the housekeeper offered her a glass of wine and fussed over her hair. "You've been out in the sun too much," she scolded her, patting her cheek. "And your gown. Surely Emmeline can afford to dress you in something a little more elegant?"

Marian had worn her simplest dress, a pale blue riding skirt without embroidery that did little to draw the eye. There were only a few reasons her father would have called her back to the city, and she had no intention of making herself any easier to marry off. She sipped her wine and looked around the room. He'd added a new tapestry since she'd left: a hunting scene, purchased to flatter the prince. Real beeswax candles adorned the sconces instead of rush lights, and she had just stood to examine the illuminated manuscript on the shelf when the housekeeper returned to tell her that her father was ready to receive her.

The climb to his study no longer carried the joy it had when she was a child, at last allowed by her nursemaid to visit her father at his work. She felt herself growing smaller with each step.

"Marian," he said when the door opened to admit her. He looked her up and down, his gaze critical, and motioned for her to stand before him.

The sheriff of Nottingham embodied his office almost as much as the office embodied him. Social class dictated he could not wear the finery of the upper nobility, but the quality of his clothes and the silver ornaments adorning his desk spoke of his wealth and the privileges his position afforded him. His dark gold tunic was embroidered with leaves, and his belt, or at least what was visible beneath his stomach, bore intricate details of boar and stag. Marian looked into her father's eyes and tried not to shudder.

She loved her father. That was part of what made it hard to look at him. His eyes no longer saw faces, only coins stacked where loved ones used to be. He could measure a person's worth by the way they tested the wind, and he had an unusual knack for bringing criminals to justice—or at least offering large enough rewards for those who turned them in and harsh enough punishments for those who didn't that the criminals appeared outside his doorstep one way or another.

"You look as though you've been out in the fields," he said, his eyes lingering on her hands. "I sent you to Emmeline to learn how to be a lady, not to work like a mule."

"Yes, father."

"Do you please her?"

"Yes, I think so."

"Good. Do what you can to coax her back into society. I want

194

as many eyes on you as possible before the winter, and with Willa of Harcourt out of the way, you'll shine next to her. Do you need a new wardrobe?"

She adjusted the fold of her riding skirts to hide the spasm of anger that twisted her face, along with the budding hope. Had he changed his mind about her betrothal? "No, father, but I did not wish to ruin a nice gown on the road."

"Any trouble with bandits?" When she shook her head, he gave a satisfied nod. "Then they've not gotten that bold yet."

"Are there many outlaws in the forest?" Marian pitched her voice as sweetly as possible.

"There are always outlaws in Sherwood. Vermin. Every now and then they need exterminating, but a few rats here and there are to be expected."

Robyn is no rat, she thought, keeping her face smooth. "Of course."

"I have a question I need to ask you, daughter," he said, folding his hands and leaning toward her. She swallowed. "You spoke with the victor of the archery contest, did you not?"

"I did."

"The widow he gave the purse to wished to give him a gift. When she could not find him, she left it with the fletcher's guild."

Marian's heart pounded in her throat.

"Did the archer tell you where he hailed from?"

She shook her head.

"A pity. I have a nice quiver of arrows for him." He reached into his desk and pulled out an arrow, placing it between them. "Does this look like one of the arrows he used?"

She stared at the shaft. Something had discolored the wood near the arrowhead, but the fletching remained intact. "I don't know," she answered, thinking of the broken arrow she kept at the bottom of her chest of clothes. "The feathers are different colors, I think."

Her father sighed. "Well, thank you for looking. I shouldn't expect you to know a fletcher's business."

"Does the widow not know him?" She couldn't help asking the question. She had not been able to bring herself to ask Gwyneth how she knew Robyn whilst she was at the priory, and the jealousy that had been eating at her ever since craved answers.

"If she does, she did not see fit to tell me."

Something in her father's voice made her blood slow in her veins. She looked more closely at his face, trying to guess the reason for the wrath beneath the surface, but he merely smiled back at her.

"No matter," he continued. "I'll be hosting a dinner party tomorrow night. Look your best. If you haven't anything else to wear, I'll have something brought for you."

Marian allowed her eyes to close just a second longer than a blink allowed. "Who will be there?"

"The viscount, of course, and a few friends."

She offered him her best curtsy and kept her eyes downcast. He gave her what she thought he'd intended as a reassuring smile, but all she saw was avarice as her flinching gaze fell on the chest sitting on a lower shelf of a cabinet. Inside, she knew, lay part of her dowry. He'd shown it to her once: silver and silks and jewels that had belonged to her mother, as well as a healthy sum of coin. The documents that would pass her father's estate on to her in the event of his death would be drawn up later. *If only I could inherit without marriage*, she thought, *but the sheriff would never allow it*.

She made her way to her room after he'd dismissed her. Not much had changed in her absence. Someone had put down fresh rushes mixed with lavender, and the curtains around the bed were tied back for the summer, a breeze from the open window stirring them. She leaned against the sill. Nottingham. Their house looked out over the wealthy quarter, home to the townhouses of the nobility, a few of the lesser gentry, and the merchant class, and the air from the top of the hill was free from the stench of the lower part of the town. She could even see the curve of Nottingham castle from here, a single turret rising into her view.

The crier announced the hour in the street below. Three hours until her father would expect her to dine with him. Three hours of sitting in the townhouse with idle hands, her mind full of arrows and archers and beautiful widows who had everything Marian currently wanted.

I should have gone with Willa and Alanna, she thought as she glared at the cold hearth. Let the viscount try to marry me then.

All the reasons this was impossible came back to her. It wasn't that simple. One missing noblewoman was a tragedy. Two could be a coincidence, but she knew her father. He would leave no stone unturned as long as his scent hounds lived, and they hadn't missed their quarry yet.

Richard may still return in time, she thought, but that wouldn't save her from dinner tonight.

And if he doesn't? Will you run then?

Chapter Twenty-Three

The merchant caravan creaked down the forest road, the wheels straining at their bearings as they jolted over roots and ruts. Two riders in light armor flanked it, and the driver carried a loaded crossbow.

"What do you think?" Robyn asked John.

John considered the caravan. "I think we just got lucky."

Will and Alanna clustered behind them. Robyn could feel the anticipation in the way they breathed. Her own lungs didn't seem capable of taking in enough air, but her blood hummed at the prospect of the coming action.

"Ready?"

"Always," said John, gripping her arm.

Robyn pulled an arrow from her quiver and nocked it, glancing over her shoulder. This was their first robbery with the new members of the band. The added numbers brought simultaneous comfort and uncertainty, as well as responsibility. John nodded in her direction, signaling for her to take the lead, and she glared at him. He'd been doing that more often of late.

"On my mark," Robyn said, meeting each of their gazes. "Remember. No one dies."

"No one dies," they repeated back to her.

She turned back to the road with her eyes on the guards. "Now."

As rehearsed, Robyn and John stepped out in front of the

caravan, Robyn with her bow, John with his staff, while Willa and Alanna took the rear. Willa put her hand on the hilt of her sword and Alanna kept her throwing knives balanced in her hands.

"Good afternoon," Robyn said to the startled driver. The horses stopped, uninterested in the humans surrounding them, and promptly attempted to browse on the nearby foliage. The driver hefted the crossbow and aimed at first Robyn, then John, clearly unsure which was the bigger threat. The guards reined up sharply.

"There's more in the rear," the one with the black beard said. He pulled a short sword from his scabbard and brandished it as he wheeled his horse around.

"Full wagon you've got there," said John, patting the nearest draft horse on the nose.

"I don't suppose you'll be getting out of our way?" the driver asked. He propped the crossbow on his knee and glared at Robyn. If he was afraid, he didn't show it.

"We will," said Robyn. "Just as soon as we help you lighten your load."

"Look," said the driver. "You steal from me, I have to answer to my boss."

"Who said anything about stealing?" Robyn asked. "Although these woods are dangerous. We just want to make sure you pass through safely."

"And that's why you've an arrow pointing at my chest?"

"You've got one pointing at mine," she said.

"Tell you what. You stand down, and my friends won't cut you down."

"Fair enough. Except that you'll still be dead before they reach us."

He scowled and flicked his eyes around him. The motion revealed his uncertainty. "Then what do you want?"

"A gesture of good faith."

"And why should I have faith in you?" he asked.

"A fair question. Have you heard about King Richard?"

"Who hasn't?"

"Then you know they're raising money to free him."

"Aye."

"We're raising money to help the good folks who have to pay that tax." The driver seemed confused, and so Robyn continued. "You serve a guildsman or a merchant, right? Or perhaps you owe fealty to a lord. He pays the tax, but where do you think he gets that money from? His coffers? No. Your pockets, your work, your blood and sweat."

"And how is that any different from what you're about to do?" said a guard.

"We'll pay you for your trouble."

The men stared at her.

"What we mean," said John, "is that we'll be taking your horses and your wagon, but we'll pay you for the time and trouble it will take you to walk back to your master and explain how you were overrun by bandits. If you choose to give that coin back to your employer, that's your decision."

"I wouldn't, if I were you," said Robyn.

"Or," said John when the men still stared at them blankly, "we could kill you all and take it anyway. Your pick."

"God's blood," said the driver as he lowered his crossbow and dropped it to the ground at the exact same time as the mounted guards sprang into action. John blocked a swinging short sword with his staff. Robyn's arrow took the other rider in his sword hand. They'd agreed to try to spare the lives of their quarry if they could; she'd had her fill of murder. Still, she flinched. Even a shallow wound could kill if it went bad.

John's attacker circled again and raised his sword. Robyn nocked another arrow. John could hold his own against a swordsman, but a mounted opponent offered significantly more risks. The horse bore down on John. He squared his stance, keeping his knees loose and at the ready, but the thought of watching him get cut down was too much.

"Mother Mary have mercy," she said under her breath as she shot the rider in the shoulder. He tumbled from the saddle in a cloud of dust. Alanna was there to grab the horse's reins, and Robyn's first mark was still shrieking in agony as he clung to his damaged hand.

"Let's get him off his horse," she said to John, pointing at the remaining rider.

The man, however, was faster. He attempted to kick his horse into a gallop, only to find John's staff unseating him with a brutal blow to his stomach. To his credit, he managed to roll into the fall, and he lunged for his sword the moment he regained his balance. His horse shied between him and Robyn, but she heard the clash of steel on steel as Will met his left-handed attack.

"John, keep an eye on the driver," Robyn shouted as she darted around the horse.

Will wore a smile as she circled the bleeding guard. Her sword snaked past his blade and slid harmlessly off his armor, but the ease with which she pierced his defenses left Robyn in no doubt of who would win.

"Disarm him," she told her. "Don't kill him."

Will engaged him in a few more parries and then shot Robyn a look that implied Robyn had ruined her fun before meeting him hilt to hilt and twisting the sword out of his hand. Disarmed, and with an arrow in his good hand, the man at last surrendered.

The second guard still lay in the dirt. Robyn noted the blood pooling beneath him with concern. "You," she said to the white-faced driver. "Can you stop the bleeding?"

He nodded, but John shook his head. "I'll be quicker."

John knelt beside the wounded man and rolled him on his side. The guard didn't protest and breathed shallowly as John probed the wound. "This will hurt," he told him, and then he sliced the fletched end off the shaft and pulled the arrow through the wound. The man bellowed.

"Cloth," John ordered. "You. Take off your shirt." The driver obeyed with alacrity. John ripped the tunic into strips and padded the wound. "You'll want to get this cleaned. Boiled wine if you can get to a tavern. Keep it clean and you might live."

"What about this one?" Robyn nodded at the other man. He backed away, only to be halted by Will's sword.

"Don't be an idiot. Let us take the arrow out and bind your wound."

Shocked, perhaps by the idea of his attackers helping him more than anything, he allowed them to remove the arrow and wrap his hand in more strips of tunic.

"Speaking of wine, see here," said Alanna as she peered into the wagon. "Wine and good leather, and I think there's some decent cloth, too."

"Leave them some wine. They'll need it for their wounds," said Robyn. "We'll take the rest."

"I thought you said you were going to pay us?" said the driver.

"That was before your friends came at us," said John.

"Anything in there we can't sell?" Robyn asked Alanna.

"Not really."

"Pity. Well, here you go." She tossed a small purse at their feet. They stared up at her in astonishment. "As I said. For your trouble."

"I still don't understand why we paid them," Will said a few minutes later. John drove the wagon, Robyn at his side, and Will and Alanna rode beside them on their stolen horses.

"Because if word gets around that it's more profitable to surrender than to fight, we're more likely to survive. A mounted man takes a foot soldier nine times out of ten," said John. "And we'll be earning it back soon enough."

He turned the willing team of horses down the road that led to the nearest market town. Nottingham would have offered them more opportunities, but they still ran the chance that someone had discovered the injured men they'd left behind, and John knew a man from his time with Siward who paid good coin for dubious wares. Besides, they had need of decent leather and cloth themselves, and a cask of wine would go down smoothly with the rabbits they'd left hanging at their camp.

The magnitude of what they'd just done did not hit Robyn until the cheerful innkeeper deposited a sack of silver into John's hands later that evening. As the four of them returned to the forest, loaded down with leather, cloth, and several skins of wine, a burst of laughter erupted from Robyn's lips.

"You all right?" John asked her as the shadows of the trees closed, familiar, around them.

"Yes," said Robyn. "Yes, I think I am." It took her another burst of laughter to realize what it was she felt: hope.

Chapter Twenty-Four

The housekeeper arranged Marian's hair in the current fashion, brushed smooth and bound with ribbons. Marian avoided her own eyes in the bronze mirror that the woman held up for her. She knew how she looked. Soft. Weak. Agreeable. The kind of daughter her father wanted her to be. She contained the rage that threatened to undo her and shoved it down into the place she shoved everything else that had to do with her betrothal. The dark moved, accommodating the new arrival.

"There. You look radiant." The housekeeper stepped back to examine her handiwork. Marian allowed her to gloat and kept her eyes downcast to hide her emotions, then raised her chin to allow Eliza to dab her neck with scented oil. The smell of roses momentarily wiped the cloistered feel of the city from her mind. Emmeline grew roses in her courtyard: leggy wild-looking things with heavy heads. Henri liked to shove his face into them and bring his mother handfuls of petals.

Harcourt isn't your home, she reminded herself. Thinking about it wouldn't get her through this dinner, either. She brushed off the housekeeper's attempt to rouge her lips and made her way downstairs to where her father waited.

"Turn," he ordered, looking her up and down.

She gave a half-hearted twirl.

"Good. Charm them." He didn't have time to issue further instructions, as the sound of horses in the stable yard signaled the arrival of his guests. She recognized a few: Lord François and his wife, Lady Adeline, baronets from Nottingham's outskirts. Baron Jacot and Baroness Cecire followed shortly behind, and her father bowed deeply to his last guest, an older man with stiff shoulders, thin lips, and gray hair. Lord Linley greeted her father and then turned to her.

No. She recoiled from the oily way his eyes stroked her body, but hid it in a curtsy.

"My lord," she said. "Be welcome."

"Anywhere you are, my dear, is a welcome place."

"You are too kind."

He took her hand and pressed his lips to it. It hardly felt like a kiss, and she withdrew her hand as soon as was polite and led the guests to the sitting room.

The conversation started off with the usual comments about the weather, the roads, and the price of grain. She listened with half her mind elsewhere, engaging when necessary, offering a witty comment when appropriate, and tried to pretend that she was riding beneath the cool branches of the forest.

". . . shipment coming soon. The caravans had some trouble with all the rain we've had, but now that the roads are dry, there isn't any reason for further delay."

"I certainly hope not," said Lord Jacot, giving his wife an affectionate pat. "I'm paying the guards enough to keep it safe as it is."

"The roads are getting worse," the viscount agreed. "I nearly lost a shipment this spring to a group of outlaws outside Kent. It seems, however, that Sherwood isn't giving you much trouble."

"Not yet, not yet. I expect we will get the usual desperadoes once the ransom is collected, but my boys are used to hunting." Marian's father smiled to himself, and Marian bit the inside of her lip.

"Ah, yes. Good King Richard," said Lord François. "One almost feels like he's avoiding spending time on English soil at all costs."

"All costs indeed. 150,000 marks. Have you ever heard of such a thing?" Lady Adeline shook her head.

"I suppose it's no less than he's worth," said the sheriff. "Or at least no less than his mother feels he's worth."

"Pity they didn't ask his lordship," said Lord Jacot.

"John might have paid them half that price again to hold on to Richard indefinitely."

Marian's thoughts drifted once more. This would be her life soon. Endless discussions about tariffs, the cost of goods, and the petty squabbles of the nobility. The room tilted at the corners of her vision, and she gripped the seat of her chair.

Get hold of yourself. The viscount watched her from across the table. Marian didn't want to show even a moment's weakness in front of him. His eyes were as hooded as Emmeline's hawks, and he watched her hungrily.

Why him? she wanted to ask her father. Why not some harmless older man who would be satisfied if she shared his bed once a week and bore him children, leaving her to her own devices the rest of the time instead of pawing at her like she'd seen the viscount do to his previous bride? She could grow to love a man like that, or at least the lifestyle it afforded her—like Emmeline, secure in her place, with a few hounds at her heels and a small estate for her children.

A pair of hazel eyes framed by dark hair flashed across her mind.

"Excuse me for a moment," she said, rising from the table. Her father waved her away with a hand, and after a curtsy she walked carefully out of the room, down the hall, and into the darkness of the larder. The cook took one look at her face and left her alone.

Settling down on a barrel of ale, Marian rested her head in her hands. Mother Mary, have mercy on me, she prayed to the darkness in her palms. Even if her father had selected a kindly old man, or a handsome, gentle youth her age, she knew she could never be content—not now, not in a world where Robyn had said, "I would like to know you better, Marian."

Anger flared in her breast and uncurled like smoke. This was her own fault. She'd helped Willa escape a fate too similar to her own, and that action, foolish in its own right, had spawned this discontent. She wanted to hit something. More than that, she wanted to run into the woods and beg Robyn to take her, regardless of the risk. None of those things could happen from within her father's pantry. She took a deep, shuddering breath and stood, composed her face, and returned to dinner.

She managed to get through the rest of the meal without thinking of Robyn. Adeline and Cecire cornered her in the salon over more glasses of wine, their affected French hurting Marian's ears.

"That is a pretty bit of embroidery. Is it yours?" Cecire asked, thumbing the sleeve of Marian's dress.

"It is," Marian admitted. She had liked the golden stags when she'd sewed them this past winter by Emmeline's fire. Now, she wished they'd frolic away down her hem and dash themselves on the floor. "Do you enjoy embroidery?"

"I've been working on a tablecloth."

"How lovely."

Marriage won't be a problem if I die of boredom, she thought as she smiled through bared teeth at the inane conversation. She forgot sometimes that most of the women at court were not like her friends. These ladies seemed to care only for their gowns and gossip.

"Have you heard anything about Richard?" she asked, desperate to discuss something of substance.

"I heard he's gone to Rome," said Cecire.

Adeline looked over her shoulder to make sure her husband could not hear her before she spoke. "My aunt is friends with Isabella. She said John and King Phillip have offered the emperor 80,000 marks to hold Richard until Michaelmas."

The French king *would* get involved, she thought. "80,000? Where do they plan on getting that?"

"Phillip perhaps? Who knows what John promised him."

"Normandy probably," said Marian.

"All I know is that we can't pay the both of them," said Adeline.

"What about Eleanor? Does she know about this?" Eleanor of Aquitaine favored Richard, Marian knew, but this went beyond sibling rivalry: it was treason.

"If she does, she hasn't moved against them. Do you think there will be fighting here?" Cecire paled at her own suggestion.

"If there is, you'll be safe," Marian told her. The impulse to comfort the other woman irritated her. Cecire *should* be frightened. War touched everybody, even ladies whose biggest concern was the embroidery on their tablecloths.

"Marian," said her father, interrupting their speculation. "Lord Linley wishes to speak with you."

She rose from her couch. Cecire and Adeline gave her sympathetic looks that only worsened her mood. Yes, pity me, she thought. Pity the poor sheriff's daughter and laugh behind her back. They dined at her father's table gladly, but loathed him when it came time to pay their taxes. She'd heard the whispers often enough to know.

"What does he want?"

"Whatever it is, give it to him." Her father patted her arm. "It's a good match, Marian."

For you, maybe.

The viscount poured her a glass of wine and joined her at the sideboard. She drank more of it than was wise for a first sip, but it helped her feign a smile.

"What can I do for you, my lord?"

"I just wished to look upon you."

"I'm afraid there's not much to see."

"The eyes of a woman will never understand what a man sees in her," said Linley. He raked his gaze up and down her body. It made her skin itch. She would have shed it if she could, writhing out of it like a snake and slithering away to a dark place where men like Linley couldn't find her.

"She looks like her mother." Her father joined them, apparently unconcerned by the viscount's visual assault on her body.

"I see it. She has her eyes. Broader hips, though."

"Yes. She should birth easily. Turn, Marian."

She stared at her father. Her cheeks burned with humiliation, and she begged him with her eyes to spare her further punishment.

"Marian, turn."

She turned slowly, a broodmare at the spring fair paraded before prospective buyers, and the light from the candles pricked tears from her eyes.

"I would like to move the wedding up," said Linley. "Before the harvest. That will give her time to see my estate before the cold sets in."

Marian's legs turned to granite. She beseeched her father with her gaze, but he considered Linley's words without glancing at her.

"You may go, Marian. The viscount and I have much to discuss."

Chapter Twenty-Five

"You're not like me," Gwyneth had told Robyn some time after Symon's birth. It was late, and neither of them could sleep with the baby fussing feverishly between them. Gwyneth still struggled to get out of bed, but some of the color had come back into her face with the poached game Robyn brought home.

"What do you mean?"

"I worry about you. I worry you'll be lonely."

"I've got you."

"For now, but I worry you're not going to like marriage when it finds you, little bird."

Robyn hadn't answered for several heartbeats, listening to the rise and fall of the baby's breaths as she tried to picture her future husband. The image kept blurring. "Perhaps I won't marry," she'd said.

"Perhaps you won't." Gwyneth had held them both, Robyn and the baby, and Robyn had renewed her silent vow to keep all of them safe. Regret gnawed at her now as the memory faded. She had not realized how much Gwyneth had protected her. Gwyneth had understood that Robyn would not marry, and she had even understood why, though they had never spoken of it outright. There were no words for such things.

She wished there had been. She wanted to tell Gwyneth about the way Marian had kissed her cheek and how the shadows beneath the trees were now limned with the blue of Marian's dress. Gwyneth would know what to do. More to the point, she would be happy for Robyn, and it would give Robyn an excuse to say Marian's name.

She shot a pheasant on her way back to their camp, plump and ready for plucking. Midge would be joining them tonight if all went according to schedule, and Robyn wanted something to send home with her besides coin. She ranged wider, eventually bringing down a duck by the river and a rabbit near the hollow tree where they stowed their dry goods.

"Good hunting?" John asked when she slipped into the little hollow by the river. She held up her prizes, and John nodded toward the string of fish smoking over the fire. "Will's good with a spear, and Alanna can catch fish with her bare hands."

"A net would be easier," Robyn pointed out.

"But less enjoyable to watch." John took a break from sharpening his knife to shoot her a grin.

"We could set a net while we're gone during the day."

"True. But then what else would we tell our scarlet friend to do with her time?"

"She could make the net."

"You're no fun tonight."

Robyn unstrung her bow and checked to make sure Will and Alanna, who were gathering wood nearby, couldn't hear her next words. "I stopped by the Harcourt Manor a few days ago."

"You *what?*" The playful tone left John's voice.

"On my hunt. I ran into Marian."

"You should have told me what you were doing. What if you'd been caught?"

"Then better you didn't try to rescue me."

"What makes you think I'd try in the first place?"

"Well, Midge would have. Any sign of her?"

"Don't change the subject. You took a risk, and I don't like it. You risk all of us when you risk yourself. And why wait to tell me until now?"

Robyn turned her back on John and took a deep breath, willing herself not to shout. John was right. That didn't mean she had to like it.

"Should I tell Will and Alanna that I saw Marian?" She ignored his last question.

"I don't see the harm." John took the rabbit and skinned it, pulling the soft brown fur off in a clean tug that left the rabbit bare and glistening in the afternoon light. "She's as good as one of the gentry."

"I know."

"What does she want with you?"

She wants me. Robyn set to plucking the pheasant with more violence than was necessary. The skin tore, and she forced herself to slow down. "We saved her. Maybe she's just grateful."

"Gratitude would have been a fat purse full of coin."

They fell silent, each lost in their own thoughts.

"Does she like you?" John asked bluntly.

Robyn focused on the feathers in her hand. "Yes," she said, running a finger along the brown and white-flecked plumage.

He reached out and placed a hand on Robyn's arm, forcing her to look up into his eyes. "Will was right about one thing. Outlaws without friends hang."

"I'm not going to use her," Robyn said.

"Why not?"

"Because . . ." Robyn trailed off. She didn't have an answer.

"You're not using her. You've caught her eye, for better or for worse, and we're harboring her friends. This could be a good thing."

"I thought you didn't like it."

"She's not the problem. It's the hold she has on you that concerns me."

"John—" She broke off.

He waited.

"I've seen the way you look at my cousin."

He withdrew his hand from her arm and rolled his shoulders.

212

The tightness around his jaw did not surprise her; the fact that he did not strike her, did. She searched for words that did not exist and tried again. "I'm not—"

"This isn't—" John looked over his shoulder toward Will and Alanna.

"That's how I look at Marian."

John stilled. Robyn felt as exposed as a rabbit in an open field, and his dark eyes searched hers. "I know," he said at last.

"Is that why you're John instead of Joan?"

John looked again at where Will and Alanna worked. She wanted to tell him that she would take his secret with her to the grave if that was what he wanted, but he spoke before she could form the words.

"I'm John because that's closer to who I am than Joan. I don't—there aren't—you know what the church would say. God never errs."

"I think he errs plenty." She thought of Michael's smile.

"I was never good at being Joan. I tried. I married. And when I killed my husband, I knew I couldn't do it anymore. It was the worst day of my life." He paused. "And it was the happiest."

Robyn tried to picture John as he must have looked then, standing over his husband's body. She couldn't. "Perhaps we're meant to be out here. You, me, and those two." She pointed her thumb over her shoulder.

"Part of God's plan?"

"If he has one."

"I would never hurt Midge. Or ruin her chances of a normal life. I swear it."

"You're the best man I know, John. She'd be lucky to have you." She clasped his forearm, as he had clasped hers moments before, and tried to tell him with her touch how much his friendship meant to her.

"Your noblewoman, though. You might be too good for her," he said.

"You think so?"

He grinned to show he was joking, and Robyn felt a part of her she hadn't known was clenched relax.

Midge arrived later than usual. Robyn saw her small form slipping through the trees, accompanied by two more shapes. She strung her bow and sent up their warning.

Her whistle alerted the others. They took up their positions behind the largest trees in the clearing and waited.

Midge's return whistle didn't soothe Robyn's anxieties. She whistled back once more, a question more than a confirmation, and Midge put her hands on her hips and glared.

"It's fine," she said. "They're with me."

"I can see that."

The two figures stumbled forward. Robyn couldn't quite make out their faces from her vantage point, but that could also have been from the bruises mottling their skin.

"Tom?" She squinted at the man, struggling to match her memory of her friend to the face in front of her. Someone had taken a fist to that face, breaking his nose badly and leaving a nasty cut across one brow. He gave a painful nod. The girl next to him looked to be no older than ten. She held Tom's hand tightly, but she met Robyn's eye without flinching. The imprint of a hand across her cheek stood out starkly.

"Lisbet," Robyn said, her voice breaking. She didn't ask what had happened. The fact that they were here told her enough. Lisbet's eyes traveled around the clearing, taking in their small fire with the fish smoking above it and the skins stretched beside it. Her child's tunic was made from good quality wool, as were her boots, but blood stained one of her knees and there were more splatters across her front.

"Two blacksmiths," Robyn said, looking over her shoulder at John.

"Tom," Tom said as he held out his hand to John.

"Little John." John winked at Midge.

"And this is Will Scarlet and . . . Alanna," said Robyn, introducing Will and Alanna. Tom shook her hand, and if he noticed that Will, like Robyn, lacked a few manly features, he didn't say anything.

"You're a minstrel," Lisbet said to Alanna in awe.

"I am. Can you sing?"

Lisbet nodded.

"Come." Alanna held out her hand. She led Lisbet to the far side of the clearing, removed her lyre from its leather wrapping, and began to play a familiar song. Lisbet joined her in the chorus and Midge gave Robyn a wide-eyed look that plainly said, *you owe me an explanation.*

Robyn turned back to Tom. He still wore his blacksmith's apron. A heavy hammer hung at his belt, and as far as Robyn could tell it was the only possession he'd brought with him. "Is anybody looking for you?" she asked.

"One of the sheriff's men went after my sister. She . . ." He looked at Lisbet. "He won't bother her again. Or anyone."

Robyn thought about the bloodstains on Lisbet's clothes and tried not to imagine what had caused them.

"I couldn't let them arrest her. I don't think they'll come after us, but we can't go back."

"She killed someone?" Will asked, her voice thick with incredulity.

"I don't know. Maybe. Probably. She got him in the stomach with a knife."

Robyn closed her eyes to dispel the anger that overwhelmed her at the thought of Lisbet, little Lisbet, needing to defend herself against a grown man. The world belonged to men, even those who preyed on little girls, and neither Tom nor Lisbet stood a chance at trial. Especially Lisbet. She prayed that the wound Lisbet had dealt her attacker festered.

"Can you hunt?" Robyn asked Tom, changing the subject before she set off at a run toward Nottingham to finish the man off herself.

215

"No. But you know I can fight."

Robyn remembered their childhood brawls. Tom had held his own, even against the older Michael.

"What about Lisbet?"

"She'll do what you need her to do," said Tom.

"I hid them in the mill when the hue and cry went up," Midge explained. "Is that pheasant?"

"Depends. You got ale in that sack of yours?" asked John.

"None for you." Midge batted at his arm and shouldered past him into the clearing, depositing her sack of ale and bread by the fire.

"How are things in Nottingham, Midge?" Robyn asked as she followed and motioned for Tom to sit. Lisbet peeled herself away from Alanna and leaned her head against her brother's shoulder. Her eyes glistened in the light of the flames, wide and dark and full of waking nightmares Robyn wished she could drive back into the shadows.

"Worse than usual. Prince John is gone again, but they say he'll be back, and either way we have to pay that damned tax. We'll be lucky to have anything left over for winter."

"This might help with that." Robyn tossed Midge a fat purse. Midge opened it and her stubborn lips parted in awe.

"Robyn—"

"Hide it somewhere safe. As for the rest, I trust you know where it's needed."

"The rest?"

John pulled three other purses out from the tree. "Small coin, all of it," he said. "Easier to explain than pounds."

Midge swallowed. It was more money than most of them had seen in their entire lives. She stroked the worn leather reverently. "I'll see to your family, too," she promised Tom.

He nodded, fatigue riding heavy on his shoulders, and gave her a weary smile. Alanna struck up a soothing melody that soon had Midge humming along with a mug of ale in her hand and a half smile on her lips. Robyn looked around the camp, taking in the tender way Will watched Alanna and how Tom's arm curved protectively around his sister. John met her eye and gave her an almost imperceptible nod, as if he knew exactly what Robyn was thinking.

Perhaps he did. Robyn felt an ache in her chest she hadn't experienced since the last time she'd seen Gwyneth. Home, she thought, as John's brown eyes promised the very thing she'd thought she'd lost forever: *family.*

All she had to do was keep them safe.

Robyn adjusted Lisbet's grip on the bow. The girl's muscles quivered as she pulled the string, but she set her jaw and kept it taut.

"Good," Robyn told her, impressed despite herself. "Did you help in the forge?"

Lisbet nodded. "I worked the bellows sometimes, and Tom showed me how to make things with a hammer."

"I'll make you a bow of your own. Smaller than this one, but you'll be able to hunt with it, and shoot anyone who comes after you before they get too close."

Lisbet pulled the bowstring again, testing the weight of the draw. "He didn't scream," she said as she sighted down an imaginary arrow. "I thought he would, but he didn't."

Robyn did her best to hide her surprise. "Sometimes they don't." Clovis hadn't screamed either.

"My brother says it's not my fault."

"What do you think?" Robyn asked, weighing her words.

"I don't know." Lisbet released the string. It snapped against her arm, but she didn't cry out, even as the welt grew visibly red.

"Lisbet, can you promise me something?"

Lisbet looked up at her and Robyn remembered with an acute stab of pain the way she'd smiled through a mouthful of bread on the day Michael died.

"Promise me that if someone ever makes you feel scared like that again, you'll do whatever you need to do."

Lisbet shrugged. It was something at least.

"Can you climb?" Robyn asked, hoping to get the girl's mind off murder.

"Yes. They sent me up for apples and chestnuts."

"Show me."

Lisbet set the bow down gingerly and eyed the nearest tree. The bark was smooth, and Robyn might have thought twice before scaling it herself. Lisbet shook out her shoulders and ran toward it, leaping onto the trunk like a squirrel and using her momentum to carry her up to the first branch.

Will clapped from somewhere behind Robyn. "She's better than a tumbler," she said, her eyes alight with curiosity. "Could you show me how to do that?"

Lisbet dropped back down, wiped her hands on her tunic, and shrugged. "I could try. Will you show me how to use that?" She pointed at Will's sword.

Will walked around Lisbet, sizing her up. "You'd do better with an axe, I think. Or a staff."

"Why?"

She grasped Lisbet's wiry shoulder. "You've got power here, like your brother. You could throw an axe quite a ways, I'd bet."

"Nobody would touch me if I had a sword."

"But nobody would question you if you carried an axe. Sometimes it's better not to look too dangerous. Now, how do I climb this tree?"

Lisbet gave Will a considering look. "Your power is in your legs," she said, deliberately mimicking Will's way of speaking. "And you're tall. When you run toward the tree, tuck your legs and grip with your hands, pushing yourself up. You won't get very many strides before your body wants to fall, so make sure you have your eye on a branch. Like this." She performed the trick again.

Robyn watched, too. Scaling a tree quickly could mean the difference between life and death, whether it was to stay out of sight of a forester or to escape an enraged boar. Will didn't manage to get more than halfway to the first branch before falling. She landed with a thump, dusted off her tunic, and tried again.

"You have to trust yourself," Lisbet said.

"I trust myself to fall." Will took a longer running jump and this time made it to the branch before dropping.

"There you go."

Robyn tried after Will, the tree bark rough and familiar beneath her hands. It didn't take her long to get the hang of it. Weeks of living rough had hardened her frame, and it wasn't difficult to imagine a wolf behind her to give her the extra push she needed. Lisbet's technique differed from her own, which involved considerably more scraping of knees and elbows, and it also boasted speed.

"Lisbet, I want you to teach everyone this. Can you do that?"

"I can try." Lisbet shot Robyn a dubious look. "Even Little John?"

"He might surprise you. He's light on his feet. I'd be more worried about your brother." Robyn had hoped to make the girl smile, but she just gave another solemn nod.

Now that there were six of them, with Midge occasionally adding to their number, Robyn's mind started turning over new possibilities. Lisbet wouldn't be much use in a fight, but she had keen eyes and a wariness about her that made her an excellent lookout. Tom, with his massive shoulders and broad frame, brought more muscle to their band. John was cutting him a stave to use as a weapon for now, although the hammer at his belt looked like it could crush a man's head just as easily, and Robyn wanted to get both blacksmiths behind a longbow once she had time to find some likely wood. Five armed outlaws and one fearsome lookout offered significantly better odds than two.

More members also meant more mouths. Game was plentiful for now, but meat alone wouldn't keep them going. She foraged for berries, greens, and mushrooms as she went, but as the days lengthened and midsummer approached, her mind strayed increasingly toward thoughts of winter. They needed a place to stay during the long, cold months, and a place to store dried meat, nuts, and fruit out of the reach of squirrels and damp.

On top of all her worries came the occasional distant baying of hounds. They scaled trees each time they heard them, stowing their few belongings in the hiding places they'd found around their camp, but the longer they spent there, the more the place looked lived in. It was only a matter of time before a huntsman stumbled upon their clearing.

A breeze ruffled her hair. She smelled deer and sap and water, and with those things the certainty of change.

Chapter Twenty-Six

Marian woke to the unfamiliar sounds of Nottingham's streets drifting in through her window, along with its smells: nightsoil, freshly baked bread, animal dung, and spices. It reminded her of her childhood, which brought still more memories. Her mother, laughing in her father's arms before a miscarriage bled her life away. Her brothers, wrestling in the street and shouting for Marian to watch to see who won, mud and dust streaking their clothes. They had died fighting in Jerusalem, along with her father's laughter and his loyalty to Richard.

She shoved off the blankets and slipped into her clothes, straightening her chemise and grimacing as she touched her hair. It would need to be brushed and braided, then rebound with ribbons, an arduous process that she didn't want to deal with. On the other hand, she thought as she pulled the rumpled ribbons from her hair, at least she could brush out the lingering scents of last night's dinner. Shame coiled within her. She wanted to bathe, anything to wipe away the lingering feel of Linley's eyes.

The comb in her room had belonged to her mother. The bone handle warmed to her touch, and she ran it through her hair in the long, even strokes she remembered, imagining the feel of her mother's hands on her scalp. So much might have been different, had she lived. So much about her father might have been different.

"Marian," said the housekeeper, announcing her presence with a soft knock. "Your father wishes to escort you back to Harcourt himself this morning."

"Really?" She couldn't help her surprise. He rarely rode with her, preferring to entrust her to Sir Gregor's company.

"I've prepared a light breakfast for you, and then you'll be on your way. Here. Let me help you with that." The woman snatched the comb from Marian's hand and proceeded to detangle her hair with cold efficiency before braiding it into the two thick ropes so popular at court. "Green or blue?" she asked, holding up fresh ribbons.

"Blue." Blue, too, reminded her of her mother.

"There." The housekeeper examined her handiwork, then adjusted the way the braids hung over Marian's chest.

I'll be riding, she wanted to say, but the woman had little enough cause to groom anyone but herself in the sheriff's house. If prettying her up made the housekeeper happy, Marian supposed it was the least she could do. Besides, arguing would just extend the process.

Her father was in the kitchen wolfing down cold sausage and bread. He greeted Marian with a greasy kiss on the cheek, which the housekeeper discreetly dabbed off when his back was turned.

"I've sent a man to let Gregor know he won't be needed. He will return ahead of us."

"He won't be riding with us?"

"There are things I'd like to discuss with you in private."

The bread turned to charcoal in her mouth. "Of course, Father," she said.

Her mare waited outside the house alongside her father's horse and a forester she didn't recognize. Marian stroked her mare's nose and gave the black stallion an affectionate scratch beneath his jaw, doing her best to ignore the man on the bay gelding. Her father had a fondness for brutes, and this one didn't look like an exception. She kept the horses between her and his line of sight until her father arrived and ordered her to mount.

"If the weather holds, we'll make good time," the sheriff said as he slapped his horse on the shoulder. The stallion nickered and reached his head around to nibble on his rider's boots, flattening his ears in a gesture Marian recognized as play anger. She amended her earlier thought. She liked one of the brutes that surrounded her father.

"Enough of that, you ruffian." He pushed the animal's muzzle gently away, and Marian's resentment wavered. She saw that side of him so rarely these days. Her own horse rolled her eyes at the presence of a stallion, and she prayed the mare didn't go into heat on their ride.

"Dinner went well," he said as they trotted down the street, forcing pedestrians to scamper out of their way. Marian winced as an old woman stumbled in her haste to avoid crossing the sheriff's path.

"Father," Marian said, hesitating before she continued. "I've been thinking."

"Oh?" His smile was tolerant.

"Would you consider sending me to the priory? The prioress is Emmeline's sister, as you know, and I think I would like it. I could learn to illuminate and read, which could be quite useful to you."

Her father didn't speak immediately, but his brows lowered as they passed the city gates. Only when they were out of range of the gate guards and a group of peasants did he turn on her.

"No daughter of mine will end up as a nun in that place, Christ as my witness. You will never speak of this to me again, and you will be grateful I do not see fit to beat you for your impudence." Spittle flew out of his mouth as he shouted the last words.

Marian froze in her saddle. Never in her life had he spoken to her with that tone, and the vitriol scalded her. Even the forester looked taken aback by the outburst.

"Now," the sheriff continued, rolling his shoulders, "let us discuss more practical matters. The viscount wants to move the date of the wedding closer to Midsummer. He's quite taken with you, and with Richard gone I think it would be best to get you settled before things get out of hand. I've had a few more offers, however. Lord Barrick has expressed interest, though I find him unsuitable, and Sir Mathurin—you remember him?—approached me just this week. He's younger than the others, better looking, too, but not in line for a direct inheritance. Still, his interest may quicken the viscount's, and who knows what he will offer?"

"Father . . ."

"It would do you good to appear more in court. You need to show off your assets instead of hiding behind Emmeline. There will be a feast on Midsummer, and you will attend. I will see to it that you have a new gown."

A gown for the viscount.

"I hate him."

Her father reached out and grabbed her horse's rein. "Say that again, daughter, and I will marry you to Lord Barrick. The viscount is a good man with good standing. Your sons will inherit his estates, and you will bite your tongue and bear it. Do you understand?"

She nodded. She did understand. She understood now just how little her happiness meant to him, and the knowledge left her cold and empty as they passed beneath the branches of the forest.

Chapter Twenty-Seven

Flies droned around their heads as the sun baked the tops of the trees, and uncharacteristic heat soaked Sherwood in thick golden rays. Robyn hoped the rest of her band felt more awake than she did. They couldn't afford to give in to somnolence, not with the road only a few feet away. She strained her ears for the sound of hoofbeats. Only the flies answered.

"Go back to hell," she muttered as she slapped one that had managed to weasel its way onto her neck for a bite. John raised an eyebrow at her from the neighboring tree. She thought about glaring, then decided that required too much energy, and returned to leaning against the trunk. Three days. Three days, and no one of means had passed by their stretch of road. A group of masons, several goatherds, and a handful of pilgrims had stirred the dust, but none were worth hanging over. They needed a fat merchant, or perhaps a member of the clergy. Their souls were already damned; picking the pockets of a priest wasn't going to make things any worse.

"Hey." John nodded toward the road. Robyn started from her stupor. The sound of hooves floated above the low hum of droning insects, and she saw Tom, Will, and Alanna stir from their positions across the road. The arrow came readily to her hand as she waited for their quarry to round the bend. Two horses, maybe three. Less than five, but a mounted man posed a significantly greater risk than men on foot, and even one

225

horse changed the balance of the odds. Too risky, she decided, and then the riders came into view.

Hatred burst from her heart like a spray of noxious vines, choking everything in its path. Three horses ambled down the lane, but Robyn only had eyes for the man on the black stallion. His belly protruded over his saddle, and sunlight reflected off the rings on his fingers and the silver thread in his collar. She stepped into the road, bowstring taut, the sound of John's muffled curses barely registering.

"Good day, Sheriff," Robyn said, leveling the arrow directly at his heart. Her pulse pounded in her ears, and the whole world contracted to the eyes bulging in outrage on the man astride the powerfully muscled horse. Michael's eyes had bulged, too, at the end, but not in rage.

"Don't be a fool," said the man to the sheriff's left. "Do you have any idea who this is?"

"He knows, Tam. That's why he called me 'Sheriff.'" The sheriff's knuckles released their bloodless grip on his reins, and he leaned forward in the saddle to scrutinize Robyn. "Remove your hood, my bold friend."

"I'd rather not, if it's all the same to you. The sun is rather bright today."

"So bright I might be tempted to overlook this grievous error, as it has clearly addled your brains. Stand down." His tone was contemptuous. Dismissive even, and Robyn seethed with murder.

"How can I stand down to someone as low as you?"

"Watch yourself, boy," said Tam.

"Wait." The sheriff held up a hand and narrowed his eyes. "You're the archer."

Robyn flexed her hand on the bowstring. It took every ounce of her strength not to release the shaft and send the sheriff straight to hell.

"The archer?" asked Tam.

"From the fair. You remember our particularly generous friend."

"The widow seemed grateful for the purse," Robyn said. "It would seem it helped her escape an unwanted proposal."

"Is that so."

"Some men just don't know when no means no."

"And some boys mistake bold words for manhood," said the sheriff, loosening his sword in its scabbard.

Will slipped out of the trees with her blade bared, and the horses shifted as John and Tom closed in their ranks from behind. Alanna remained in the tree, ready to deliver a knife to a throat if needed.

"Only one of you has a bow," Tam said. "We'll gut you like pigs."

"Not before I kill you." Robyn's words were for the sheriff. He gave her a thin smile.

"You would kill a man in cold blood in front of his only daughter?"

Robyn's heartbeat slowed. She tore her eyes from the sheriff's face and forced herself to glance behind him.

On a small bay mare rode Marian.

His words did not immediately make sense to her. Marian was not the sheriff's daughter. *Could* not be the sheriff's daughter. Surely Robyn would have known. You knew he had a daughter, she thought, but she had not seen the girl in years. Yet as impossible as the thought was, her mind presented her with a list of things that had not added up about Marian. There was the fair, where Marian had stepped onto the field to speak to Robyn, and the comments she had brushed off but nonetheless overheard. Perhaps Marian had assumed that Robyn already knew who she was. Nottingham wasn't large enough that she should have missed that. *Sheriff's daughter.* The words repeated in her mind, and Will filled the silence.

"No one needs to die," said Will, and Robyn detected the quaver in her voice, "as long as you give us your purses."

No, thought Robyn. This is wrong. This is all wrong. For a moment she hated them all: the sheriff, Michael, and Marian. The sheriff for killing her brother. Michael for dying. And Marian, Marian she hated for spoiling her revenge. Just shoot him, she urged her fingers. Nothing else matters. Her finger itched to release the arrow and free Michael's ghost. He would do it for her if their roles were reversed, damning the consequences.

Her eyes slid back to Marian's. If she loosed this arrow, she'd be condemning Marian to that same nightmare. She would fall asleep, as Robyn did, watching someone she loved die over and over and over again.

"Marian," the sheriff said, never taking his eyes off Robyn. "What was the archer's name, again?"

"Robyn Hood." Marian kept her tone even, what little emotion she betrayed attributable to fear, not familiarity, but there was a plea there.

"Yes, Robyn Hood. A fine archer. A man like you could have made a decent living, and yet here you are."

"And a man like you could have made a fine husband, only she wasn't interested, was she?" Rage twisted his face at her words. It sent a thrill of vindictive pleasure through her. "She got as far away from you as she could."

"You will pay for that," said the sheriff in a deceptively calm voice.

"I believe I did."

"Your purse," said John from the rear. "A small price for your life, don't you think?"

"Yours too." Will pointed at Tam with her sword.

"The lady may keep hers." Robyn was careful not to let her hand waver on the arrow. "We do not tax those who cannot pay here."

The sheriff gave a humorless laugh. "Everyone can pay," he said. "Even my daughter." He undid his purse and tossed it to the ground at his horse's feet. "Give it up, Tam. Marian."

"Sir—" said Tam.

"Do it."

Tam glared at his employer, then spurred his horse toward Robyn. She released the arrow on instinct. It took him in the sword arm, punching through the muscle of his biceps and burying itself nearly to the fletching. He roared with pain as Robyn dodged out of the way of the horse, whipping another arrow from her quiver.

"I said, give the boy your purse, Tam."

"Are you mad?" Tam shouted. "Why should we yield to this coward?"

"Because," said the sheriff, a vicious smile on his lips, "I would not shed even this coward's blood in front of my daughter. But I promise you, Robyn Hood, I will not forget this, nor will I forget what you have stolen from me. We will meet again."

"I look forward to it."

"Now, Tam, I won't tell you again. Your purse."

Tam flung his purse into the woods. Marian, too, let her purse fall. Robyn did not move to return it.

Sheriff's daughter.

"Good day then," she said, forcing herself to step out of the road and make way for the riders. The sheriff smiled at her as he spurred his horse on. She recognized that smile. She'd felt it on her own face on the occasions she'd allowed herself to fantasize about this moment, only those fantasies had involved a slow drawing and quartering and the sheriff's agonized screams, not the much more personal agony of watching him ride away unharmed, vengeance upon her fresh in his mind.

She didn't look at Marian. Nothing in the other woman's eyes could change what she should have already known: *sheriff's daughter.* The sound of hooves faded. Tom poked around a sprawl of brambles to retrieve the purse, while John watched Robyn closely.

"We should get off the road," Robyn said at last. "He'll be back, and now he knows our faces."

"Let him come," said John. "We'll be ready."

Chapter Twenty-Eight

Her father rode in silence toward Harcourt. Tam kept up a steady string of curses as blood dripped from his arm, but Marian paid him no mind. Only the sheriff mattered. The sheriff, and perhaps Robyn. She saw Robyn's face again: eyes burning beneath the shadow of her hood, mouth twisted in hatred as she pointed her arrow at Marian's father's heart.

That naked loathing had stripped away her own anger toward him. She'd never seen someone look at another person like that, and when Robyn's eyes had met her own, she'd felt the white heat scorch her.

She had meant to kill him. Would have killed him, had Marian not been there. Her entire body ached at the thought as if she'd come down with a fever. Tears spilled down her cheeks. Whatever anger she held toward her father, she didn't want him dead. His broad shoulders filled her vision on the road ahead, still strong despite the weight he'd added over years of rich eating. She'd loved those shoulders as a girl. He'd carried her around their manor on them, pretending to be a warhorse while the serfs shook their heads at their lord's indulgence and her mother smiled.

What happened to that man?

She didn't know the person on the horse in front of her.

She did, however, know that Robyn would hang for this. Her father would never forgive this slight against his pride. The feverish feeling grew. Maybe she didn't know Robyn either.

A concerned servant helped her from her horse when they arrived at the manor. Her father remained mounted, too lost in thought to notice her or his wounded employee.

"Do you wish to join us for supper?" she asked him in a flat voice. She saw Emmeline coming toward them across the yard, limping more heavily than usual.

"I cannot stay. There is work that must be done." His eyes focused on her face, and a flicker of something that might have been love lit them briefly. "No outlaw will harm you on our roads again, my dear. That I promise." He turned his horse with a nod to Emmeline and trotted back toward the forest. Tam followed, cursing more loudly than ever.

Marian handed her mare off to the stable boy and caught Emmeline's arm.

"Tell me," the lady said as she searched Marian's face.

"My father—" To Marian's horror, she burst into tears. Emmeline led her to the garden and sat her on a bench. The smell of roses filled her nostrils, and she thought again of Robyn. The story spilled out of her. Not all of it, but enough. The viscount, the ambush on the road, and Robyn Hood.

"He . . ." She fought a wave of hiccups. "He saved me in the forest. I never told you."

"Alanna had it right then," said Emmeline. She gave Marian a warm smile, her gentle teasing reassuring. "But Marian, love, you've had a terrible shock."

"He'll kill him." Marian let out a miserable sniffle. "My father will hunt him down and kill him, just like he always does."

"Your Robyn sounds like both a fool and a clever man. Perhaps he'll leave the forest."

Marian nodded, though this did little to assuage her worry. Robyn leaving was almost as bad as Robyn dead. She wished she could tell Emmeline the whole truth. Robyn's gender, however, might be all that saved the outlaw if it came down to it. She doubted her father would spare a woman, but if he was searching for a man, Robyn stood a chance.

"Marriage might not be so terrible," Emmeline said, interrupting

Marian's thoughts. "It would get you away from your father, and the viscount is an old man. He could be dead within the year."

"I don't *want* to marry anyone." Her outburst echoed around the small garden. Emmeline studied her, fair brows knitted together.

"Even your Robyn?"

"She—he's not my Robyn. And even if I did, that would be impossible." *In so many ways.*

"We are allowed to feel," said Emmeline, taking Marian's hand in hers. "It is only how we act that matters to others. You are not married yet, Marian, and a great deal can happen in a short period of time. And if nothing else, marriage will give you children, God willing, and you will love them as you have never loved anyone or anything."

Is that all I have to hope for? A child to love? Not such a terrible thing perhaps, but if so, she prayed that child was a boy.

Men could take what they wanted.

Chapter Twenty-Nine

Robyn waited by the mill, jumping at the slightest sound. She trusted her instincts deeper in the wood, where she knew which crack of branch meant human and which meant deer, but here she swore she could feel the sheriff's eyes upon her no matter where she stood.

Smoke rose from the mill's kitchen. The front door stood open and the sound of a screaming baby drifted out over the late summer morning. Robyn's chest ached with the palpable chaos of family. A woman stepped out of the door, laughing over her shoulder at something from within the house. Mallory, one of Midge's older sisters. Robyn shrank further behind the tree.

"Come on, Midge," she whispered.

A grinding noise made her jump again. She wiped sweating palms on her tunic as the water wheel sprang to life, powering the millstone that ground the grain Robyn had eaten all her life. Longing for the taste of bread joined the other aches.

"I'll be back later."

Robyn's head jerked as she heard Midge's voice. Her cousin kissed Mallory and turned to head down the rutted road. Robyn followed, careful to leave enough space between them until they were out of earshot of the mill.

"Midge," she said, stepping out from behind a tree. The forest was sparse here, and Midge noticed her immediately.

"What are you doing here?"

"I came to warn you not to come today."

"Robyn, we've been over this before."

"This time is different. Listen to me. You have to promise to listen."

Midge folded her arms across her chest and waited.

"I . . ." The words piled up, but Robyn found she could not say them. Things had been going so well. Now she'd ruined everything. Again.

"You what?"

"I nearly shot the sheriff."

Midge listened to the story with uncharacteristic patience, nodding in the right places and resisting her usual urge to interrupt.

"Then I mentioned Gwyneth."

"You what?"

"I said . . . damn it, I don't remember what I said, but I brought her into it. He may try and question her again, and I can't have you getting dragged—"

"Why would I get dragged in?"

"I don't know. You're my cousin. He might . . . Oh, God, Midge." Robyn grabbed her cousin's shoulder to steady herself.

"What?"

"The arrow."

"What are you talking—"

"I shot Tam."

"He's a bastard. So what?"

"So, the sheriff now has one of my arrows. What if he—"

"He already knows you bought arrows from Gwyneth. You said as much at the fair."

Robyn's heart raced as she considered this. Midge was right, but that didn't explain the sick feeling in her gut. "I never retrieved the arrow that killed Clovis."

"Jesus, Robyn. It's an arrow. You tie a bunch of feathers to the end of a pointy stick. How can he track that back to you?"

"Is that really what you think fletching is?"

"Am I wrong?"

"Not entirely, but Midge . . ." She clutched the back of her neck, frustrated by her inability to articulate the sense of foreboding flooding her veins.

"Hang on. What I don't understand is why you didn't just shoot him."

"In front of his daughter?"

"How many people did he hang in front of *their* families? How many people, despite the law, did he sentence to death before they could get to the courts?" Midge's voice rose and cracked. "Robyn, if you had killed him, we might finally have stood a chance."

Sick fury uncoiled inside her, desperate for the chance to strike at someone other than herself. "And if the next sheriff was just as bad? He'd still collect the ransom tax, Midge."

"But he wouldn't know your face."

"It doesn't matter. I know the woods seem large to you, but there are only so many places to hide. That's what I came to tell you. I'll try and bring you coin and food when I can, but I can't risk them linking me to you, and I can't risk you getting caught. You can't come looking for us anymore. We're moving camp."

Midge's eyes widened in disbelief. "So that's it? You're vanishing again?"

"To protect you—"

"No. To protect yourself so that you don't have to feel guilty."

"Think about your family, Midge."

She glared at Robyn. "You are my family."

Robyn removed the sheriff's purse from her belt and shoved it into her cousin's hands. "This should be enough to get you through. I love you, Midge. Take care of yourself." She stumbled away from her cousin before she could change her mind, Midge's stricken face burned into her memory.

"Not as much as you seem to love the sheriff's daughter," Midge said, nearly shouting the words as Robyn fled back into the shelter of the trees.

I had no choice, she told herself. I have to keep them safe. She walked as fast as she dared, sprinting when she could, aware that

235

the forest would soon be overrun by workers harvesting fallen wood, mushrooms, and the first of the nuts and fruits to ripen on the trees. Any one of them might recognize her, even in Michael's clothes with her hair worn loose and short. Or, worse, she might run into one of the sheriff's men, and then everything would come undone.

Not as much as you seem to love the sheriff's daughter. She flinched anew as she remembered Midge's words. Midge couldn't understand, though, what it was like to lose a father or a brother. None of her sisters had died in front of her, and both her parents were hale and strong. No matter how much Robyn hated the man, she couldn't do that to Marian. *Or anyone.* Even if that meant risking her own life.

But what about Gwyneth and Midge? *Didn't you just put their lives in danger, all to spare Marian a few nightmares?* Robyn ran faster, trying to outrun the voice in her head. There were no good choices. That was just the way of it. Wishing things were different didn't help.

She did need to think about how to hide her band from Nottingham. Today, tomorrow, or a month from now, the sheriff would return. They needed to keep a watch at all times and stay out of sight as much as possible. Feeding themselves would be challenging, but they'd eaten well over the past few weeks as the forest ripened around them. They could afford a few days of hunger. A brace of pheasants scurried through a clearing ahead of her. She resisted the urge to bring one down and skirted the open land, keeping to the shadows. They'd have to leave their camp near the river. Too much traffic to and from the water left trails, and the longer they were in plain view, the more likely the risk of capture.

"Damn," she cursed under her breath, picturing the lazy loops of the river as it wound through the woods. Their current camp had everything they needed. Shelter from prying eyes, a thick canopy to keep off the rain, and proximity to water. No other spot boasted so much. Moving, however, was necessary. They had no way of knowing how many eyes might have seen smoke from their fires. They needed higher ground—harder to get to, easier to keep an eye on. That meant abandoning the stretch of road near Harcourt and moving deeper into the woods, closer to Siward and away from Marian.

Siward. Tom and his sister hadn't fleshed out their numbers that much, but she vowed to bring it up tonight over the fire. Perhaps one of the others would have an idea that wouldn't end with all of them dead.

"So," said Will later that night as Robyn prodded the embers of the fire with a stick. "Siward."

"Siward," she agreed. John and Tom sat staring into the flames with identical expressions of longing that Robyn assumed came from missing the forge, while Tom's sister stood watch outside the bright circle of firelight. "We're still too few to take him on directly."

Will tapped her fingers on her thigh as she thought. "My brother hated strategy. I attended those lessons for him until we got too old to pull it off. Our tutor actually applauded him when he discovered what we'd been up to. Him, mind you, not me. Called it a bait and switch."

"Did you get the switch, too?" asked John.

"I couldn't sit for a week." Will shuddered at the memory. "What I'm wondering, though, is if there is some way we can pull a bait and switch on both Siward and the sheriff."

"We're listening," said Robyn.

"Siward has a large band, right?" Will asked John. He nodded, and she continued. "That means he has a lot of mouths to feed. He might be willing to take more risks than we are, and that could work in our favor."

"It will also make him more dangerous," said John.

"If Siward caught wind of a wealthy caravan, do you think he'd take it?"

"Hard to say. He might, if he thought the odds were in his favor."

"And if the sheriff were to hear a reliable rumor that Robyn Hood had plans to ambush said caravan, do you think he would come in person?"

Robyn remembered the look in the sheriff's eyes as he rode away from her. "He'd come."

"Then we get them in the same place, and while they're at each other's throats, we take them out." Will's voice did not shake as she suggested killing Marian's father.

Robyn pressed her boots deep into the ground to keep from clenching her fists and pretended she did not feel John's eyes on her. He had to know the agony she was in. Her feelings for Marian complicated everything, but she could not put them in front of the lives of the other people she cared about. She and Marian had never had a future anyway.

"How do you propose we drop these hints?" Robyn asked Will.

"I'm not sure yet."

"Siward is easy. He knows me. I could go to him," said John.

"Is that safe? Won't he ask where you've been?" said Robyn.

"We'll think of something to tell him."

"What about the sheriff?" asked Tom.

"That will be harder. Are you sure Midge is out? Because—" asked Will.

"Yes." Robyn and John spoke at the same time.

"Then one of us needs to drop a hint to a forester."

Robyn thought of Cedric and said nothing. He would listen to her if she could bring herself to betray him. He could also ruin everything.

"I could," said Alanna.

They all turned to look at her.

"I'm a minstrel. I can go where I please with fewer questions asked."

"Alanna—"

"It's a start." Robyn cut Will off before she could protest. "But we have no way of discovering when a caravan will come through."

"But we do." Will turned green eyes to Robyn, and she did not miss the challenge there.

"How?"

"Marian."

"No." Robyn stood. "You would have me ask her to plot her own father's death?"

Will paled beneath the vehemence in Robyn's words. "I didn't mean—"

"Then what did you mean? She's the daughter of the sheriff of goddamn Nottingham, Willa of Maunnesfeld, or did you forget?"

"Enough." John's deep voice growled over Robyn's. "There will be time to deal with Siward and time to deal with the sheriff, but not if we are at each other's throats."

"Then perhaps we should not have brought a fox into our midst."

"Robyn."

She glared at John. "Tomorrow we move camp." A part of her hoped Will would argue further, but the redhead sank back down to her spot before the fire and refused to meet her eyes.

Chapter Thirty

Midsummer loomed on the horizon, and with it everything Marian dreaded. Emmeline had regained some of her good humor, though she still brooded over Willa and Alanna's absence. Without the minstrel and her quarrelsome lover, however, there was little to distract Marian from her future. She missed Alanna's soothing voice, and even Willa's temper would have brought a welcome relief from the monotony of sunlit afternoons. The darning needle in her hand slipped, piercing her finger, and she winced and sucked on the bright bead of blood.

She had too many unanswered questions. What had the exchange between Robyn and her father meant? What did the widow have to do with anything? She wished there was someone she could ask, but she did not know any of the men who worked for her father well enough to pry, and court gossip hadn't carried any news to Harcourt.

Robyn wanted her father dead. That was another thing. How could she accept that? How could she reconcile the woman who had saved her in the woods with the hate-filled archer on the Sherwood road?

Her finger ached where she'd pricked it, and she set down the dress so as not to bleed on it. The heady smell of roses washed over her as she stood and accidentally jostled the blossoms behind her. *I can't even speak with Emmeline.* She stared at the courtyard walls. Never before had Harcourt felt like a trap. I shall go mad, she thought, and she understood with a sinking feeling how Willa had mustered the courage to leave everything behind. It wasn't courage. It was desperation, a bone-deep, feral need to run that made her marrow itch and the air come too quickly to her lungs.

I could fake my death like Willa. Or pretend I've run off to France with a nobleman's son or gone to sea with a merchant. She could do it. A note, a carefully placed word in the right maid's ear—her father would rage, no doubt, but at least he would not come looking for her in the woods. *And then what?* How long could she survive in Sherwood? How long could any of them? Winter wasn't that far off, and even if they survived this winter, or even the next, there was no future. She'd seen outlaws brought to justice after years of rough living. Ragged, lice-ridden, filthy men and women weak with hunger and barely able to protest the noose.

I am not like Robyn. I cannot wield a sword or shoot a bow. I can embroider and spin and run a household, but I have only rarely plucked a chicken and I have no brother's clothes to steal away in. I am my father's daughter in all the ways that might have made a difference, and in none of the ways that would have made me happy.

Emmeline found her then. Henri's small hand was in hers and dust stained his knees. When she saw Marian's face, she scooped her son into her arms and limped toward her. Henri's weight offset the hitch of her gait.

"Shall we go for a ride?" she asked, rubbing small circles on the boy's back. "This one is ready for a nap, and I'm covered all over with horse already."

Marian nodded, mutely grateful for her friend's quiet understanding.

They were mounted a short time later. Late summer opened its arms to them as they cantered down the manor lane, the fields burdened with waving sheaves of wheat and the pointed peaks of haystacks. Laborers stopped their work to wave as they rode by, and they passed a wagon full of firewood coming back from the forest. Harcourt owned a scant few acres of woodland on the borders of Sherwood, just enough to keep the fires lit all winter and to supply the manor's building needs. Emmeline made note of the trees, slowing her horse to a walk to examine a large chestnut. Some of the spiny, green fruits were opening, the dark red shell of the nuts inside gleaming in the sunlight. *Soon,* they promised, and Marian's mouth watered in anticipation.

Fat squirrels scampered in front of their horses' hooves. The road was wide here, the banks sloping upward into roots and trees and sprays of grass and brambles. Ivy tumbled here and there, attended by mosses and pale yellow flowers. Some of the panic ebbed away as she breathed in loam and soil.

"Emmeline," she said, reining closer to Emmeline's horse. "Do you ever wish you could leave everything behind? Just, I don't know, run away? Not forever. Only for a while, until things felt more . . . manageable."

Emmeline gave her a sad smile. "Oh, Marian, we all feel that way. No, I don't mean to chide you," she added, seeing Marian's face. "It is a terribly lonely feeling. I think my husband felt that way before he left. Perhaps, I've often wondered, that was why he left. It is harder for us to run. A man can find work. But a woman . . ." She trailed off, gazing into the forest. "We have children, and if we don't have children, we have husbands, fathers, or brothers to think of. Too many people need us."

"I think about Willa a lot," Marian said. The truth hovered at her lips, jostling like horses at the starting gate. "I wonder if she got away."

"I like to think that she did." Emmeline bowed her head. Her blue eyes rested on the pommel of her saddle. "It makes it easier to bear the rest of it."

"If we could find her, help her in some way, would you?"

Emmeline did not look at Marian directly. She kept her eyes first on her saddle's pommel, then on her horse's mane, and then at last on the road ahead. "You know very well I would, Marian." Marian shifted uncomfortably at the weight of Emmeline's words. *Do you know? Do you know how much I've hidden from you, despite all you've done for me?*

"Sometimes I think I see her hawk," Emmeline continued. "When I'm hunting deep in the woods. I know it cannot be. There are a hundred birds like hers, but still we always look for signs of the people we've let go. It doesn't get easier with time, Marian, but you learn to bear it, and the joys are greater too when tasted with the bittersweet."

Joy. She rolled the word around in her mouth, sampling it carefully. When had she last felt joy? Sometimes out in the fields or riding with Emmeline she'd feel a great swooping in her stomach as the colors of the sun and wheat and leaf and grass went to her head like wine. Those moments always felt fleeting, changing as quickly as a spring day and impossible to hold on to for long. She thought she might have felt joy that day with Robyn beneath the willow, but now the memory twisted like a knife.

"What if I cannot learn to bear it?" she said, half to herself and half to Emmeline.

"You will. And if you don't, the pain will become your companion, and there is comfort to be found even there."

I want more than that. She tasted the words in her mouth, keeping them locked behind her teeth, but Emmeline heard them all the same. She reached out across the space between their horses and clasped Marian's hand with hers.

I'm here, the gesture seemed to say.

For so many years, that had been enough. Now, though, despite the dearness of her friend, she searched the forest for another pair of eyes.

243

Chapter Thirty-One

Robyn chanced upon their new camp by accident. She'd climbed a tree to get a better view of the hills and had instead seen the fall of rock on the far side of the river. Her body tensed like a sight hound about to give chase. Rock did not bear the imprints of boots, and while she could see little past the thick layer of leaves, the land looked promising.

John came with her to explore.

"It's a hard climb," she said, eyeing the moss-covered boulders. "Impossible on horseback from this approach at least."

"And close to the Meden river."

They scaled the rockfall, weaving through the gnarled trees that had put roots down in the inhospitable ground, until they came to the bare stretch of rock Robyn had seen from her tree. Stone towered above her and rose into the sky.

"I don't think we need to worry about anyone coming on us from that direction," she said. John gave a grunt of assent and ran his hands over the rocks at their feet.

"It would be too much to ask for a cave, I suppose," she said, scanning the trees. "But we might find something. An overhang, at least, to keep off the rain."

They split up to search. Robyn leapt from boulder to boulder, noting the depth of some of the narrow ravines she crossed. Good hiding places for weapons, she found herself thinking, among other things. The moss felt springy beneath her feet. Kneeling, she peeled some of it away, and a heavy scrap of verdant carpet came off in her hands. *Easy to cover a trail.*

"Robyn." John's voice jerked her attention away from the flora. She replaced the moss and picked her way back, using her staff for balance.

"John?" she called out. She didn't see him anywhere, and the familiar dread uncoiled in her belly.

"Here."

She studied the direction his voice had come from. Still nothing.

"Here," John said again as he stepped out from behind what had looked like a solid wall of rock. A huge grin split his face. "It's not quite a cave, but it will do just fine."

Robyn pushed past him. What had looked like solid rock concealed a cleft that curved back in on itself, open to the sky but nearly invisible until the viewer came directly upon it. The cleft was only five feet wide, but it wound back into the cliff for a good thirty feet before it narrowed. Her mind immediately set to work. They would cut branches to create a roof and thatch it as best they could before the winter rains set in. Nothing would be as dry as a cave, but they had time, and they could store firewood here, and game. Midge could build an oven out of nearby stones . . . she stopped herself. Midge would never see this place. But she, Robyn, could build an oven, pounding leached acorns into flour and baking flat, brittle bread.

This cleft was life.

"It's perfect," she said to John.

"I know. Closer to Siward than I'd like, though."

"Then we lie low for now. We have a lot of work to do before winter, and I don't want anyone taking risks. I'll do as much of the hunting myself as I can. The sheriff will be happy with me if I'm caught, and he won't go looking for the rest of you."

"And Siward?" John asked.

Robyn paused, her argument with Will fresh on her mind. "We keep out of his way and hope for the best."

"You don't think there's any merit to Will's plan, then?"

The casual way he phrased the question didn't escape Robyn's notice. "I am not bringing Marian into this."

"I agree. Blood wins out, and he's her father. We don't have to do it Will's way, however."

"Do you have a better idea?"

"I might have something."

"Then I'll hear it."

John tapped the solid wall of the cliff before he spoke. "I've been thinking about Tuck."

"I bet you have," Robyn said, raising an eyebrow suggestively.

"We could hide you in a nunnery, if it came to it. You, Will, Alanna, Midge, and Lisbet."

"What about you?"

"I'll be fine. Tom and I could draw the sheriff away from you. What I'm thinking, however, is that he and I could go back to Siward. I could tell him I was captured and released, but that I heard a few things."

"And how will you hear those things?"

"Alanna's right. A minstrel can go places the rest of us can't. Inns. Taverns. Markets. She doesn't have a memorable face, either. She could ask questions without raising any."

"Fair enough. Tom isn't going with you, though. I am."

"You know the risks."

"And I got us into this. If I had just let him ride past—"

"You should have. But he killed your brother and hunted your sister-in-law. I don't think any of us would have acted differently."

"He's Marian's father."

John put a hand on her shoulder. "I'm sorry."

Robyn pressed her forehead against the cliff. A real wall, solid, enough to keep the wind away. They'd start the roof at the narrow end, sloping it down. Water would run off toward the opening, where they'd collect it in the wooden buckets sealed with pitch they'd make over the next few weeks. They'd build the fire in the narrow end, too. Smoke would rise up the natural chimney of the cliff, dispersed by the wind, and they'd trap heat from the fire with hides and willow hurdles. Over time, perhaps they'd even reinforce the cleft with timber and stone, chipping shelves out of the rocks and building cots and chairs to prop around the fire.

Over time. Time that she needed to buy for them with human lives, for all that the thought made her ill.

"What if he doesn't have to die?"

"Who?"

"The sheriff."

"I don't follow."

"What if we can make him believe I am dead?"

"How?"

"If he thinks I'm with Siward."

"That could work."

"But?" said Robyn, hearing the unspoken word in his voice.

"But you need to be prepared for the fact that it might not. And if it comes to that, it will be his life or ours."

It took less than an hour for them to remove all evidence that they'd ever been at the old camp.

"Well," she said, looking around the gentle bowl between the hills that had sheltered her for the better part of two months. A mound of freshly turned earth, covered by leaves, was all that remained where their fire had burned. Tom and Alanna had made short work of the latrine, and John, Will, and Robyn had removed all the caches of food they'd squirreled away around the clearing. "You can come down now, Lisbet."

Lisbet dropped to the ground with a muted thud. It unnerved Robyn how quickly the girl had taken to the forest. She'd make good on her promise to craft the girl a hunting bow once they got settled into their new home. *Home.* An odd lump rose in her throat. Home had been Gwyneth and the baby and the shop, not open woodland and the company of strangers, and yet she felt an ease out here she'd never experienced in Nottingham.

"Time to go." John slung an arm around her shoulder, but like her he seemed reluctant to leave. Not strangers, she amended, leaning into him. And, of course, there was Midge.

"Midge won't be able to find us," she said quietly enough that only he could hear her.

"I know." He squeezed her. "But we can find her when it's safe."

"You don't think she'll come looking?"

"Oh, I'm sure she will. And if she tracks us down, we'll know we still have a lot to learn about hiding our tracks. Come on. We need the daylight."

They followed the Rainworth river, crossing back and forth where it allowed to further disguise their trail, until they came to the place where it joined the River Maun. There, eyes darting around the trees, they forded it downstream of the main bridge, and emerged, soaking but unseen, into the forest on the far side. Their clothes dried as they walked on. This time, Robyn did take down an unwary pheasant, and Lisbet gathered mushrooms and greens as Robyn had shown her while John and Tom collected firewood. Will and Alanna brought up the rear, keeping an eye out for pursuit.

The climb up wasn't any easier this time around. Robyn and John had scoured the hillside looking for the gentlest routes, but they'd been forced to conclude that the gentlest route was the one that ended the most quickly, regardless of the incline.

"This better be worth it," Will said from the back of the line. She bore the largest of their pots on her back, a great, hulking kettle that Midge had dragged into the forest for them earlier that summer.

"Just wait." Robyn paused to extend Will a hand, noting the new calluses as she hauled the other woman up. Will shot her a grateful smile, which faltered as they both remembered their earlier argument.

Lisbet, to no one's surprise, made it to the top first. John followed, and after a few more scrambling moments the rest of them stood on the rocky stoop outside the cleft.

"This is it," John said. Robyn schooled her expression, letting him have his fun.

"This?" Will looked around, sweat pouring down her face. Alanna held her own counsel as she surveyed the scene.

"Come off it," said Tom, a hesitant grin on his lips, as if he suspected there was a joke in here somewhere, but wasn't sure enough to bet on it.

"First one to find it doesn't have to haul water," Robyn said. She and John stood back and let the others poke around. "My money's on Lisbet," she told John.

"Mine would be, too, if she were going in the right direction."

Robyn watched Lisbet scale the rock wall. "If she finds a better cave up there, you're hauling water until spring."

"Deal."

They shook on it as Will let out a shout of triumph. Lisbet slid down the rock face and into her brother's arms as they filed into the cleft. It didn't feel quite as large with the six of them inside, but there was still plenty of space to move around.

"I wish I was a mason." Tom ran his hand along the wall in admiration.

"We wish you were too," said John. "One less blacksmith around the place."

"And masons get to go wherever they please," added Lisbet.

"Next time we're out recruiting, I'll be sure to put out a call for masons." Robyn set down her satchel, which contained a poorly wrapped bundle of hides, her cloak, and the fishing nets they'd deemed worth saving. "Let's get a fire going so we have something to eat. Who wants to go down to the river?"

An ill-fated game of stones left Robyn with the task. She collected the waterskins and the kettle and made the descent, already hating this new addition to their routine. John and Lisbet accompanied her, leaving Will, Alanna, and Tom to look for wood for the fire. Robyn set Lisbet to gathering rushes for the floor.

"We'll build proper beds later on. Plenty of willow down here, and while we don't have sacking, we'll make do with hides and leaves and dried grass."

"Might be clay farther up the bank, too." John let silt from the riverbed run through his fingers. "Good for the roof. We don't want to harvest too much of anything close by, though. Which means we've got some climbing ahead of us."

"The more we climb, the stronger our legs, and the better chance we stand." Robyn rubbed at her calves as she spoke, doubting the wisdom of her own words.

"Lisbet," said John, looking back up at the wall. "Do you think you could scale that?"

"Yes." Lisbet didn't bother looking up and went right on cutting rushes, her dark head bent to the task.

"Maybe we can get a rope up there. It's not much, but if we're cornered it would be nice to know there was another way out."

"Unless they have archers," Robyn pointed out.

"Ever the optimist."

"We'll need to establish a secondary rallying point. Somewhere we can all find that isn't here. The old camp will do for now, but ideally someplace else. And a new watch rotation. Should we post watches from the cleft, or farther down?"

"Farther down, I think. And we already have a rallying point. The priory." John helped lift the kettle and together they began the ascent back up the hill, Lisbet following behind.

Thanks to the coals they'd carried from the previous camp, Will and Tom had a good blaze going by the time Robyn, John, and Lisbet returned.

"We'll need to keep an eye on the smoke," Robyn said as she set up a spit over their new hearth. "But first, let's eat."

Lisbet added the wild onion and dandelion greens she'd found to the pot, and Robyn emptied the crumbled store of mushrooms from her belt before she began plucking the pheasant. She'd roast the bird, she decided, then add the bones and leftover meat to the pot to thicken their meager stew. Her stomach rumbled. One pheasant would not go far split six ways.

"I wish we had some porridge," Lisbet said.

"We'll have to make do without porridge for a bit. Or bread." Robyn's stomach grumbled in disagreement.

"What *are* we going to do?" Tom asked. He twirled his hammer idly.

"Well," said Robyn, shooting John a glance, "about that . . ."

As she lay awake in their new home hours later, however, her mind traveled over river and hill to Harcourt. *She's the sheriff's daughter.* Repeating that fact didn't lessen the yearning that pierced her lungs. If anything, it made it worse. Marian had risked her father's wrath to save Will, and each time she spoke with Robyn, Marian committed treason. *As if she would speak to me now.*

What would Marian think if she knew Robyn had plotted to kill her father? Blood always won out in the end. She would not choose Robyn. She hardly knew Robyn. A few words meant nothing.

She trusted me with her friends' lives, and I've trusted her with mine.

Surely, that was worth more than a few words. The memory of Marian's lips brushing the corner of her mouth came back to her, and once again she watched Marian wading into the stream as she returned to Harcourt. Marian had asked her to name her reward; she had spoken truth when she answered, but not the whole truth. "I would like to know you better," she had said. She had meant, "I would like to call you mine."

The knowledge came to Robyn as a crescent moon waned over the slice of sky visible from the cleft. She would have to walk away from Marian, but first she needed to see her one last time.

Chapter Thirty-Two

Hounds milled about their horses' hooves. Their tails wagged as the kennel master struggled to maintain order above the din of the enthusiastic pack. Emmeline, striking in dark green chased with gold embroidery, gave him the signal, and he set off with his tangle of leashes toward the forest. Emmeline didn't have a gift of chase beyond her own lands, but she did have right of warren, which meant she could hunt fox and hare and pheasant in the king's wood even if she couldn't hunt deer or boar. Marian didn't care what they hunted; the promise of a day's ride and the feast to follow offered a break from the monotony of emotional turmoil that had defined her life both within and without the walls of Harcourt since she'd helped Willa and Alanna escape.

She could see the huntsman ahead, running alongside his hounds as they dispersed into the trees in search of game. Emmeline's hawk flapped her wings. Gregor carried bow and spear behind his saddle, and Marian herself had a lady's light hunting bow. Perhaps I'll take a few squirrels, she thought, idly watching the little brown bodies scrounging through the leaves.

It took the better part of the morning for the hounds to pick up the scent of a fox. The huntsman released them with a loud cry that sent Marian's heart racing, and her mare leapt to keep up with the other riders.

This time, I will not run into a hornets' nest, she vowed, leaning low over her horse's neck. The woods here remained open, grazed by pigs and sheep and deer, and she wasn't overly worried about her horse pulling up lame or tripping on a root. Burrows, on the other hand, posed a greater risk.

"Hole," one of the riders called out ahead. She reined away from the rabbit warren, wishing they'd scared a rabbit out of the brush but grateful for the warning.

"Hole," she shouted over her shoulder, only to discover that she'd ended up at the rear of the hunting party and no one remained to heed her warning. She slowed her mare, not enough to lose sight of the rest of the party, but enough to buy herself a little more space.

Her horse didn't seem to mind. She trotted along, then broke into a walk, pausing to browse each time she felt Marian's attention slipping. The woods closed in around them. Marian could hear the hounds, still within a short canter's distance, but the birds had resumed their song and she felt the solitude like a kiss. When, she wondered, was the last time she had been alone? Really alone? Dappled sunlight flowed over her skin. She held a hand up to the light and caught the shadows in her open palm.

The snap of a twig caught her attention. Off to her right, lit by the same dappled sunlight, stood a fallow deer. The dapples on his hide moved with the light, and his antlers, fresh with the first hints of velvet, lent gravity to the slow movements of his head. Marian sat frozen on her horse. The deer paused to crop at the lower branches of a coppiced elm, then pricked his ears forward.

I'm downwind of him, she realized. He'd see her soon enough, or hear the heavy, even breathing of her horse, but for now she watched him pick his way through the woods.

"Marian."

The voice caught her by surprise and her horse spooked beneath her as she jolted upright. The deer fled with a launch of powerful haunches, his antlers vanishing into the trees while Marian struggled to calm her horse. When she finally succeeded, two people stood before her, for all that she could have sworn she was alone.

"Willa?" she asked the one nearest her. The redhead smiled,

looking entirely at her ease, and placed a reassuring hand on Marian's reins. The horse snorted once, then settled. Marian remained in the saddle for a moment longer as she studied the noblewoman. Willa's loose, short red hair framed a face tanned by weather and sun and smudged with dirt, and in her brother's clothes she looked every inch the rogue. It suited her. Marian swallowed her envy and dismounted to embrace her, laughing in relief.

"I didn't hear you coming," she said, turning from Willa to Robyn. Her heart thudded uncomfortably at the sight of the outlaw, the momentary relief that came with seeing Willa dispelled by the memory of their last encounter.

"We made something of an effort," said Willa.

Robyn didn't say anything, and Marian couldn't read the expression on her face. Her dark hair was tangled here and there with twigs. Marian wanted to wrap her hands in it, and she also wanted to shake Robyn's shoulders and shout at her for ruining everything. *If you'd stayed out of my father's way we might have had something.* Now, any time spent in Marian's company put Robyn further at risk, and Marian couldn't think about her without also remembering the arrow pointed at her father's heart.

"It isn't safe for you here," she said to Robyn.

"It isn't safe for us anywhere."

She still couldn't read the other woman's expression. The frustration she'd been trying to keep at bay snarled. "And whose fault is that?" she said, leaving Willa with her reins as she advanced on Robyn. "He'll never stop looking for you. He doesn't forgive things like that." Robyn didn't back down, and Marian was forced to halt a few inches from her face. She glared up at Robyn. "You should have just shot him."

The words burned her throat as they poured out of her. I don't mean it, she thought, but that wasn't entirely true, and she hated herself for even considering the possibility.

"I couldn't." Robyn smelled like leaves and crushed mint, a sweet, wild, heady scent that made it hard to understand her words. "I couldn't do that to you."

She seemed so solid, standing there, her clothes the greens and browns of summer, the leather of her jerkin smooth and the oiled wood of her bow golden over her shoulder.

Willa cleared her throat. Marian took a hasty step back from Robyn. She didn't like the knowing look in Willa's eyes.

"We have an idea to get your father off our backs, and to rid Sherwood of dangerous outlaws." Robyn's voice flowed over her skin much like the sunlight had a few moments earlier, carrying the same heat.

"I assume you are not these 'dangerous outlaws?'"

"No." Robyn's lips curved in the barest hint of a smile. "There is a group of brigands south of here. They're brutal, and more of a threat than we are. John used to run with them. If we can make the sheriff think I'm with them, we can set him on their trail. That should keep everyone occupied and give us time to feed our families and get ready for winter."

"And you want my help."

"No. I don't want you involved at all." Robyn dropped her eyes. "But you deserve to know, and I wanted . . . I wanted to apologize. For scaring you."

"I could help you."

"I can't let you—"

"Why not? It's not like I'm good for anything else, besides breeding, of course, which will happen soon enough if my father has his way."

Robyn flinched. Marian turned on Willa.

"And you. Do you have any idea what it's been like? Lying to Emmeline? She suspects something, I think, with Alanna gone, but that trick you pulled with your dress was cruel. I hear your brother is trying to drink himself into the grave, too."

"Doesn't matter. The less they know, the safer they'll be." Her flippant tone was undermined by the tremor in her lower lip.

Easy enough for her to talk about safety, Marian thought, unable to swallow back the envy that nearly knocked her off her feet. Out here Willa didn't have to lie to Emmeline's face. She didn't spend her days waiting for a summons from her father, aware that each evening brought her closer to a marriage she loathed. Willa was free. So what if she was caught or killed? At that moment, Marian would have given her own life gladly for the chance to trade places.

"And what about me?" At Willa's blank expression, Marian pressed on. "Has it occurred to you that I am risking everything, too? And for what? So that I can lie to my friend? What do you think she will do when she finds out I've been keeping this from her? I will lose my place, which may not seem like much to you, but Emmeline is the only thing between me and my father."

"Marian—"

"Emmeline would do anything for you. You should trust her," she finished. Willa looked to Robyn, and Marian let out a derisive laugh. "Do you let her speak for you now, Willa of Maunnesfeld? Have you taken her to husband instead of Alanna?" The insult, so close to what she herself desired, felt good leaving her lips. She watched it slap the other women in their faces as she settled back on her heels, and the frustration of the past few weeks left her body. A languid heat took its place. She would never have dared speak to Willa like that in her previous life, but out here Willa's birth carried little weight.

"I speak for myself," said Willa, but her voice wavered.

"Leave us, Will," said Robyn.

"What?"

"Keep a lookout and let me know if anyone comes within earshot."

Willa frowned, but obeyed, handing the reins back to Marian. Her easy acquiescence surprised Marian. She had seen Willa exhibit that sort of deference only to Emmeline, and Robyn was only a commoner.

"I didn't know you were the sheriff's daughter," Robyn said when Willa was out of earshot.

"How could you not?"

"I've had other things on my mind. Besides, you might have told me."

"And you might have held me for ransom if I had, the first

time we met. Or worse. Would you still have rescued me if you'd known who I was?"

Robyn didn't answer.

"What do I have to gain by turning you in? There will be no reward for me. My father will consider it his due, and besides, he will ask how I came by the knowledge, and that will discredit him in the eyes of his employers. If he can't keep his own household in line, how can he keep a city? And turning you in would expose Willa and Alanna. I owe you my life, and I want you free and alive just as much as you do. More perhaps, though it may damn me."

She felt out of breath at the end of her speech, uncertain of its effect and painfully aware of just how much of her heart she had laid bare.

"And your father? What do you think he will do when he discovers you have befriended an outlaw?"

"Is that all I am to you? A friend?"

Robyn took half a stride toward her, then stopped herself. "Marian, I would have killed him the other day if you weren't with him. I should have killed him."

"I know." Her throat closed up. "I know what he is, Robyn, but he is still my father. If I promise to help you in any way that I can, will you promise me that you will not kill him?"

Robyn stared at her for the space of ten slow heartbeats before she spoke. "Even if I did, I cannot make that promise for my companions."

"Then make it for yourself," Marian pleaded, taking Robyn's hands in hers.

"Why?"

"Because he is my father."

"Why does it matter to you that I am not the one to kill him?"

Her father would see Robyn hanged if he had his way, Willa and Alanna with her. She'd known this since that day on the road. When, and not if, he cornered them, she knew who she wanted to walk away, for all that her soul threatened to split with the knowledge.

"Do you really not know?" she asked Robyn.

A shout echoed down the hills. The baying of a hound followed. Robyn made no move to leave or to answer, but flecks of green shifted in her eyes.

"Swear to me that you will not kill my father, and I will meet you at the priory in three days' time," she said, her voice strange to her own ears. "I will tell you then if you cannot guess."

"Marian."

She felt Robyn's hand on her face, warm and rough, cupping her jaw as her thumb brushed Marian's cheek. Marian leaned into her touch, aware of the distant sound of hooves. They didn't matter. Willa didn't matter either, for all that she might be watching.

Robyn's lips brushed hers. There was no hesitation this time, or any possibility of accident. She tasted Robyn: sunlight on skin, the lingering tartness of summer berries, and another taste that had no name but that she savored, craving more, until Willa's warning whistle broke them apart.

"Robyn, we need to go, now."

The outlaw released her with reluctance evident in her every move. Marian felt her own legs might not hold her weight.

"I swear to you, Marian, that I will not be the one to kill him."

"Will you still meet me at the priory?"

"I would meet you anywhere."

"Then I will see you in three days," said Marian. Her lips felt foreign and alive to the rush of her breath and the warm summer air.

"Three days," Robyn repeated, and she gave Marian one last look before she turned to follow Willa back into the forest.

Chapter Thirty-Three

It took less time than Robyn had anticipated to set up the new camp. John and Tom had rafters felled and wedged by the end of the first day, and Lisbet climbed up the rock face like a squirrel to lay the beginnings of thatch with Alanna, who was almost as nimble. The thatch itself wasn't much to brag about: evergreens instead of straw, but it would do for now to keep the rain off. Meanwhile, Will and Robyn hauled stones for the hearth and cut willow withies to size for the wickets that would shield the opening of the cave from the wind and the firelight from watching eyes.

"I'm worried about the smoke," Robyn confessed as she laid the last of the hearthstones in place. "We'll have to be careful not to burn green wood, and no fires on clear days if we can help it. We should do most of our cooking after dark."

"Banking the coals will help. The hearthstones should keep us warm enough, or at least that's what my nurse used to tell us." Will eyed the stones with a dubious expression.

"Have you ever been cold? Truly cold?"

"We got caught in the open in a storm once coming back from Nottingham. The wood was too wet to catch when we tried to stop, and we were soaked through before the rain turned to snow. It was awful."

But have you known the kind of cold that lasts for days, never leaving your bones? The cold that only comes when the wood runs low and the snow lies too heavy to travel far beyond the town gates? She didn't give voice to these thoughts. Will would learn soon enough, for there was only so much they could do to fortify their shelter for the winter months. The damp would creep in, and with it cold and fever and chilblains and all the other curses that accompanied winter. At least the sheriff would not waste energy chasing them during the bitterest months, but that would not be much of a comfort. Any strange outlaws who stumbled on their camp would try to wrest their shelter and stores from them, and desperation would lend the strangers strength.

"We'll need to get warmer clothes before then. Fur would be best, or sheepskin."

"And mutton?" Will asked hopefully.

"I'd rather not steal from my neighbor's flocks."

"What about Maunnesfeld's flocks?"

"You would steal from your own people?"

"They're hardly my people now."

"Will." Robyn took a steadying breath. "Your father won't suffer for a missing sheep. The shepherd, however, will. Do you follow me?"

Will groaned. "Yes, Robyn, I follow you. I'm too much the noblewoman, and my entitlement makes you ill."

"Precisely."

"Speaking of noblewomen."

Robyn tensed. Will had been silent thus far about what had transpired in the forest, but something about the glint in her green eyes made Robyn suspect that restraint was coming to an end. "Yes?"

"What you feel for Marian, and I'm not casting judgment," she added quickly as Robyn opened her mouth to protest, "I just wanted to tell you that that's part of the reason I had to run."

Robyn's suspicions had not been unfounded, then. "Alanna?" Will nodded.

"She's a hard one not to love."

"I know. She's composed a few songs about you, by the way."

"What?" Robyn asked, confused.

"Well, us. You. This." Will gestured to the forest. "The one about you and John fighting on the bridge is my favorite."

"I hope she omitted the part where I fell into the water."

"Ask her to play it for you."

"Midge was involved in this somehow, wasn't she?"

Will shrugged. "She may have contributed a few verses."

"Why am I not surprised."

Will looked up at Robyn shyly. "I wanted to thank you again," she said. "For helping us."

"It's nothing." Robyn met Will's gaze. "You've grown on me, for all that you're a noblewoman."

"Marian's part of the gentry, too."

"Marian is . . . Christ, you won't mention what you saw, will you?"

"Not likely. Ladies sometimes get overfond of their handmaids, but kissing the sheriff's daughter is another thing entirely."

"Thank you for that reminder."

"Does . . . does anyone else know?" Will asked.

"John," said Robyn.

"Not your cousin?"

"Not about Marian. She and Gwyneth know I don't want to marry, but—"

"Robyn," John called from the far end of the cleft.

"What?"

"There is something you need to see."

Dread poured down the back of her throat. She grabbed her bow and sprinted toward him with Will on her heels. He stopped her at the entrance.

"Down there."

Robyn strained her eyes. A small figure stood at the base of the cliff, its hands on its hips and its head tilted up toward them.

"Can he see us?" Robyn asked John.

"I don't think so. Nor do I think he's a he."

"What do you mean?" But even as she spoke, she knew. Something about the way the person stood, radiating fury, struck a familiar chord. "Midge."

"The one and only."

"How did she find us?"

"She must have been watching us. We left no trace, of that I'm sure." He watched Midge with a hint of a smile. "What would you like to do about it?"

"Do you think she knows where we are?"

"Do you really want to let her corner you when she gets up here? We haven't rigged an escape yet."

"Damn it. I just wanted to keep her safe."

"I know you did. I think, however, that you should be more worried about your own safety. I've never seen someone so small so full of hellfire."

"It isn't funny, John."

"No, it's not." He sighed, a deep echoing bellows of air that vibrated through his body into hers. "But she's here, and I don't think you should try to send her away again."

"She's still a child."

"She's not. She's old enough to starve, and she's old enough to marry. She's no more a child than you are."

For the first time she thought about how she would have felt if it had been Michael in the woods, telling her to stay home while he risked his life to care for their family.

"Damn it," she said, and set off down the slope.

Midge greeted her with balled fists and a punch to the shoulder, followed by a wordless scream that hissed out between her clenched teeth. Robyn covered her head with her arms and let her cousin vent her fury, surprised, as ever, by her strength.

"Welcome back," she said when Midge had spent the worst of her ire.

Midge pointed a trembling finger at Robyn, and her lips worked soundlessly as she struggled to find words to express the depths of her outrage. Eventually she gave up and settled for a glower.

"You know I was just trying to protect you."

Midge's glare deepened.

"I'm sorry, cos."

"Send me away again and I'll stab you in your sleep."

"Fair enough."

"Did you know Siward raided Papplewick?"

"What?"

"Shot one of Eric's sons. He might live. They stole some of our grain, too. What were you saying about keeping me safe?"

"I—"

"My father sends his greetings."

"Does he know where you are?"

"Sent me here actually. Thinks I'm safer with you, not that you care. What's this place?"

"New camp."

"Is John here?"

"Yes."

"Good." She pushed past Robyn, her pack absurdly large on her small frame, and made her way up to the cleft. Robyn watched her climb while her mind reeled. She settled on the only thing she could process without a drink. Regardless of the sheriff, Siward had to go.

Chapter Thirty-Four

Marian delayed until the rest of the household had gone to bed before approaching Emmeline.

"My lady," she said, hesitating as she folded Emmeline's gown. "There is something I need to tell you."

Emmeline looked up from the piece of embroidery she'd been staring at for the better part of the evening without working on. "Yes?"

"It's about Willa. Well, more than Willa." She'd waited half of the summer to get these lies off her chest, but now that the moment had arrived, she couldn't find the words.

"Has there been some news?"

"Not exactly." Marian took a deep breath. "The outlaw that I told you about, Robyn, is a woman." Emmeline frowned, but Marian pushed on. "I sent Willa and Alanna to her."

Emmeline's embroidery clattered to the floor. "Willa's alive?"

"She ordered me not to tell you where she was. I swear to you, my lady, that we wanted to, but Willa did not wish to put you in a position where you had to choose between her and the crown." Rarely had Marian seen Emmeline angry, and fear curdled on her tongue. She dropped to her knees and pressed her forehead into Emmeline's empty hands. "Please don't dismiss me."

"Dismiss you?"

"I cannot go back to my father."

"It is not you I am angry with, though you should have told me."

Marian didn't dare raise her head.

Emmeline stood, forcing Marian to edge out of her way, and paced the room. "I should have anticipated this. She always did like to play at being her brother. But it's folly, running off to Sherwood. What will she do in the winter? And she doesn't have the training to stand against a real opponent."

"I told her we'd meet them in three days' time at the priory—"

"My sister, my closest friend, and my handmaid," said Emmeline, shaking her head. "I don't suppose you've had word from my husband? Has he taken a new wife and turned from me as well?"

"Emmeline—"

"Very well. We'll go to the priory. You I shall forgive, for I don't see what other choice you could have made, but my sister is another matter."

"Forgive me, my lady, but Willa invoked sanctuary."

"Which ended when she left the church. Tuck does what she wants and damns the consequences. She always has. Have I not been made to worry enough? The Lord knows I have a husband at war and tithes to pay before the winter, which is trial enough for any woman."

"I am so sorry."

"Not as sorry as my sister shall be."

Marian lay down to sleep some time later, replaying the evening in her mind. Emmeline now knew all the truth save for the one Marian held close to her chest in the darkness: the kiss she'd given Robyn beneath the trees. It did not matter if Willa had seen. Willa was equally guilty of this sin, and unlikely to reveal it so long as she depended on Marian to keep her own secret. Lady Emmeline, however, might draw the line at this last aberration.

That did not stop her body from aching for the outlaw's touch.

Robyn was not the first person she'd kissed. There had been boys before that, and a few girls. She and her cousins had taken turns playing at husband before Sara's marriage, and Chelsea, the cook's girl, had taken a liking to her one summer before she'd died giving birth to twins. There had been no harm in kissing

265

girls as a child, for nothing could come of it, and besides, everyone knew that women needed stimulation to prevent suffocation of the womb. Unmarried women could seek out a midwife to do the job for them until they could find a husband. If she mentioned her feelings to Emmeline, that would be her suggestion. Find a midwife, get the lust out of her system, and return to her senses.

The real sin was not the kiss in itself, though that was a sin of the flesh once a girl flowered. No—the sin she'd be called to penance for came from desiring a woman more than she desired a man. She'd be shamed, publicly and privately, and she did not want to think about what kind of man her father would find to take her if the depth of her depravity was known.

But nothing about Robyn felt depraved. Marian smiled into her pillow, glad for the summer heat that prevented her from sharing Emmeline's bed. She remembered how Robyn's lips had felt beneath her own. She deepened the kiss in her recollection, burying imaginary hands in Robyn's hair and wondering what it would be like to lie beside Robyn, not as she lay beside Emmeline each night, but as a lover might, their bodies and fingers intertwined and Robyn's heart beating in time with hers.

Chapter Thirty-Five

The priory walls loomed through the morning mist. John and Robyn paused at the tree line, Midge, Alanna, and Will on their heels. Robyn had managed to convince Tom and Lisbet to stay behind and keep an eye on the camp, but Midge had flat-out refused to follow a single order since her arrival unless it came from John.

"This is as good a place as any to wait," he said, looking at Robyn for confirmation. "We've a clear shot of the road, we're close to the priory, and the trees offer good cover."

Robyn nodded and reflected, not for the first time that morning, on how easily Marian had swayed her away from her decision to bid her farewell. One kiss. That was the price of her resolve.

They'd chosen a stand of oak. She began to climb the nearest one, her boots scuffing against the bark. She paused at the second split and settled into the crotch to check the forest floor below for visibility. Most people didn't look up, but it only took one aberration.

Leaves obscured most of the view. Someone standing right at the trunk might glimpse her, but farther out the view was blocked by leaves and clusters of green acorns, save for an opening that looked out over the priory wall into a garden. Candles burned in some of the windows. Robyn watched the flames until the bell tolled for morning prayer.

Waiting in trees had little to recommend it. Her back stiffened over the course of the next few hours, and the occupants of the priory did little save weed between the cabbages. She had almost given up on Marian when the distant sound of hoofbeats floated through the still midsummer air. She could hear the voices of the riders as they dismounted.

"Lady Emmeline."

"I've come to see my sister."

"Sister Tuck is brewing, but I can fetch her."

"Thank you, Magdalena. We'll see to the horses ourselves."

"Very good, my lady."

Robyn rubbed the blood back into her legs and waited for the sound of the gate opening and shutting before edging further down the tree. They had agreed that only one of them would approach the nuns at first, in case Marian had brought unwanted company. Of the five of them, Robyn was the least recognizable, save for Midge, but Robyn had drawn the line at her cousin's participation in this part of the plan. The sheriff only wanted Robyn, and they needed Midge to remain undetected for as long as possible in case they needed to get a message to someone in Nottingham.

She landed on thick loam. Generations of leaves had fallen and moldered around the roots, aerated by the foraging noses of swine and squirrels. The soil absorbed the impact and muffled the sound. None of the distant peasants looked up from their toil, and Robyn walked across the narrow strip of green to the small side gate in the priory wall.

An older nun answered her knock.

"May I help you?" She looked down a long and somewhat pointed red nose at Robyn.

"I'm here to see the prioress."

"I am afraid the Reverend Mother is receiving visitors at the moment."

"Will you let Marian know that her friend is here to speak with her, then? She is expecting me."

"This is a convent. Not a place for trysts, young man."

"My business is entirely platonic." Robyn decided that the sister must be nearsighted, for she squinted at Robyn with watery eyes.

"We'll see about that. Wait here." She shut the door in Robyn's face, leaving her alone with the same goat that had greeted her and John on their last visit.

"Where did you come from?" she asked the animal as she scratched it between its horns. It belched appreciatively and leaned into her.

Standing in the open, even with the shade of the wall shielding her from sight, made Robyn's skin crawl. The dirt around the gate had been packed down by visitors, and she resisted the urge to look over her shoulder every few seconds in case more visitors showed up—visitors whose eyes were not as weak as the sister who had greeted her and who might recognize the fletcher from Nottingham. Her fingers itched for an arrow.

The door swung open. "Well met, my young friend," said Tuck. Robyn braced herself against the almost palpable sense of well-being that radiated from the nun.

"Reverend Mother."

"Did you come alone? My sister is most anxious to speak with the Lady Willa."

"Did the Lady Emmeline come alone?"

"Her man-at-arms is in the stable, but Marian is within, pretending she didn't just hear my beloved sister damn me to the seven hells."

"Then it is a good thing you have already pledged yourself to the Lord."

"Indeed. Call your friends. They will come to no harm here. You have my word, and I know Gwyneth is anxious to see you."

"And I her."

Robyn whistled. Will was the first to drop from her tree, followed by John, Alanna, and Midge.

"My good friend blacksmith," Tuck said as she clapped John on the shoulder. "Good to have you back. And who is this?" She surveyed Midge.

"An introduction I would be happy to make inside if it pleases you," said Robyn.

Tuck stepped back to make way for the group. Robyn ducked past the larger woman and let out a breath when the door shut behind them. Inside, the buzz of bees in the kitchen garden droned out the shouts from distant laborers, and Robyn inhaled the scent of fresh herbs.

"I'm Midge," said Midge.

"Reverend Mother. Tuck, if you will. Come this way. And John, I've a bit of mending that needs seeing to before you go."

"Reverend Mother," he said, offering her a slight bow.

"She's like a bear," Midge whispered to Robyn, momentarily forgetting her anger. "Her thigh is as big around as I am."

"She's a man-crusher," Robyn agreed. "I think you'll be safe, though."

"I wouldn't be so sure." Will leaned in so that only Robyn could hear her. "I overheard some queer things about the sister while I was here."

"Like what?"

"Things." Will smirked.

Robyn contemplated pressing the issue, but decided against it as Tuck led them along the cloisters. Their footsteps echoed faintly in the covered walkway surrounding the courtyard. A few vines climbed up the pillars, bobbing in the morning breeze. John ran his hand along the stone as they walked.

"Solid work," he said.

"We could use a mason."

"That, alas, I am not."

Tuck shrugged and led them onward. A nun on her knees pulling weeds looked up curiously as they passed her. A scar marred her face, mottling the skin and lifting the edge of her mouth. A burn, perhaps, most likely from hot oil. Robyn gave her a slight nod. The girl had probably been deemed unmarriageable and her dowry gifted to the convent in exchange for taking her off her family's hands. In place of motherhood, she'd learn how to read and write and would probably live a significantly longer life than her married peers. Robyn wondered if she considered herself lucky. *If only Marian had ended up in a place like this.* The fantasy flitted briefly through her head. Out here things were possible. She could scale the convent wall and visit Marian in the garden or meet her as she harvested mushrooms on the forest paths. No husband would demand her attention and her time and her body.

She hardly noticed the interior of the priory as they passed through it. Stone walls and stone floors, filled with the low murmur of women's voices. She might have found it soothing in another frame of mind.

"And here we are," said Tuck, waving them through another doorway and into the priory parlor. "Allow me to introduce you to my sister, the Lady Emmeline of Harcourt."

A tall blond woman rose to her feet and wrapped Will in a tight embrace. Robyn moved out of her way just in time and came to a halt beside Marian.

"Consider yourself lucky that you missed our initial welcome," Marian whispered. "My lady nearly flayed her sister with her tongue."

Emmeline still had Will in her grasp. Robyn couldn't hear the words the lady murmured into Will's ear, but she saw the emotion contorting Will's face and looked away. John and Midge hovered behind Tuck in the doorway, equally unsure of how to handle this display of affection, while Alanna chatted with Tuck.

"I don't know," said Robyn. "That sounds like something I might have liked to see."

"I swear dust came out of the mortar. I thought the walls might come down."

"That would have been a pity."

"Indeed. You would never have gotten to meet my lady."

"Or seen you again."

"Would that grieve you?"

"Marian," Robyn started to say, but Emmeline had turned to them.

The proper thing to do when confronted with nobility was a

display of deference. Robyn froze, torn between a curtsy and a bow, until the moment had passed and her indecision translated to defiance. "M'lady," she said, accepting her fate.

"I owe you a debt, it seems. Twice now you have rescued friends of mine from harm."

"Anyone in our position would have done the same," Robyn said, but it was a lie and they all knew it. "This is John, and my cousin, Midge."

"I am glad to meet you all. Sister, will you bring us some of the mead you are so fond of?"

Tuck leaned her head out of the door and called out for another nun. Emmeline's lips pressed together in a thin line, and Robyn had a suspicion she had been hoping Tuck would fetch the mead herself.

"I've sent for a flagon," Tuck said. "This is the house of God, Emmy, not Harcourt."

"And you do make such a lovely bride of Christ. The Lord must be ever so pleased with your . . . devotion." Emmeline turned her attention back to Robyn. "Name a reward and it is yours as long as it is in my power."

"A reward?" Robyn repeated, glancing at John. A thousand wants flashed across her thoughts. Safety for Midge's family. Warm winter clothing. The sheriff's head on a pike. Marian. A place to winter, with food and fire and shelter. In other words, nothing she could reasonably request.

"My friends mean a great deal to me. I would be honored to repay you," Emmeline pressed.

Something Will had said came back to Robyn. *Outlaws with noble ties do not hang.* She wished she had a moment to talk with John and Will or even Marian, but Emmeline's cool gaze waited, and so she did the same thing she'd been doing ever since she loosed that fatal arrow: she gambled.

"My friends mean a great deal to me, too. The greatest reward I can think of would be to count you among them." She didn't dare look away from Emmeline to gauge the reactions of her companions, but the words felt right.

"Well said," said Emmeline. "And I confess I am curious about you. Should we ever get that mead, I would love to hear how a yeoman's daughter ended up in Sherwood."

"It is not a terribly interesting story, m'lady."

"Don't worry," said Marian. "Alanna will embellish it for you. She has a knack for making dragons out of housecats."

"A gift, we minstrels call it," said Alanna.

"Gwyneth, thank you," said Tuck as Gwyneth entered the room bearing a flagon and mugs on a tray. Robyn stared. Gwyneth looked different than she had when last she'd seen her: brighter, lighter even, and her eyes had lost a little of their shadow. She served in silence before greeting Midge quietly, and when Robyn offered her an uncertain smile, Gwyneth returned it.

"Your widow," said Marian in a whisper near Robyn's ear. Robyn tore her eyes away from Gwyneth to glance at Marian. Her face gave nothing away, but some of the warmth had left her gaze.

"Gwyneth," Robyn said, unsure what Marian wanted from her.

"Gwyneth." Marian repeated the name. "Yes, we've met."

For the first time, Robyn wondered if Marian was aware of her father's interest in Gwyneth.

"My father asked about her," Marian said as if reading Robyn's mind. "He said she left a quiver of arrows for you with the fletcher's guild."

"What?"

"From the fair," said Marian, as if this should be obvious.

"She didn't leave me any arrows."

Marian's brow creased.

"Did your father say anything else?" Robyn asked.

"He showed me an arrow and asked me if I thought it was yours."

"What did you say?"

"I said I didn't know." Marian still had a cold look in her eyes. "But it was yours. I recognized the fletching."

"What color were the feathers?" Robyn asked, closing her eyes as she visualized the arrow that she'd left in Clovis's chest.

"White, except for half of one."

Damn. "Did he say *anything* else?" Keeping her tone level took all her concentration. She wanted to grab Marian by the shoulders and demand that she tell her everything she knew.

"Just that I must attend a banquet on Midsummer, where I am to be paraded like a broodmare for the viscount and all of Nottingham."

Robyn knew she should have grabbed the arrow. Damn Cedric and his mercy. If she had shot him, too, she might have made a clean break. Banquets and marriages were nothing next to that.

"Robyn?" Marian reached out a tentative hand and touched the inside of her wrist, breaking her train of thought. "Is everything all right?"

"No." Nothing was all right. "He can trace that arrow back to the shop, and if he does that, he can figure out who I am."

"All this from one arrow? Didn't Gwyneth sell to other people?"

"A few maybe, but your father made it nearly impossible." At Marian's look of confusion, she hesitated. "Do you not know?"

"Do I not know what?"

"Your father wants to marry my sister-in-law, Gwyneth. That's why he had my brother hanged, and that's why I had to win the archery contest."

"Your brother?"

"Michael." She felt his name in her mouth like a memory of light. "He was hanged without a trial."

"But—"

"Your father hated him. A neighbor turned him in for poaching."

"Robyn, I am so sorry." Marian's stricken eyes met hers. "I didn't know."

"You didn't tie the noose."

Marian bit her lip. "I had two brothers. They were much older than me, and we were not close, but I loved them. They went on Crusade with Richard, and—" She broke off and swallowed, hard.

Robyn's panic receded at the pain in Marian's voice. "Then I, too, am sorry."

Neither spoke for a moment, but Robyn felt Marian's presence within the space of her grief, and the broken half of her soul trembled at the touch.

"Gwyneth is your sister-in-law?" Marian asked eventually.

"My brother's widow. Yes."

"Oh. I thought . . . it doesn't matter what I thought." She touched her lips, her dark brows furrowing in thought. "My father never told me he was courting."

"Well, he wouldn't, would he? She was born a peasant. Michael was a step up for her, but marrying your father would have been several stories. Only a fool would have turned him down. But she and my brother were in love, and I don't think either of them realized what would happen."

"My father does not like to be told no."

"No." *Though he enjoys saying it.*

Marian shook her head and exhaled sharply, as if she had been about to laugh or sob. "He would have married a peasant, and yet he won't let me join the priory or choose my suitors."

"He's not overfond of priories these days," said Robyn, remembering the fight she'd overheard between the sheriff and Tuck.

"Nor is he overfond of me. I will get the arrow for you. It might be too late, but if he keeps it in his study then I could take it. I have to go to Nottingham tomorrow anyway."

"To be paraded like a broodmare."

"Yes," said Marian, glancing up at Robyn through her lashes. Robyn's pulse quickened, and for a moment the sheriff and her errant arrow ceased to matter.

"I could meet you," Marian suggested.

"In Nottingham?"

"Why not? It will be like the fair. With the bonfires going, who would recognize you?"

"Your father."

"I could slip away."

"Marian," said Robyn, recalling the brush of her lips and forgetting that they stood in a priory surrounded by their friends. "What are you asking me?"

"Meet me outside the town gates at half past eleven tomorrow. I'll have the arrow."

"Are you asking me to meet you at the fires?" said Robyn, lowering her voice.

Marian's breath caught, and Robyn felt a flush rise in her cheeks as her own breathing grew suddenly more difficult.

"Yes."

The word sent a jolt through Robyn. Michael had courted Gwyneth at the fires, arriving home early in the morning with a smile that nearly spanned his entire face. She'd rolled her eyes then, but now all she could think about was how smooth Marian's skin would feel against her lips as she kissed her neck in the light of the bonfires, music and laughter whirling around them as the night air promised the full strength of the summer to come.

"I'll be there."

"Good," said Marian, and as they turned back to the rest of the group, she slid her hand into Robyn's, concealing the gesture behind the folds of her skirt. Robyn noted the strength in her fingers as they interlocked with hers. What was it John had said? It wasn't Marian he worried about, but the hold Marian had over Robyn? She looked around the room, noting the warmth between Will, Alanna, and Emmeline, and the way Midge stood close to John. Only Gwyneth watched Marian and Robyn. When she caught Robyn's eye, she smiled, an expression in her blue eyes Robyn couldn't read. Marian's thumb stroked the palm of her hand as Emmeline addressed them, and Robyn dropped Gwyneth's eyes to listen.

"I extend my friendship to you all, and I have no desire to see any of you hang."

"Thank you, m'lady," said Robyn.

"Furthermore, I encourage you to take advantage of the hospitality provided to you thus far by my sister. There are places a nun can go that an outlaw cannot. Willa, I am sure the prioress would be happy to send messages to me on your behalf."

"M'lady," said John, "do not put yourself at unnecessary risk."

Emmeline gave a hollow laugh. "Risk. Come the harvest, I shall have to beggar my estate to pay this ransom, leaving my son with little more than a heap of stone and a few surly peasants. My husband is gone, most likely dead, and should Prince John make an attempt at the throne I shall have to turn over the rest of my estate to his forces. Once the civil war is over, the winner will either reward me for my loyalty, or strip me of my title. I might be in need of assistance from you then, if only to put food in my son's mouth. I take no risks, John. I merely hedge my bets."

Silence followed Emmeline's words. The gentle aroma of lavender and thyme drifted up from the rushes to mingle with the beeswax from the candles. Robyn glanced at Marian, who looked troubled, and then at Tuck. The nun's expression surprised her. Tuck's face glowed with pride as she observed Emmeline, and the hope that had filled Robyn ever since they found the cleft in the rocks threatened to overflow its banks.

With friends like these they might just stand a chance.

"One more thing. Alanna, I have not dismissed you from my service. You will return to Harcourt with me. I will not hold you against your will, but I cannot excuse your absence indefinitely."

"Emmeline," said Will, her face stricken.

"I can come and go between you," Alanna said. "I've composed some new songs I'd like to try out on an audience, and Harcourt is forgiving."

"Will you sing one now?" asked Midge.

"Only if you'll accompany me."

Midge downed her mead. "But of course."

Alanna unslung her lyre from her back and cradled the instrument between her knees as she tuned the strings to her liking. When she was satisfied with the sound, she nodded at Midge, who cleared her throat. Together they sang.

"There dwelt in Sherwood an outlaw
By the name of Robyn Hood,
And he ruled beneath the branches
Of his majesty's greenwood.

Deer and fox and maiden fair
All fell before his bow,
And the sheriff cursed and the sheriff swore
He would see the thief brought low."

Robyn's hand closed around Marian's in horror. John burst into laughter, joined shortly by Tuck, and even Gwyneth smiled.

"There's more," said Midge, fixing Robyn with an evil grin.

"I don't doubt it. Tell you what. You keep singing. I'm going to get some fresh air before I give in to the overwhelming urge to strangle my favorite cousin."

"And at the faire he met a maiden fair . . ." Alanna sang, drawing out the notes for emphasis.

Robyn felt her face flame as she shook her head, unsure whether she was annoyed or amused, but positive that she did not want to listen to another word. She gave Emmeline a short bow, then withdrew her hand from Marian's and fled.

"Wait," Marian called from behind her.

Robyn paused as Marian gathered her skirt and ran after. The leather soles of her boots were almost silent on the stone. "You don't want to listen to 'The Ballad of Robyn Hood'?"

"Oh, I do," said Marian as she caught up. "But I'll ask Alanna for a private recitation."

"You wouldn't."

"How exactly do you intend to stop me?"

"I could get Alanna lost deep in the forest."

"Then I'd be forced to make up my own lyrics. It's a memorable tune, don't you think?" She hummed a few bars.

"And who exactly do you think the 'maiden fair' is supposed to be?"

"Your sweet sister-in-law. That part was obvious."

Robyn pulled her into an alcove, enjoying the feel of Marian's body close to hers as the summer breeze drifted in through the window. "Is that really what you think?" she asked.

Marian tilted her face up and searched Robyn's eyes. "Is there a reason I should think otherwise? She's quite lovely."

"Marian." Warmth spread from their clasped hands up into her chest, where it curled around her ribs and made it hard to breathe. A tendril of Marian's hair had come loose from its ribbons, slightly damp from the summer air. Something about the way it brushed Marian's cheek made the tightness in her chest grow, and she thought of the kiss they'd exchanged in the woods—brief, fleeting, but indelible. A nun passed them at a sedate pace, her eyebrows rising into her wimple as she observed how close they stood to one another.

"Is there anywhere here where . . ." she couldn't bring herself to finish her sentence, but Marian understood her meaning.

"The stable."

Robyn waited until the nun's footsteps had passed, her breathing too loud in her ears, then stepped out of the alcove. She didn't let go of Marian's hand.

"Keep up," said Marian, tossing a smile over her shoulder as she pulled Robyn along the hall to the cloisters, then through a side door and at last into the warm darkness of a long row of stalls. The smell of hay and horses washed over them.

"Isn't your guard here somewhere?"

"Gregor?" Marian called out. There was no response beyond a few curious snorts from the horses. "Last I saw he was talking with some of the villagers. It's just us and the horses."

"Which one is yours?"

"This one." Marian stroked the neck of the mare Robyn remembered from their earlier encounter in the woods. The horse twitched her ears lazily, enjoying the comfort of the stable and the hay in the manger.

"She's pretty." Robyn did not bother looking at the horse. Now that they were alone, her heart hammered, the earlier certainty of the pull between them overwhelmed by the paralyzing fear of the consequences. Their sex aside, an affair with the sheriff's daughter was suicide for them both. What am I doing? she asked herself as her eyes fell from Marian's, drawn to the girl's mouth. Her body answered the question for her. The world narrowed to the full curve of Marian's lips and the slight dimple in one cheek

279

when she smiled. Her boots had rooted themselves to the stable floor. In the stable's dim lighting, Marian looked older, no longer a girl but a woman capable of things Robyn had only allowed herself to imagine late at night as she stood watch, boredom and solitude breaking down the inhibitions she might have felt during the day. She didn't look like the sheriff's daughter, here. She looked . . . she looked like the answer to a question Robyn had been asking herself her whole life.

Marian's hand fell from the mare's shoulder. Robyn watched, transfixed, as she reached out. Her fingers brushed Robyn's neck, and then Marian's lips pressed against hers with a fierceness that belied the lightness of her touch. Robyn caught herself on the wood of the stall as Marian fell against her, her lips obliterating conscious thought. The mare gave a startled snort behind them. Her mouth moved against Marian's and responded to the intensity of the kiss with a power that left her shaking. She wrapped her arms around Marian's waist, feeling the other woman's breath come just as quickly as her own. Marian's fingers buried themselves in Robyn's hair, eliminating any possibility of coming up for air, and Robyn pulled her closer still and gave in to the demands of lips and tongue.

Marian whimpered as Robyn pressed her up against the wall with her hips. The sound undid Robyn. She pulled her lips away, eliciting a gasp of frustration that turned into a soft moan as Robyn kissed the curve of her jaw and down the smooth skin of her neck. Marian's breath came quick and hot in her ear, and she tightened her grip on Robyn's hair as Robyn reached the base of her neck.

"Oh, God," Marian cried out. The words vibrated in Robyn's ear.

The resulting ripple of desire nearly blinded her. Marian's skin tasted like sunshine and clean sweat, sweet and warm and with a hint of rosewater. She could kiss that skin all day. Nothing else mattered. Not the sheriff, not the precariousness of their position, and certainly not their half-baked plan to take down Siward.

The sound of a distant door shutting threatened to shatter this illusion. Marian turned her head toward the door, still in Robyn's arms, and Robyn's lips brushed her ear. Marian shivered and nestled deeper into her embrace as the sanctuary of the stable remained undisturbed. "I need you, Marian," Robyn murmured. Her lips found the hollow above Marian's collarbone, then the swell of breast beneath it, and she would have gladly followed that course if John hadn't cleared his throat loudly from behind her.

She whipped around, blocking a disheveled Marian from view, and prayed her glare would turn her friend into a pillar of ash. It didn't. John crossed his arms over his broad chest and smiled widely.

"I came to check on a horse," he said.

"I hope it kicks you."

"There's a trough of cold water in the yard. You might consider dunking yourself," John offered. "And the lady."

Robyn wished John would stop smiling. The satisfaction in his grin only highlighted Robyn's own frustration, and while a part of her was dimly aware that she should be grateful it was John who had walked in on them and not a nun or Emmeline, that part was very small and not inclined to argue.

"Give us a moment," she said.

"You don't have a moment. Emmeline's man-at-arms is on his way."

"I should have drowned you in the stream the day I met you," she said.

"You could have tried. Oh, and you have straw in your hair, Robyn Hood."

Robyn cursed as she ran her hands through her hair. Marian had restored order to her own clothing, although her cheeks were flushed and her eyes glowed. Robyn paused, caught by the desire to kiss her again even with John watching.

"Gwyneth wanted to talk to you," John added when Robyn had collected herself as best she could. "And Emmeline was asking after you, Marian."

"Let us go, then," said Marian, and she tucked her hand into the crook of Robyn's arm with more dignity than Robyn could have dreamed possible. She let Marian tow her out of the stable and tried to keep her own face composed; her lips, however, kept curving upward, and she wanted to run like a child through the priory halls, shouting at the top of her lungs with the joy threatening to burst out of her like a summer storm.

Robyn joined Midge, John, and Gwyneth when she and Marian returned, leaving Marian to Lady Emmeline and company.

"I will make you listen to the entire song one day," Midge said. "You can't run forever."

"My legs are twice as long as yours. All I have to do is keep out of your range."

"Not if I tie you to a tree."

"You'd still have to catch me, first."

"Oh, I wouldn't need to do that. John?"

"Sorry, Robyn. I'm going to have to side with your cousin on this one. And I am faster than you."

"Traitor. I will promise to plug my ears with wax."

"Not until you've heard the verse about you and 'Little John.'"

Robyn shook her head in defeat and turned to Gwyneth. "Have you forsaken me, too?"

Gwyneth put her hands on her hips and looked Robyn up and down, her eyes lingering on Robyn's clothes. "You look so much like your brother," she said. The change in subject shifted the climate of the group, but Gwyneth didn't seem to notice. Her eyes shimmered with unshed tears. "I have something for you."

She left the room, leaving Robyn sober and silent, and returned with a long, thin parcel wrapped in supple leather. Robyn recognized the shape. Her hands shook as she accepted the gift and removed the wrappings to reveal a bow.

The wood gleamed, polished smooth by familiar hands and waxed with beeswax from her uncle's hives. She stood the longbow on one end of its stave and ran her index finger down it, memories of her brother overwhelming her. This was one of his bows, carved by his hands and tested with his arm. Robyn blinked past the sudden prickling in her eyes. *Let them fly, little bird,* she heard him say from the depths of her memory. The grip warmed to her palm, a perfect curve, strong, powerful like Michael's shoulders had been and supple as the muscles she had prodded with curiosity as a child, jealous that her own body did not have his shape.

"Thank you," she said past the lump in her throat. Gwyneth closed the space between them and placed her small hand over Robyn's.

"It's a heavier draw than yours, but it will shoot farther. Michael was making it for you. I finished it."

The lump in her throat grew into an ache that filled her lungs. *Michael.* She put her other hand over Gwyneth's. Midge, too, stepped closer, wrapping her arm around both of their waists as they stared at the bow between them. John kept a discreet distance.

"It's . . ." She wanted to tell Gwyneth how perfect it was, and how much she had needed it, but her tongue refused to form the words. She felt Michael's love in the smooth grain of the wood, and now that she looked she noticed that this wood bore a higher polish than their usual stock. She pictured Gwyneth rubbing it with an oiled rag by the fire while Robyn was hunting, using some of her carefully hoarded strength to finish the gift her husband had started.

"I miss him," she said instead. "I miss him so much, Gwyn."

Gwyneth pulled her hands free from Robyn's and embraced her, resting her head on Robyn's chest. Midge joined her. Robyn looked down at their heads, one blond, one brown, both precious. Her family. She held them tightly to her. Lying to Gwyneth and pushing Midge away had been a mistake. These were her people, and the things that had happened to them were none of their faults. Taking the blame for their circumstances onto her own shoulders wouldn't change that. There was only one person to blame for the pain the three of them carried, and she would make him pay for their tears in blood.

Chapter Thirty-Six

Midsummer dawned with clear skies and a hot bath. Soaking was a rare privilege, and if Marian submerged her head in the copper tub so that only her nose and mouth remained above the surface, she could tune out the sounds of the maid fussing over her gown in the next room and think about what lay ahead.

Tonight, after the banquet and the dancing and the inevitable suitors, she would see Robyn. Her body thrilled at the thought. She had been able to think of little else since she'd left the priory with Emmeline and Alanna. Every time she closed her eyes she felt Robyn's mouth on her skin, and her fingers remembered the feel of Robyn's hair tangled between them. Beneath the water, she ran her hand over her ribs and across her breasts, trembling as her palms brushed her taut nipples.

"Marian?" Alanna said.

Marian emerged from the water with a splash, spraying Alanna.

"Sorry if I startled you," Alanna said, holding her hands up to ward off more water. "Emmeline told me to bring you some of her bath oil."

Marian hoped the heat from the water explained the flush in her cheeks and accepted the bottle. Alanna turned to go.

"Wait."

The tub had been drawn in the small bathing room in Emmeline's quarters in Nottingham castle. The stone made each splash echo, and she sat in the copper tub with her knees drawn up to her chest as Alanna leaned against the wall. Alanna had bathed earlier, and her dark hair was still damp in its braid.

"Want me to wash your hair?" Alanna offered.

"That would be nice," said Marian, though that was not why she had asked Alanna to stay. She relaxed as Alanna rubbed the oil into her hair, her nimble minstrel's fingers massaging her scalp.

"Have I told you how much I missed you?" she said.

Alanna laughed. "You could have asked a maid to do this for you."

"It wouldn't be the same."

"True. I do have a gift." Her hands worked on a knot at the base of Marian's skull. "Can I ask you something, Mare?"

"As long as you keep doing that."

"Robyn."

Marian opened her eyes. "Robyn?"

"I'm a minstrel. I watch people and make up songs about them for a living."

Marian hummed the opening bars of "The Ballad of Robyn Hood."

"Are you sure you know what you're doing?"

"I'm taking a bath."

"Are you sure you know what you're doing with Robyn?" Alanna sluiced water over Marian's head to rinse out the oil, giving her a moment to think about her answer.

Her body knew what it was doing—or at least what it wanted. She'd been trying very hard not to think beyond that, because the answer to the question was a resounding *no*. Robyn was not just a woman. She was an outlaw, and not even just any outlaw. She was an outlaw who had stolen directly from the sheriff of Nottingham, which made her the last person in the world Marian should entangle herself with. She raised her shoulders in a helpless shrug.

"I didn't think so," said Alanna. "Here." She pushed Marian's hair over one of her shoulders and poured a handful of oil onto Marian's skin, rubbing it in deftly. Her touch was intimate and comforting, and it occurred to Marian that she'd never thought of Alanna as anything other than a friend, for all that they both desired women. There was so much she didn't understand about this new part of herself.

"I can't help it," she said. "I didn't mean for it to happen, but when I see her, I—"

Alanna squeezed her shoulder. "I understand."

"How did you know, with Willa?"

"I didn't at first. Remember when she kept getting those horrible spots?"

"She even had them on her rear. I remember her complaining about them to Emmeline."

"That's when I knew."

"Really?" Marian turned in the tub to give Alanna a look of horror. "But she was hideous."

"Willa of Maunnesfeld has never been 'hideous' a day in her life."

Marian sighed, partly in jealously, partly in amusement. "You don't need to remind me. Do you know what my father said when she went missing? 'At least she won't outshine you anymore.' Or something like that."

"During her spotty phase, I found her crying on the stairs because her brother wouldn't let her borrow his sword. She shouted at me to leave her alone."

"That sounds like Willa."

"And that's when I knew."

"That she was a terror?"

"That I could never leave her alone."

"You fell in love with Willa because she yelled at you?"

"I fell in love with Willa because she's not afraid."

"Not because she's beautiful?" Marian asked, raising an eyebrow.

"There are lots of beautiful women, and all women are beautiful in their own way. Even I."

"Alanna," said Marian. She'd never heard Alanna talk about herself like this, and it twisted her gut.

286

"I have my voice. Willa has her will. And you, my love," Alanna said, taking Marian's chin in her hand and shaking it gently, "are a little bit like her."

"I am not like Willa."

"You're not willful? You don't act on impulse? You don't fall for the one person in the entire world you shouldn't?"

Her words were so close to Marian's own thoughts that she almost questioned whether Alanna had spoken them aloud.

"I haven't fallen for anyone," she said, but lying to one of her closest friends, while naked, was significantly harder than lying to herself.

Alanna's lips quirked in amusement. "Well, you did fall off your horse. I'm working on a song about that bit, but I think I'll leave out the hornets."

"Probably for the best. I'm not sure what rhymes with *grotesque*."

"*Statuesque?*"

"My point exactly."

"I just want you to be careful, Mare. Your father wants her dead. You know that."

Which reminded her that she needed to steal the arrow from his house. She didn't have a plan for that, yet. She'd been too caught up in the prospect of seeing Robyn again.

"My father wants a lot of things."

"Your father is the sheriff of Nottingham. Unlike the rest of us, he can get what he wants."

"Then what do you think I should do?"

"I don't know. Just tread carefully."

"She's coming here tonight."

Alanna listened while Marian explained about the arrow and its implications.

"You could have just burned it," Alanna said when she finished. "There's no real reason for her to meet you here."

"I know." The bathwater had grown cold, and goose bumps erupted on her skin. "I just . . . It's Midsummer. The viscount wants to marry me soon, and I just want something that is mine before it is too late." She hated the hot tears that pricked her eyes.

"You want Robyn."

"Yes."

"Well, if she agreed to come, then she's as much a fool as you. Luckily," she added, holding out a towel for Marian, "you have me. I'll help you get out of the castle."

The rest of the day dragged on. The feast day, in theory, was in honor of Saint John the Baptist, but saints were far from Marian's thoughts as she sat through multiple courses of food and drink at Emmeline's side. She felt her father's eyes on her throughout the afternoon, and periodically men asked her to dance in increasingly drunken revels. Flushed from wine, she didn't even mind, and laughed at their jokes as her mind conjured images of Robyn. Even the viscount couldn't spoil her mood; she let him paw at her through three consecutive dances before breaking away.

Then, toward evening, a terrible thought struck her. What if Robyn didn't come? What if she thought better of her decision and realized how foolhardy it was to set foot in Nottingham? She set down her goblet and stared at the crowded banquet hall, fear making the laughter raucous and the music shrill. Robyn would come. She'd promised. Her unease offended Sir Horace, who left her in a huff when she failed to respond to his question three times in a row. She felt her father's disapproving gaze as the knight stalked off.

"Marian?" asked Emmeline, taking Horace's place at her side. "Are you all right?"

"I'm fine. I just think I need some air." She pushed herself away from the table and stumbled toward the doors and away from her friend. Her feet felt too light and her head too heavy. I drank too much, she realized, leaning against a wall to catch her breath. Servants passed her carrying still more trays of food. Boar, deer, rabbit, duck, pheasant, cabbage, pies, pastries, tarts, sugared carrots, bowls of peas and baby onions, anything and everything available this time of year.

I can't stay here a moment longer.

She knew she should go back and tell Emmeline and Alanna that she was leaving and, more importantly, make some excuse to her father, but her feet carried her down the corridors and out of the castle.

Nottingham, too, celebrated. The streets were packed, and she was jostled with every step, the hem of her gown muddied and her skirt stained from brushing past dogs and sheep and dirty children. None of that mattered. She let herself into her father's house and shut the door behind her, breathing heavily.

No one stirred. Even the housekeeper seemed to be out celebrating, an image she amused herself with for a moment before climbing the stairs to her father's study. The handle of the door was cool beneath her hand. She pushed it open, bracing herself for a shout, but it too was empty, and the room smelled of leather and parchment and wax. The door shut behind her with a comforting click as the latch fell into place.

She'd never been allowed into her father's study alone. Here he did the king's business, and the king's business was far too important for girls to meddle in. She touched the wood of the desk with the tip of her finger. Solid. Imposing. Furniture trying to assert its influence on the room. Her giggle took her by surprise. She clapped a hand to her mouth and looked around her, terrified someone might have heard, before she reminded herself that the house was empty. Get hold of yourself, she thought.

Drawers, shelves, cabinets, and chests lined the walls. Marian searched them all. Most of them contained papers: warrants, accounts, and lists she could barely read, for her father hadn't thought it necessary for her to learn her letters. Emmeline had taught her what little she knew. *Shipments.* She recognized that word and paused, perusing a list that only made partial sense to her, and pocketed it. Perhaps it would help Robyn.

There was a pile of warrants on his desk, too, held down by a carved figurine of a wolf. She moved it to one side and the picture on the first sheaf drew her attention. The artist had clearly never seen his subject. He'd kept his lines vague, relying on shadow to convey the ominous effect of the broadsheet. Marian read the words as ice settled in her belly.

Wanted: The man calling himself Robyn Hood.
Reward 10£, dead or alive.
5£ for his associates.

She stared at the parchment until her eyes watered. The likeness was poor. That wouldn't matter. Ten pounds was more than most people could hope to make in four years. Bounty hunters would seize upon this opportunity like hounds to the chase, and there was nothing Marian could do to stop them except warn Robyn before these pages were posted all over the shire.

Suddenly the arrow didn't matter. It never had. Her father was determined to see Robyn hanged, regardless of her identity. One more piece of evidence wasn't going to make a difference. The important thing was warning Robyn. She took one of the drawings and folded it carefully into her belt, then stared around the office.

Her eyes fell on the locked chest in the cabinet. She hadn't looked in there for the arrow, but she knew what it contained: her dowry. A mad urge struck her. Dowries were intended as incentive and security. Her children would inherit her wealth, but if her husband died, or if she could prove grievous mistreatment, she could fall back on her dowry. She willed her mind to tell her where he'd hidden the key. He didn't keep it on his person. She remembered that; it was somewhere in here. Somewhere her mother wouldn't have approved of, he'd said.

This time, she didn't bother trying to put things back where she'd found them. She tore apart his office, pulling scrolls and books off the shelves and searching behind them and inside them. Nothing. Outside, the town crier called the hour: eleven. Robyn might be here any minute, risking her life because Marian was a selfish fool.

The tax records.

Her heart leapt as she pulled the large book out of its drawer and turned the pages. Lords, ladies, knights, landowners, guildsmen—even land-owning peasants paid taxes, and their names and the amount they paid and owed were all here.

At the back, sewn into a tiny pocket in the binding, she found the key. It felt cool and heavy in the palm of her hand. She stroked the tarnished silver and fitted it into the chest's lock, easing the lid open. A bolt of silk lay on top of the contents. Blue, of course, but finer than anything she'd ever worn. Nestled underneath it sat two silver goblets, a strand of pearls, and her mother's golden ring. She touched each and wondered how they measured up to her worth.

The other object in the chest was a leather purse. The leather was old and cracked, but the coin inside gleamed. She raised a hand to her mouth in awe. How many pounds sat in her hand? Ten? Twenty?

A door slammed downstairs, interrupting her count. She clutched the purse to her breast and shut the chest, forcing herself to walk, not run, to the study door and lift the latch.

"Come here, you," said a gruff male voice. Marian nearly shrieked before she realized the command was not aimed at her, but at the housekeeper, who laughed almost girlishly. The laughter subsided into a series of grunts and sucking noises that let Marian know exactly what was going on. She eased herself down the staircase one step at a time, praying that the couple was too engrossed in their activities to notice her as she dashed across the landing and flung herself out the door.

Twilight still colored the sky, faint purple and gold wreathing the clouds above the thatched roofs of Nottingham. She shoved the purse and the key into her belt and melted into the crowds.

Chapter Thirty-Seven

Robyn waited by the gate, far enough away that the gate guard paid little attention to her, but close enough that she could keep an eye on traffic. Her hood shadowed her face and no one seemed to pay her any heed at all, not even the stray dogs. She'd walked past church processions and plays and fires of wood and bone, nodding when someone offered her food or drink, smiling when necessary, all the while knowing she shouldn't have come. That didn't stop her heart from leaping each time she saw a half-familiar woman turn toward her. Her frustration grew each time it wasn't Marian. A group of boys raced by her, rolling a giant wheel and screaming with glee as they sped off down the sloping hill toward the town below. She stepped out of the way, and when she looked back up at the gate, she saw her.

Robyn didn't know much about fabric. Noblewomen wore too many layers; tunics and breeches were good enough for Robyn. Seeing Marian forced her to reassess her opinion. The blue and gold gown clung to her hips, and while she found the sleeves ridiculously long, her eyes caught on the expanse of skin revealed by the gown's open neck. Marian looked over her shoulder behind her toward the gate, and Robyn noted that she was not the only one fascinated by the ringlets cascading down her back. A group of young men paused to stare. One of them nudged the other, but Robyn crossed the distance between them before he could get any ideas.

"Shouldn't you be at the castle, parading yourself in front of a more refined line of drooling boors?" she asked, slipping her arm through Marian's.

"And shouldn't you be in the forest, chasing down slavering boars?"

"Usually it is the boar chasing me."

"A sentiment I couldn't agree with more. Can we get out of here?"

The flush across Marian's cheeks highlighted the brightness of her eyes, and it took Robyn several heartbeats to formulate a response. "We can go anywhere you like."

"How about there?" Marian pointed to a distant hill where a line of fires lit the evening sky.

"Isn't that a bit far?"

"We can't get far enough away from here," said Marian, leaning into Robyn as she pulled her down the hill. "Have you had anything to drink?"

"I crossed a stream on my way here."

Marian raised a brow, looking up at Robyn through her lashes in a way that made the temperature of the night air rise several degrees.

"Then let me buy you a drink."

"I don't need—" she began, but Marian pressed a finger to Robyn's lips and halted in front of an alewife with a ready cask, paying the woman extra for a drinking horn.

"Yes, you do. Now drink."

Drinking was a bad idea if she wanted to keep her wits about her. This was Nottingham. Everyone watched everyone else, and it would take just one pair of eyes and a shout to summon the sheriff's men at a run. Marian lifted the horn to Robyn's lips and waited, a challenge in her light brown eyes.

Robyn placed her hands over Marian's and drank deeply. The ale slid down her throat and went straight to her head, reminding her that she hadn't had enough to eat today, then burying that realization with a rush of confidence she recognized as idiocy and didn't care. Marian took her arm again and looped it around her waist, her fingers still entwined with Robyn's.

293

"What if someone sees you?" Robyn asked. In her court clothes, Marian stood out. Even if she wasn't recognized as the sheriff's daughter, it was clear to anyone still half sober that she didn't belong with Robyn.

"Let them."

Unlike Midge and Gwyneth, Marian was nearly as tall as Robyn. She didn't have to shorten her stride to keep pace, and before long they had passed out of the press around the city gates and down the comparatively empty road. Marian sighed in the silence.

"Was it that bad?"

"The food was fine, and I suppose the music was enjoyable," Marian said. "I danced with enough men to please my father, as my toes can attest to."

Robyn's jaw clenched at the idea of men dancing with Marian. There wasn't a man alive worthy of that honor.

"But I don't want to think about that," Marian continued.

"You don't have to." Robyn could do that for her. Visions of handsome men with groping hands seethed behind her eyelids.

"Tell me something about you. Did anyone ever ask you for your hand?" asked Marian.

"Just one."

"Did you like him?"

"He was sweet, I suppose. Shy. He bought my arrows even when your father didn't want him to." *And he saved my life.*

"You didn't answer my question."

"I'm sure he'll make someone else a good husband."

"Robyn Hood," said Marian, stepping in front of her to block her path. Robyn's arm still held her, and she could smell the sweet wine on Marian's breath.

"Of course I didn't like him. Not in the way you mean."

"Was that so hard?"

What was hard was refraining from kissing her in the middle of the road.

"What about you? Did you ever fancy anyone?" Robyn asked,

buying herself time to catch her breath. The memory of their last kiss hung heavy in the air between them.

"There was a squire I was sweet on when I was nine, but I think I just liked his horse. Your turn."

"My turn for what?"

"Have you ever been in love with anyone?"

"That's not fair," said Robyn. "There's a big difference between fancying someone and being in love."

"Love, lust, a silly crush—take your pick."

"I don't know. My brother always had girls around him. His brain stopped working the minute one smiled at him, and I promised myself I wouldn't ever be like that." A promise she'd broken the first time Marian had looked at her, once the swelling from the hornets went down.

"Men," Marian scoffed.

"And then there was always so much work to do, and I had Michael and Gwyneth and the sheriff to worry about."

"What about Gwyneth?"

"What about her?"

Marian pulled back a half step. "Did you ever have feelings for her?"

"She's my brother's wife."

"You do not answer my question."

"Gwyneth . . ." Robyn took a deep breath, unsure what Marian wanted to hear and equally unsure of her answer. "It's possible, I guess. In a dumb, young, silly way. She knows how I am, and she's never judged me for that. Of course I love her, but it's different. She's my sister."

"She's beautiful."

"Not as beautiful as you."

Marian smiled. "Then you're blind."

"I can see very well."

"Even in the dark?"

"Is it dark?" Robyn gently pulled Marian back to her, ignoring the whistle of a man leading a laden donkey toward the city.

"Because I see you everywhere." The words felt thick in her throat and she didn't recognize her roughened voice.

Marian bit her lip and stared at Robyn out of darkened eyes, moonlight illuminating the perfect arch of her brows and the shadows of her lashes. A distant pipe played a familiar tune as a group of revelers made their way up the road. Robyn had heard that tune at festivals for as long as she could remember. Usually she hated the song. It was about a lord and a shepherdess and didn't mention the fact that the lord probably left the woman with a bastard child to care for when he returned to his castle and his wife, but without the words it had a pleasing lilt. She just wished Marian would say something so that she felt less like a fool for standing there on the road with her heart exposed between them.

Instead, Marian kissed her. Her lips pressed against Robyn's with an intensity that knocked her off balance. She caught herself as her body responded, opening to Marian without a shred of resistance, and she reeled when Marian pulled away.

"Let's get off the road," said Marian.

Robyn nodded, still dumbstruck, and followed Marian into a field occupied by a herd of grazing sheep. The music grew louder, accompanied by torchlight and the high, excited voices of dancing children.

"Dance with me?" Marian asked.

"What if I step on your toes?"

"I don't care."

Marian laced her fingers through Robyn's and pulled her into the quick step of the jig. The last time Robyn had danced with anyone had been with Midge; this was different. Marian moved with a careless grace that took Robyn's breath. Dancing with her was easy, and she couldn't have stopped the smile from spreading across her face if she had wanted to.

"Is this how you dance up at your castle?" she asked as Marian twirled away from her.

"Hardly. That's more like this. Here. I'll be the nobleman, you be the lady." Marian put her hand on Robyn's waist before Robyn could protest. "Put your hands on my shoulders. See? I get to guide you."

She pulled Robyn in a tight step that forced her to pay attention to her feet. Marian, meanwhile, stepped wide, her skirts brushing against Robyn's breeches as she commanded Robyn's movements. Flustered, Robyn fought, only to discover that Marian knew exactly how to manipulate her weight so that she fell into the pattern of the dance whether she wanted to or not.

"How are you doing that?" Robyn asked, laughing.

"Just trust me. Remember, you're a fancy lady in a fancy gown."

"Am I?" Robyn eyed her worn leather jerkin.

"Lady Robyn. You look simply ravishing tonight." Marian pulled her in tightly. Robyn found herself tumbled in a position she would very much have loved to have had Marian. Perhaps sensing this, Marian smirked.

"Thanks?"

"You're supposed to simper."

"I don't think I even know what that means."

"'Oh, Sir Marian, you're too kind. And so strong.' Like that."

"You are strong."

Marian relaxed her hold on Robyn. "Better."

The music faded behind them, and with it Marian's smile. "I have to tell you something," she said, avoiding Robyn's eyes. "About my father."

Robyn didn't want to talk about the sheriff of Nottingham. Not with Marian in her arms and the summer sky wheeling overhead.

"I couldn't find the arrow, but I did find something else. My father's put a price on your head. Ten pounds for you, and five for anyone found in your company."

Chapter Thirty-Eight

Marian watched her words blow all the joy of the evening away. Robyn's jaw tightened, and she stiffened in Marian's arms. The muscles of her stomach hardened beneath Marian's hands.

"I'm sorry, Robyn."

"Ten pounds."

"He really hates you." Ten pounds was more than someone like Robyn could hope to make in a year, if not several years. It was also the amount of money in the purse Robyn had won at the archery contest, which didn't strike Marian as a likely coincidence.

"Then you shouldn't be here with me. It isn't safe," Robyn said.

"My father isn't going to collect money on my head." She brushed off Robyn's concerns. "And he hasn't announced it yet."

"That's why you wanted to get out of the city."

"I know I should have told you sooner, but . . ." *But I didn't want you to leave.*

Robyn raked a hand through her hair and broke free of Marian's embrace. The warm night air chilled her in the sudden emptiness where Robyn had stood.

"Robyn." Her voice broke. Robyn's profile stood out stark against the sky, her straight nose and firm jaw cut from starlight and the high, pale clouds.

"Do you remember Clovis?"

Marian shuddered. Clovis's death had come as a relief to her. He brought out the worst in her father, and she hadn't liked the way he looked at her. "I remember him."

"I was a fletcher once. He caught me poaching. I shot him. That's why I had to leave Nottingham. I killed Clovis, and Cedric, the boy I told you about, saw me."

"The one who loved you."

"Yes."

"And he didn't tell anyone?"

"I faked my death before he could."

"Robyn—"

"My life isn't one of Alanna's songs, however clever they are. I'm not a hero. I'm a murderer and an outlaw."

"And I'm the sheriff's daughter."

Robyn smiled faintly, turning back to Marian. "And you're the sheriff's daughter."

"What do we do?"

"You marry a rich nobleman, and I hang."

"I think I prefer Alanna's version."

"I'm sorry I dragged you into this, Marian."

"I'm not. And if I recall correctly, I dragged *you* into most of it. If I hadn't fallen off my horse, you wouldn't have had Willa dumped into your lap."

"She's growing on me."

"Robyn." Marian held out her hand. Robyn took it, but her face was still twisted with pain. "I don't care that you killed Clovis, and I hate that my father ruined your life, but I am glad I met you."

Marian saw her words fall into Robyn slowly. Robyn's hand tightened on hers, and her hazel eyes widened. It made her look suddenly young. Marian lifted Robyn's hand to her cheek and held her eyes, waiting to see if Robyn planned to stay or go. *Stay,* she prayed. *Stay with me.*

"Marian."

Robyn's voice sounded raw as she said her name. She thought about everything Robyn had lost—a brother, a home, a life—and she hated the world for taking all of that from her. She hated her father.

"I won't let you hang," she said, and Robyn's lip curled in a crooked smile as she brushed Marian's mouth with her thumb. The touch was tender; the effect it had on Marian was not. She shivered as reverberations of the caress traveled down her body, weakening her knees and any reserve she might have had left. She turned her mouth to Robyn's hand and kissed the skin of her wrist, tasting tree sap.

Robyn watched her with slightly parted lips. Marian could see the flush darkening her tanned skin even in the pale light of the moon. She kissed her wrist again, this time moving toward her palm. Robyn's breath came faster. She ran her lips over the base of Robyn's thumb with her eyes still on Robyn's, intoxicated by the way Robyn's pupils dilated and the thrall her touch held over them both.

"I like your hands." She let her lips brush Robyn's fingers as she spoke.

"I like your mouth."

The calluses on Robyn's palms scratched her face and sent another shiver down her spine. She wanted those hands, rough though they were, on her body. The fabric of her gown chafed against her breasts, and she let her lips close over the tips of Robyn's fingers as her tongue tasted the archer's calluses. Robyn gasped in response. The sound went through Marian like lightning. She pulled Robyn's hand away and reached for her face, but Robyn was already there, kissing her, holding her, her mouth hot and willing as Marian wrapped her arms around her neck.

A cool, evening breeze stirred their hair. Robyn's hands rasped against the smooth fabric of Marian's dress, and then her hands were on Marian's bared shoulders, pushing the gown down, her palms warm and rough on her skin. Marian could barely breathe. Desire like this was completely foreign to her, and she gasped for air as Robyn traced the neckline of the dress.

"Take it off," Marian said. She turned in Robyn's arms and

presented the laces. Robyn tugged at them, her normally deft fingers fumbling as she loosened the bodice enough to let the gown slip off one shoulder. Marian leaned back into her as Robyn kissed her neck and then down the newly bared skin, barely able to stand. Robyn's mouth left a trail of need as she slid the gown still lower. The hem caught her nipples as it passed over her breasts, and she cried out in surprise at the shock the sensation sent between her legs.

"Are you all right?" Robyn asked in her ear.

She answered with her body, yanking off the gown with impatient fingers and untying her belt, which was heavy with the dowry purse, before turning back to face a Robyn struck dumb; she stared at Marian with a look that suffused her with a heady draught of power.

Robyn didn't protest when Marian drew her down to the ground. The grass of the meadow was summer soft against her skin. Robyn undid her jerkin and ripped her tunic off over her head, leaving only her undershirt, and laid the tunic down on the grass before pressing Marian into it. The feel of Robyn's weight against her, on top of her, with the stars overhead and the sweet summer air whispering through the grass, was exquisite. Robyn braced herself on one elbow, freeing her other hand to stroke the skin of Marian's waist. The touch was almost too much. Her hips pushed against Robyn of their own accord and she grabbed a fistful of grass.

"God, you're perfect," said Robyn.

Marian's heart ached at the words, and in that moment, she believed them. She was perfect. This was perfect. Robyn was perfect. Robyn would be so much more perfect if she would just touch her, and she arched her back as Robyn's hand cupped her breast at last. When her thumb trailed over her nipple, something in Marian broke free. This moment didn't belong to her father or her station or any misguided sense of duty. It was hers, and so was Robyn, and for the first time in her life she felt in control of something that mattered.

She rose against Robyn and rolled her into the grass so that she could straddle her with her hips as she pulled the undershirt over Robyn's head and tossed it to the ground. The binding underneath was more difficult, and she tugged at it until Robyn sat up and allowed her to unwind it as best she could with Robyn's mouth on her breast.

The feel of Robyn's tongue nearly brought her to the brink. She bucked her hips, and the leather of Robyn's belt rubbed against her. Her breath came fast and shallow. Robyn's breasts were smaller than Marian's, firm where Marian's were full and heavy, and Marian stared in fascination as they met. Robyn's stomach was hard and muscular beneath. She sat back, releasing her grip on Robyn as she took her in. She'd mussed Robyn's hair, and it lay tousled over one eye. Robyn's chest rose and fell as quickly as Marian's, and the curve of her biceps made something inside Marian tighten almost painfully. She'd touched herself enough to know what she wanted, and the strength in Robyn's arms promised release.

First, though, she wanted Robyn. She loosened Robyn's belt and let her hair fall across Robyn's stomach. Robyn lifted her hips for her to slide her breeches down, and Marian felt her kick off her boots, followed by her breeches, while Marian stared at the long, lean muscles of Robyn's legs. If she had legs like those, she'd never stop running.

"Come here," Robyn said.

She lay down, memorizing the feel of their bodies connecting at the breast, hip, and leg. The pulse in Robyn's abdomen pounded against her own as she buried one hand in Robyn's thick hair, the other stroking the smooth skin over Robyn's ribs. The kiss Marian gave her was slower than their others. Deeper. The stars were behind her eyes, this time: a swirl of colors as she poured her heart into the woman beneath her. Robyn smelled of wood smoke and sap, and underneath the forest fragrance was a hint of apples.

"Marian," Robyn said when Marian slid inside her. She tightened her grip on Robyn's hair as Robyn's hips rose to meet

Marian's hand. She stroked her, at first gently, then harder, until Robyn came with Marian's name on her lips and Marian pressed her forehead against hers, sharing her breath as Robyn tightened around her hand, then relaxed, her face smooth and perfect and in this moment, at least, hers.

She lay in Robyn's arms with her discarded gown spread over them as the night air cooled. Robyn smoothed the damp hair on Marian's forehead.

"I wish we could stay here," she said, circling her finger around the hollow of Robyn's collarbone.

"Will they be looking for you?"

"It doesn't matter."

Robyn pulled her closer. "Ten pounds says it does."

Marian curled herself under Robyn's chin and listened to the beat of her heart. Her father had undoubtedly noticed her absence by now, as had Lady Emmeline. Her only hope was to sneak back into the city and feign a stomachache or too much drink. She could pretend to have passed out in a storeroom for a few hours, which would also explain her disheveled appearance.

Or I could run away. She let herself fall into the daydream. Like Willa and Alanna, she'd leave court for the forest, hunting with Robyn and lying like this beneath the stars every night with Robyn's arms around her. The longing that accompanied the thought made her shudder.

"Are you cold?"

"No."

She couldn't go with Robyn. Her father would hunt her down to the ends of the earth, and when he found them, hanging would seem like a kindness compared to what he'd do to Robyn. The thought sobered her.

"There's something I want you to have," she said into the warmth of Robyn's neck.

"You don't need to give me anything, Marian."

"I want to." She forced herself to sit up and reach for her belt.

303

The purse clinked in the pouch. "Here," she said as she pulled it out and thrust it into Robyn's hand.

"What is this?"

"Open it."

"Marian . . . is that . . . is that silver?"

"Yes. I don't know how much it is."

"I can't take this—"

"You can. My father stole your life from you. I can't fix that, but this will help your family pay the tax."

"It's too much."

"It's nowhere near enough."

"Where did you even find this much money?"

"It's mine," said Marian, defiance rising in her voice. "It's my dowry."

"Your . . . dowry?"

"Most of it, anyway. The rest is in a locked chest, and the key is in the purse, too."

"I can't take your dowry, Marian."

"Why not? It's mine, isn't it? And if anyone should have it, it's you, because you're the only one I want."

Robyn set the purse down and cupped Marian's face in her hands.

"It's not fair," Marian continued. "I hate the man my father has sold me to. He's vile and old and cruel, and—" She felt the tears rising in her eyes and tried to blink them away, but one fell down her cheek. Robyn wiped it with her thumb.

"Listen to me," Robyn said. "Nothing is ever fair for people like us. We have to make our own justice."

"But I want to marry you."

Robyn closed her eyes, and Marian wished she could take back the words. Idiot, she told herself. She doesn't want to marry the sheriff's daughter, even if she could. You're just a stupid girl, and you're lucky you can't get pregnant.

"God, Marian." Robyn's eyes were still closed, and she took a long, shaking breath.

"I'm sorry. I shouldn't have said anything. I'm stupid, and—"

Robyn kissed her. Marian tumbled over a cliff she hadn't seen coming and landed in Robyn's arms, Robyn, her Robyn, her brave, doomed Robyn.

"I want to marry you, too," Robyn said when she pulled away. "More than anything."

"Then keep the money and the key. We'll find a way. We'll go to France, or Scotland—someplace my father can't find us."

"You know I can't leave."

"You're an outlaw. Of course you can leave."

"Maybe someday." She kissed Marian again, this time with a hint of regret. "Things like that take planning."

"Then I'll wait."

"Your life would be easier if you married a nobleman."

"My life would be empty, you mean. Maybe I'd love my children, if I didn't die in childbirth. Maybe I'd even learn to like my husband, if he was kind. None of that matters without you."

"You don't know that. You don't know what you're giving up."

"Because you do?"

"I can't go back, Marian. I will never have a chance at a normal life again. Not here at least. You could. You could marry, and I could see you sometimes, if we were careful." The pain in Robyn's voice twisted in Marian's chest.

"Is that what you want?" she asked.

"I can't ask you to do what I want."

"But if you could?" She willed her to speak the truth.

"I'd ask you to come with me, right now, into Sherwood, and I'd kill anyone who tried to stop us."

"Then let's go." Marian tried to stand, but Robyn held her down, her eyes weary.

"I can't ask that of you."

"I'm not asking you to. My father will look for me, but he won't know where I've gone until it's too late. I won't slow you down. If Willa can do it, so can I." She ignored the voices of reason clamoring for her attention.

"What if we wait a few days? That way you can think about it, and you can't run away in this, anyway," said Robyn as she plucked at the gown. "Find yourself some hunting leathers and a warm cloak."

"What if you change *your* mind?"

Robyn gave her an incredulous look. "Then I'd be a fool. Come on. Let's get you back to the city before they release the hounds." She stood and offered Marian a hand. Marian rose reluctantly, letting Robyn wrap her into one more embrace before she pulled her gown back on and did her best to fix her hair. Robyn's clothes had been rumpled to start with and didn't look the worse for wear, but her hair was mussed beyond saving. She pulled her hood over her head with a rueful grin.

"Hey," said Marian, touching Robyn's cheek. "I see you everywhere, too, Robyn Hood. Promise me you'll come back for me."

"I will."

"When?"

"Meet me at the priory in five days. If I'm not there, wait for me. Tuck will hide you from your father."

"I'll be there." She closed Robyn's fingers around the purse. The broadsheet with Robyn's likeness and the list of taxes owed were tucked inside. "But take this. Please."

"It's yours, Marian."

"I told you—"

"But I will keep it safe for you, and perhaps one day it will buy us that passage elsewhere." Robyn secured the purse in her belt pouch.

"There is one more thing I would give you." Marian slid her silver ring off the middle finger of her right hand and onto Robyn's ring finger. The band fit as if it had been made for her. Robyn stared down at it, and Marian saw the moonlight glinting on the metal reflected in her eyes.

"I have nothing to give you in return."

"I have the arrow from the fair."

"You're worth far more to me than a broken arrow."

"Then give me this." She kissed Robyn and let her lips linger, memorizing the way they yielded beneath hers. So much of Robyn was hard edges. This surrender, though, belonged to Marian alone.

Robyn left her at the city gates with a squeeze of her hand, but neither of them dared more than that, even with the rollicking crowds within. Marian dodged drunken revelers as she wound her way toward the castle. Her feet floated over the cobbled streets of the merchant quarter, past her father's house and through throngs of men and women dancing to street music while the drink flowed freely.

I'd ask you to come with me, right now, into Sherwood, Robyn had said. Her body ached with the aftermath of pleasure, and everything her eyes touched seemed brighter, glazed with a holy light that filled her to the brim and made her want to shout or weep with joy. This, then, was what the singers sang about. Everything was different now. She'd do as Robyn said—plan for a few (eternal) days, finding clothing and supplies, and then she would join Robyn in Sherwood. Emmeline would miss her, but she could see her at the priory, and besides, Linley's estates were a far cry from Harcourt. She'd see more of Emmeline as an outlaw than she would as the viscount's wife.

An outlaw.

With a sickened start, she recalled the state she'd left her father's study in. She quickened her stride. It was crucial he didn't guess she was to blame for that. Plenty of other people had cause to hold a grudge against the sheriff, and Midsummer was a perfect opportunity for burglary. She chewed on her lower lip as sweat pricked her palms. Sobriety had returned, bringing its cousin, clarity, with it. Foreboding filled her mouth like ash. She had taken a terrible risk.

The guard at the castle gate waved her through without a second look. Please don't remember me, she prayed, ducking into a servant's passageway at the first chance she got. From here, she'd make her way back to the banquet hall and pretend she'd fallen asleep in a pantry somewhere. That would explain her disheveled appearance, and the flush in her cheeks could be attributed to wine.

Servants passed her laden with trays of soiled linens and dirty dishes. That was a bad sign; it signified that the banquet was dying down. By the time she reached the great hall, she was nearly running.

Music assaulted her ears as she rounded the corner to the open doors. She sagged against the wall in relief. Music meant the feast had continued, even if food had been replaced with ale. The singer closest to her had a large group gathered around him. Most were servants, pausing in their errands, but a fair number of young lords, ladies, and all the gentry in between hung on the singer's words. A refrain floated toward her.

"... and at the fair he met a maiden fair
With golden roses in her hair.
She swore she'd seen no truer mark
Than Robyn Hood of the Greenwood."

Alanna. She pushed through the listeners to find a drunken Alanna seated on a stool, strumming her lyre with half-closed eyes.

"Alanna," she said, nearly shouting.

Alanna's eyes snapped open in alarm. Upon seeing Marian, she bowed to the crowd and excused herself with a few gracious nods, dissipating the rumbles of displeasure.

"What are you doing?" she demanded of the minstrel.

"Where have you been?"

"I—"

"Your father's looking for you."

Sweat did more than prick, now. It trickled down her back in a river of cold fear. "Where is he?"

"I don't know. He realized you weren't here about an hour ago. The viscount is angry, too. Where did you go?"

"I met Robyn."

"You should have told me you were leaving. I could have covered for you."

"There wasn't time. Alanna, I have to talk to you." Skipping over the majority of the evening, she told Alanna about the price on Robyn's head, and the price that hovered over the minstrel's as well.

"I'm worth more than five pounds," said Alanna when she finished. "At least seven."

"It gets worse."

"How?"

"I stole my dowry."

Alanna's mouth opened, then shut, then opened again. "Why?" she managed at last.

"I don't know."

"That's a terrible answer."

"I can't marry Linley. I just can't. I was drunk, and it was there."

"I'll drink to that," Alanna said, but her voice was solemn. "What will you tell your father?"

"That I had too much to drink and fell asleep in a broom cupboard."

"Do you think he'll believe it?"

"I've done it before. Remember Leonne's wedding?"

"Does anyone?"

"Alanna—"

"You've been spotted. Good luck and good night. I'll see you next time I'm in Harcourt." She retreated into the crowd with a sympathetic grimace before Marian could tell her that she'd agreed to meet Robyn at the priory, leaving her to face her father.

"Where in the seven hells have you been?" He hissed the words. Combined with his wine-red face, she concluded the only thing between her and the back of his hand was the surplus of witnesses.

"The dancing and the drink," she said, gesturing in what she hoped was a helpless manner. "I needed air, and then I sat down, and the next thing I knew I woke up and came here."

"You have disgraced me." He gripped her wrist.

"You're hurting me."

"I needed you here."

"And I was. I danced with your suitors and I drank what they brought me so forgive me, father, if I was too agreeable. Lord Linley pours liberally."

A cough from behind her surprised them both. She looked over her shoulder, unable to turn with her arm still trapped in her father's grip, and up into Linley's eyes.

"It's true, Pierrot. I may have given her too much to drink." He touched the small of her back in what he seemed to think was a solicitous manner. Caught between her father and the viscount, she quivered like a bowstring. "She's still just a girl." His fingers brushed low across her waist. The difference between his touch and Robyn's spanned centuries. She would burn this gown, she decided, smiling up at him in forced gratitude, along with anything else of hers he'd touched. *I will die before I marry you,* she thought as she apologized again. Her father's face relaxed as Linley accepted her apology with a smug smile. *And if it comes to it, my lord, Robyn will kill you for me.*

"She won't be a girl much longer."

She glanced up at her father, confused by his words. Linley wore an anticipatory smile that made her queasy.

"I've formally accepted Lord Linley's proposal on your behalf. You'll be wed in three days' time."

"Three days?" she asked, her voice faint.

"It's the soonest I can arrange," said her father. "My lord, will you excuse us? I wish to speak to my daughter about the ceremony."

"Of course. My lady." He kissed Marian's hand with lips that lingered far too long. She shivered with revulsion as he pulled away.

"Now," said the sheriff, smiling through clenched teeth as he spoke, "you will explain to me why one of my men reports to have seen you at the city gates."

"I . . ." Terror stole her voice. "I wasn't."

"And yet Cedric says you were. With a *commoner*." He spat the last word.

"Cedric must be mistaken." The name reverberated in her skull. *Cedric*. Robyn's Cedric? If so, had he recognized the outlaw?

"I've been too lax with you. Until the wedding, you'll be staying under my roof, locked in your room if need be. I will not have you vanishing like your friend Willa on the eve of your wedding."

Robyn, she thought, wishing she could call her back with her mind. "Yes, father," she said as meekly as she could. The more she fought him, the more his suspicions would deepen. "Might I say goodnight to Emmeline at least and tell her this joyous news?"

Her father had never directed the look he now wore at her before, but she recognized it: it was the look he reserved for those he hanged.

"Do you take me for a fool?" He closed his hand roughly on her arm. "I will have one of my men escort you home, where he will remain until I return. We will talk then."

Home. Home to the house she'd ransacked earlier that night. She curtsied as best she could while still in her father's grip and prayed.

Marian sat by the cold fireplace in her father's receiving room. The guard, a man named Hob, hadn't let her retreat to the shelter of her bedroom where she might at least have changed out of her gown. He sat across from her with a puzzled expression on his face, as if he couldn't identify what manner of creature lashed its tail in the undergrowth before him. She wished she had a tail to lash, or claws, or a boar's great raking tusks. Anything to help her break past him. Hob, however, stood a full head taller than she, and he was almost as broad through the shoulders as a steer. He could probably stop her from fleeing with one finger. The housekeeper glowered at Marian as she brought Hob a mug of ale. No doubt they'd disrupted her plans for the rest of the evening, but Marian didn't feel a shred of pity.

She needed a story. What reason, however, could she give for leaving the city in the company of any man, let alone a man beneath her station? Nothing that wouldn't soil her reputation as well as her ruined gown. She'd have to continue to deny it. Cedric, she'd say, was mistaken.

She glanced at Hob. If only he'd been one of her father's dumber thugs. Hob, however, was reliably intelligent. His puzzled look deepened into a frown as he caught her gaze. She thought he wanted to ask her a question, but he held his tongue. She wished he'd speak. The silence turned the waiting into agony.

I fell asleep in a broom closet, she told herself. I'll say it must have been another girl. Keeping the lie simple might save her. What, she wondered, would Robyn do? Or Willa? She dug her nails into her palms. They would both fight their way out. Robyn had killed a forester rather than be taken captive, and Willa had faked her own death and run away in her brother's clothing. Marian didn't know how to fight like that. She'd never wanted to know. "Words and tears are woman's weapons," her father had said, once. She didn't remember the context, but she recalled the dismissive tone of his voice. Now even words had failed her. Nothing she told Hob would convince him to leave her unguarded.

Footsteps on the stairs and the sound of the door swinging open struck her mind dumb. Fear keened at the edges of her hearing like an evil wind, and she pressed her back into the chair as her father strode down the hallway. Hob stood as the sheriff entered, followed by an unfamiliar young man with a bad case of acne. Marian remained where she sat. Her father glowered down at her.

"Explain," he said.

Fear had dried her mouth and her tongue rasped against her lips like an autumn leaf. "I don't understand," she managed eventually.

"Where were you tonight?"

"I told you. I fell asleep. Too much wine." She stuttered over the words.

"Liar."

She jumped at his shout. Veins pulsed in his forehead. Never, not once in her entire life, had she seen him this angry.

"You will tell me even if I have to beat it out of you."

"Father!"

"I have done everything for you. Everything." His voice dropped from a shout to a malevolent whisper on the last word. "Do you think the viscount will want to marry you when he finds out you've been rolling in the mud with pigs like a common whore?"

"I haven't. I—"

"You will not contradict me. Cedric, you saw my daughter?"

The pock-faced man—Cedric—looked between the sheriff and Marian, and she pleaded with her eyes for him to lie.

"Yes, m'lord."

"You are sure?"

He hesitated. She held her breath, hoping, but he nodded.

"And did you recognize who she was with?"

Panic strangled her breath. Please, she prayed. Please, Mother have mercy on Robyn, if not on me.

"He wore a hood, m'lord. I did not see his face." Her flash of relief retreated as the man's eyes darted away from hers and back to her father's. "But—"

"Speak, lad."

"I believe it was the archer. From the spring fair."

Marian felt her stomach might heave up all the food and drink she'd consumed that night. Fury twisted her father's features into something animal and alien.

"Very well. You may leave us. All of you."

No, she almost begged Hob and Cedric. She didn't know the man before her. Her father wouldn't speak to her like this. Her father loved her. This man was deranged with wrath.

"It matters not." His voice was the flat calm of ice before the thaw. "You will wed Linley, and if you bear the vermin's bastard, you will tell the viscount it is his, do you understand me?" He gripped her shoulders and shook her, hard. "John means to make him an earl when he succeeds his brother. You will not disappoint me in this."

"I didn't," she began, even as her mind screamed Robyn's name, but he shook her again. She squeaked as she muffled a scream. "I would never lie with a man." The words tumbled out of her before he could hurt her again. "I swear it, Father. I swear it on her grave."

He froze. Tears leaked down her cheeks as she forced herself to stare up at him. She didn't need to name her mother. They both knew who she'd meant. Rage and grief clashed behind his eyes. Abruptly his hands loosened. He looked down at them as if he didn't recognize them, and she felt the skin begin to bruise where he'd held her.

"Marian," he said in a choked voice.

She quaked before him, and the sound of her chattering teeth filled the air, the ghosts of words she wished she had the strength to scream into his face.

"Go," he said, finally, stumbling back from her as if she'd struck him.

She fled. Her feet pounded up the stairs and she threw herself into her room and slammed the door, sliding down to sit with her back to it and her feet braced against the uneven slats as if she feared he might change his mind and batter it down. Bile rose in her throat. She clasped her hand over her mouth to keep it down, not wishing to remember the thing she'd seen wearing her father's skin. Had the monster always been there? The trembling became violent, and she lowered her hands from her mouth to wrap them around herself, for fear her skeleton might shake itself apart.

Things she'd heard over the years came back to her. People feared her father. She'd always told herself it was his power and position that made people avert their gaze in the street. Respect and fear often wore the same cloak, and a sheriff could not be too well loved, or he would not be able to carry out his duties. Nottingham required a firm hand. Those who crossed him did not always deserve their fates, she knew, but strength required sacrifice.

And I have never crossed him until now.

The truth of it temporarily stilled the shaking. As a child she'd misbehaved, but since coming of age she hadn't been under his roof long enough to garner more than his mildest displeasure. She'd concealed all acts of defiance, as would anyone, but not because she feared her father. Not because she hated him.

"I don't hate my father."

She made herself say the words aloud and tasted them for truth. *No.* The man she'd seen downstairs was hateful, but she didn't hate him. Instead, the turmoil in her chest solidified into the weight of betrayal.

". . . if you bear the vermin's bastard."

That is what I am worth to him then, she realized, recounting his words. That is all he will ever see. A vessel for his bloodline. A measure of his pride. He'd find out just how much she was worth when he tried to open the chest that held her dowry. She wished she'd taken all of it: the cups, the golden ring, the pearls, and the silk. She listened to his feet mount the stairs. Any second now he would discover the wreckage of his study. She waited for his bellow of rage to rend the air, torn between dread and satisfaction at the prospect of thwarting him still further. There was nothing left for her to lose.

Silence dragged on. No shout came from the hall. Instead, as the minutes passed, she heard a different sound: a careful measured tread on the boards beyond her door, and then the click and rattle of a lock being fastened. A lock to keep her here, in this prison of a room where once she'd slept with the wide, trusting eyes of a child secure in the knowledge of her father's love. She had not realized she held room for further betrayal. The wood of the floorboards bit into her seat and thighs as she remained, motionless, as locked into her position as surely as the door. She wanted to beat her fists upon it. She wanted to scream at him to let her out—that he could not do this to her, that she was his only child, and that he could not hold her prisoner—but the thought of his glinting satisfaction stayed her.

She woke up in a haze of early sunlight with her hands raw and her throat rawer. Her resolve had not held in the end, and she'd flayed herself as she cursed him in the small hours of the morning. No one had come to silence her.

Very well.

She forced shrieking muscles to unclench as she stood to take an inventory of her possessions. She still wore the clothes from the banquet, but she had little else in her wardrobe. All of her traveling clothes were with Emmeline, for that was where she'd planned on returning after the feast, and all that remained was one old shift, a dressing gown, and a red cloak. None would serve her current purpose. A basket of embroidery lay on a side table, along with a dusty skein of wool. She eyed the needles. Perhaps they'd serve as a weapon in desperation. *If I can get to the kitchen, I can take a knife.* Finger combing her hair back into place, she knocked on her door. No one answered.

"Hello?" she called out.

Distant footsteps scurried toward her. Someone fumbled with a key until at last the door opened to reveal the housekeeper and Hob, wearing her father's livery and a neutral expression.

"My lady," said the housekeeper. Marian had never been so glad to see Eliza in her life. "Perhaps you'd like some breakfast? Some water to wash?" Eliza's haughty demeanor had been replaced with nervous sympathy.

"No," Marian said. "I'd like to see my father."

"Oh." The woman raised her hands to her face, then lowered them. "Very well. He's . . . he's in his study."

The guard followed them down the hall. His heavier footfalls emphasized the mounting tension in the corridor, and Marian wondered what he would do if she made a run for it, veering toward the staircase instead of standing obediently outside the study door. Grab her probably, and then she'd never get a second chance. This was her only choice. She knocked.

Her father bade her enter in a calm, if chilly, voice. Inside, the study was unrecognizable from the mess she'd left it in. Everything once again lay in its place.

Everything except the small chest.

The monster in her father's skin met her eyes. The housekeeper curtsied hastily and shut the door behind her, leaving Marian alone in the room with the man she'd come running to for help for most of her life.

She took shelter in insulted dignity and outrage. "I am to be locked up then?"

"That is generally what I do to thieves and traitors."

"Pray tell me, how have I robbed you, Father?" She hid her shaking hands in her skirts.

"Three people knew about the key that unlocks this chest. One of them is in the ground. The other two are in this room."

The chest drew her eyes. Play dumb, she told herself. "My dowry?"

"You are perhaps not aware that I kept a spare key in the event the first was lost. It is a well-made chest. I had no desire to break the lock, and it seems my foresight was . . . fortuitous." He drew out the last word.

"I . . . I don't understand."

He picked up the key and slipped it into the lock. It turned with a click, and he lifted the lid with careful fingers. "I asked myself what kind of thief would overturn this room yet take so little. I can't account for any losses besides this."

"W-what?"

"Did you know your dowry contained twenty pounds in coin? You're worth more, of course, with my estate behind you and no male heir, but coin is easily liquidated. The viscount will not be pleased."

She didn't say anything. She didn't trust her tongue.

"Then I asked myself what kind of thief would take a bag of coin, a few papers, and leave the rest. There is silver aplenty in this room, and yet they took it from your dowry chest, almost as if they hoped I wouldn't notice. Tell me, when you ran away with your outlaw, did you think I wouldn't find you?"

She felt what blood remained in her face drain away. "I didn't—"

"Do not lie to me." Disgust twisted his mouth. She searched for the words that would get her out of this, the indignation that would redeem her, but nothing came. The sheriff of Nottingham had stood before hundreds of men and women like her. *I know a liar when I see one,* said his expression, *and you cannot fool me, daughter.*

"I would not—" she began, but her voice broke on the words and went high and brittle.

"Where is the money?"

"I don't have it." That, at least, was the truth. He seemed to guess it, for his brows lowered further over his eyes.

"You have shamed me, robbed me, and dishonored yourself, but you are still my daughter. You will do your duty if I have to lead you to Linley's bed with your hands bound, do you understand? I will make up the loss, but I assure you I will also find the filth who has soiled you, and when I am through with him . . ." His face turned a dangerous shade of purple, and he pounded the desk, as if there were no words to describe the horror awaiting Robyn. "And you will obey, because if you do not I will tell your husband what you have done, and his displeasure will shadow you all of your life." He took a deep breath and then softened his voice. "You may think me cruel, Marian, but I am your father. I want what is best for you."

She saw that he believed his own words, and she saw that there was nothing she could say to convince him of her innocence. Only one path was left to her. Hating herself, she let the tears come and dropped to her knees. "Please, I'll be good. Please don't tell him. Please don't let him hurt me, Father."

His chair scraped the wood as he stood and rounded the desk to stand over her. It didn't take much to make herself redouble her sobs and clutch at his boots, staining the dark leather with her tears. He let her weep, prostrate, for several moments before crouching down to lift her up. She blinked the tears away and let her shuddering breaths speak for her.

"Please," she said when she could once again draw air. "I'll marry him. I'll be good. I'll be *good.*"

"Of course you will." He searched her face then pulled her to him, and she sobbed into his chest as he stroked her hair, full of self-loathing and the bitter satisfaction that her tears at least still had power, even if the shame of it cut her to the bone.

Chapter Thirty-Nine

Robyn made her way down the road with her heart more whole than it had been since Michael's death. Her body still hummed from Marian's touch, and the promise of more nights to come drove out the doubt that circled her mind's borders. "Marian." She said the name out loud to the darkness. It didn't matter that she was the sheriff's daughter. It didn't matter that loving her was madness, suicide even, because holding her outweighed every possible consequence. Later, maybe, she would second-guess her heart's direction. For now, she let herself walk with a lightness to match the forest deer.

A snatch of song from a cluster of revelers caught her ear. The tune seemed familiar somehow, and she hummed along until she realized where she'd heard it: Alanna. She paused. The singer's voice bore all the hallmarks of intoxication. It bellowed off key and was punctuated with laughter from the man's fellows, but the lyrics were clear enough. As she listened, she heard a glorified retelling of her own shooting at the spring fair, followed by her encounter with Gwyneth. The implication was not, however, that the two of them had fallen in love, but rather that this fictional Robyn had acted out of chivalry. No mention was made of Gwyneth's rebuke. But, she heard to her horror, there was a line about the sheriff's daughter. Surely Alanna wouldn't have been foolish enough to put that into song. She waited for more, but the song changed into an older tune as if the singer were unaware of the difference in his subject matter. His audience didn't seem to care, either, and they cheered him on.

Robyn quickened her pace. Nobody would recognize Robyn the fletcher, but if songs were being sung about Robyn the archer, then she needed to get out of the city and to a place where she could strangle Alanna out of sight of witnesses.

Did Marian know? Had the song penetrated the upper echelons of society, or had Alanna saved it for markets and villages? Somehow, she found that unlikely. Tension replaced the languor suffusing her body. Perhaps the sheriff wouldn't put any store by the song. Or songs. How many had Alanna composed while Robyn wasn't paying attention? Yes, the rich were often the subject of ballads, and many of those songs centered around love scandals, but Robyn knew the sheriff. The suggestion that his daughter might be engaged in any sort of relationship with a commoner would gall him. The song doesn't say I'm a commoner, she reminded herself, although she hadn't heard the entire thing. It also doesn't say I'm an outlaw. Confirming the exact nature of the content would be the second thing she did once she found Alanna, after she'd satisfied the itching in her fingers.

Damn her. It didn't surprise Robyn that the song had spread. Anything that put the sheriff in an uncomfortable light was bound to attract public attention, and there were those who knew of his courtship of Gwyneth. That his daughter might also be wrapped up in a scandal would be oil tossed in the flame.

Stopping the spread of the song was impossible, she realized as she broke into a jog. The damage couldn't be mitigated. She'd just have to ride it out and forbid Alanna from composing so much as a rhyme about her or Marian for the rest of her life. Her short life, she amended. She'd let Alanna's easy smile and steadying presence fool her. Minstrels were dangerous. More dangerous than noble ladies dressed in their brother's clothes or an outlaw with a bow.

She arrived back at their camp with the rising sun. Midge and John waited for her at the entrance to the cleft with worried faces. Both visibly relaxed when she came into view.

"Unnecessary," Midge said the minute Robyn was close enough to hear her. "There was no reason for you to go to the city. None."

John, who understood exactly why Robyn had gone, didn't say anything. He did, however, frown at the look on Robyn's face.

"Is Alanna back yet?"

"No. Is everything all right?"

She explained about the song in a low and angry voice, doing her best to keep her temper.

"I thought you knew," said Midge when she finished.

"Knew that she was planning on spreading it all over England?"

"Well, you heard her singing."

"I didn't realize she was going to sing it in front of *other people*."

"Robyn has a point," said John. "We're trying to avoid attracting attention."

"Did it say anywhere that Robyn Hood is a supposedly dead woman hiding in the forest?"

"No, but she could have at least changed my name."

"We know about a dozen Robyns," said Midge dismissively. "It's a common name."

"It's a risk. A risk we really, really don't need," said Robyn, "and if Alanna continues, I'll send her back to Emmeline."

"You will not," said Will. She'd emerged from the cleft in time to catch the last few exchanges.

"She's putting us all at risk."

"She's saving your ass."

Robyn blinked at Will.

"No one will go out of their way to help an ordinary outlaw. They'd turn you in as soon as they saw you, hoping for a reward. But Robyn Hood? Don't you see what Alanna is doing?"

"Enlighten me."

"She's making you a hero."

Robyn's head spun as she stared at Will, unable to comprehend the meaning of her words. "I'm not a hero," she said at last. "I'm a poacher and a murderer and a thief." Marian's dowry hung heavily in her purse, reminding her of a few more crimes she could add to the list.

322

"That doesn't matter. Alanna always says people don't want to hear the truth. They want something bigger than they are. That's why singers always lie."

"They can lie about someone else, then."

"It's too late for that," Midge added, not at all helpfully, in Robyn's opinion.

"Did you get the arrow?" John asked.

"What?"

"The arrow. That's why you went, isn't it?"

"Marian couldn't find it." She remembered the things Marian had found, however, and looked over her shoulder. "Let's get inside. I have things to tell you."

"Five pounds?" said Midge in outrage when Robyn finished her story. "We're worth just as much as you."

"If we're captured, you can take it up with the sheriff," said John. He furrowed his brow at the drawing. "It's not a good likeness."

"Does it matter? Between this and Alanna's ridiculous ballad, we'll be lucky to still be alive by autumn."

"This could apply to any outlaw out here," said Will as she studied the picture. Tom and Lisbet listened with wide eyes, and Robyn hated that they'd come to her for safety, only to find themselves even more hunted than before.

"And now any outlaw out here is at risk. All someone has to do is say, 'I found one of Robyn Hood's companions,' and they can try to claim their reward," said John. Robyn appreciated that he, at least, understood the gravity of the situation.

"So, we give them an outlaw."

They all turned to Will.

"Are you volunteering?" said Midge.

"Hardly. Siward, remember? The sheriff is looking for someone to hang. He can claim Siward is you, for all that it matters to us. He'll get his blood, we'll get rid of Siward, and the woods will be safer for everyone."

Robyn wanted to argue. She wanted to point out that the woods would never be safe, and that drawing the sheriff into a fight now was idiocy, but she couldn't deny the logic of Will's plan. "Marian said you would be able to read this," she said, handing the illegible list to Will.

Her green eyes scanned the parchment. "Robyn," she said when she finished. "Do you know what this is?"

"If I did, I wouldn't be asking you."

"This is the list of taxes still owed for the ransom tax, and the dates they're due."

She was too tired and full of conflicting emotions to sort out why, exactly, this had Will so excited, and she waited for Will to explain.

"Some of these manors are on the other side of the forest. They'll have to cut through to get to Nottingham."

"Bringing them directly to us," Robyn finished for her, a smile creeping across her face.

Chapter Forty

Words and tears are woman's weapons. As she continued her feigned act of contrition, she wondered if her father had realized how effective tears could be under the right circumstances. He let her break her fast in the dining room instead of her bedroom. The housekeeper kept her lips thinned to a narrow slash as she brought Marian honeyed bread and fruit from the kitchen, though Marian heard her scolding a maid behind the closed door. She didn't know who the woman disapproved of—Marian, or the sheriff. Either way, she didn't have a friend in Eliza or Hob. He remained nearby and his gaze made the back of her neck prickle.

Getting a message to Emmeline wasn't possible. No one here would deliver it for her, and what could her friend do? Her father was within his rights to marry her off and to keep her locked up until then. Alanna couldn't help either. Besides, she might go to Robyn, and that would end in disaster. She had no intention of seeing Robyn hanged.

Her only hope was to create a distraction. She surveyed her surroundings as she slowly ate her meal. Leaving under the cover of darkness had its advantages, but by then she'd be locked up in her room. Escaping out the window wasn't an option. The drop was too great, and her father's men guarded the street. Unless she developed squirrel-like climbing skills, that route was out.

She paused with the bread halfway to her lips. Yes, the drop to the ground was too far. If she could manage to climb up the thatch, however, she might be able to make her way to the cross street and the stable. The steep pitch of the roof loomed in her mind's eye. At least she'd die instantly if she slipped. Alternatively, she could wait until after her wedding to make her escape. Surely she'd have more freedom then. That plan, however, required spending her wedding night with her husband, and the thought of the repugnant viscount touching her was untenable.

Setting the bread down, she reached for the honey and the knife. Amber liquid dripped from the short blunt blade as she spread it over the remaining slice on her plate. Too dull to do much damage to anyone, she mused, eyeing the edge. Maybe it could punch through flesh if she shoved hard enough, but she didn't think it would be able to puncture leather. Even a straw dummy stood a chance of beating her, with this as her only weapon.

Straw. Her hand tightened on the hilt. If she could get this back to her room somehow, she might be able to use it to get a grip as she climbed. Excitement raced through her, followed by sharp terror. This was madness. The long sleeves of her gown hid her trembling hands from Hob's sight, and she forced herself to eat. She would need her strength.

The housekeeper bustled in with a mug of ale for Hob just as she was finishing her meal, giving Marian her chance. She slipped the sticky blade up her sleeve and hoped the honey would do its part to keep it glued there for the length of time it would take to return upstairs. A maid followed the housekeeper, glancing at Eliza nervously as she cleared away Marian's plate. In her obvious distress, the girl didn't notice the missing utensil, and Marian allowed herself to breathe as she stood and turned to face her jailors.

"I would like to return to my room now," she said. "And would you bring me some water for washing?"

The housekeeper nodded, and Hob took a swig of ale before gesturing for her to lead the way. She kept her head bowed and meek and her arms wrapped around herself as she walked the short distance to her chamber, the façade helping to keep the knife in its hiding place. Once inside, she shoved it beneath her mattress and arranged herself on the stool by her washbasin. An ewer of hot water arrived moments later. Thanking the maid before she dismissed her, she proceeded to wash her face and hands. Cleaning the knife took a matter of seconds. She secreted it in the stays of her bodice, unwilling to risk losing it should her father decide to move her elsewhere, and looked around. One blade wasn't enough. She opened the wardrobe again.

The red traveling cloak was old and out of fashion. She'd worn it as a younger girl, and the dark red color reminded her too much of blood. That didn't matter. It had a hood and it would hide her fine clothes, even if it did catch the eye. Her mother's comb lay on the shelf above the hooks. The bone handle was rounded, and the teeth still contained strands of her hair. Could they bite deep enough into the thatch to support her weight? No other option presented itself.

She unlatched the window shutter and peered out into the street. Business went on as usual below: hawkers shouting about their wares, animated discussions between friends, quarrels creating little stirs of movement amid the crowd as people pushed to get out of harm's way. A herd of sheep trotted below, followed by a rider on horseback who hurled invectives at the young shepherd to get them out of his way. She frowned. The rider wore the prince's livery, and he pulled up sharply at her father's door. Normally, she would have done her best to overhear the news a messenger brought. His haste, and the brutal way he shoved the reins at one of the guards, suggested bad news. Perhaps the king had escaped and was on his way back to England to thwart John's plans. She no longer cared. The messenger's arrival provided her an unlooked-for opportunity. The guards argued about who should hold the horse, which seemed inclined to nip, and Marian swallowed her fear. Nobody in the street was looking up. It had amazed her, as a child in this room, how infrequently people bothered to raise their heads above eye level. She would have to trust to that now while her father's men were distracted. She grabbed the cloak, put the knife between her teeth and the comb in her bodice, and stood at the edge of the window. The hardest part would be getting over the lip of the thatch, which jutted out above her. Nothing in her life had prepared her for this. She'd need to dangle in midair, then haul herself up using nothing more than the knife and the beam.

I can't do this, she thought as she measured the distance. Nor could she bear the alternative. She moved slowly so as not to attract attention to herself as she edged out onto the sill. She could barely close her hand over the lip of the thatch. The coarse straws provided little grip, but the beam beneath them did. Marian said a prayer, and only the certainty of her future if she stayed spurred her into the uncertainty of open air as she swung out over the street three stories below.

No one gasped as she hung suspended. They would see soon, though, if she didn't move, but pounding terror stripped her of her senses. Her fingers ached with the weight of her body and her feet reached uselessly for the ledge she'd left behind. I'm going to die, her mind gibbered at her, splattered with the shit and rotting food and piss that filled the street below. The seconds passed, each one increasing the likelihood of her exposure.

Shouts erupted from the ground. Mother have mercy, she prayed, and took one hand away from the beam and turned herself to face the building. She couldn't see anything in the street, but the shouting continued. The knife handle between her teeth still tasted sweet in her dry mouth. Whimpering, she released her hand again, this time to take the knife, and prayed her other hand would hold her weight. It did, though barely, and she swung herself back just enough to stab the blade into the thatch above the crossbeam.

It held. Shaking with panic and effort, she dared to haul her body up enough to place her other hand on the hilt. It held again. A laugh, born of fear and insanity, escaped her lips. The sound gave her the strength she needed to pull herself up far enough to swing one leg over the edge. The pitch of the roof didn't give her much leverage, but it was enough. She pulled the comb out of her bodice and jammed it into the thickly woven straw with all her strength. It sank an inch in, and she hauled herself fully over the edge.

Her sense of victory faded as she appraised the slope above her. It seemed as tall as a mountain, and her arms already felt as if they had reached the end of her strength. Climbing the rest of the way, only to descend on the other side unnoticed, was inconceivable. She glanced down. A crowd milled below her, but they weren't looking up. They were shouting at each other and at the messenger, who had returned to his horse and was having difficulty getting past them. Whatever news he'd brought had clearly stirred them up, and Marian stared, unwilling to believe her luck as her father's guards did their best to keep the crowd away from the door. No one noticed the girl in the red cloak clinging to the roof like a drunken bat. Her relief lasted as long as it took for her muscles to remind her that they objected to this kind of use. Gritting her teeth, she continued her climb.

The comb snapped halfway to the peak. The force sent her sliding back down, and her feet in their felt dancing shoes scrabbled at the thatch for purchase that did not come. Straw flitted to the street below. Desperate, she shoved the jagged, broken handle into the roof. Her fingers strained with the effort of keeping her tenuous grip on the bone. Above her, the remnants of the comb stuck out from the straw like jagged fangs.

I will not die here.

Her right foot found a knot of fibers. Working her toe in, she shoved off, and the ground ceased to pull at her with such vehemence.

Sweat poured down her face and stung her eyes as she reached the peak of the roof and looked down. The buildings on this side tapered more slowly, and she saw the roof of the stable to her left. She'd deal with the drop from the first roof to the second when she got there. For now, she focused on lowering herself carefully, making sure her knife and comb were firmly sunk into the thatch at each move. The stable roof thankfully hid her from anyone's glance, as it extended over most of the street. She skidded down the thatch as the comb came loose again. The motion pulled the knife free but she managed to sink it in before she had fallen more than a few feet. Her already heightened nerves screamed at her, and her shoulder ached from the wrench. At least the drop had brought her closer to the stable. She eyed the distance between her and the next roof. She couldn't get an accurate measurement from this angle, but she knew it was more than she wanted to drop willingly. A broken ankle wasn't an option.

The problem gnawed at her until a movement across the street sparked her attention. A woman stood in an open window with a bucket in her hands and her jaw hanging open. Marian froze. The woman, by all rights, should have raised the hue and cry the moment she spotted one of her neighbors potentially breaking the law. Failure to do so implicated her in the crime. Marian held a finger to her lips and silently begged the stranger for mercy. The woman emptied the bucket slowly, still staring at Marian, and then backed into her home. It was the first prayer she'd had answered in what felt like years.

Marian let herself plummet to the stable roof without further deliberation. She tried to take the jolt loosely. The impact knocked her breath out of her chest and she barely caught herself from rolling all the way off. She wheezed until her lungs stopped seizing and then edged toward the alley. Several bodies lay in the darkness, probably drunk or possibly dead. They didn't matter. She dropped again, this time lowering herself as far as she could before letting go.

Filth spattered around her. One of the bodies stirred. She didn't wait around to find out what he would do, and hurried into the street with her hood up. Taking a horse from these stables wasn't an option. The men there would recognize her and alert her father as soon as she attempted to ride away. Her own mare was stabled with Emmeline's horses at the castle. That wasn't an option either. She chewed her lip as she walked, dodging through the crowd with her eyes down to avoid drawing attention. The smell of ale hit her as she passed a tavern. Customers still rowdy from the night before milled in the streets, and one man collapsed against his horse before slumping to the ground with a hand still on his stirrup.

She didn't give herself time to question her decision. He'd already untied the horse from the post, and the animal seemed more than willing to get away from his wasted owner as she gathered the reins in her hand and backed the gelding up enough to mount. Her tired arms barely managed to pull her body into the saddle, and she had to make three attempts before she gained enough momentum to flop over the horse's back. He stood patiently while she floundered, and once upright, to the amusement of several onlookers, she sat awkwardly in her skirts.

"Too much to drink?" a man asked her in a voice so slurred she barely understood him.

Nodding, she pointed the horse's nose toward the city gates. Moving in the post-festival traffic chafed at her already panic-stricken mind. Traveling at anything more than a walk would draw unwanted attention, and while the lack of pursuit was so far comforting, she knew better than to trust it would last.

A few people commented to each other on her peculiar appearance as she shoved her way through the crowd. Her skirts were not divided for riding and showed more leg than was proper. Only the people right next to her noticed, however, as the press of bodies remained tight right up to the city gates. She joined the mass of people exiting the city. The hood fell over her eyes, and she hoped the guards would credit the choice with a hangover.

After the appalling odor of the city, the breath of fresh air that wafted over her outside the gates took her by surprise. She looked back over her shoulder at the walls of the place that had once been her home and searched her heart for regret.

She found none.

Marian urged her stolen horse into a trot and rode toward Sherwood.

Chapter Forty-One

Alanna returned later that day with a smile on her face, which faltered when she saw Robyn's expression.

"You," Robyn said, rising from the rock where she'd been fletching an arrow.

"I'm glad to see you made it back safely," Alanna said cautiously.

"I need to talk with you."

Alanna unslung her instrument from her shoulder and waited.

"You can't sing about me anymore."

"People love the songs."

"We're wanted."

Alanna's expression sobered. "I know."

"And you still think this is a good idea?"

"I think," Alanna said, keeping her low voice calm, "that we need it more than ever. If anything, I must sing that song louder and more widely."

"Don't feed me any horseshit about how eager people will be to help us. I know how eager they are. People love blood far more than they love songs."

"Unless the songs are about the man who will get them their money back from the sheriff."

Robyn felt all the blood drain from her face. "What are you talking about?"

"You've been helping your family and friends. Have you thought about helping the rest of Nottingham?"

Her heart beat unnaturally loudly in her own ears, and she recalled the children she'd given feathers to on the day of the fair so very long ago. "There's nothing we can do."

"Everyone knows the sheriff skims off the top of the king's taxes for John's purse and his own. They hate him, Robyn, even more than they love a good hanging. Find a way to give them back some of their coin, and even some of the nobility will want to kiss you."

"That's impossible," she said, but her mind flew back to the piece of paper Marian had given them.

"It's not." Alanna said the words simply, as if she already knew where Robyn's thoughts had strayed. "Trust me, Robyn. I would never do anything to put you or Willa in danger. You saved us. Let me save you."

Robyn set out with John early the next morning, leaving the rest of the band to continue work on the camp while they scouted out Siward's territory and delivered their message.

"Here," said John, stopping by the river to smear mud under his eyes. Robyn did the same, aware of how visible a pale face was amid the trees.

"If we're stopped, we will be hard-pressed to explain ourselves," she said.

"If we're stopped before we get to Siward, mud will be the least of our problems."

She ceded John the point with a frown. "How far is it, anyway?"

"Six miles, or at least it was last I knew. Let's just hope he hasn't moved camp."

That didn't seem likely. From what John had told her about his previous winter in Nottingham, the limestone caves where Siward camped were dry, defendable, and spacious. She doubted the self-styled outlaw king would give up such territory without a fight.

"What do you think of Alanna's reasoning?"

John took a moment to ponder the question. "I don't know.

You and I come from a different world than she and Will. I've never heard of a song saving anyone's life."

"Me neither."

"But I also know this: if I got wind of a man—or woman— willing to risk their neck to spite the sheriff of Nottingham, I'd do what I could to keep him out of the gibbet."

"Even if it meant your own life?"

"No. But I wouldn't go out of my way to turn him in, even for a reward that large."

"You wouldn't turn me in for ten pounds?"

"I haven't yet."

"We can't count on everyone being as thick as you."

"And not everyone's as mistrustful as you. The sheriff was going to be after us no matter what. If Alanna wants to turn us into heroes, I say we should let her. We're ready for him."

They walked on. Robyn turned John's words over in her head, along with Alanna's. If they really could convince Siward to ambush a tax collector or a trade caravan, perhaps her band could find a way to take the money once the sheriff thought she was dead.

And how, exactly, are you going to arrange that?

She'd figure it out. He'd want to believe her vanquished, and he hadn't gotten a clear view of her face, thanks to her hood. Any man of a similar build would do.

And if your plan fails?

Then she'd do what she had to do.

"John," she said, thinking of the promise she'd made to Marian. "If this goes awry, promise me you'll kill the sheriff."

"You stand a better chance of that, archer."

"I can't."

"You can't?"

"I made a promise."

"Not all promises should be kept," he said, but Robyn heard the resignation in his voice.

"Do you—" She broke off, unable to frame the rest of her question for fear of the answer.

"Do I what?"

"Do you think I'm damned?"

"For which crime? You've got a few to your name now."

"Marian."

"For loving a woman? God should be grateful we can find any love at all in His world."

"Even the sheriff's daughter?"

John stopped to face her, and the mud did little to obscure the seriousness of his expression. "I want that man dead as much as you do, Robyn, but if we can't have that, then it gives me great pleasure to think that Robyn Hood will be the one to despoil his daughter."

Robyn hesitated. She opened her mouth to tell John about the pact she'd made with Marian, but faltered. This wasn't the time. They needed to stay focused on the task at hand.

They came upon the first signs of Siward's camp as the midday sun began to sink toward the western horizon.

"Here," said John, pointing at a mark slashed near the base of a tree. "That's one of his boundary markers. The foresters know them, and they leave him alone."

"Tell me more about Siward."

"I don't know much about where he came from. He was a soldier once. He's clever, unpredictable, and cruel. So are his men."

"Are we any better?"

"When I left Siward to join you, I made a choice. It wasn't death. If I hadn't thought there was more to you than met the eye, I would have brought you back with me to Siward's camp and done my best to keep you safe there. Instead, I followed you."

"You didn't follow me. I followed you."

"And yet the minstrel isn't singing songs about Little John."

"Give her time," said Robyn darkly. "Midge said she was working on one."

"Look. I'm not good with words. That's Alanna's business. But what you've done means something."

"I haven't done anything. Except maybe kill Clovis."

"You stood up to the sheriff. Twice."

"Which has done us so much good."

"Don't be so sure. I know Midge has been angry with you

335

about moving the camp, so I don't know how much she's told you about things back in Nottingham, but no one's forgotten the archer at the spring fair who gave away the prize to save Michael Fletcher's widow from marriage to the sheriff of Rottingham."

"Rottingham?"

"That's what Midge has started calling it."

"I don't see your point."

"I'm saying it isn't just about your family anymore, or Tom's, or any of our friends. We could do something lasting out here."

"Alanna's wrong." Robyn shook her head. "You're the hero."

"I'm not pretty enough to be the hero."

"Shut up."

"It's true." John reached out and ruffled Robyn's hair beneath her hood. She pointed in silence at a branch broken off at eye level. "We're close." John motioned for her to halt and pointed to a ridge ahead. "They'll have someone on watch. We should be able to get around, but if we're caught, remember to follow my lead. He won't trouble us so long as we pay the proper respect."

She nodded. Discovery on someone else's terms wasn't a contingency she relished, but as she and John had endlessly discussed, it had merits of its own.

"This way."

They were halfway up the ridge, shielded from view by a low brow of rock, when an arrow thudded into the tree directly ahead of them. Robyn had an arrow of her own nocked a second later as she crouched and scanned the trees for their attacker.

"Hold," said John, stepping in front of her. "It's John. I've come to see Siward."

A shape detached itself from a nearby elm and made its way toward them. Robyn noted the unkempt hair and tattered tunic, along with the gaunt cheeks and yellowed eyes.

"John?" the wraith of a man said. "Thought you were dead."

"Thought I was dead, too."

"Who's this?"

"Friend of mine."

"What are you doing sneaking around then?"

"Trying not to get shot by the likes of you."

The man chewed on this quite literally, gnawing on a ragged wisp of beard as he weighed John's story. "Looks like we're full of visitors these days."

John's eyes flickered over to Robyn's, but neither questioned this strange statement.

"Siward's holding court in the greenwood. You know the way."

"What's to stop the rest of you from turning us into hedgehogs?" asked John.

"Better hope your luck holds. Where've you been anyway?"

"I'll tell you after I tell Siward."

"Suit yourself."

Robyn waited until the man was out of earshot before speaking. "The greenwood?"

"The woods by the caves. You'll see. It's not far from here."

They were challenged twice more, once by another bearded man, and once by a woman. The female sentry eyed Robyn with suspicion.

"That's Yvette," John said when they'd left her behind. "She likes killing." The way he said it suggested John had witnessed more than he'd wanted to of Yvette's hobby. "I don't know where she came from. She knows how to use a knife, though, and I've seen her gut a man for looking sideways at her."

Their path led them over a ridge and Robyn's mouth worked in silent envy as she took in Siward's territory. Crags rose on either side of a long lake overgrown with trees, and she saw a pair of swans swimming in the distance. The natural enclave offered shelter, fresh water, and a vantage point to watch for unwanted visitors. John followed a game trail along the slender strip of land between the crags and the water's edge until the ground opened up to reveal a clearing. Robyn knew at once why it was called the greenwood. The trees and rocks dripped with moss, the brilliant green carpeting every surface and muffling their steps. A massive oak dominated one end. At its base sat a man wearing a wooden crown, and at his side, her eyes wide with shock, sat Marian.

Chapter Forty-Two

The rope cut into Marian's hands as she clenched her fists to keep from shouting Robyn's name. Siward shifted beside her on his makeshift throne, a tortured thing built of twisted wood and deerskins. He was a slender man, something that had led her to believe at first that he was harmless until she'd looked deeper into his pale blue eyes. What she'd seen there had pricked a cold sweat all over her body. Now, he lounged at his ease, considering the outlaws before him. Marian bit her lip until blood blossomed in her mouth. She stared at Robyn and tried to communicate with eyes alone everything that needed to be said. The mud that smeared Robyn's cheeks concealed the fury that flushed them, which Marian alone recognized. John, also smeared with earth, offered Siward a bow with a carefully neutral expression on his face.

"I see you've found yourself some company in my absence, your highness," John said.

Siward tried to stroke Marian's hair. She pulled away fast enough to hurt her neck. He chuckled. "Little pigeon got lost in the forest."

"I hope you haven't harmed her," said John. "She looks valuable."

Robyn's eyes searched Marian's, and Marian gave her head a minuscule shake. No, Siward had not harmed her, or not in the way she had feared when he grabbed her horse's bridle on the road to Edwinstowe. That he was capable of such harm she didn't doubt. The fact that he'd held off was entirely due to the quality of the gown she wore and the ribbons in her hair.

"She'd be a fitting queen, don't you think?" he said.

John made a show of looking Marian up and down, then shrugged. "If you like highborn ladies. I find they tend to scream, and you never know who's listening out here."

Robyn glared at her companion and opened her mouth to say something, but John cut her off with an elbow to the rib cage and Robyn's words ended in a whistle of lost breath that Marian could hear ten paces away. Eleven of Siward's people surrounded them, but Marian knew at least five more lurked in the limestone caves nearby. She was not entirely sure how many brigands Siward had under his command. Sixteen, at least, but she suspected the number was closer to twenty, and Yvette, who scared her far more than Siward, counted for two. Robyn and John didn't stand a chance in a fight.

"Where've you been, John?"

"Got caught. Spent the summer rotting in Nottingham, but they never got around to hanging me. Old friend of mine here got me out."

"Did you bring me anything?"

"News."

"Silver would have been better."

Robyn interrupted John before he could respond. "What are you doing with her?"

"I plan to ransom her back to her mistress after we've had our fun. Not that it is any business of yours."

"If you touch a hair on her head, you piece of horseshit, I will put an arrow in your eye faster than you can say 'Mother Mary.'"

Marian cursed inwardly at Robyn's outburst. An ugly silence fell over the greenwood. The assembled outlaws bristled, waiting for Siward's command. John shifted his grip on his quarterstaff and Robyn, good as her word, had an arrow nocked, drawn, and pointed at Siward's skull. Marian hadn't even seen her draw it, but she'd seen that same look in Robyn's eye before. Then, the arrow had sought her father's heart. Marian wouldn't mind if Robyn's finger slipped on the bowstring this time, so long as none of the other arrows in the clearing found their mark in Robyn's chest.

The tableau before her stretched as the seconds passed. She knew what would happen if Robyn killed Siward. Siward's band would slaughter Robyn and John where they stood, and when they were finished, they would turn to Marian.

"Wait," she said, all hope of escape draining from her body. "Robyn, tell him who I am."

"Get behind me, Marian," Robyn ordered.

Marian didn't move. She had chosen to identify herself as simply a highborn lady's handmaid, marking her as one of the lesser gentry, rather than the sheriff's daughter. Unlike her first encounter with outlaws, this was not because she feared reprisal for her father's deeds. It was because she feared her father. However, the sport the brigands might have had with a handmaid was one thing; invoking the wrath of the sheriff of Nottingham was another. They wouldn't dare touch her. Not if they valued their lives.

She raised her chin and repeated her command. "Tell him who I am."

Siward, far from showing signs of alarm at the naked threat in front of him, leaned back further in his chair and crossed one long leg over a bony knee. Jeweled rings, all no doubt stolen, adorned the hand that rested on his thigh, and the other hand—the one that had tried to touch her—toyed with a loose tuft of hair from a deer hide. If anything, he seemed amused.

"She's no one," said Robyn. "Let her come with us."

"Your friend's manners leave a lot to be desired, John." Siward stood in a languorous motion and placed his hands on Marian's shoulders, positioning her body between him and Robyn. Robyn lowered her bow. "You bring me nothing, and yet you demand I give you my latest treasure."

"She's the sheriff's daughter, Siward," said John. "And if you hurt her, it will be on all our heads."

"You're joking." Siward's rings dug into Marian's shoulders as his hands tightened.

"On my honor," said John. "And my mother's grave."

Siward spun Marian around. "You're the bastard's bitch, then?"

"I am the daughter of the Sheriff of Nottingham, in service to the Lady Emmeline of Harcourt, and betrothed to Lord Linley."

"Tell me more about this Linley, pigeon. Would you say he was a wealthy man?"

"Yes. And even if he wasn't, my father will pay you. Maybe he'll even pardon—"

"Do I look like I want a pardon, pigeon?" He shook her, and her bound wrists knocked against his chest. "Why would I go back to Nottingham, when I am king of Sherwood?" He laughed, and the sound had a manic edge. "Maybe I'll give my men a taste of the sheriff's justice. Yvette, too, of course. She won't pass up a slice of pigeon pie. Then we'll send what's left of you back to Lord Linley with a bastard in your belly."

"You'll be drawn and quartered," she said, though a part of her wondered if her father would even care.

"Perhaps. Or perhaps not. Maybe Linley will thank us for—"

"Ransom her," said John, mercifully cutting short whatever Siward had been about to say next. "Untouched. It would show your goodwill. How'd you end up with her, anyway?"

"She rode right to me. Almost as if she was looking for trouble." He pulled Marian a little closer, forcing her to choose between staring at the wiry, no doubt lice-infested hair at the open neck of his shirt or craning her head to look up at his face. She chose his face.

"Did it occur to you that someone might have followed her?" John asked.

"Then they're still following that gelding of hers, all the way to the horse market at Maunnesfeld."

"He'll pay a hundred pounds to see me alive and unspoiled."

Siward released her in shock and she stumbled backward, tripping over the dais of roots. Robyn's hand steadied her. At her touch, some of the color came back into the world. She smelled

341

the thick earthy scents of moss and rotting logs, and felt a breath of summer air stir the clearing. *I will not be cowed by this man.* She lifted her chin and met Siward's incredulous gaze.

"A hundred pounds?"

"He'll lose face if something happens to me in his county."

"A hundred pounds is—"

"You've heard about the king?" John asked Siward.

"I am the king."

"The other king."

"Good riddance."

"The sheriff will have his hands on Nottingham's share of the ransom tax soon enough. We've got the records, which is actually why we're here. I don't know if the girl is worth a hundred pounds, but he might pay dearly for your cooperation—and for your silence," said John.

"Hmm." Siward folded his arms over his chest and considered the three of them. "First, I want to know why your friend here seems so fond of the slut."

"He's got a soft spot for maidens in distress," said John. "Likes to play the hero. You should try it sometime. Excellent results." He leered convincingly.

"She knew his name."

"My lord," said Yvette, twirling a long wicked knife in her hand. "I could get the truth out of him."

"I'm sure you could, my love," said Siward.

Marian stepped away from Robyn. Maybe she couldn't find her way through the woods or fight off outlaws, but she'd grown up in Nottingham. She could lie. "Robyn was a forester," she said. "He worked for my father before he got caught poaching."

"Fancied you, did he?" one of Siward's men said.

"What's not to like?" Siward held out his hand, and Marian forced herself to place her bound wrists in his grasp again. Robyn growled behind her. "Soft skin. Lovely lips. And a hundred pounds between you and the sweet spot between her legs."

"She's got a pretty mouth," said the same man.

"And teeth." Marian snarled the words, snapping her jaws to illustrate her point.

Siward laughed as the man recoiled. "Well, John, since you've brought me news, can I trust you to take a message to the sheriff? Tell him that I have his daughter and that she will remain unharmed so long as he brings me a hundred pounds, a cask of his finest ale, and a feast worthy of a king by the day after tomorrow. I can't guarantee her safety any longer than that."

"Of course, my lord," said John. "Robyn and I—"

"I'll be keeping your friend, of course, until then."

"Of course." John's lips thinned and he exchanged a long look with Robyn that Marian couldn't decipher. "Why don't we send Robyn, and I'll stay?"

"I think not. Besides, I want to hear all about how he sprung you from the Nottingham jail. Resourceful lad."

"Siward," John tried again. "Listen to—"

"Go, or I'll geld him before you return."

John gave Robyn one last look before turning and walking away from the greenwood, leaving Robyn surrounded by Siward's men and Marian still trapped in his embrace.

Chapter Forty-Three

They tied Robyn to a tree with her arms and legs spread and her face pressed against the moss. Her view of the clearing was limited to what she could see over her shoulder, and that view mostly contained Yvette. The outlaw sat with her head leaning against Siward's throne and her evil-looking knife on her knees, studying Robyn.

At least with her back to them, the attributes Robyn lacked were not on display. She had no doubt that the reserve Siward's men showed when it came to valuable hostages would not apply to female outlaws dressed as men. John had said as much when they first met.

The sound of someone striking a flint caught her ear, followed by the smell of wood smoke. She couldn't see the fire or Marian, and the ropes dug into her wrists and ankles while the muscles in her shoulders ached with the unaccustomed abuse.

Nothing about the situation made sense. Marian still wore the dress from Midsummer. Robyn had left her at the city gates, where she should have been safe enough. What had happened between now and then that had left Robyn tied to a tree with Marian at the mercy of the very man Robyn had hoped to use to eliminate the sheriff?

"Please, let me speak with him," she heard Marian say.

"You can speak to him from where you are," Siward's unmistakable voice replied.

Marian didn't say anything else. The conversation around the fire ranged from speculation about how the sheriff would respond to their demands to the bleak returns from the latest hunt. From what Robyn gathered, they'd picked this part of the forest nearly clean, which explained the gauntness of the band, and why they raided the villages so frequently. Robyn thought about the lushly inhabited stretch of woodland she called home and silently dared Siward to set foot on her territory. Lisbet and Midge would eat him alive.

Midge. Had John gone back to camp to consult with the others, or had he done as he had assured Siward and headed straight for Nottingham and the sheriff? Robyn ran the scenarios through her head. It seemed highly unlikely that John would take the news to Nottingham himself. If she were him, she would alert the others and then find the prioress, who would notify Emmeline, who would be the best positioned to inform the sheriff of his daughter's absence. And if John had gone to Tuck, then Robyn could be nearly certain he was on his way back to Siward's camp even now. All Robyn had to do was keep their attention on her and off Marian until he returned.

Yvette seemed to read her thoughts, for she stood to stretch, her eyes fixed on Robyn. "I've an idea," the outlaw said. She hefted the hilt of her knife in an experimental fashion and tossed it in the air, catching it deftly before she passed out of Robyn's peripheral vision. "Since we've money coming our way, we should decide how we're going to split it."

"Evenly," someone said to a chorus of boos.

"Let's throw for it."

Robyn gritted her teeth. At least her outlaws didn't gamble. They were honest thieves. The thud took her by surprise. She didn't even have time to flinch as the knife quivered in the trunk a few scant inches from her nose.

"God's blood," said Marian. The rest of the brigands cheered, and Robyn smelled Yvette's musky odor as she leaned in to pluck the knife out of the trunk.

"Didn't wet yourself, did you?" the woman asked, groping Robyn between the legs.

Robyn stiffened, straining a muscle in her thigh and lower back. Yvette's breath fell hot on her ear. There was no way the other woman could miss the absence that hung between Robyn's legs. She waited for Yvette to call her bluff.

Yvette said nothing as she retreated. Robyn didn't know whether to find that comforting or more alarming. The brigand didn't seem the type to put much stock in sisterhood.

The next knife nicked Robyn's hand. She swore as blood collected against the ropes, grateful that it was her left hand, and not the one that pulled a bowstring. She would need that hand to finish off Siward.

"Nothing for you," said Yvette to the thrower.

"Sorry about that, lad," the man said as he retrieved his knife. He patted Robyn roughly on the back, making her shoulders scream with pain, but at least he didn't grope her. Maybe she'd spare his life. Robyn turned her head to face the tree and leaned her forehead against the mossy bark, breathing in the smell of wood and rot as missiles lit into the trunk all around her.

"Stop," Marian shouted after the fifth knife. "Please."

"You've upset the pigeon, Yvette," said Siward.

"Of course I'm upset," said Marian. Robyn flinched at the steel in her voice. "Robyn took the archery prize at the Nottingham Fair. If you want to see true marksmanship, give him his bow."

"We'll need a target," Yvette said, her words a dark promise.

"Use me."

The silence that followed had a keen edge. Scattered applause broke it, and Robyn sucked in her breath. The girl was mad. Stark, raving, mad. They weren't at a market fair where, at close range, performers fired blunt arrows at fainting maidens to the sound of clinking coins. They were in a darkening wood, and Robyn had no intention of risking Marian's life for the sport of this lot.

The ropes that held her arms gave as Yvette sliced through them, and she fell backward, her feet still bound. The relief was agonizing. She forgot about Marian and the sheriff and Siward as blood flowed back into her arms, stabbing each nerve as it went by. She hardly noticed when her feet were freed.

"Robyn." Marian knelt before her, resolve in her dark eyes. Firelight flickered across her face and Robyn, still dazed from the sudden freedom from pain, almost reached out to touch her cheek. Marian seized her injured hand and turned it over in the firelight.

"It's not deep," said Robyn.

"Hold still." Marian ripped a strip of cloth from her dress and bound the wound.

"This is madness."

"You won't miss."

"You don't know that."

"I saw you shoot."

"That was for a purse," Robyn said. "This is different. I can't shoot at you."

"You have to."

Yvette did not let her pursue the argument. She grabbed Marian by the arms and hauled her to the tree Robyn had just vacated. Several pairs of hands restrained Robyn when she launched herself to intervene, and Marian shot Robyn a look of warning.

Marian didn't understand. Seeing her restrained reminded Robyn too much of Michael's fate. Letting the sheriff deal with Siward no longer seemed sufficient. She would end him herself, as she had Clovis.

Marian raised her head over Yvette's rough binding to glare out at the clearing. The gesture, haughty and defiant, calmed some of Robyn's blind rage. Marian looked in control despite the ropes and her stained gown, and the look she turned on Robyn was full of trust.

"Fetch the lad his bow," ordered Siward.

Robyn tried one last tactic. "If I miss and she dies, the sheriff will see us all dead."

"I don't think so. If you miss, then we deliver you to the sheriff along with the girl's body and collect the reward for her murderer."

Sweat trickled down Robyn's back.

"We've all seen how it's done." Siward dismissed Robyn with a wave of his hand. "We need something to put on her head. Alex, fetch a bladder of ale."

The crude bindings exaggerated the curves of Marian's body, and Robyn noted the eyes that roamed freely over Marian and vowed to pluck them out when this was over. Someone handed her back her bow. Another man strung his own and trained an arrow at her chest in case she decided to aim anywhere besides Marian. Robyn ground her teeth together. Marian deserved so much more than this mockery of a tourney sideshow. At least they hadn't ripped Marian's bodice, she consoled herself, but that brought cold comfort.

The man she took to be Alex—a short, broad man with a jerky way of walking—produced a pig's bladder half full of ale and rested it on top of Marian's head. "Chin up," he told her, brushing his knuckle beneath her chin to illustrate his point.

Marian kept her eyes fixed on Robyn's face. "Let's give them a show," she said, offering Robyn a small smile.

She knows what she's doing, Robyn realized. She reached for an arrow. *She knows what this looks like, and she knows what they want.* Robyn glanced at the faces around them, lit by the fire in the dying evening light. Yvette watched Marian with contempt and satisfaction. Alex, former owner of the bladder, leered. Ecstatic hatred mingled with lust and poorly suppressed rage from the rest. Beaten men and women all, and Marian stood for everything they'd lost and everything they'd lacked all of their miserable lives. In the heat of their envy, Marian glowed.

I have to contain this fire before it burns us all, Robyn thought, whatever the cost. Still, she could not but admire the naked courage in Marian's face as she gambled for their lives with her own. *Like me.* The last thought shook her, and she thought briefly of Gwyneth's anger at the risks Robyn took, understanding at last the price Gwyneth paid for Robyn's heroics. Marian's bravery pierced her heart like an arrow. *But I must see this through.*

"Ten paces back." Siward gestured at the short space between her and Marian. "A dog could make this shot."

He urged her on until she paused at the far side of the clearing. From there, she could still make out the details of Marian's face, but the shot was far less sure.

"How many arrows?" she asked.

"One," said Alex.

"Three," said another man.

"As many as it takes," said Yvette.

Siward settled the matter. "Three."

Three arrows. She couldn't hit the bladder on the first shot. That wouldn't satisfy the need that drove this spectacle. Nor could she hit it on her second, but each miss had to be spectacular. Marian's chest rose and fell as the seconds passed. Robyn nocked her arrow, aimed, and loosed.

The arrow landed a finger's breadth above the bladder. The brigands cheered and heckled her shot, but Marian remained stoic.

She chose another arrow. This time, she aimed lower, feeling the breeze against her cheek as she sighted off an irregularity in the bark a hair's breadth to the left of the bladder. Any increase in wind strength would send it into the ale, but if it landed where she aimed, she'd know she had the feel of the distance.

The shaft vibrated against the bladder but did not pierce it. Marian flinched and bit her lip but did not cry out.

"I'll let Yvette take her if you miss," said Siward.

Robyn lowered her bow as she nocked her last arrow and looked at Siward. A grotesque smile twisted his lips, and the eagerness in his pale eyes repulsed her.

She turned away from him and fired without pausing.

Ale sloshed down Marian's face and soaked the bodice of her dress. She sputtered beneath the shower, and Robyn forced herself to walk instead of run to her side.

"A waste of good ale," a man muttered, but the rest didn't seem to share his opinion. They cheered and uttered bawdy comments that Robyn ignored.

"Are you all right?" she asked as she leaned her bow at the base of the tree and plucked the arrows out of the wood, briefly shielding Marian from view. She didn't dare touch her with Siward watching.

"Is there any ale left?"

"A bit," Robyn said as she freed the bladder.

"Give it to me."

Robyn raised the bladder and poured the remaining ale down Marian's throat. Marian closed her eyes as she swallowed, and the pulse in her throat fluttered with the panic she had not let herself show. Robyn tossed the empty bladder back to Alex when Marian had drunk her fill.

"I'm untying you," she told her as she pulled her spare knife out of her boot, uncaring that by revealing its presence it would doubtless be confiscated. She sliced the ropes that bound Marian's arms before anyone could protest. Yvette hadn't bothered to tie her feet, and Marian pulled away from the tree with a shudder.

Robyn gave their audience a mock bow, flourished her arrows, and presented Marian to them with exaggerated ceremony, alive and unscathed and dripping with ale. With luck, that would be the only harm that befell her before this nightmare ended.

Chapter Forty-Four

Idiot, Marian berated herself as she sat with her back to the cave wall, surrounded by the sleeping bodies of men and women who were no doubt dreaming of the ways they would make her suffer in the morning. Robyn remained tied up outside the cave's mouth, guarded by Yvette and soaked from the insistent drizzle that had descended as the night drew on.

I should have stayed in Nottingham. She could have run to Emmeline when the coast had cleared. Emmeline could have helped her come up with a plan to cover her tracks, and then she could have waited for Robyn at the priory as they had planned.

And then what? You'd run into her arms and change your skirts out for hunting leathers and shoot foresters of a summer's day? You've never been good with a bow, and unless Robyn needs her clothes embroidered, you're worse than useless. You're a liability and a burden.

Siward snored on a bedroll beside her. The rope that circled her neck and wrist was wrapped around his sleeping hand, and she'd already discovered that he slept lightly. *If only I could wrap it around his throat.*

The rain abated, then intensified, coming down in a solid sheet. At least the cave was dry. She couldn't make out much in the darkness, but she knew the cavern was at least as large as Emmeline's hall, and she could only guess at what lay in the caves deeper in the hill. Gold? Food? If there was food, there

351

wasn't much of it. Hides were curing somewhere nearby; she could smell them, along with the sour stench of unwashed bodies and urine. At least the sound of the rain covered the worst of Siward's snores. She cautiously raised her hands, slowly so as not to wake him, and pressed them to her face. Even the rope stank. The coarse fibers irritated her chafed skin, and she knew she'd have to pick fragments of it out of her wrists later on. If there was a later on. Perhaps even now her father rode toward them, his face distorted with rage, hell-bent on wiping Siward from the face of the earth. Rescue wouldn't help her, though. She tried to gain some slack in the tightly knotted rope.

I have to get out. If she could somehow escape, then perhaps her father would blame Siward for her disappearance, and she could spend the rest of her life . . . where? Out here in the woods with Robyn? The past few hours had shattered that illusion. Back to the priory then, where perhaps she could persuade her father to let her pledge her troth to God in the wake of her disgrace. The walls of the cave closed in around her as all options faded. The sheriff would never let her join a convent, not when her children could guarantee him a position of favor in the years and wars to come.

So I marry then and tell myself that this was all a child's dream, fueled by a minstrel's song and too much ale. Try as she might, though, she could not reconcile herself to that fate.

Siward rolled over in his sleep, his back bumping up against her thigh. Her skin twitched with revulsion and she was about to move away when a stray gleam caught her eye. His belt knife lay almost within her reach. All she had to do was loosen the rope that connected her hands to her neck enough to allow her to grab it. Her fingers, swollen from the ropes as they were, edged their way around her throat, but they could get no purchase. If she pulled too hard, she knew, the rope would tighten, cutting off her air. She bit her lip in frustration. The knife was so close. She only needed a few inches, and he could roll over at any minute, depriving her of her chance.

A few inches. Her fingers found her hair, fingering the frayed ribbons binding the plaits. She tugged, and the knot, already pushed past its limits of endurance, gave. Her hair fell over her shoulder as she gathered the ribbon clumsily in her hands to make a loop. Sweat and oil had stiffened the silk, and she held her breath as she coaxed it toward the hilt. It took a few tries to catch. When at last the ribbon gained purchase on the shallow groove between hilt and blade, she paused, hardly daring to believe her luck.

Gently, she tightened the ribbon around the blade. Years of wrapping Emmeline's hair had given her both skill and patience. When the ribbon felt tight enough, she pulled. The knife slid out of the scabbard in well-oiled silence, hardly putting up a fight at all. She paused after each inch of progress to make sure Siward's breathing remained steady, until all that held the knife in place in its scabbard was the tip. Please, she begged whatever deity might be listening. The knife swung loose. She pulled it up by the ribbon until her fingers closed around it and she could flip the blade against her wrists.

Freeing her hands took another century. She could not saw away with any vigor, for that would make too distinctive a noise, so she had to time her efforts with Siward's snores and the coughs of the man nearby. Eventually, however, the first rope broke beneath the blade and she eased the coils free, careful to maintain the same tension on the line that connected her to Siward.

He rolled over as she began working on the rope around her neck. In the dark, she couldn't tell if his eyes were open. She stared at his face until another snore shook his chest, and then she gathered her courage, sliced the remaining fibers, and appraised her next obstacle: Yvette. The woman was just a silhouette against the dim starlight filtering through the rain clouds, but the entrance to the cave was far too narrow for Marian to sneak past. The hopelessness of her situation hit her again. She was just as trapped as she had been before. If she were Willa, she might have tried fighting her way out, now that she had a knife and free hands, but she was Marian. All she knew how to do was run.

Or hide. She strained her eyes to see the back of the cave, where, earlier, torchlight had illuminated the low tunnel that led to God only knew where. She remembered something her father had said once about Sherwood's outlaws.

"If they get into the goddamn caves, it's over. They're warrens, and once the rats get below ground we can't flush them out."

I could be a rat. Wandering through the caverns offered risks of their own, but at least she'd be free to die of starvation or thirst, instead of her current alternatives. She had a vivid image of herself crouching by an underground lake, gnawing on the carcass of a rat or perhaps a bone-white fish, pale from eons of living out of the sight of the sun. Was that really better than waiting for her father?

Yvette stood, cutting off her speculations. Marian held her breath as the outlaw stepped out into the rain, perhaps to relieve herself or check on her other captive. I might not get another chance, Marian thought, and she gathered up her skirts and felt her way cautiously to the wall. She kept her hand on the rough limestone, and when it encountered empty air she turned, keeping her hand outstretched, and vanished down a tunnel that smelled of damp earth and stone. Her shoes scraped on the uneven floor and her breath sounded loud to her ears in the silence. Sometimes the echo of her footsteps rose, and she had the impression of open space around her. Once she passed through a shaft of muted light coming from a narrow crack, only the absolute blackness of the cave distinguishing this glimpse of stormy night sky from her surroundings. She peered up, breathing the cool night air and pausing to lick some of the rainwater that filtered through the rock before continuing.

Keep turning right, she told herself as she went along, but she knew that her turns were random and that there were passageways she must have missed. Sometimes she had to crawl, and once she wedged herself into a shaft that promised light at the end but proved too narrow for her body. She reached for the sky with her hand and let the rain cool her fingers.

The last skylight she found lit a small chamber filled with a large stalagmite. She could tell by the grayness of the light that it was nearly morning, and her body ached from sleeplessness and running. She sank to the cave floor with her back to the lumpy pillar and watched the gray dawn break through the cleft in the rock until her eyelids grew heavy and she dozed with her cloak wrapped around her, unable to keep herself awake any longer.

Chapter Forty-Five

The rain had at last penetrated every fold of skin and warm secret crevice Robyn's body possessed, leaving her too miserable even to shiver. They'd taken her knives and they'd bound her tightly, a fact that the rain compounded as the rough fibers of the rope swelled until she couldn't feel her hands beyond the sharp, pulsing pain of thwarted blood. *Come on, John, come on.*

Marian and the rest of Siward's band were in the cave, blocked from her sight by darkness and the rain. Only Yvette remained, sitting just out of reach of the weather, sharpening Robyn's belt knife with proprietary strokes. The woman didn't seem to need sleep. She also hadn't responded to any of Robyn's questions, taunts, or threats.

They'll untie me before the sheriff arrives, she assured herself, but the thought only renewed the panic gnawing at her insides. She had no guarantee they'd do anything of the kind.

John, she willed into the darkness. *Get your ass back here.*

An owl cried from somewhere down the lake. Yvette glanced up from her knife and stared at Robyn, who did her best to remain impassive. Did owls hunt in the rain? She didn't know, and neither, it seemed, did Yvette, who studied the dark forest with sharp eyes. It could have been an owl. It also could have been her band. All of them knew that call.

The sound came again, this time closer. Yvette rose and stalked out into the rain, keeping her hand on the hilt of the knife as she approached Robyn.

"Friends of yours?" she asked in a low hiss.

A flash of white passed overhead, followed by the sound of wings.

Robyn shrugged, sending a cascade of water down her back. "It's an owl."

Yvette made a displeased sound in the back of her throat and turned back to the cave.

"You could always kill the sheriff," Robyn said, seizing on the first thing that came to her mind. She needed to keep Yvette in the open. Once back in the cave, she could sound the alarm, which would ruin Robyn's chances of escape. Yvette might have been willing to overlook the anatomical differences of various birds in the darkness, but Robyn had recognized the goshawk, and knew that her handler couldn't be far off.

"Kill one, another gets appointed," said Yvette. "I'd rather have money."

"He'll want revenge for his daughter."

"He'll have the girl back. Untouched."

"He'll still want revenge. He's not a man of his word. I could help you if you untie me."

"With what?"

"You saw me shoot."

Yvette crouched down in front of Robyn. "I know what I saw and I know what I felt. The rest of them might have sheep shit between their ears, but trust me when I tell you that you're better off out here than in there. They get a whiff of a woman, and . . ." she trailed off.

"You're a woman."

"I'm a man-killer, girl, just like John. That's why I'm out here. They know it, I know it, and we all sleep easy at night."

Robyn kept her eyes trained on Yvette, but she saw the shapes moving in her peripheral vision. John moved silently when he wanted to.

"I've killed a man, too."

"Not like I have." Yvette's smile would have chilled Robyn if it had been possible for her to feel any colder.

357

"Speaking of killing," said John, choking off Yvette's breath with his staff, "want to tell me why my friend is bound to a tree?"

Yvette made a harsh gagging sound.

"Drop the knife and I'll let you speak."

Yvette stabbed toward his legs with the hand that wasn't clutched at his staff. He tightened his grip and dodged her blow. The knife landed in the mud.

"Hey, cos," said Midge from behind Robyn as she began to fight the rope that bound Robyn to the tree.

John loosened his hold on Yvette enough to let her draw a breath when Robyn stumbled to her feet. Her bow was in the cave, as were her other weapons, but she was willing to kill Yvette with her bare hands. Or her knife. John kicked it toward her, reading her mind.

"Siward didn't trust—" Yvette began in a strangled whisper.

"He doesn't trust anybody," John said. "Didn't mean you had to leave Robyn in the rain."

"Did you get in touch with a forester?"

"They'll be at the river at midday."

"Let me get Siward then."

John hesitated. Robyn saw the decision in his mind: kill her or let her go? If he killed her, or at least bound and gagged her, they could make a clean escape, but they'd have to leave Marian behind.

"Let her go," said Robyn.

John thrust the brigand from him in disgust, and Yvette stalked back to the cave.

"You all right?" he asked Robyn.

"Fine. Who's here?"

"Will's in the trees with Alanna and Tom. Lisbet's keeping watch."

"What the hell are we going to do?" she asked, keeping her voice low.

He didn't get a chance to answer. Yvette's shout broke the silence, followed by the sound of half-awake men mobilizing hastily, stumbling over one another in the process.

"Where is she?" they heard Yvette say. "Where the fuck is she?"

"Marian," said Robyn, sprinting the few steps to the cave with John and Midge behind her.

Inside, chaos reigned. Someone fanned the coals of the banked fire until a torch flared to life, casting shadows that were almost as confusing as the darkness. Siward clutched a handful of rope with a murderous expression while Yvette snatched the torch from the bearer and thrust it into the corners of the cave. "She didn't get out the front," she said, and Robyn noted that she made a point of staying out of Siward's reach as she searched. "Must have gone in."

"Robyn," John said, pulling her back into the open.

"What does she mean, in?"

"The caves are a maze." He shook his head, worry and admiration evident in his furrowed brow. "Either she got loose herself, or someone cut her loose and took her back there. Any idea how many men Siward had?"

"We can't count now," said Midge, peering around the lip of the cave mouth. "Half of them have already gone in."

"Are there any other ways in or out?" asked Robyn.

"Yes."

"Then let's go."

"We've got bigger problems," he said, keeping a firm grip on her arm. "We need to get out of here."

"I'm not leaving her here."

"She isn't here," Midge pointed out.

"They have my bow."

"We brought your spare."

"Marian's in there." Robyn tried to yank her arm free, but John didn't budge.

"He's coming, Robyn. We need to get out of here. Now."

"Let go of me." Robyn froze as his words sank in. "You actually went to the sheriff?"

"This is what we wanted, remember? Siward and the sheriff. Everyone wins, Robyn. Marian goes home safely, we get him off our backs, and Siward is no longer a threat."

Marian goes home safely.

"No," she began, planning to tell him what she and Marian had decided, but Midge interrupted her.

"Robyn, let's go. Or do you want to die? What will happen to Gwyneth if he finds out who you are? Or my family?"

Gwyneth. The name snapped Robyn back to her senses. Gwyneth and Symon depended on her in a way Marian didn't. Her loyalties were first to them, and second to her band. She couldn't afford to split them any further, but neither was she willing to leave Marian behind.

"You said there was another way out," she said as she let John pull her away. "Take me there."

"Robyn—"

"Dammit, John, I'm not leaving her."

"Then it's time to run." He set off, and Robyn and Midge followed just as Siward's angry voice asked Yvette, "where is the goddamn archer?"

John skidded to a halt beside the mossy trunk of a fallen giant ten minutes later. Shelf mushrooms as large as shields grew from the dead oak, and its gnarled, decaying roots played host to spiderwebs larger than Robyn's arm span.

"This is the other entrance to Siward's cave," he said. "There are other caves in the cliffs, though. If she stumbles into one of them she could come out anywhere."

Robyn knelt to peer beneath the trunk. A dark passageway barely wide enough for a man and no taller than her waist met her eyes.

"How well do you know the caves?" Robyn asked. The others gasped for breath as they joined them, and Lisbet crawled into the entrance and back out, looking thoughtful.

"Well enough."

"Can you find Marian?"

John looked around at their band as he considered his response. "The caves are dark. With a torch, maybe I could. Without one, no."

"What about the sheriff?" asked Tom. "We don't want to be

in there, dealing with brigands and the sheriff's men at the same time."

Will and Alanna turned on Tom, but Robyn cut them off. "He's right," she said. "John and I will go. The rest of you will get out of here while you still can."

"No," Will said flatly.

"We shouldn't go in," said Lisbet. They all turned to stare at her. "They'll send in the hounds if they find out Siward doesn't have Marian. Like hunting rabbits. We should stay by the exits and see what the dogs flush out."

Hounds. Robyn looked into Lisbet's dirt stained face and pictured the massive boarhounds favored by the nobility snarling down a cold, dark tunnel.

"She might be right," said John. "And we'll have no way to know if Marian's escaped by a different way once we're inside. If she's even in there at all. Getting ourselves lost won't help her, and it certainly won't help us."

"We have to do something." Robyn hated the cold logic of their words, even as she knew they were right.

"There's nothing we can do." John's expression hardened. "She's the sheriff's daughter. It's up to him to see that she isn't harmed."

"Or Siward will kill her to spite him," said Robyn.

"Charging in there blind will only get you killed. Think about it."

"I'm going in." Robyn moved toward the cave.

John blocked her way. "You're not," he said.

"Let me by."

"You'll die in there for nothing. Her father is coming. We should use this opportunity."

"How?" She considered striking John.

"We kill the sheriff after he kills Siward." John's eyes glittered with resolve. "One good shot. That's all it would take."

Silence met his words. Robyn held John's gaze and thought of Michael and Gwyneth and the life the sheriff had stolen from her. What was a promise worth, compared to that? Her brother would never see his son's first step. Gwyneth—laughing, sunlit

Gwyneth—now spent her nights alone and her days in silent prayer and hard work, and Robyn would never again walk among her friends and neighbors. She would never see her brother's smile.

None of that would change with the sheriff's death. She could, however, prevent the sheriff from harming anyone else ever again, including her band. Dead men might haunt, but a ghost couldn't wrest Gwyneth from the priory. A ghost couldn't skim money off the top of their taxes, getting fat and rich while the rest of them starved. In the chaos to come, they'd have their chance at last, and Robyn was the best shot. She'd asked John to kill him as an alternative when there had been time for another plan. Now she resigned herself to the reality that unless they got lucky and the sheriff died in battle, she needed to be prepared to act.

"Will," she said, "I want you and Alanna to stay here. If Marian finds her way out, bring her to the priory. Tom, get Lisbet out of here and go to back to the priory right now. Midge, you're going with them. Don't argue—Gwyneth will not lose two family members this day. Explain to Tuck that we might need sanctuary. We'll regroup there."

"What will you do?" asked Midge.

"John and I will head back to the main entrance and see if Siward's found Marian, and then we'll take out the sheriff."

She turned and headed back the way she had come before any of them could raise further protests. John caught up with her in a few strides. Her heart, which had thundered painfully on her flight, now settled into a steady rhythm. *Kill him, kill him, kill him*, it beat, and her legs no longer burned with cramped exhaustion. She felt fleet as a deer and sure of her purpose. This was where she belonged. Who she was. A hunter.

They slowed as they approached Siward's camp. Thick moss muffled their footsteps, and both of them moved in a crouch by the lake until they could just make out the clearing through the reeds.

Nearly twenty brigands paced the space in the gray morning light. They looked over their shoulders every few seconds as they waited for their leader to give them instructions. Siward, how-ever, stood still. It would have been a clean shot if shooting would not have exposed them to a return volley.

"We should get the hell out of here," one of the brigands said. "We don't have the girl. He'll kill us."

"Yvette will find her," said Siward.

"Yeah, but what if she doesn't?"

"Then we'll stick you in a frock and send you out to the sheriff instead."

"It was that bastard John, wasn't it?" said another man. "Wanted the reward for himself. He knows the caves. Could have come in the back way."

The others agreed in a loud chorus. Siward raised his hand and they quieted. "If it was John, then we will find him and his friend and . . ." he trailed off, and his head whipped around to face the east. Robyn felt it, too. Faint, almost past hearing, but unmistak-able through the bedrock. *Hoofbeats. Horses must have died last night to get a message to Nottingham that quickly.*

"In," Siward said with a snarl. His men obeyed him at a dead run. Siward remained in his court a minute longer. His thin, wiry shoulders looked fragile from her vantage point. One day, if she was lucky enough to survive that long, this was how she would look. Gaunt. Undernourished. Aged prematurely from a life of constant watchfulness and driven mad by loss, all of it thanks to the man riding toward them. Would she also grow cruel, as Siward had, stealing from neighbors who already had little enough for their own families? She wouldn't prey on village girls, though, she reminded herself. Nor would she style herself a queen.

"They don't have her," she said. She wasn't sure whether to be relieved or more worried.

"They will soon if Yvette's on her trail. We need to find cover."

"Where?" The lake at their back offered no room for retreat.

"There." John pointed up the face of the crag to the tree cover above. It would provide them with a clear view of the ground below.

"Do we have enough time?" she asked.

"We don't have any choice." John crawled through the reeds for five more paces before breaking cover and sprinting for the rock. Robyn followed with the bow slung over her back.

The rock face was three or four stories high, but there were natural fingerholds and toeholds beneath the vines. Robyn thought of Lisbet and their cleft camp and tried to channel as much of the girl's squirrely spirit as she could. The wound on her left hand broke open and began to bleed as she worked her way up after John. They passed a shadowy alcove that gave her pause.

"Trap," John said when he noticed her slowed progress. "No way out."

Robyn climbed on.

They gained the summit just as the sound of hooves reverberated across the lake. John pulled Robyn over the lip of the rock, and they lay in the undergrowth panting as the line of riders came into view.

At least thirty men and horses filled the valley. Leather and mail creaked in the morning air, and the horses let off clouds of steam from their flaring nostrils.

"Here, my lord," said one of the riders. His clothing identified him as a forester, but Robyn stifled a hissing breath. She recognized that voice: *Cedric.*

"Siward," another man called loudly. She didn't recognize him, but his massive shoulders and metal helm suggested he was a professional soldier.

No answer issued from the cave.

"Establish a perimeter," the soldier ordered. Half of the riders took off, crossbows loaded on their hips. The other half remained at the cave's mouth. Hounds gathered behind the riders. Scent hounds, with their long ears and low bodies, snuffled at the ground. Marian's scent was all over the clearing. The remainder of the dogs made Robyn very glad to be high out of reach. Ten towering alaunts strained at their leashes, foam dripping from their jaws. While they were normally used to hunt large game, she'd heard of alaunts being set on men before. These dogs seemed eager to give chase to the first thing that moved.

"Siward," the soldier called again. "Show yourself, or we'll set the dogs on you."

Robyn imagined running from one of those beasts down a dark tunnel. Siward, apparently, had the same visceral reaction to the idea, for he spoke from the depths of the cave.

"You'd set hounds on your own daughter, Pierrot?"

A man spurred his horse forward. The black stallion arched his neck, and Robyn's fingers tightened on the bow. She loosened an arrow in her quiver and laid it along the string.

"Bring her forth," said the sheriff.

"And lose my leverage? I think not."

"Without proof that you have her, I'll give the order to flush you from your filthy den like the vermin you are."

"If it's proof you want . . ." A stone flew from the cave mouth. Robyn strained her eyes to see what was attached to it, but saw only a flash of blue. Cedric bent to pick it up and handed it to the sheriff.

"A blue ribbon," said Cedric.

The sheriff clenched his fist around the silk. "Let me see my daughter, and I will spare your life."

"I believe I requested silver."

"I do not bargain with rats."

"Even rats that have your sweet, sweet girl? Thus far I've managed to keep my men from spoiling her, but desperate men do desperate things. I promised them silver. Without that, they may take their own reward."

"I will have any man who touches her drawn and quartered."

The bickering continued. Robyn surveyed the trees around her, keeping her eye out for reinforcements. Grim lines etched John's face.

"Siward doesn't stand a chance," he said.

Robyn and John had never accounted for a hostage situation in their plans to eliminate their enemies. Thirty soldiers would not have been dispatched to prevent a robbery. A rescue mission, however, was different.

The voices ceased their exchange. Breath held, she watched the sheriff turn to the soldier. She couldn't hear what they said, but their gestures suggested they were devising a strategy.

Marian was somewhere in the caves below. The circumstances of her appearance came back to Robyn: the Midsummer gown; her solo ride; the discrepancy in the time frame she and Robyn had agreed on. Something had gone wrong. She strained her eyes to better see the sheriff. Had he discovered that Marian had stolen her own dowry? Had someone seen Marian leaving the city in Robyn's company? Whatever the reason, she'd fled from her father. Robyn was certain of that much. *Promise me that you won't be the one to kill him.* The arrow burned in her fingers.

Do you see now, little bird? Michael's ghost whispered on the wind. She closed her eyes at the irony. Unwittingly, she'd made the same fatal mistake as her brother. The sheriff would never let his daughter run away with an outlaw, just as he couldn't accept Gwyneth's refusal. Marian's capture had set into motion things Robyn couldn't control. He'd hunt them until his last breath or Robyn's, regardless of the cost.

Robyn almost wanted to laugh. If she killed the sheriff, she and Marian would be free, but Marian would never forgive her. If she spared the sheriff, he'd hunt her to the ends of the earth. There was no world where they lived happily ever after. That only happened in Alanna's songs. Robyn focused on the place where the sheriff's chain mail gapped at the neck.

She couldn't have Marian.

But she could have revenge.

She pulled back the arrow and took aim, preparing to release, and then the sheriff bellowed a command that split the morning air and sent her arrow skittering over the surface of the lake as she recoiled in dismay.

"Release the hounds."

Chapter Forty-Six

Marian woke with her face pressed against the stone and no idea of how much time had passed. Silence met her ears. No one shouted her name, and no searching footsteps stirred the stones, just the soft plink of dripping water and the grumbling of her belly.

Well, she thought, rubbing her sore wrists. I suppose this is an improvement. Sunlight flitted overhead, interrupted by passing clouds that sent shadows flying across the uneven surface of the stone surrounding her, but she could not tell if it was morning or afternoon. She knew she was lost. Exactly how lost remained to be seen, but the silence pressed against her ears, along with the uncomfortable knowledge of the crushing weight of the earth above her. Maybe Robyn will find me, she told herself.

Is that who you want to be?

The thought was so foreign to her she almost believed that someone else had spoken. "I haven't been here long enough to go insane," she said aloud.

Just long enough to lose your self-respect. No one is going to rescue you. No one is ever going to rescue you, sheriff's daughter. There must be a way out, and you must find it.

Fibers from the rope had embedded themselves in her skin, just as she'd suspected. She ignored the voice in her head as she did her best to pluck them out. Her clothing was damp and torn, and half her hair hung loose and tangled. She finger combed the worst of the knots and rewrapped her hair into one long plait. *I could cut it off, like Willa. Pretend I'm a boy.* Unlike Willa, however, she didn't have a narrow frame or a twin brother's angular face. Her body had decided her fate for her at the age of twelve, when hips and breasts had forced themselves upon her, along with the unwanted attention of men.

She peered into the low tunnel extending in either direction and wondered what it would feel like to be free of fear. Was Robyn free? She looked it, with her hunter's grace and her bow. What would it be like to know that she could take care of herself without relying on the man she hated and loved in equal parts?

Her head ached with too little sleep and hunger as she stood. She couldn't change her sex and she couldn't change her lineage, but in the quiet, chill damp of the cave the spur that had goaded her out of Nottingham struck again, biting into her sides with its urgency, and she realized with a gasp of pain that there was one thing, at least, she knew for certain: she wasn't going back. Not to Harcourt, not to Nottingham, and not to her father. If they caught her, so be it, but at least she would have chosen. At least she would have fought with her own words and her own will so that when they shut the bars of her cage she would have the comfort of knowing she'd tried to be free, instead of locking the door on herself.

Both tunnels looked the same. She thought she'd come in from the one on her left, but she couldn't be sure, so she chose the right tunnel anyway, crouching low to avoid scraping her skull on the ribs of the earth as she took the first steps toward her new life, whatever form it would take, come whatever hell it would bring.

Footsteps whispered behind her not long after. Marian flattened herself in the nearest crevice and held her breath to listen. One pair of boots, no more. A light step. Her stomach clenched as her instincts told her who approached: Yvette.

Marian still had Siward's knife. Aware that it was futile, she held it with both hands in front of her. The most violent thing she had ever done with a knife was cut meat at table. What was she going to do, kill Yvette, who could probably skin a man alive in her sleep? She didn't even know where to stab. The footsteps paused. Her chest hurt from holding her breath, and she fought against the urge to breathe.

Her pursuer sniffed the air. Dread filled Marian at the sound. Could Yvette actually smell her? No, she told herself, but she hadn't bathed in days and the sweat of acrid fear stained her clothes.

"Come out, m'lady," said Yvette.

The footsteps came closer, stalking her in the darkness. *What do I do?* She wanted to run. Her legs trembled with the urge to flee, but she'd likely knock herself out on a rock. Her only hope was to remain as still as the stone around her until Yvette passed and pray that she didn't hear the thundering of Marian's heart. If she did, well, she had the knife. Maybe she'd get lucky.

Yvette drew nearer. In the darkness, blind, Marian found that she could smell Yvette. Wood smoke and sweat clung to the other woman and filled the passageway. If Marian smelled as strongly, she stood no chance.

"Come out," Yvette said again. She had to be no more than a few feet away by now. Marian allowed a small stream of air to escape her nostrils as the need for oxygen overwhelmed her fear. If only she had something to throw, something to distract her pursuer. All she had was the knife. The footsteps stopped directly in front of her. She could hear Yvette's breathing and imagined her turning her head this way and that like a dog on a scent, searching.

A real dog barked. It sounded faint, but Marian felt the brush of air as Yvette spun around. She recognized the catch in the other woman's breathing. It was a gasp. *Fear.* The dog barked again.

"Alaunts," Yvette said under her breath. Then she ran.

Marian listened to her receding footsteps with her mouth open, unable to believe her luck. One second more and Yvette would have found her. She lowered the knife. The next bark was still distant, but the noise echoed strangely.

Oh. Oh no. Suddenly, she understood. The dogs were in the caves. And they were after anyone inside.

She shoved the knife into her belt and fled after Yvette. Alaunts wouldn't care that she was the sheriff's daughter. Once loosed, only the huntsman could call them off, and the dogs she'd stroked and played with as puppies would be too caught up in the chase to recognize a familiar scent.

"Yvette!" She no longer cared about avoiding capture. Hiding wouldn't do her any good when it came to dogs. The footsteps ahead slowed, then stopped, and she put out a hand to avoid running into the brigand.

"Keep up," Yvette said when Marian's fingers touched her shoulder. How Yvette knew her way in the blackness was beyond Marian, but she followed, stumbling, hands outstretched, and ducked when Yvette told her to duck until they came to an echoing cavern.

"Damnit," Yvette said. Marian heard her turn as her feet scuffed a circle on the stone. She's lost, she realized. Water dripped in the silence.

"How far do these caves go?"

Yvette didn't answer. The barking was closer now, and more savage. And now screams came to their ears.

"Siward." The venom in Yvette's voice forced Marian back a step. "I told him to leave you where he found you. Your kind bring only ill luck."

Marian didn't know what to say to that.

"I will not die here." A hand seized Marian and pulled her close. "Do you want to live?" Yvette asked.

"Yes."

Yvette felt down her arm to her sleeves. "Then take off your cloak and gown. We'll leave it for the dogs."

Marian didn't bother with her laces. She sliced through the bodice with her knife and stepped out of the crumpled remains, clad only in her shift and felt dancing shoes.

"This way."

She let herself be towed along, aware that Yvette planned to use her as leverage once they were out of the caves, but unable to think of an alternative. All the while the sound of fighting grew closer. Eventually she understood that was because they were running toward it.

"I said, keep up," Yvette growled when she stumbled. "We're almost there." She slowed, and Marian heard the soft whisper of skin against rock. She put out her own hand to touch the wall and felt the grooves gouged into the stone at regular intervals. *So this is how she finds her way.* Yvette strode ahead of her with more confidence. Abruptly, Marian realized she could make out the outline of her body. Sunlight.

Now what? Do I stab her while her back is to me?

The growl sent Marian flinching to the side. The dog leapt past her and onto Yvette. Yvette screamed as teeth dug into her shoulder, and Marian wished she was back in the darkness, deaf to the agony in Yvette's voice. Yvette fought, scrabbling at the huge dog with her bare hands. She must have dropped her knife when it lunged, Marian realized. This was her chance. She could leave Yvette to die, torn to pieces by hounds, and get out of these godforsaken caves.

Yvette screamed again.

"Hold," said Marian. She put all the authority she could into the command. The dog hesitated. It recognized a hunter's voice, even if it didn't know the hunter—or perhaps it did recognize some aspect of her scent or sound from years ago. "Hold," she said again. Yvette panted in the quiet. The dog still had her in its jaws, but it no longer savaged her. *"Here."* She threw her weight behind the word, and the alaunt dropped its prize and trotted over to her. She felt its hot breath on her hand. "Good," she told it. The dog shook itself and sat at her feet to await further orders.

Thank you, she prayed to whoever might be listening. She placed her hand on the dog's back. Its short hair was damp, per-haps from water, perhaps from blood. Hard muscles quivered with excitement. "Stand slowly," she instructed Yvette. The dog growled. "Easy," she told it, and grasped its leather collar.

Yvette rose. She clutched her shoulder, and the arm attached to it dangled loosely. Marian couldn't tell the extent of the dam-age in the darkness, but Yvette was lucky the arm was still attached.

"Do you have it?" Pain tightened Yvette's voice.

"I can hold it if you don't make any sudden movements."

Yvette began to laugh. The hair on the back of Marian's neck stood up at the sound.

"Run back to your father then, girl," Yvette said.

"Shut up." The dog backed her up with a snarl. "I'm not going back to him. Is this the way out?"

Yvette nodded, still laughing.

"Then let's move." She stepped toward the brigand and waited. The dog vibrated beneath her hand. Yvette let out one more choking burst of laughter, then set off at a limping crouch with Marian and the alaunt at her heels. She paused in the shadows at the tunnel's mouth.

"We don't know who could be out there," Yvette said. In the brighter light, Marian could see the blood soaking the leather of her jerkin and running down the sleeve of her tunic.

"Stay by me."

Yvette glanced up at her in surprise. Marian didn't blame her. *Why am I helping her?* Yvette had been nothing but cruel to Marian in the days she'd helped Siward hold her captive. Still, she couldn't forget that it *had* been Yvette who had counseled Siward to hold off his men, warning him that Marian's value would decrease if they despoiled her. And even if Yvette hadn't offered her that small mercy, she couldn't leave Yvette for the dogs. No one deserved that fate. Taking a deep breath, she crawled out into the sunlight with her hand firmly clasped around the hound's collar. The sharp brightness of the shady woods assaulted her eyes and she shielded them with her other hand, nearly slicing her forehead with the knife.

Movement above her startled the dog. It whirled and lifted its lips to reveal wicked teeth, jerking her with it.

"Marian?"

She looked up into Willa's eyes. Sweat and dirt streaked her friend's face, but that red hair was unmistakable. Alanna emerged from a bank of ferns behind her with knives in hand.

"Hold," Marian said quickly to the overeager dog.

"God's nails." Willa took in the alaunt with wide eyes. Marian didn't blame her. Blood slicked its white fur and mingled with the dark detritus of the caves. It looked like a creature out of a nightmare, and she clung to its neck, not sure of her ability to prevent it from lunging if it chose to snap.

"Are you all right?" Alanna asked.

"I'm fine."

"You're bleeding."

Blood did indeed stain her shift. "It's not mine," she said. "It's hers."

Yvette straightened from her pained crouch. Her shoulder sat strangely in its socket, and the brigand's face had turned the pale unhealthy color of the mushrooms growing at their feet.

"You." Willa slid from the fallen trunk and bared her sword. "Get away from—"

"We don't have time for this," said Marian. "Where's Robyn?"

"Looking for you. We'll meet her later," Willa said. "Alanna told me about your dowry. Does your father know?"

"Yes. I'm not going back."

"Then we need to move. Your father's men are all over these woods. It's only a matter of time before the lymers pick up your scent."

Lymer hounds. Of course. He wouldn't have brought only alaunts. Her heart beat faster. Losing the scent hounds would be nearly impossible on foot.

"You need a horse," Yvette said, echoing her thoughts. She pulled open the laces of her jerkin as she spoke and eased leather and cloth over her shoulder. Puncture wounds and bruising mangled the flesh, and the angle of the bone made Marian queasy. Yvette set her jaw.

"Hold my arm," she said. Alanna stepped forward to obey. Yvette grimaced, took a breath, and twisted. The joint popped. Alanna steadied Yvette as she staggered. When she righted herself, however, her shoulder sat normally in the socket, and her pale face was rigid with determination. "As I said. You need a horse."

Willa sheathed her sword with reluctance and looked around the woods. "Plenty of riders. Too bad they're all in mail."

373

"Doesn't matter. We need to get away from the cave." Shouts from the caverns punctuated Yvette's words.

"What do you want to do with her?" Alanna asked Marian.

Marian met Yvette's cold gaze. "You'd leave me behind if our places were switched, wouldn't you?"

"Yes."

Somehow, the fact that Yvette didn't bother lying made Marian's decision more difficult.

"She's not our problem," said Willa.

"She knows Marian escaped, though," Alanna countered.

Marian could still hear Yvette sniffing in the back of her mind, and she suspected that sound would haunt her dreams for weeks to come. She'd saved Yvette's life, rescuing her from the dog. Any debt she owed Yvette for protecting her from Siward was paid. Yvette wouldn't get far, though, with her wounds. The dogs would smell the blood, or one of her father's men would ride her down.

Her father. A vicious pang shot through her chest. Had he known she was in the caves? And even if Siward had lied about her whereabouts, would he really have risked her life on a brigand's word?

Yes. The answer came with aching clarity. She'd shamed him, disobeyed him, and stolen from him and, in so doing, decreased her own worth. Linley would not want her once he discovered what she'd done, and there was little hope of her father concealing her transgressions now.

"Can you stop the bleeding?" she asked Yvette. Betrayal thickened her voice. "We can't afford a blood trail."

"Give me some of your shift."

Marian sliced a wide strip from the hem and handed it over.

"What are you doing?" Willa sked.

"We're not leaving her." *Because I am not my father.*

"She just admitted she would leave you."

"Then that's the difference between us. Let's go. I need to talk to Robyn." She held on to the dog as she stepped forward into the trees. If she wanted a new life, then she would have to take it, regardless of the cost.

"Marian," Willa said, catching her by the arm. "Robyn will meet us later. What happened to your clothes?"

"It doesn't matter."

"Did they . . ." Willa trailed off, but the eyes that searched Marian's face were full of worry. Marian shook her head as she realized what Willa was asking.

"No one touched me. I left the dress for the dogs. At Yvette's suggestion."

"Good thinking." She dropped her hand. "We'll head north and loop around to the priory. I saw a few riders heading that way, but most of your father's men are in the other direction."

"Where's Robyn?"

"She'll meet us there."

Willa started walking, but Marian remained where she stood. "Willa."

Her friend didn't turn around.

"She went to kill my father. Didn't she?"

Alanna shifted her feet and glanced at Willa, which confirmed Marian's suspicions. She waited to feel something: betrayal, or maybe fear, or at least sadness. Instead she found herself at the center of a strange calm. There was no going home. She had known that when she took her dowry, but if Robyn killed her father—even if he had knowingly condemned Marian to death—neither of them would ever be free of him. Death only bred death.

"Marian—" Willa began.

"I have to stop her."

Chapter Forty-Seven

"Shoot him," John said over the sounds of screaming coming from the cave below.

Robyn fumbled for another arrow and strained her eyes for the sheriff's horse. The clearing had erupted into chaos. Siward's men fired arrows from the cave's mouth, and some of the sheriff's men had dismounted to pursue the dogs into the tunnel. A few fell beneath the brigands' volley, but the sound of screaming soon won out over battle cries as the dogs savaged any outlaws who had lacked the good sense to flee immediately.

Five ragged men burst from the cave with swords raised. The horsemen fell on them in a surge of pounding hooves and gleaming castle-forged steel, and Robyn, despite her search for the sheriff, watched in horror as blood spattered the mossy ground and the trunk of a nearby tree. Siward's men should have been able to hold their position in the caves with relative ease. Darkness and topography were on their side, but the dogs had clearly broken their discipline, and now they scattered.

"I can't find him," she said, raising her voice over the melee.

"There." John pointed. A contingent of riders broke away from the fight to ride north, and the sheriff rode at their head. Robyn released her arrow, but the distance and the angle of her shot worked against her. It struck his helm instead of his back, where it might have punctured the chain mail or at least bruised him, and spun harmlessly into the reeds.

"Seven hells," she swore as she stood to get a better shot.

John tugged her away from the ledge. "He's trying to cut them off. We need to move."

"Will and Alanna," said Robyn, realizing the reason for the set of his jaw. The sheriff was riding right toward them, and if he somehow knew about the other exit, they would be cornered.

John sprinted through the tangled vines and shrubs growing on top of the limestone ridge. A misstep here could send them plummeting, but they needed every second haste could buy them.

A trail so narrow Robyn thought she imagined it wound along the ridge. She saw it in glimpses, no more than patches of bare earth beneath a blur of green, and she willed her feet to find it, relying on instinct instead of her eyes to tell her where to place each fleeting footfall. Alanna and Will stood no chance against a mounted party, but that was not the only panicked thought clawing for purchase in her mind: Marian was in these caves. Marian and a pack of dogs, and the sheriff was headed for Robyn's best chance of getting in to find her. *As I should have done in the first place, damn their logic and damn my cowardice.* Marian, to Robyn's knowledge, had no weapon, and even if she did, what hope did she have against a dog bred to bring down wolf and boar, alone in the dark? What did revenge matter if Marian lay ripped to ribbons?

Ahead of her, John leapt over a chasm nearly as wide as Robyn stood tall. She sped up and flung herself over the vine-choked rift to land, her arms windmilling, on the far side. John paused just long enough to make sure she'd made the leap before continuing. Blood was running down her face and hands from brambles and whipping branches by the time he skidded to a halt along a natural chimney.

"Way down," he said, panting.

Water dripped along the steep slant. What Robyn would have hesitated to call steps on her most generous day periodically interrupted the drop, but short of trusting to one of the flimsy vines trailing over the sheer expanse of limestone in full view of any onlookers, this was their only choice.

Robyn didn't wait for John. She braced her hands on the slick walls and slid, heedless of her gathering speed, using the steps only to prevent herself from falling outright. A screen of leaves shielded the base of the chimney from view. Robyn rolled right through it and landed in a crouch, already nocking an arrow to her bowstring. John broke cover seconds later. Robyn was grateful for his presence, even as a part of her wished he'd had the sense to remain behind, hidden in the crevice.

Before her, mounted on his foam-flecked stallion and surrounded by his soldiers, rode the sheriff of Nottingham.

"So kind of you to join us, Robyn Hood."

She held her arrow steady while she struggled to control her breath. The run had winded her, and she wanted nothing more than to take a moment to regain the ability to breathe. John shifted behind her, also panting, and she knew he had just raised his staff.

Not that it would do them much good.

The sheriff made no move atop his horse, but the other three riders all had crossbows trained on her and John. Her eyes darted around them. Death on horseback, come to claim her.

Cedric looked back.

Pain and recognition filled his eyes. She saw his lips form her name before he clenched them together, but she did not care. It hardly mattered now if the sheriff knew her true identity. Both she and John would die here.

She turned her gaze back to the sheriff.

"My lord," she said, buying herself time to think with words. She could take him out before he gave the command for his men to shoot her, of that she was sure, but if there was any chance that either she or John could make it out of this alive, she had to try to find it.

"I should have known you were behind this," said the sheriff. "Tell me, what did you promise my daughter? What poison did you put in her head?"

"Nothing that was not already there. As for promises, she makes her own choices. I did not promise her anything." *Except that I would not kill you.*

378

"Where is she?"

"In the caves." Robyn's voice broke on the words. The sheriff flinched, and his horse tossed its head. Had he not known? Truly? What had he thought then? That this was all some ploy, driven by greed and vengeance? She looked into his face and tried to imagine what it must be like to be this man. As she looked, as she watched confusion turn to fear and grief, she understood. He *had* thought this was a bluff. How could he think otherwise, when greed and ambition ruled his world? How could he understand how other minds worked when his was so far down the path of corruption that rot bloomed in his footsteps? Almost, she pitied him.

"She loved you," she told the man she hated with every drop of blood that passed through her heart. "She begged me once not to kill you. If I had shot you on the road, she would have been free, instead of—" She couldn't finish. *Instead of bleeding out in the darkness, alone, betrayed at the last by all who claimed to love her. Marian, I should have run to you at once. I should have taken you with me on Midsummer as you asked. I should have read the danger all around us.*

"You. You took her from me." His face purpled as his fists clenched. "You took my daughter." She heard the unspoken words that followed: *and Gwyneth.*

"I took nothing. You drove them both away. This is your harvest, my lord."

He spurred his horse forward so that the stallion's teeth clacked in Robyn's face and green-flecked foam sprayed her cheeks.

"Let me go," she said. Her arrow still aimed at the sheriff. This close, it would punch through his mail and end him, and he would fall from his horse to the ground like a sack of rye flour. She savored the image but did not shoot. If there was a chance, even a slim one, that he would let her find Marian—

"Why in God's name would I do that?"

"Let me find your daughter. There is another entrance to the caves not far from here. I will go in, and I will find her, and you can kill me when I return. I swear it."

"Your word means nothing."

"Every second we waste here the dogs get closer to her—if they haven't found her already." She fought to keep from shouting. "Do you love her at all? At least let me show you to the cave so that you can send in your men."

"My lord." Cedric spoke in a voice that no longer cracked. "If there is a chance he speaks the truth, should we not listen?"

Robyn saw doubt in the sheriff's eyes.

"This—" he spat at Robyn's feet, "this creature plans to lead us into an ambush."

"My lord—"

"The sheriff has no bow." The whisper in her ear distracted her from the argument taking place between the sheriff and his men. Robyn stilled. The sheriff had a sword and mail, yes, but no long-range weapon. Cedric and the other two riders all bore crossbows, but at the moment they were focused on the sheriff, not Robyn and John. She understood John's meaning. If they struck now and disabled the crossbowmen, they stood a chance.

Robyn spun, putting the sheriff's horse between herself, Cedric, and the second rider, and took aim at the third. Her arrow sank into his unprotected throat and his horse sidestepped as he flailed. No time for regret, she told herself as she nocked her second arrow. John's staff moved in a blur beside her as he blocked the downward swing of the sheriff's blade, shielding her from harm.

She aimed at the second rider as his crossbow bolt slammed into her thigh. Her hand released the bowstring in pain, but he had not been quick enough with his shot, and her arrow had been trained on his heart. He too fell.

John stood over her as she sank to the ground and nocked a third arrow. Her thigh shrieked with agony and black spots danced around her vision. The sheriff's wordless bellow echoed in her ears, but John did not back down before the sheriff's charge, and the end of his staff slammed into the horse's nose. The stallion shied and reared.

Robyn's fingers shook as she raised her bow and pointed the shaft of her arrow toward Cedric while the sheriff fought to control his wounded mount. "Drop your bow," she told him.

Cedric hesitated. *Please,* Robyn begged him. *Don't make me shoot you, too.* But Cedric's face settled into bleak determination, and she knew he would give her no choice.

"Robyn," said John. She heard it: hoofbeats pounded on the trail. *Reinforcements.* John hauled her to her feet as the sheriff's horse reared again, bugling his pain. Cedric's crossbow remained trained on her chest. He hasn't shot yet, she told herself.

"Give me the bow and take my staff. You can't walk on that leg and we need to go. I'll take care of the boy and the sheriff," said John.

"Hold." A rider galloped into the clearing and wheeled his horse around in a spray of soil and leaves. Robyn was forced to lean into John as she stumbled backward, and the arrow Cedric loosed in her direction thudded harmlessly into a nearby hawthorn. Robyn looked up at the mailed and helmeted figure and felt the hope she'd harbored die. She'd never get to Marian now. It was over.

Chapter Forty-Eight

The mounted scout picked his way along the path. He had removed his helmet to get a better view of the forest, and sweat plastered his dark hair to his forehead. The dog whined in recognition as Marian stepped out onto the path.

"Sir," she said in a falsely grateful tone. "Oh, sir, you've saved me."

The man's grizzled face went slack with surprise. Then, as she'd anticipated, he dismounted and strode toward her with reassuring words on his lips. Willa's sword pressed against the scout's throat, cutting off his assurances of safety. Yvette flanked Willa, dagger bared, and Alanna came up behind him with another knife.

"What the hell is this?"

"Shh," said Willa. "Don't touch your dagger. Shout for help, and you die. Listen, and you'll live."

"We don't have time for this." Alanna moved as she spoke and brought the hilt of her dagger down on top of the man's skull. His eyes rolled back in his head and he fell to the ground. Alanna grabbed the horse's reins before it could spook away.

"Efficient," said Willa, sounding impressed. "Marian, help me get this off him."

Wrestling the unconscious man out of his mail shirt, quilted padding, leathers, tunic, and breeches made sweat stream down her face. He weighed twice as much as she did, and his dead

382

weight was clumsy. After longer than any of them liked, however, they had him stripped down to his underclothes. The clothing reeked of sweat, horse, and rancid grease. Marian pulled it on over her shift and tried not to breathe as the sweat-soaked cloth and padding released its foul odor. His helmet remained tied to his saddle. Alanna jerked it free and jammed it on Marian's head. With all her hair piled up on top of her head, it nearly fit.

"Someone's coming." Yvette's warning gave Marian's arms strength as she pulled herself into the saddle. The tunic hung ludicrously far past her knees, but at least the quilted padding beneath the mail hid her curves from view. Alanna, Willa, and Yvette hauled the unconscious soldier into the undergrowth and out of sight.

A second rider appeared around a bend on the trail from the opposite direction. Marian swung the horse around to face him. "Anything?" he asked.

Marian shook her head, not daring to speak. Alanna, Willa, and Yvette crouched behind the trees on either side of the path. It was up to Marian to get rid of the rider, and she needed to do it quickly, because the helmet only hid her hair and nose, not the rest of her face. He frowned at her.

"You're not Martin," he said.

Willa crept around her tree to approach the rider from behind. Marian needed to buy her time.

"He went that way," she said, deepening her voice to a low rasp. It sounded painfully false to her ears.

"That's his horse you're riding."

He drew his sword. Marian did the only thing she could think of and dug her heels into her horse's sides. It lunged forward as she struggled to pull the heavy sword from her stolen scabbard. While the man's attention was on her, Willa leapt from hiding and seized him by the back of his shirt and hung on. Her weight unbalanced him as Marian's horse slammed into his, and the point of her sword skidded off his mailed chest harmlessly, but not without adding another shove to his upset. He landed heavily on the ground.

"Don't move," Willa said as she scrambled out from beneath him and leveled her sword at his throat. He slammed it out of the way with a gauntleted fist and would have plunged his blade into Willa's stomach if Alanna hadn't thrown her knife. It flashed in Marian's peripheral vision on its way to its mark. The hilt quivered in his eye socket. He tried to scream, convulsed, then lay still. None of them spoke. Alanna's face had turned white with shock, and Willa stared at her with her mouth open.

"Christ," said Yvette. "Get on the damn horse."

Willa mounted. Alanna vomited into the bushes, then clambered up after her. Yvette shook her head in disgust and pulled the knife out of the man's head. She wiped the blade clean on his pants and handed it back to Alanna before turning to Marian. "Good luck," she said.

Marian looked at her pain-drawn face and nodded. "Go to the priory in Edwinstowe and ask for the Reverend Mother. Tell her I sent you. She'll take care of your shoulder and she won't ask any questions. Take the dog for protection. Talk to it like I did. Can you make it that far?"

"Worry about yourself," said Yvette. She held Marian's eyes, and the cruelty in her gaze parted for a fraction of a second. Then she turned and vanished into the woods with the alaunt at her heels.

"Let's go," Marian said to Willa and Alanna. Willa looked as if she wanted to argue, but as Marian turned her horse away, she heard the sound of Willa's horse's hooves following. They spurred their mounts back toward the greenwood. Her horse tried to seize the bit in its teeth. She fought it, mustering strength from reserves she didn't know remained, and attempted to think of a plan. Nothing came to her. Exhaustion and adrenaline warred inside her skull and left no room for anything else. All she knew was that she had to stop Robyn from killing her father, and more importantly she had to stop her father from killing Robyn.

The horse seemed to know where to go. She let it choose the path, though not at the pace its arched neck suggested it would prefer. Shouts rang out periodically from farther down the lake as her father's soldiers hunted down Siward's gang. *How am I going to find Robyn in the middle of this?* Her stolen clothing caught on branches and she gripped the horse tightly with her legs. Ahead, a low-hanging limb threatened to knock her off entirely. She ducked. With her face pressed to her horse's mane, she glimpsed a small clearing. Riders surrounded two figures on foot. One of them was Robyn.

She pulled up on the reins, ignoring her horse's snorts of protest, and burst into the clearing with Willa arriving behind them in a shower of dislodged moss.

"Hold," she shouted as she wheeled her horse around. She took in the scene as quickly as she could. Cedric, the man who had identified Robyn to her father, stared at her with relief writ across his pimpled face. The other man shouted at his horse. Blood streamed from its nose, and she recognized the stallion a split second before she recognized her father.

"Marian?" Robyn gaped up at her. Blood and scratches covered her face, and Marian saw more blood seeping from the crossbow bolt sticking out of her leg. Her own thigh tightened in sympathetic pain.

"Kill him," ordered the sheriff. He still had not looked up from his horse's anguished head.

"No." Marian interposed her horse between her father and her friends. Her father stiffened at the sound of her voice, and his horse hung its head in blowing defeat.

"Marian?"

"Father."

"Marian, what—"

"Listen to me."

"You should have—"

"Listen to me." Her shout silenced him. Had she ever shouted at him? Certainly not in front of his men, and certainly not with the vehemence that now filled her voice. "You sentenced me to die."

"I—"

"I was in those caves. Did you think to rid yourself of me? Is the price of your pride that high?" Her voice did not break.

385

"Never. Marian, I swear I did—"

"Don't lie to me. You knew there was a chance I was in there. You knew what might happen, and you set the dogs loose anyway."

"Outlaws lie. Come back to Nottingham, daughter."

She laughed. "I am not your daughter. I haven't been in years, but I didn't know it until today. Thank God mother died before she could see what you've become." Her words leached the color out of his cheeks.

"How dare you speak of her like that."

"How dare I?" Her horse sidestepped as her legs tightened. "I asked you to choose me another husband. Then I asked you to send me to the priory. You denied me, as is your due, but when I disobeyed, you set your dogs on me as if I were vermin. I would have been torn to pieces if one had not recognized me. Do you hear me?"

He opened his mouth.

"I will not come back to Nottingham. Not with you, and not with any other. Tell your men I died here. That should satisfy your pride."

"You would choose this outlaw over me? Over the life I gave you?"

"Yes. A thousand times, yes."

The sheriff turned to Willa. If he'd hoped to find support from that quarter, he was mistaken. She saw recognition flicker in his eyes. "I see," he said. "Nottingham's daughters now play whore to filth. I shall tell your father, Lady Willa, and we—"

"What will you do, m'lord?" said Willa. "Hunt us? Bring us back and punish us? What will that bring but your own disgrace?"

"Mark my words."

"No," said Robyn. "Mark mine." Marian looked down and saw Robyn push back her hood so that the morning light fell full over her face. Cedric stirred. The sheriff frowned.

"What is this?" said her father.

"Do you not know me, my lord?"

"The archer from the fair."

"I am more than that to you, surely. I begged your mercy once, and you threw me back into the street."

Horror, followed by understanding, curled his lip. "You're the sister."

"Are you afraid to speak his name? Yes, I am Michael Fletcher's sister. Did you not wonder what had happened to me, or did you assume that I had starved, as you intended?"

Marian had never seen her father truly speechless. His eyes bulged and his lips worked, but no sound passed them as Robyn spoke.

"Hear me now. You will not have Marian, and you will not have me, and you will not have anyone under my protection. Hunt us if you will. If we are captured, however, know this: you were thwarted by a woman. That will be what Nottingham remembers. Not my death, and not the justice you claim to work. They will remember that Nottingham's daughters rose up against you when no one else dared. Will you rule them then with fear?"

In the silence that followed, Cedric dropped his crossbow to the ground.

"Dismount, m'lord," said John. "Your horse wants tending."

"You can get off your horse, too," Willa told Cedric. "We'll be borrowing it."

Cedric dismounted; the sheriff did not. He sat, immobilized, as Cedric handed his reins over to John. Marian studied her father. This might not be the last time she laid eyes on him—fate was rarely that kind—but it was the last time she would look at him through a daughter's eyes. She began to memorize the bulk of his shoulders and the set of his jaw, then she stopped herself. This was not how she wanted to remember him. Instead, she thought of the man who'd smiled to see her mother laugh and whose arms had lifted her onto the back of her first horse, guiding her hands on the reins as he beamed up at her with pride. She would remember that man, not this one.

"Robyn," Cedric said. Accusation filled his voice.

"I am sorry to meet you like this again," said Robyn. "It was never my intention to hurt anyone."

"Pol. Brendan."

Marian followed Cedric's gaze to the bodies she'd overlooked before. Robyn's arrows protruded from their wounds.

"And Clovis." Exhaustion crept into Robyn's words. "I know. I'll carry them with me until the end of my days."

"I believe you," said Cedric.

"You're a good man, Cedric. Much better than your master. Don't let him make you cruel."

Cedric nodded and backed away, looking lost. Marian spared him no further glance. "Get her on my horse," she told John. John helped Robyn up behind Marian's saddle. The feel of Robyn's arms around her waist drove away some of the emptiness in her chest, and she turned to her father one last time as John mounted.

He watched her out of haunted eyes.

"Good day, sheriff," she said, and then she dug her heels into the horse's sides. There would be time for reckoning later, when they were far away from here.

John led the way out of the valley. They passed the bodies of brigands near the tunnel she'd emerged from. Some sported man-made wounds. Others bore the marks of teeth. Had Siward perished in the darkness, or had he clawed his way to sunlight at the end? Once, she thought she recognized his body, or at least his ringed hand, but the corpse's face was too mangled to say for sure and she did not stop to check. It did not matter if he lived or died. His reign was over.

They heard riders only once. John led them off the path to a stand of firs, where the boughs blocked them from view, and then they rounded the cliffs and entered the forest.

John kept them to game trails. The horse's tracks would be easy to follow, but it was faster than breaking through the under-growth, and they needed speed. Robyn breathed rapidly behind her. The wound had to hurt badly. Crossbow bolts were thicker than arrows, and the jarring of the horse's hooves must have felt like a knife in the wound, but there was nothing Marian could do for her except get her to the priory as swiftly as possible.

"Should we take the road?" she asked John.

"They'll have it watched. We'll loose the horses at the river to throw them off our trail, and walk from there."

"Robyn can't walk." Marian wanted to turn in the saddle to see Robyn, but the mail made that impossible.

"She'll have to," said John.

"But—"

"I'll be fine."

Marian felt the effort the words cost Robyn in the tightening of the arms around her waist. She was grateful for the foreign leather and mail between them, for all that it reeked of unwashed man. The reality of Robyn was suddenly too much. What if Marian had arrived in the clearing even a moment later? Who would have been left standing? *Don't,* she warned her mind. She could not afford doubts until they were safe, and besides, she'd arrived in time. If Robyn suspected some of the turmoil riding pillion with her, she didn't let on. Instead, her head sagged against Marian's back. Twice she nearly slid off the horse.

The second time this happened, Marian halted and turned in the saddle. Robyn's face had changed from pale beneath the bloodstains to gray. She looked like she might pass out at any moment.

"Stay with me," Marian said. They'd been riding for only twenty minutes, with at least an hour more to go before they hit the river. Robyn struggled to focus her eyes.

"Damn." Willa brought her horse alongside Marian's, although the closeness of the woods here made it difficult. Blood dripped down Robyn's leg and onto the leaves. Marian heard the double meaning in the curse. Robyn was not only losing blood too quickly, but they were leaving a blood trail.

"Get her off the horse," said Alanna.

"No." Robyn shook her head slowly, as if the effort hurt. "If I get off, I might not be able to get back on. I need . . ." she trailed off, blinking rapidly. "I need something to stop the bleeding."

"We should have seen to this before. Here." Alanna sliced a strip of cloth from the saddle skirt. "Tie your leg off above the wound."

Robyn hissed as she tied the tourniquet. The blood slowed to a trickle, which Robyn stanched with her hood. She looked vulnerable without it covering her head. "Nothing we can do about the blood trail now," she said, "except ride and hope no one comes looking for us."

Morning faded to afternoon. They had left the tangle of the woods around Siward's cave behind. The trees here spread their branches high and wide, blocking the sunlight from all but the most ambitious of saplings. Vines curled around their trunks, and sweet ferns rustled in the shade.

"We're near the road here," said Willa. "We'd make better time."

"John said to stay off it." Alanna craned her neck to stare at Robyn as she spoke.

"She's lost too much blood. We need to get her to safety."

"Willa's right," said John. "Come on."

Marian directed her horse through the trees toward the road and strained her ears for the sound of voices. Only birds chorused. "Hold on, my love," she said to Robyn, who slumped against her. She urged her horse into a slow canter, fearing a trot would be too jarring for Robyn. Willa stayed on her other side so that Alanna could keep an eye on their casualty while John scouted ahead. They hadn't ridden for more than a few minutes when a group of traveling stonemasons came into view. She felt their eyes as they cantered past, hands raised in greeting.

John brought his horse down to a walk as they rounded the next bend and stared at Marian, wordless. She nodded. They led the horses off the comfortingly rutted surface of the road and into the forest once more, letting the trees swallow them from sight.

"We have to assume they'll tell someone," Alanna said. "Nothing travels faster than a secret."

"I know." John's frustration carried over into his mount, which shied at a passing branch. "We'll make for the river as we planned."

Marian's arm throbbed from the awkward effort of keeping Robyn in the saddle. She clenched her teeth and endured. On top of pain and blood loss, neither of them had had anything to eat or drink since the day before, and she doubted Robyn had slept while she had been tied up. It was a miracle she'd held on to consciousness this long.

She smelled the river before she heard it. A breeze wafted the rich smells of mud and damp, and her taxed salivary glands ached at the nearness of water. The horses smelled it too. Sweat dampened their flanks, and she knew her father's men had ridden them hard to reach the cave by dawn. All of them needed a drink.

"We dismount in the water," said John as they crested a low hill overlooking the reedy riverbank. "We leave no tracks. And we'll release the horses and move downstream before we go the rest of the way on foot."

The horses scrambled down the banks and slurped greedily at the reedy stream. This deep in the forest, the water flowed over fallen leaves and silvery fish, who flitted away from the disturbance created by the horses' hooves. Willa and Alanna dismounted with a splash. John's landing was quieter, and he patted his horse's shoulder.

Marian stayed mounted.

Willa cut the other two horses' reins with her knife, leaving only a foot or so of leather dangling from the bridle. "This way it won't catch on a tree," she said, pocketing the leather straps. "I'll help you with Robyn." She waded closer while Alanna searched the horses' saddle bags for anything of use. John moved to help Willa.

Robyn jerked into consciousness when Willa placed a hand on her wounded leg.

"We need to get you down," Willa told her.

"John—" Marian felt Robyn look around for the man.

"I'm here," John said.

Robyn tried to swing her other leg over the cantle and the back of the horse, which was difficult enough for a hale rider. "Wait," Marian told her, and swung her own leg over the horse's lowered neck. The water filled her shoes the instant she landed.

Together, she, John, and Willa helped Robyn off the horse. Marian looped her arm around Robyn's waist and bore the brunt of her weight while Willa repeated the process with the reins. John offered to take Robyn from Marian with a gesture, but Marian shook her head. She could not loosen her hold on Robyn. Not now, and perhaps not ever again.

"We'll head downstream and then we'll splint your leg," John said to Robyn. "Can you manage that?"

"Yes," Robyn gasped.

Marian half supported, half carried Robyn as they waded through the river. She couldn't take Robyn into the deepest part of the stream because she didn't want to get her wound wet, but that meant staying in the muddier shallows. The ground sucked at her thin-soled dancing shoes, and she lost both in a matter of minutes. They hadn't been much use to her anyway out here, and there was no time to fish them out.

The horses, freed from their riders, trotted off, urged on by Alanna, who slapped their rears and forced them across the stream. With luck they'd lead any pursuit deep into the forest before someone found them. She didn't have time or strength to pity the animals. Her stolen clothing grew quickly sodden, and the mail shirt weighed her down even further.

"Let me take her for a bit," said John when he noticed Marian struggling.

"I can walk on my own," said Robyn.

"And I'm the king of England." John gripped his friend around the middle. "Just a bit farther, and then we'll see to your leg. We've got to get that bolt out."

Just a bit farther took them around several bends in the river, until they came to a narrow stretch. The water coursed between two boulders, and the exposed roots of a massive elm offered a shallow cave out of sight from watching eyes. John and Marian lowered Robyn onto the muddy bank.

"I'll keep watch," said Alanna.

"Still with us?" John asked.

"I've been better. I'm thirsty."

Willa filled her hip flask from the stream and handed it to Robyn, who emptied it. Marian resisted the urge to quench her own thirst until after Robyn had drained the flask a second time. Only then did she kneel to drink her fill of the sweet, clear liquid, removing her helmet and splashing more water onto her face. When she turned back to Robyn, John had sliced away the cloth around the wound. Robyn lay on her side propped up on her elbow with a gray expression. Marian folded herself down to sit beside her, and Robyn leaned her head against Marian's ribs.

"Just pull it out," said Robyn.

"It's through and through. First I have to cut the fletching."

"Do it."

Marian had not had a chance to take a good look at the wound back in the clearing. Now, she saw that the bolt had bit through the large muscle of Robyn's thigh. The barbed head protruded at an angle from one side, and the bloodstained fletching from the other. John pulled out his knife and examined the bolt. Robyn reached for Marian's hand.

"This is going to hurt," said Willa. "If only we had some of Tuck's mead to give you."

"You think?" Robyn managed a grimacing smile. "Fuck the lord and all his angels," she swore as John trimmed the fletching off the crossbow bolt. If even that slight pressure hurt, Marian did not want to think about the next step. Sweat sprang out on Robyn's forehead, and she turned the color of day-old porridge. Her grip nearly broke Marian's hand. Willa, too, looked queasy.

Only John kept his composure. "Are you ready?" he asked.

"No," said Robyn.

John wrapped the point with a bit of cloth, then braced himself and with one steady movement, pulled the shaft out. Robyn stifled a scream by biting her lip hard enough to make it bleed. When John held up the bolt, Robyn slumped her head onto Marian's lap and lay there, breathing shallowly. Marian brushed the hair back from Robyn's face. "It's over," she told her.

Robyn lifted their clasped hands to her face and pressed her forehead against their interlocking fingers.

"I need to remove the tourniquet, but first I need something to stanch the bleeding. Preferably something clean," said John.

They all examined their persons. Nothing on Marian's body had been clean in some time. The soldier's clothing stank, and her shift was soaked with sweat beneath it. Willa and Alanna were in somewhat better condition. John matched Robyn stain for stain.

"Use my hood," said Robyn.

"It's already soaked in blood."

"Then we'll use mine," said Willa.

"Your hair is too easily recognized. Just because the sheriff knows who you are now doesn't mean the rest of Nottinghamshire needs to know. Besides, leather won't work as well as cloth." Alanna pulled her tunic off and handed it to John.

"Thanks." John folded it into a thick pad, then untied the cord from Robyn's leg. Robyn groaned in pain. John pressed the pad to the wound and secured it in place. "Now we need something to splint your leg with so you can walk without using that muscle."

Alanna climbed the roots of the tree and returned a few minutes later with a stout rod.

"Perfect." John tied the splint to Robyn's leg with the severed reins. "Let's move."

"I'd move faster without this," Marian said, gesturing at the mail shirt and helm.

"You'd also be more recognizable," said Alanna. "But the helmet catches sunlight. Give it to me."

Marian handed over the helm. Alanna dug a hole in the stream, filling the helm with the dislodged mud and pebbles, then plunged the helm into the hole. "No one will find it here."

"Brilliant." Willa smiled wearily. "Okay. We can leave the river now, I think. John?"

"No." Robyn shook her head before John could answer. "A bit farther."

"It will be harder for you."

"So will getting shot again."

No one argued with that logic. Alanna and Willa led the way while John and Marian supported Robyn on either side, through the boulders and onward as the river flowed through Sherwood Forest toward the priory and safety.

Chapter Forty-Nine

Robyn woke to the gray light of morning and the sound of voices arguing. Every part of her body hurt. Squinting against the ache in her head, she opened her eyes.

She didn't recognize her surroundings at first. The stone walls pressed in on her, somehow different from their home in the cleft, and distant voices sang—a sharp contrast to the voices hissing at each other above her.

"She's awake," a familiar voice said at her shoulder. Midge's face hovered into sight. She looked cleaner than Robyn had seen her in a while, and her curly hair fell loosely around her shoulders. Robyn herself had been bathed and cosseted in clean bed linens.

"Robyn." Gwyneth leaned into her field of vision with concern twisting her face.

"Gwyn? Where am I?"

"You're at the priory of course. Don't move," she added as Robyn tried to sit up.

"I'm fine."

"Like hell you are," said John.

Robyn's head whipped around to locate him, and she ignored the pain it caused her. "Did everyone make it?" she managed to ask.

"We all did."

Something about his words mattered. She looked back at

Gwyneth, then around the room, counting Midge, Will, Alanna, Tom, and Lisbet. "Where's Marian?"

"With Tuck," said Will. "And the lady Emmeline."

"And she's . . ."

"Fine. We're all fine, which is a miracle, considering."

"Did they track us here?" Robyn's head felt clearer by the minute. Gwyneth held a cup of water to her lips, and she drank gratefully.

"Not yet," said John. "And we'll be out of here soon enough. Tuck thinks you'll be able to move by this afternoon, although she doesn't recommend it."

"You should stay here in case the wound festers," said Gwyneth with a glare at John.

"And put you and the baby in danger?" Robyn raised a hand to Gwyneth's cheek. "You know I can't."

Gwyneth frowned but didn't argue.

"I'll go let them know you're awake," said Alanna.

Dread and hope filled Robyn's chest. With everything that had gone wrong, Marian couldn't possibly want to stay, despite what she'd said to her father, but it was enough that she was alive and unhurt.

"What happened? The last thing I remember is the river."

"You passed out just after we got out. Marian and I carried you most of the way here," said John. "You could stand to lose a few pounds."

"I'll be sure to remember that next time we get a deer," Robyn said. "And thank you."

"Good morning," Tuck said in her resonant voice as she entered the room. "Glad to see you're still among the living."

Robyn nodded, but her eyes passed over the nun and the blond woman beside her to land on Marian. She had a vague memory of Marian in mail, but now she wore a simple tunic and leggings, and her hair hung in a single braid over her shoulder instead of bound in ribbons. Despite the exhaustion evident in the dark circles beneath her brown eyes, Robyn hadn't ever seen anything so beautiful.

Marian met her eyes with a look full of anguish, longing, and hope. She didn't blame Marian for the former; at least Robyn knew her family had loved her before she'd lost them. The latter two emotions, though—could she trust them? Robyn had failed to save her from Siward, and while they had escaped the sheriff, surely her ordeal had made her reconsider a life of outlawry. "Marian," she said.

Emmeline placed a hand on Marian's shoulder, and Robyn saw Marian lean into the support. "Would you have killed him?" she asked.

"When I thought he'd killed you? Yes." Robyn pushed herself into a sitting position, shaking off Gwyneth's attempts to keep her lying down. "But I missed."

Marian folded her arms over her chest.

"I watched the sheriff set dogs on the caves when you could have still been in there."

"I *was* in there."

Robyn flinched. She'd been right, then, to fear for Marian's life. She wanted to ask how Marian had escaped, but it was not the time. First, she had something she needed to say.

"For months, I've dreamed of killing your father, Marian. I thought he took everything from me: my brother, my home, and Gwyneth's happiness and safety. And he did take those things. But he also gave me you."

Marian's expression melted fractionally.

"And the sheriff didn't pledge Willa in marriage to a man who might have killed her, one way or another. The sheriff is not the only reason John is here, nor Lisbet, nor is he why Alanna left the comfort of Harcourt. The sheriff did not levy the tax. I've hated him for so long that it blinded me. When he cornered John and me today, I could have killed him. If I had, though, it would have condemned John, and it also might have condemned you, Marian. I thought he might at least let me lead him to the cave exit so that he could call off the dogs and buy you time. Do you see?

"Killing the sheriff won't change everything. They'll just

replace him with another man, and for all we know his replacement could be worse. Alanna is right." All eyes swiveled to the minstrel. "There is more we can do. We can help people. Not just our families, but everyone the sheriff and the crown like to grind under their boots. Even you, m'lady." Emmeline nodded her head in recognition. "We can flush venison and boar into your holdings, and perhaps we can even take back some of the seed grain taken from you for the ransom tax." As Robyn spoke, her voice and her conviction grew stronger.

"The sheriff killed my brother for trying to feed his family. I killed a man because Michael's death left us hungrier than ever, and as a result I had to abandon Gwyneth. Michael would have wanted me to help her, not take revenge for him. If we can prevent other people from having to make the choices he and I were forced to make, isn't that a better way of remembering him?" She turned to Gwyneth. Her sister-in-law's eyes were dry, but the look she gave Robyn shone with love. She held that gaze, knowing both of them were remembering her brother's laughter and his warm, strong arms.

"We might die trying. You all know that. Most of us were dead anyway. I'd rather die here in Sherwood, or if I have to hang, then at least I'll hang knowing I did something to stick it up their asses, with the people who matter most to me beside me."

Tuck's laugh rumbled. "Love thy neighbor, sayeth the Lord."

"But I think we stand as good a chance as anyone. Better, even. I intend to make it to next spring."

"You can winter in Harcourt," Emmeline offered without pause. "We're snowed in more often than not anyway, and the roads are too wet and muddy for much travel. No one will be dropping in unexpectedly, and my people are loyal."

"Thank you." Robyn didn't protest. They needed help if they were going to do this, and that meant accepting that others understood the risk and were willing to share it.

"We can fortify the caves in the spring," said John. "There's plenty of room there to house anyone who might need our help, and perhaps we can arrange for more peaceable relations with the neighbors: hides and meat for grain, instead of raiding them as Siward did. The cleft will serve as an alternate camp."

"Yes. But the first thing we're going to do once I can walk is figure out how to take out the tax caravans. Tuck," she said, meeting the nun's eyes, "do you know how we might smuggle goods back to their rightful owners?"

"As long as it's small enough to fit in a cask, I think we can find a way. I must ask, however, if you've thought this through. To right one wrong with another is a slope you may find it hard to climb back up."

"I know." Robyn considered her next words carefully. "And I wish there was another way. Perhaps we'll find one someday. I do not wish us to become like Siward, nor do I wish us to meet the sheriff with his own weapons. It would please him to paint us as lawless brigands."

"Might he have a point?" said Tuck.

"We need to make our own justice. If we steal, we give something back. If we must take a life, we find a way to grant life elsewhere. More than that, I want us to believe that there is a place here for all of us to exist as we are, instead of how others wish us to be. It won't be easy. We'll provide coin and safe passage to those who want to start over elsewhere. If any of you wish to leave, I—"

"Oh, shut up," said Midge and John in unison.

Robyn couldn't help the smile that spread across her face at their looks of disgust.

"I've been waiting for this moment for a while," said John as he shook his head.

"We all have," said Midge.

"What are you talking about?"

"For you to realize what you're capable of." Midge clapped her on the shoulder. "Alanna's right about you."

Robyn's face heated with embarrassment. "Come off it."

Midge broke into a rousing chorus of "The Ballad of Robyn Hood," which intensified Robyn's discomfort. She couldn't look at Marian, though she felt her eyes.

"That's it. That's all I had to say," she said when Midge subsided. "If we're all in agreement."

"That's not it."

They all turned to look at Marian. Robyn couldn't read her expression, and her heart stilled. Marian was about to tell her she was leaving. She steeled herself, trying to convince herself it was for the best.

"Tuck," Marian said, breaking eye contact with Robyn to face the nun. "Can you marry me and Robyn?"

Robyn expected a wave of shock or outrage from the nun and Emmeline, and perhaps from some of her friends. Instead, Tuck considered first Marian, then Robyn. "It's not necessarily within the scope of my authority," she said. "And there is the matter of the law. But as long as that doesn't bother you, I don't see why I can't."

Robyn hardly heard her. She pushed herself to her feet, wobbling unsteadily on her bad leg while her head spun with dizziness and disbelief. John helped her up by the elbow as Marian turned back to Robyn with defiance radiating from her blazing eyes, as if daring her to try to turn her away.

"Are you sure?" Robyn asked. Or at least, that's what she meant to ask. Instead, the only word that left her lips was Marian's name.

Marian closed the distance between them before she could add anything else. "I'm staying," she said, and then she kissed Robyn with an intensity that drove the pain from her body and left only sweet, aching love.

Chapter Fifty

Tuck ushered them into the church an hour later. Marian still wore her new clothes, which had been left by a previous guest of the priory, and Robyn walked with the support of John's quarterstaff, dressed in the clothes Gwyneth had cleaned and patched and dried over the fire the night before. None of that mattered. Marian thought with amusement of the elaborate ceremony her father had planned. In truth, she'd married Robyn that night on the hill. This was just a formality, and—if she was honest with herself as she looked at Robyn's scratched and bruised face—a way of ensuring Robyn didn't try to send her back out of misguided concerns about her safety. Robyn raised an eyebrow at her as if she guessed her thoughts and held out her hand. Marian laced her fingers through hers as they stood before Tuck at the altar.

Lady Emmeline and Gwyneth carried flowers picked from the priory garden. Gwyneth had woven hers into a crown for her son, who looked up at his mother with round eyes. The rest of the bedraggled company stood around them. Marian moved closer to Robyn.

"You know no words need be said before me. Any pact made in sight of the Lord is binding."

"I know," said Marian. Robyn gave her assent with a nod and a squeeze of Marian's hand.

"Do you take each other in our most sacred of covenants?"

Marian looked into Robyn's eyes and searched for the flecks of green that reminded her of the way sunlight filtered through the summer leaves. She wondered if she should be feeling scared or uncertain at the magnitude of what they were about to do. Even if her father and the church never recognized this marriage as binding—and they would not—she'd take these vows in the eyes of her God. *He* would know, and the knowledge filled her heart with a joy so immense she thought she might burst, light spilling out of her into the church. This felt right in a way nothing else ever had. Robyn's callused hands gripped hers, and she smiled as she spoke the words.

"I do."

They each repeated the words three times, and with each utterance the joy within her grew as she expanded to contain it.

"Have you prepared any vows?" asked Tuck.

They hadn't had time. Marian hadn't even known what she was going to do until she'd heard Robyn's speech.

"Yes," said Robyn, startling her out of her thoughts. "I swear to love you from this day and for all my days, and I swear, too, to trust that you know your own mind. I will not try to choose your path for you, and I will walk that path with you for as long as you want me by your side. In this way, and in all ways, I am yours."

Tuck's eyes crinkled at the corners. She waited for Marian, who couldn't breathe. She wanted to wrap her arms around Robyn and hold her so close she forgot where she ended and Robyn began, but the expectancy in the air grounded her.

"I . . ." she began, uncertain, and then the words flowed out of her. "I vow to love you, come winter or spring, beneath these trees or beneath this earth, until our souls meet again in the next world. I will keep our home—even if it is a cave—filled with light and happiness. I will care for you and comfort you in times of pain and trouble. I will love you as no one on this earth has loved you, and I will do so with a glad heart, for I shall know myself strong within your love."

"Amen," pronounced Tuck. "Now let's have some mead and get our archer off her feet before she faints again." She steered them firmly toward a bench. They sat, and Marian nestled into Robyn as the others gathered around them. Emmeline smiled at Marian with an understanding she realized had been there for years, far longer than Willa's suspicions, and longer even than she'd understood herself.

"The sheriff will come for you again," Emmeline said quietly. "And when he does, I'll be there to hide you."

The sound of barking dogs filled her memory. "I don't think he will," Marian said, and sadness crept in to dim some of her joy as she accepted the truth she'd known since she'd heard the alaunts baying for blood through the caves. "I think he'll say I died in the forest at the hands of outlaws." Robyn's arm tightened around her, and Marian knew Robyn understood the price she had paid for her freedom.

"You still have family," said Emmeline in a fierce voice.

The others nodded, and Midge gave her an appraising look. "I've never lived with a lady before. Do you snore?"

"If she does, it will only be to drown you out," said Robyn. Then she turned to Marian. "Do you snore?"

"Sometimes she does," said Emmeline. "But I promise she stops if you kick her."

The sharp edge of Marian's loss receded at the playful teasing, and she scowled at Emmeline in mock outrage.

"We'll have to teach her to shoot," John said to Robyn. "She can act as lookout with Lisbet for now."

"She's not a terrible shot," said Willa. "Not as good as you, of course, but I've seen her take down a rabbit from horseback once or twice."

"I think I might be able to hit you from here, in fact. And I won't even need a bow." Marian couldn't keep the smile out of her voice. No matter what happened next, she'd found, at last, a place where she belonged.

Six Weeks Later

Robyn crouched behind the thick trunk of a beech tree. A wagon wound laboriously through the stand of oaks between her and the road, the bridle of the cart horse jingling in the still summer air. Two mounted guards rode alongside it. Both held crossbows loosely at their side, lulled by the soporific quality of the afternoon. Only the forest insects seemed keen on making their industrious presence known.

Across the road Robyn knew Lisbet waited with her slingshot primed and her young eyes trained on the nearest horse's flank. Tom and Will crouched near her, while John, Alanna, and Marian accompanied Robyn. This was their fourth tax strike, and news of the fresh forest threat had not yet reached the manors on the far side. Had it, Robyn knew the guards would never have allowed themselves the luxury of drifting off in the saddle.

She whistled. The bird call drifted over the still air in a series of trills and warbles that often fooled the real birds it mimicked. She didn't see Lisbet move, but the horse on the far side of the road snapped its head up as a small stone stung its haunches. Its rider struggled to maintain control, and his struggle distracted the other guard long enough for everyone but Lisbet, who would remain in the trees for her own safety despite the girl's protests, to step into the road.

Robyn, Marian, John, and Tom held longbows, their arrows

trained on the guards. At this distance, even Marian, whose delicate palms and finger pads now bore the blisters of practice with both bow and staff, couldn't miss. Will's naked sword glinted in the sunlight and Alanna's throwing knives rested easily in her hands. The guards froze. Even the startled horse paused its sidestepping and head tossing to eye the outlaws ranged across the road ahead.

"Good afternoon, worthy men," said Robyn in as cheerful a voice as she could muster. She'd found that unsettled men liked this more than outright aggression. "Drop your crossbows. You won't be needing them today."

One of the guards—there was always an idiot like him—raised his weapon to take a shot. Lisbet's next stone took him in the back of the head. He pitched forward in the saddle and the quarrel went wide, zinging its way into the trees. Robyn smiled. The illusion of even more outlaws lurking in the shadows also served their cause.

"Drop it," she said, "or the next thing that hits you won't be so gentle."

"How do we know you won't just kill us?"

"Because I'm Robyn Hood."

The driver, who had so far kept himself as small as possible on the seat, leaned forward with a look of interest.

"Who in God's name is Robyn Hood?" asked the guard.

"He's the one they're singing about," said the driver. "I heard it last time I was in town. They say he never misses, but he only shoots when necessary."

The guards exchanged uneasy glances. "We're on the king's business," the one nearest Robyn said. The other rubbed the back of his head with a glassy expression.

"Funny you should mention that. So are we," said Robyn. "The way we see it, a king should protect his people, not beggar them."

"Fuck I know about it," said the injured guard.

"Tell you what." Robyn adopted a conspiratorial tone. "I know you don't get paid shit for this work. We could kill you all right now and take everything, and where would you be then? But, if

406

you cooperate, we'll leave you with a little extra for your trouble. You just tell the sheriff outlaws took everything they could carry, and he won't ask any questions about what you might have in your purse."

"To hell with it." The injured guard dropped his empty crossbow to the dirt. "Do it, Ben. I want to get home to Lise tonight."

"Smart man," said John.

The second guard hesitated for another moment, then tossed his own weapon to the ground.

"Dismount, if you'd be so kind. I don't fancy getting run over," Robyn told them.

The men obeyed and handed their horses over to Alanna, who led them off the path and looped their reins over a branch.

"Sit down by Will Scarlet over there. He's the one with the sword. You can leave your weapons by your horses. That's it, just take off your sword belts. No need to take anything out of the sheath. You're safe with us now."

John and Tom approached the wagon. The driver shrank back from them, but John shook his head. "We're not going to hurt you. Hop on down and go sit with your friends."

"Seeds, coin, and ale," said Tom as he peered at the cargo.

"Ale's for the sheriff himself," one of the men said.

"Might take a piss in it then," said John as he leapt over the side of the wagon. He heaved several sacks of grain out of the back, followed by four sacks of coin. "Coin was in the grain. Clever."

"Let's grab a bit of that ale, too." Robyn edged around the wagon and tossed a grin at Marian over her shoulder. Marian's hood shadowed her face and kept her dark braid hidden, but Robyn could see her full lips curve.

She assessed the goods in the dust. They needed to move quickly now, before anyone else came down the road. Tom and John could carry a sack of grain apiece. The rest of them could manage the coin easily, and they'd rigged a way of carrying heavier items between two of them using a litter. That would cover the ale she intended to drink later in celebration.

407

"We'll leave two purses. That should keep the queen happy."

"I doubt it," said Will.

"Don't bother," said the driver. "The prince has declared himself the rightful king. The queen will never see a shilling of it."

Robyn met John's eyes and nodded. "In that case, we'll leave him something to drown his sorrows." She hopped into the back of the wagon and uncorked all but two of the casks. Ale trickled through the slats and onto the thirsty earth, where it pooled around the wheels.

"Where are you coming from?" she asked as she landed lightly in the ale mud.

"Maunnesfeld."

Will didn't so much as blink at the mention of her home.

"And how is our lord of Maunnesfeld?" asked John.

"Hale and whole."

"Glad to hear it." Robyn picked up one of the purses and scattered a handful of coins over the ground. The guards and the driver would have to work to find them all, which would buy Robyn and her band time to make their escape. "It's been a pleasure doing business with you. See to it that the driver gets his share, won't you? Or else next time, it won't be a rock that hits you in the ear."

The men grumbled their agreement.

"Give our regards to the sheriff," said John. He heaved two of the sacks over his shoulder, and Tom followed suit. Blacksmiths had their uses. Marian and Alanna lifted an ale cask together. Will remained standing guard over the men while the rest of the band carried off the goods to the litters waiting in the trees with Lisbet. Robyn kept an arrow trained on the men as well. She took no chances.

John's whistle came a few seconds later. Will backed away while Robyn covered her. "Bill," Robyn said, speaking to the imaginary outlaw they'd invented for this purpose. "Stay here and keep an eye on them. If it looks like they might come after us, shoot this one first." She pointed at the injured guard with her arrow. He paled.

They slipped away through the trees in single file. Tom and John shared one litter, and Alanna and Will shared the other. Lisbet led the way, followed by Marian, who had the bags of coin slung over her shoulder in a sack. Robyn took the rear. She kept an arrow at the ready in case the men decided to pursue them, but she wasn't worried. When push came to shove, fear of immediate death almost always won out over fear of future retribution. She hoped the sheriff didn't punish the men too harshly when they arrived in Nottingham.

The afternoon wore on as they picked their way along the forest paths. Robyn switched out with Will, who had become almost as adept at moving quietly as Robyn, and enjoyed the burn in her arms from the weight of the grain. That burn meant Maunnesfeld's serfs would eat.

She called a halt at the outskirts of Edwinstowe. The villagers surrounding the priory might turn a blind eye, but that was another risk she wasn't willing to take. Breathing deeply in the twilight, she hooted.

Midge's answering hoot floated over the sound of crickets and tree frogs, accompanied by Midge herself, a donkey pulling a small cart, and Yvette, who had made her way to Edwinstowe shortly after Robyn. According to Gwyneth, Yvette had taken one look at Tuck and decided to stay—along with the dog, who she forgave for savaging her arm after it defended her from an angry boar on her journey—to offer the nuns additional protection. Now, the brigand rarely left Tuck's side and, while her devotion to the Lord might be suspect, no one doubted her devotion to the prioress.

"Good haul?" Midge asked as she ducked into the shadows where they stood. The donkey lipped at a low-hanging branch, and Yvette scowled. Some things, at least, remained the same.

"See for yourself."

Midge surveyed the loot approvingly. "I just got back from Papplewick. My father's willing to mill the grain for us, and Tuck and I came up with a better way of getting coin around."

"What?"

"Baking it. A shilling a loaf."

"Midge," said Robyn, pulling her cousin into a hug. "You're brilliant."

"I know." Midge squirmed out of the embrace and turned to Alanna. "They're singing about us everywhere."

"Good," Alanna said. "How is the sheriff taking it?"

"He's furious, of course, but he's too busy with the prince's revolt to do much about it at the moment. Have you heard?"

"One of our new friends told us after we relieved them of their burden," said John. "So it's true?"

"As I live and breathe."

"Will he make a stand here?" asked Will. Robyn could see her mind beginning to weigh the strategic pros and cons of Nottingham castle.

Midge shrugged.

"We'll need to prepare ourselves," said John.

"Not necessarily," said Marian. "Midge is right. They'll be too focused on the throne to think about outlaws."

Robyn considered her wife. *Wife.* It still didn't seem real, nor could she believe that they'd committed any sin. Loving Marian felt too much like an answered prayer. That, and Marian's intuition had proved invaluable as they planned their strategy for the coming months. She rivaled even Will in her ability to guess the motives and reactions of the sheriff's men.

"Any chance that ale is for us?" asked Yvette.

"As soon as we're in the priory."

"Right. Here." Midge reached under the canvas covering the back of the cart and pulled out seven habits and cloaks.

"I hate this part," said Tom. "It's all very well for you to dress like men. Our clothes are comfortable."

"But you look so fetching," said John as he pulled the stiff wool on over his clothes. The habits were winter weight, but if they protected Tuck from suspicion, a little sweat was a price Robyn was happy to pay. They loaded the goods into the cart along with their weapons.

"Let's go get you drunk, little one," John said to Midge.

"We'll catch up," Marian said as the group split. "To avoid suspicion."

"Sure." Will smirked at Marian before following Midge, who had broken into song. Robyn and Marian watched them leave in silence.

"I'm sorry about Richard," Robyn said when she was sure the cart and their friends had made it safely to the priory. "I know you were close."

"He favored me on the rare occasions he bothered sleeping on English soil." Marian shook her head. "I thought him a friend before I knew what true friends were."

"And now?"

"Now he is merely a king, and I," she paused to give Robyn a slow kiss, "am the Lady of Sherwood."

"What does that make me, m'lady?"

Marian considered her. "Who you've always been: Robyn."

"That hardly seems fair."

"But you're my Robyn. Isn't that worth something?"

Luck favors the rich, little bird, whispered Michael. Robyn smiled. She understood now that she'd always been rich in the ways that mattered. "I suppose, since I can't have a castle, that I'll settle for that."

"You don't want a castle. Very drafty, lots of upkeep, and always too many people about. I much prefer our cave."

"You don't regret it then? Choosing this?"

Marian pressed her lips to Robyn's before speaking. "I've never been happier."

They walked into view of the priory some time later. The sounds of the village settling in for the night drifted past them, along with the rustling and calls of the forest animals. In the darkness, silvered only by the light of the distant stars, Marian took Robyn's hand.

411

Acknowledgments

Nottingham was the first book-length project I ever attempted. The first draft, circa 2014, is a very different story from this one, and I have quite a few people to thank for that. First and foremost my wife, who has read more versions of this story than anyone, and who has put up with a seemingly endless cycle of "I'm burning it for real this time," followed by, "what if I tried working on *Nottingham* again?"

Secondly, to the team at Bywater Books, who supported this project through all its (many) bumps and believed it had a place in our literature, and to my editor, Elizabeth Sims, who helped me find my way out of the woods (figurative and literal—she made me draw a map). Ann McMan of Treehouse Studio has, once again, outdone herself with the cover. This will come as no surprise to those who know her work.

My early readers—you are my band of merry people. Rachel, Samara, Alessandra—this book is better because of you, and your emotional support was (and is) critical to my writing.

One of the things I learned the hard way during this process is that England is, in fact, a real place, with history and geography that obeys certain rules. Meg is the friend and medievalist every writer needs in their corner, and she graciously answered all my burning medieval questions. All historical and geographical discrepancies are entirely my fault. You can thank her for the accuracies. (Also, on that note, my Siward bears no relation to the historical figure. I simply liked the name.)

Books, whether we write them or read them, serve as markers in our own histories. While finishing *Nottingham*, I lost one of my oldest and dearest friends. If the friendships in these pages resonate with you, it is in large part because of El, who taught me about friendship and loyalty and the value of a "hey, buddy," whenever it was needed. I like to think El would have gotten a kick out of a group of queers establishing an intentional community in the woods and challenging an unjust social and economic system. El fought to make the world a brighter, safer, and more welcoming place for the queer community, and I will miss their light more than I can say.

About the Author

Raised in Upstate New York, Anna Burke graduated from Smith College with degrees in English Literature and Studio Art. She holds a certificate from the International Writing Program at the University of Iowa and was the inaugural recipient of the Sandra Moran Scholarship for the Golden Crown Literary Society's Writing Academy. She's currently pursuing an MFA from Emerson College. *Nottingham* is Anna's third novel, following her spectacular debut novel, *Compass Rose*, and her breathtaking fairy tale, *Thorn*.

Bywater BOOKS

At Bywater Books we love good books about lesbians just like you do, and we're committed to bringing the best of contemporary lesbian writing to our avid readers. Our editorial team is dedicated to finding and developing outstanding writers who create books you won't want to put down.

We sponsor the Bywater Prize for Fiction to help with this quest. Each prizewinner receives $1,000 and publication of their novel. We have already discovered amazing writers like Jill Malone, Sally Bellerose, and Hilary Sloin through the Bywater Prize. Which exciting new writer will we find next?

For more information about Bywater Books and the annual Bywater Prize for Fiction, please visit our website.

www.bywaterbooks.com